FRITZ LEIBER

SELECTED STORIES

Fritz Leiber with wife Jonquil, Beverly Hills, 1937

WITHDRAWN

FRITZ LEIBER

SELECTED STORIES

INTRODUCTION BY NEIL GAIMAN

EDITED BY JONATHAN STRAHAN AND CHARLES N. BROWN

NIGHT SHADE BOOKS
San Francisco

"Smoke Ghost," first published in *Unknown Worlds*, October 1941.

"The Girl with the Hungry Eyes," first published in *The Girl with the Hungry Eyes and Other Stories*, Avon, 1949.

"Coming Attraction," first published in *Galaxy Science Fiction*, November 1950.

"A Pail of Air," first published in *Galaxy Science Fiction*, December 1951.

"A Deskful of Girls," first published in *The Magazine of Fantasy & Science Fiction*, April 1958.

"Space-Time for Springers," first published in *Star Science Fiction Stories No.4*, Frederick Pohl. ed., Ballantine, 1958.

"Bazaar of the Bizarre," first published in *Fantastic Stories of Imagination*, August 1963.

"Four Ghosts in Hamlet," first published in *The Magazine of Fantasy & Science Fiction*, January 1965.

"Gonna Roll the Bones," first published in *Dangerous Visions*, Harlan Ellison, ed., Doubleday, 1967.

"The Inner Circles" (AKA "The Winter Flies"), first published in *The Magazine of Fantasy & Science Fiction*, October 1967.

"America the Beautiful," first published in *The Year 2000*, Harry Harrison, ed., Doubleday, 1970.

"Ill Met in Lankhmar," first published in *The Magazine of Fantasy and Science Fiction*, April 1970.

"Midnight by the Morphy Watch," first published in *Worlds of If*, July-August 1974.

"Belsen Express," first published in *The Second Book of Fritz Leiber*, DAW Books, 1975.

"Catch That Zeppelin!" first published in *The Magazine of Fantasy & Science Fiction*, March 1975.

"Horrible Imaginings," first published in *Death*, Stuart David Schiff, ed., Playboy Paperbacks, 1982.

"The Curse of the Smalls and the Stars," first published in *Heroic Visions*, Jessica Amanda Salmonson, ed., Ace, 1983.

First Edition

ISBN: 978-1-59780-180-5

Night Shade Books
Please visit us on the web at
http://www.nightshadebooks.com

CONTENTS

INTRODUCTION

NEIL GAIMAN

I MET FRITZ LEIBER (it's pronounced Lie-ber, and not, as I had mispronounced it all my life until I met him, Lee-ber) shortly before his death. This was twenty years ago. We were sitting next to each other at a banquet at the World Fantasy Convention. He seemed so old: a tall, serious, distinguished man with white hair, who reminded me of a thinner, better looking Boris Karloff. He said nothing, during the dinner, not that I can remember. Our mutual friend Harlan Ellison had sent him a copy of *Sandman* #18, "A Dream of 1000 Cats," which was my own small tribute to Leiber's cat stories, and I told him he had been an inspiration, and he said something more or less inaudible in return, and I was happy. We rarely get to thank those who shaped us.

My first Leiber short story: I was nine. The story, "The Winter Flies," was in Judith Merril's huge anthology *SF12*. It was the most important book I read when I was nine, with the possible exception of Michael Moorcock's *Stormbringer*, for it was the place I discovered a host of authors who would become important to me, and dozens of stories I would read so often that I could have recited them: Chip Delany's "The Star Pit" and R. A. Lafferty's "Primary Education of the Camiroi" and "Narrow Valley" and William Burroughs' "They Do Not Always Remember," J. G. Ballard's "The Cloud-sculptors of Coral D" not to mention Tuli Kupferberg's poems, Carol Emshwiller and Sonya Dorman and Kit Reed and the rest. It did not matter that I was much too young for the stories: I knew that they were beyond me, and was not even slightly troubled by this. The stories made sense to me, a sense that was beyond what they literally meant. It was in *SF12* I encountered concepts and people that did not exist in the children's books I was familiar with, and this delighted me.

What did I make of the "The Winter Flies" then? The last time I read it I saw it as semi-autobiographical fiction, about a man who philanders

1

and drinks when he is on the road, whose marriage is breaking down, and who interrupts a masturbatory reverie to talk a child having a panic attack back to reality, an action that, for a moment, brings a family, fragmenting in alcohol and lack of communication, together. When I read it as a nine-year-old it was about a man beset by demons, talking his son, lost among the stars, home again. And both ways of reading it were, I suspect, as right as they could be.

I knew I liked Fritz Leiber from that story on. He was someone I read. When I was eleven I bought *Conjure Wife*, and learned that all women were witches, and found out what a hand of glory was (and yes, there is sexism and misogyny in the book and in the concept, but there is, if you are a twelve-year-old boy trying to make sense of something that might as well be an alien species, also the kind of paranoid "what-if-it's-true?" that makes reading books such a dangerous occupation at any age). I read a 1972 issue of *Wonder Woman* written by Samuel R. Delany, featuring Fafhrd and the Gray Mouser and was disappointed that it felt nothing like a Chip Delany story, but had now encountered our two adventurers, and, from the magic of comics, knew what they looked like. I read *Sword of Sorcery*, the Fafhrd and the Gray Mouser comics that DC comics brought out in 1973, and finally found a copy of *The Swords of Lankhmar* at the age of thirteen, in the cupboard at the back of Mr. Wright's English class, its cover (I would later discover) a bad English copy of the Jeff Jones painting on the cover of the US edition; and I read it, learned what the tall barbarian and the little thief were like in Leiber's glittering, half-amused prose, and I loved it, and I was content.

I couldn't enjoy Conan the Barbarian after that. Not really. I missed the wit.

Shortly after I found a copy of *The Big Time*, Leiber's novel of the Change War, a war across time and space being fought by two incomprehensible groups of antagonists who use human beings as pawns, and I read it, convinced it was a stage-play cunningly disguised as a novella, and when I reread it twenty years on I enjoyed it almost as much (aspects of how Leiber treated the narrator bothered me) and was still just as convinced it was a stage-play. Some of Leiber's better SF tales were Change War stories.

Leiber wrote some great books, and he wrote some stinkers: the majority of his SF novels in particular feel dated and throwaway. He wrote some great short stories in SF and fantasy and horror and there's scarcely a stinker among them, even when the SF elements feel tacked on or redundant or protective colouration for the fantastic.

He was one of the giants of genre literature and it is hard to imagine the world of tales we read today being the same without him. And he was a giant partly because he vaulted over genre restrictions, sidled around them, took them in his stride. He created—in the sense that it barely existed before he wrote it—witty and intelligent sword and sorcery; he was the person who put down the foundations of what would become urban horror; and he wrote SF that resonated in its time for its readers, and some that did more than that.

Leiber at his best has themes that repeat, like an artist returning to his favourite subjects—Shakespeare and watches and cats, marriage and women and ghosts, the power of cities and booze and the stage, dealing with the Devil, Germany, mortality, never repeating, usually both smarter and deeper than it needed to be to sell, written with elegance and poetry and wit.

Good malt whisky tastes of one thing; a great malt whisky tastes of many things. It plays a chromatic scale of flavour in your mouth, leaving you with an odd sequence of aftertastes, and when finally the liquid has gone from your tongue you can still find yourself reminded of, first, honey then woodsmoke, and bitter chocolate or of the barren salt pastures at the edge of the sea. Fritz Leiber's better short stories do the thing a fine whisky does, but they leave aftertastes in memory, an emotional residue and resonance that remains long after the final page has been turned. Just as the stage manager he describes in "Four Ghosts in Hamlet," we feel that Leiber had spent a lifetime observing, and he was adept at turning the straw of memory into the bricks of imagination and of story. He demanded a great deal of his readers—you need to pay attention, you need to care—and he gave a great deal in return, for those of us that did.

Twentieth-century genre SF produced some recognised giants—Ray Bradbury being the obvious example—but it also produced a handful of people who never gained the recognition that should have been their due. They were caviar (but then, so was Bradbury, and he was rapidly taken out of SF and seen as a national treasure). They might have been giants, but nobody noticed them; they were too odd, too misshapen, too smart. Avram Davidson was one. R. A. Lafferty another. Fritz Leiber was never quite one of the overlooked ones, not in that way: he won many awards; he was widely and rightly seen as one of our great writers. But he was still caviar. He never crossed over into the popular consciousness: he was too baroque, perhaps; too intelligent. He is not on the roadmap that we draw that takes us from Stephen King and Ramsey Campbell back to H. P. Lovecraft in one direction, from every game of Dungeons and Dragons with a thief in it back to Robert E. Howard, in another.

He should be.

I hope this book reminds his admirers of why they love his work; but more than that, I trust it will find him new readers, and that the new readers will, in turn, find an author they can trust (as much as ever you can trust an author) and to love.

Neil Gaiman
In Transit
February 2010

SMOKE GHOST

MISS MILLICK WONDERED just what had happened to Mr. Wran. He kept making the strangest remarks when she took dictation. Just this morning he had quickly turned around and asked, "Have you ever seen a ghost, Miss Millick?" And she had tittered nervously and replied, "When I was a girl there was a thing in white that used to come out of the closet in the attic bedroom when you slept there, and moan. Of course it was just my imagination. I was frightened of lots of things." And he had said, "I don't mean that traditional kind of ghost. I mean a ghost from the world today, with the soot of the factories in its face and the pounding of machinery in its soul. The kind that would haunt coal yards and slip around at night through deserted office buildings like this one. A real ghost. Not something out of books." And she hadn't known what to say.

He'd never been like this before. Of course it might be joking, but it didn't sound that way. Vaguely Miss Millick wondered whether he mightn't be seeking some sort of sympathy from her. Of course, Mr. Wran was married and had a little child, but that didn't prevent her from having daydreams. She had daydreams about most of the men she worked for. The daydreams were all very similar in pattern and not very exciting, but they helped fill up the emptiness in her mind. And now he was asking her another of those disturbing and jarringly out-of-place questions.

"Have you ever thought what a ghost of our times would look like, Miss Millick? Just picture it. A smoky composite face with the hungry anxiety of the unemployed, the neurotic restlessness of the person without purpose, the jerky tension of the high-pressure metropolitan worker, the sullen resentment of the striker, the callous viciousness of the strike breaker, the aggressive whine of the panhandler, the inhibited terror of the bombed civilian, and a thousand other twisted emotional patterns? Each one overlaying and yet blending with the other, like a pile of semitransparent masks?"

Miss Millick gave a little self-conscious shiver and said, "My, that would be terrible. What an awful thing to think of."

She peered at him furtively across the desk. Was he going crazy? She remembered having heard that there had been something impressively abnormal about Mr. Wran's childhood, but she couldn't recall what it was. If only she could do something—joke at him or ask him what was really wrong. She shifted around the extra pencils in her left hand and mechanically traced over some of the shorthand curlicues in her notebook.

"Yet, that's just what such a ghost or vitalized projection would look like, Miss Millick," he continued, smiling in a tight way. "It would grow out of the real world. It would reflect all the tangled, sordid, vicious things. All the loose ends. And it would be very grimy. I don't think it would seem white or wispy or favor graveyards. It wouldn't moan. But it would mutter unintelligibly, and twitch at your sleeve. Like a sick, surly ape. What would such a thing want from a person, Miss Millick? Sacrifice? Worship? Or just fear? What could you do to stop it from troubling you?"

Miss Millick giggled nervously. She felt embarrassed and out of her depth. There was an expression beyond her powers of definition in Mr. Wran's ordinary, flat-cheeked, thirtyish face, silhouetted against the dusty window. He turned away and stared out into the gray downtown atmosphere that rolled in from the railroad yards and the mills. When he spoke again his voice sounded far away.

"Of course, being immaterial, it couldn't hurt you physically—at first. You'd have to be peculiarly sensitive even to see it, or be aware of it at all. But it would begin to influence your actions. Make you do this. Stop you from doing that. Although only a projection, it would gradually get its hooks into the world of things as they are. Might even get control of suitably vacuous minds. Then it could hurt whomever it wanted."

Miss Millick squirmed and tried to read back her shorthand, like books said you should do when there was a pause. She became aware of the failing light and wished Mr. Wran would ask her to turn on the overhead light. She felt uncomfortable and scratchy as if soot were sifting down on to her skin.

"It's a rotten world, Miss Millick," said Mr. Wran, talking at the window. "Fit for another morbid growth of superstition. It's time the ghosts, or whatever you call them, took over and began a rule of fear. They'd be no worse than men."

"But"—Miss Millick's diaphragm jerked, making her titter inanely—"of course there aren't any such things as ghosts."

Mr. Wran turned around. She noticed with a start that his grin had broadened, though without getting any less tight.

"Of course there aren't, Miss Millick," he said in a sudden loud, reassuring, almost patronizing voice, as if she had been doing the talking rather than he. "Modern science and common sense and better self-understanding all go to prove it."

He stopped, staring past her abstractedly. She hung her head and might even have blushed if she hadn't felt so all at sea. Her leg muscles twitched, making her stand up, although she hadn't intended to. She aimlessly rubbed her hand back and forth along the edge of the desk, then pulled it back.

"Why, Mr. Wran, look what I got off your desk," she said, showing him a heavy smudge. There was a note of cumbersomely playful reproof in her voice, but she really just wanted to be saying something. "No wonder the copy I bring you always gets so black. Somebody ought to talk to those scrubwomen. They're skimping on your room."

She wished he would make some normal joking reply. But instead he drew back and his face hardened.

"Well, to get back to the letter to Fredericks," he rapped out harshly, and began to dictate.

When she was gone he jumped up, dabbed his finger experimentally at the smudged part of the desk, frowned worriedly at the almost inky smears. He jerked open a drawer, snatched out a rag, hastily swabbed off the desk, crumpled the rag into a ball and tossed it back. There were three or four other rags in the drawer, each impregnated with soot.

Then he strode over to the window and peered out anxiously through the gathering dusk, his eyes searching the panorama of roofs, fixing on each chimney, each water tank.

"It's a psychosis. Must be. Hallucination. Compulsion neurosis," he muttered to himself in a tired, distraught voice that would have made Miss Millick gasp. "Good thing I'm seeing the psychiatrist tonight. It's that damned mental abnormality cropping up in a new form. Can't be any other explanation. Can't be. But it's so damned real. Even the soot. I don't think I could force myself to get on the elevated tonight. Good thing I made the appointment. The doctor will know—" His voice trailed off, he rubbed his eyes, and his memory automatically started to grind.

It had all begun on the elevated. There was a particular little sea of roofs he had grown into the habit of glancing at just as the packed car carrying him homeward lurched around a turn. A dingy, melancholy little world of tar paper, tarred gravel, and smoky brick. Rusty tin chimneys with odd conical hats suggested abandoned listening posts. There was a washed-out advertisement of some ancient patent medicine on the nearest wall. Superficially it was like ten thousand other drab city roofs. But he always saw it around dusk, either in the normal smoky half-light, or tinged with red by the flat rays of a dirty sunset, or covered by ghostly windblown white sheets of rain-splash, or patched with blackish snow; and it seemed unusually bleak and suggestive, almost beautifully ugly, though in no sense picturesque; dreary but meaningful. Unconsciously it came to symbolize for Catesby Wran certain disagreeable aspects of the frustrated, frightened century in which he lived, the jangled century of hate and heavy industry and Fascist wars. The quick, daily glance into the half darkness became an integral part of his life. Oddly, he never saw it in the morning, for it was then his habit to sit on the other side of the car, his head buried in the paper.

One evening toward winter he noticed what seemed to be a shapeless black sack lying on the third roof from the tracks. He did not think about it. It merely registered as an addition to the well-known scene and his memory stored away the impression for further reference. Next evening, however, he decided he had been mistaken in one detail. The object was a roof nearer than he had thought. Its color and texture, and the grimy stains around it, suggested that it was filled with coal dust, which was hardly reasonable. Then, too, the following evening it seemed to have been blown against a rusty ventilator by the wind—which could hardly have happened if it were at all heavy. Perhaps it was filled with leaves. Catesby was surprised to find himself anticipating his next daily glance with a minor note of apprehension. There was something unwholesome in the posture of the thing that stuck in his mind—a bulge in the sacking that suggested a misshapen head peering around the ventilator. And his apprehension was justified, for that evening the thing was on the nearest roof, though on the farther side, looking as if it had just flopped down over the low brick parapet.

Next evening the sack was gone. Catesby was annoyed at the momentary feeling of relief that went through him, because the whole matter seemed too unimportant to warrant feelings of any sort. What difference did it make if his imagination had played tricks on him, and he'd fancied that the object was crawling and hitching itself slowly closer across the roofs? That was the way any normal imagination worked. He deliberately chose to disregard the fact that there were reasons for thinking his imagination was by no means a normal one. As he walked home from the elevated, however, he found himself wondering whether the sack was really gone. He seemed to recall a vague, smudgy trail leading across the gravel to the nearer side of the roof. For an instant an unpleasant picture formed in his mind—that of an inky, humped creature crouched behind the nearer parapet, waiting. Then he dismissed the whole subject.

The next time he felt the familiar grating lurch of the car, he caught himself trying not to look out. That angered him. He turned his head quickly. When he turned it back, his compact face was definitely pale. There had only been time for a fleeting rearward glance at the escaping roof. Had he actually seen in silhouette the upper part of a head of some sort peering over the parapet? Nonsense, he told himself. And even if he had seen something, there were a thousand explanations which did not involve the supernatural or even true hallucination. Tomorrow he would take a good look and clear up the whole matter. If necessary, he would visit the roof personally, though he hardly knew where to find it and disliked in any case the idea of pampering a whim of fear.

He did not relish the walk home from the elevated that evening, and visions of the thing disturbed his dreams and were in and out of his mind all next day at the office. It was then that he first began to relieve his nerves by making jokingly serious remarks about the supernatural to Miss Millick, who seemed properly mystified. It was on the same day, too, that he became aware of a growing antipathy to grime and soot. Everything he touched seemed gritty, and he found himself mopping and wiping at his desk like an old lady with a morbid fear of germs. He reasoned that there was no real change in his office, and that he'd just now become sensitive to the dirt that had always been there, but there was no denying an increasing nervousness. Long before the car reached the curve, he was straining his eyes through the murky twilight determined to take in every detail.

Afterward he realized that he must have given a muffled cry of some sort, for the man beside him looked at him curiously, and the woman ahead gave him an unfavorable stare. Conscious of his own pallor and uncontrollable trembling, he stared back at them hungrily, trying to regain the feeling of security he had completely lost. They were the usual reassuringly wooden-faced people everyone rides home with on the elevated. But suppose he had pointed out to one of them what he had seen—that sodden, distorted face of sacking and coal dust, that boneless paw which waved back and forth, unmistakably in his direction, as if reminding him of a future appointment—he involuntarily shut his eyes tight. His thoughts were racing ahead to tomorrow evening. He pictured this same windowed oblong of light and packed humanity surging around the curve—then an opaque monstrous form leaping out from the roof in a parabolic swoop—an unmentionable face pressed close against the window, smearing it with wet coal dust—huge paws fumbling sloppily at the glass.

Somehow he managed to turn off his wife's anxious inquiries. Next morning he reached a decision and made an appointment for that evening with a psychiatrist a friend had told him about. It cost him a considerable effort, for Catesby had a peculiarly great and very well-grounded distaste for anything dealing with psychological abnormality. Visiting a psychiatrist meant raking up an episode in his past which he had never fully described even to his wife and which Miss Millick only knew of as "something impressively abnormal about Mr. Wran's childhood." Once he had made the decision, however, he felt considerably relieved. The doctor, he told himself, would clear everything up. He could almost fancy the doctor saying, "Merely a bad case of nerves. However, you must consult the oculist whose name I'm writing down for you, and you must take two of these pills in water every hour," and so on. It was almost comforting, and made the coming revelation he would have to make seem less painful.

But as the smoky dusk rolled in, his nervousness returned and he let his joking mystification of Miss Millick run away with him until he realized that he wasn't frightening anyone but himself.

He would have to keep his imagination under better control, he told himself, as he continued to peer out restlessly at the massive, murky shapes of the downtown office buildings. Why, he had spent the whole afternoon building up a kind of neomedieval cosmology of superstition. It wouldn't do. He realized then that he had been standing at the window much longer than he'd thought, for the glass panel in the door was dark and there was no noise coming from the outer office. Miss Millick and the rest must already have gone home.

It was then he made the discovery that there would have been no special reason for dreading the swing around the curve that night. It was, as it happened, a horrible discovery. For, on the shadowed roof across the street and four stories below, he saw the thing huddle and roll across the gravel and, after one upward look of recognition, merge into the blackness beneath the water tank.

As he hurriedly collected his things and made for the elevator, fighting the panicky impulse to run, he began to think of hallucination and mild psychosis as very desirable conditions. For better or for worse, he pinned all his hopes on the doctor.

"So you find yourself growing nervous and… er… jumpy, as you put it," said Dr. Trevethick, smiling with dignified geniality. "Do you notice any more definite physical symptoms? Pain? Headache? Indigestion?"

Catesby shook his head and wet his lips. "I'm especially nervous while riding in the elevated," he murmured swiftly.

"I see. We'll discuss that more fully. But I'd like you first to tell me about something you mentioned earlier. You said there was something about your childhood that might predispose you to nervous ailments. As you know, the early years are critical ones in the development of an individual's behavior pattern."

Catesby studied the yellow reflections of frosted globes in the dark surface of the desk. The palm of his left hand aimlessly rubbed the thick nap of the armchair. After a while he raised his head and looked straight into the doctor's small brown eyes.

"From perhaps my third to my ninth year," he began, choosing the words with care, "I was what you might call a sensory prodigy."

The doctor's expression did not change. "Yes?" he inquired politely.

"What I mean is that I was supposed to be able to see through walls, read letters through envelopes and books through their covers, fence and play Ping-Pong blindfolded, find things that were buried, read thoughts." The words tumbled out.

"And could you?" The doctor's expression was toneless.

"I don't know. I don't suppose so," answered Catesby, long-lost emotions flooding back into his voice. "It's all so confused now. I thought I could, but then they were always encouraging me. My mother... was... well... interested in psychic phenomena. I was... exhibited. I seem to remember seeing things other people couldn't. As if most opaque objects were transparent. But I was very young. I didn't have any scientific criteria for judgment."

He was reliving it now. The darkened rooms. The earnest assemblages of gawking, prying adults. Himself sitting alone on a little platform, lost in a straight-backed wooden chair. The black silk handkerchief over his eyes. His mother's coaxing, insistent questions. The whispers. The gasps. His own hate of the whole business, mixed with hunger for the adulation of adults. Then the scientists from the university, the experiments, the big test. The reality of those memories engulfed him and momentarily made him forget the reason why he was disclosing them to a stranger.

"Do I understand that your mother tried to make use of you as a medium for communicating with the... er... other world ?"

Catesby nodded eagerly.

"She tried to, but she couldn't. When it came to getting in touch with the dead, I was a complete failure. All I could do—or thought I could do—was see real, existing, three-dimensional objects beyond the vision of normal people. Objects they could have seen except for distance, obstruction, or darkness. It was always a disappointment to Mother," he finished slowly.

He could hear her sweetish, patient voice saying, "Try again, dear, just this once. Katie was your aunt. She loved you. Try to hear what she's saying." And he had answered, "I can see a woman in a blue dress standing on the other side of Jones' house." And she had replied, "Yes, I know, dear. But that's not Katie. Katie's a spirit. Try again. Just this once, dear." For a second time the doctor's voice gently jarred him back into the softly gleaming office.

"You mentioned scientific criteria for judgment, Mr. Wran. As far as you know, did anyone ever try to apply them to you?"

Catesby's nod was emphatic.

"*They* did. When I was eight, two young psychologists from the university here got interested in me. I guess they considered it a joke at first, and I remember being very determined to show them I amounted to something. Even now I seem to recall how the note of polite superiority and amused sarcasm drained out of their voices. I suppose they decided at first that it was very clever trickery, but somehow they persuaded Mother to let them try me out under controlled conditions. There were lots of tests that seemed very businesslike after Mother's slipshod little exhibitions. They found I was still clairvoyant—or so they thought. I got worked up and on edge. They were going to demonstrate my supernormal sensory powers to the university psychology faculty. For the first time I began to worry about whether I'd come through. Perhaps they kept me going at too hard a pace, I don't know. At any rate, when the test came, I couldn't do a thing. Everything became opaque. I got desperate and made things up out of my imagination. I lied. In the end I failed utterly, and I believe the two young psychologists lost their jobs as a result."

He could hear the brusque, bearded man saying, "You've been taken in by a child, Flaxman, a mere child. I'm greatly disturbed. You've put yourself on the same plane as common charlatans. Gentlemen, I ask you to banish from your minds this whole sorry episode. It must never be referred to." He winced at the recollection of his feeling of guilt. But at the same time he was beginning to feel exhilarated and almost light-hearted. Unburdening his long-repressed memories had altered his whole viewpoint. The episodes on the elevated began to take on what seemed their proper proportions as merely the bizarre workings of overwrought nerves, and an overly suggestible mind. The doctor, he anticipated confidently, would disentangle the obscure subconscious causes, whatever they might be. And the whole business would be finished off quickly, just as his childhood experience—which was beginning to seem a little ridiculous now—had been finished off.

"From that day on," he continued, "I never exhibited a trace of my supposed powers. My mother was frantic, and tried to sue the university. I had something like a nervous breakdown. Then the divorce was granted, and my father got custody of me. He did his best to make me forget it. We went on long outdoor vacations, and did a lot of athletics, associated with normal, matter-of-fact people. I went to business college eventually. I'm in advertising now. But," Catesby paused, "now that I'm having nervous symptoms, I'm wondering if there mightn't be a connection. It's not a question of whether I really was clairvoyant or not. Very likely my mother taught me a lot of unconscious deceptions, good enough even to fool young psychology instructors. But don't you think it may have some important bearing on my present condition?"

For several moments the doctor regarded him with a slightly embarrassing professional frown. Then he said quietly, "And is there some... er... more specific connection between your experiences then and now? Do you by any chance find that you are once again beginning to... er... see things?"

Catesby swallowed. He had felt an increasing eagerness to unburden himself of his fears, but it was not easy to make a beginning, and the doctor's shrewd question rattled him. He forced himself to concentrate. The thing he thought he had seen on the roof loomed up before his inner eye with unexpected vividness. Yet it did not frighten him. He groped for words.

Then he saw that the doctor was not looking at him but over his shoulder. Color was draining out of the doctor's face and his eyes did not seem so small. Then the doctor sprang to his feet, walked past Catesby, threw open the window and peered into the darkness. As Catesby rose, the doctor slammed down the window and said in a voice whose smoothness was marred by a slight, persistent gasping, "I hope I haven't alarmed you. I saw the face of... er... a Negro prowler on the fire escape. I must have frightened him, for he seems to have gotten out of sight in a hurry. Don't give it another thought. Doctors are frequently bothered by *voyeurs*... er... Peeping Toms."

"A Negro?" asked Catesby, moistening his lips.

The doctor laughed nervously. "I imagine so, though my first odd impression was that it was a white man in blackface. You see, the color didn't seem to have any crown in it. It was dead-black."

Catesby moved toward the window. There were smudges on the glass. "It's quite all right, Mr. Wran." The doctor's voice had acquired a sharp note of impatience, as if he were trying hard to get control of himself and reassume his professional authority. "Let's continue our conversation. I was asking you if you were"—he made a face—"seeing things."

Catesby's whirling thoughts slowed down and locked into place. "No, I'm not seeing anything… other people don't see, too. And I think I'd better go now. I've been keeping you too long." He disregarded the doctor's half-hearted gesture of denial. "I'll phone you about the physical examination. In a way you've already taken a big load off my mind." He smiled woodenly. "Good night, Dr. Trevethick."

Catesby Wran's mental state was a peculiar one. His eyes searched every angular shadow and he glanced sideways down each chasmlike alley and barren basement passageway and kept stealing looks at the irregular line of the roofs, yet he was hardly conscious of where he was going in a general way. He pushed away the thoughts that came into his mind, and kept moving. He became aware of a slight sense of security as he turned into a lighted street where there were people and high buildings and blinking signs. After a while he found himself in the dim lobby of the structure that housed his office. Then he realized why he couldn't go home—because he might cause his wife and baby to see it, just as the doctor had seen it. And the baby, only two years old.

"Hello, Mr. Wran," said the night elevator man, a burly figure in blue overalls, sliding open the grillwork door to the old-fashioned cage. "I didn't know you were working nights now."

Catesby stepped in automatically. "Sudden rush of orders," he murmured inanely. "Some stuff that has to be gotten out."

The cage creaked to a stop at the top floor. "Be working very late, Mr. Wran?"

He nodded vaguely, watched the car slide out of sight, found his keys, swiftly crossed the outer office, and entered his own. His hand went out to the light switch, but then the thought occurred to him that the two lighted windows, standing out against the dark bulk of the building, would indicate his whereabouts and serve as a goal toward which something could crawl and climb. He moved his chair so that the back was against the wall and sat down in the semidarkness. He did not remove his overcoat.

For a long time he sat there motionless, listening to his own breathing and the faraway sounds from the streets below; the thin metallic surge of the crosstown streetcar, the farther one of the elevated, faint lonely cries and honkings, indistinct rumblings. Words he had spoken to Miss Millick in nervous jest came back to him with the bitter taste of truth. He found himself unable to reason critically or connectedly, but by their own volition thoughts rose up into his mind and gyrated slowly and rearranged themselves, with the inevitable movement of planets.

Gradually his mental picture of the world was transformed. No longer a world of material atoms and empty space, but a world in which the bodiless existed and moved according to its own obscure laws or unpredictable impulses. The new picture illuminated with dreadful clarity certain general facts which had always bewildered and troubled him and from which he had tried to hide: the inevitability of hate and war, the diabolically timed mischances which wrecked the best of human intentions, the walls of willful misunderstanding that divided one man from another, the eternal vitality of cruelty and ignorance and greed. They seemed appropriate now, necessary parts of the picture. And superstition only a kind of wisdom.

Then his thoughts returned to himself, and the question he had asked Miss Millick came back, "What would such a thing want from a person? Sacrifices? Worship? Or just fear? What could you do to stop it from troubling you?" It had now become a purely practical question.

With an explosive jangle, the phone began to ring. "Cate, I've been trying everywhere to get you," said his wife. "I never thought you'd be at the office. What are you doing? I've been worried."

He said something about work.

"You'll be home right away?" came the faint anxious question. "I'm a little frightened. Ronny just had a scare. It woke him up. He kept pointing to the window saying, 'Black man, black man.' Of course it's something he dreamed. But I'm frightened. You will be home? What's that, dear? Can't you hear me?"

"I will. Right away," he said. Then he was out of the office, buzzing the night bell and peering down the shaft.

He saw it peering up the shaft at him from three floors below, the sacking face pressed close against the iron grille-work. It started up the stairs at a shockingly swift, shambling gait, vanishing temporarily from sight as it swung into the second corridor below.

Catesby clawed at the door to the office, realized he had not locked it, pushed it in, slammed and locked it behind him, retreated to the other side of the room, cowered between the filing cases and the wall. His teeth were clicking. He heard the groan of the rising cage. A silhouette darkened the frosted glass of the door, blotting out part of the grotesque reverse of the company name. After a little the door opened.

The big-globed overhead light flared on and, standing just inside the door, her hand on the switch, he saw Miss Millick.

"Why, Mr. Wran," she stammered vacuously, "I didn't know you were here. I'd just come in to do some extra typing after the movie. I didn't… but the lights weren't on. What were you—"

He stared at her. He wanted to shout in relief, grab hold of her, talk rapidly. He realized he was grinning hysterically.

"Why, Mr. Wran, what's happened to you?" she asked embarrassedly, ending with a stupid titter. "Are you feeling sick? Isn't there something I can do for you?"

He shook his head jerkily, and managed to say, "No, I'm just leaving. I was doing some extra work myself."

"But you *look* sick," she insisted, and walked over toward him. He inconsequentially realized she must have stepped in mud, for her high-heeled shoes left neat black prints.

"Yes, I'm sure you must be sick. You're so terribly pale." She sounded like an enthusiastic, incompetent nurse. Her face brightened with a sudden inspiration. "I've got something in my bag that'll fix you up right away," she said. "It's for indigestion."

She fumbled at her stuffed oblong purse. He noticed that she was absent-mindedly holding it shut with one hand while she tried to open it with the other. Then, under his very eyes, he saw her bend back the thick prongs of metal locking the purse as if they were tinfoil, or as if her fingers had become a pair of steel pliers.

Instantly his memory recited the words he had spoken to Millick that afternoon. "It couldn't hurt you physically—at first… gradually get its hooks into the world… might even get control of suitably vacuous minds. Then it could hurt whomever it wanted." A sickish, old feeling came to a focus inside him. He began to edge toward the door.

But Miss Millick hurried ahead of him.

"You don't have to wait, Fred," she called. "Mr. Wran's decided to stay a while longer."

The door to the cage shut with a mechanical rattle. The cage creaked. Then she turned around in the door. "Why, Mr. Wran," she gurgled reproachfully, "I just couldn't think of letting you go home now. I'm sure you're terribly unwell. Why, you might collapse in the street. You've just got to stay here until you feel different."

The creaking died away. He stood in the center of the office motionless. His eyes traced the course of Miss Millick's footprints to where she stood blocking the door. Then a sound that was almost a scream was wrenched out of him, for he saw that the flesh of her face was beginning to change color; blackening until the powder on it was a sickly white dust, rouge a hideous pinkish one, lipstick a translucent red film. It was the same with her hands and with the skin beneath her thin silk stockings.

"Why, Mr. Wran," she said, "you're acting as if you were crazy. You must lie down for a little while. Here, I'll help you off with your coat."

The nauseously idiotic and rasping note was the same; only it had been intensified. As she came toward him he turned and ran through the storeroom, clattered a key desperately at the lock of the second door to the corridor.

"Why, Mr. Wran," he heard her call, "are you having some kind of fit? You must let me help you."

The door came open and he plunged out into the corridor and up the stairs immediately ahead. It was only when he reached the top that he realized the heavy steel door in front of him led to the roof. He jerked up the catch.

"Why, Mr. Wran, you mustn't run away. I'm coming after you."

Then he was out on the gritty tar paper of the roof. The night sky was clouded and murky, with a faint pinkish glow from the neon signs. From the distant mills rose a ghostly spurt of flame. He ran to the edge. The street lights glared dizzily upward. Two men walking along were round blobs of hat and shoulders. He swung around.

The thing was in the doorway. The voice was no longer solicitous but moronically playful, each sentence ending in a titter.

"Why, Mr. Wran, why have you come up here? We're all alone. Just think, I might push you off." The thing came slowly toward him. He moved backward until his heels touched the low parapet. Without knowing why or what he was going to do, he dropped to his knees. The black, coarse-grained face came nearer, a focus for the worst in the world, a gathering point for poisons from everywhere. Then the lucidity of terror took possession of his mind, and words formed on his lips.

"I will obey you. You are my god," he said. "You have supreme power over man and his animals and his machines. You rule this city and all others. I recognize that. Therefore spare me."

Again the titter, closer. "Why, Mr. Wran, you never talked like this before. Do you mean it?"

"The world is yours to do with as you will, save or tear to pieces," he answered fawningly, as the words automatically fitted themselves together into vaguely liturgical patterns. "I recognize that. I will praise, I will sacrifice. In smoke and soot and flame I will worship you forever."

The voice did not answer. He looked up. There was only Miss Millick, deathly pale and swaying drunkenly. Her eyes were closed. He caught her as she wobbled toward him. His knees gave way under the added weight and they sank down together on the roof edge.

After a while she began to twitch. Small wordless noises came from her throat, and her eyelids edged open.

"Come on, we'll go downstairs," he murmured jerkily, trying to draw her up. "You're feeling bad."

"I'm terribly dizzy," she whispered. "I must have fainted. I didn't eat enough. And then I'm so nervous lately, about the war and everything, I guess. Why, we're on the roof! Did you bring me up here to get some air? Or did I come up without knowing it? I'm awfully foolish. I used to walk in my sleep, my mother said."

As he helped her down the stairs, she turned and looked at him. "Why, Mr. Wran," she said, faintly, "you've got a big smudge on your forehead. Here, let me get it off for you." Weakly she rubbed at it with her handkerchief. She started to sway again and he steadied her.

"No, I'll be all right," she said. "Only I feel cold. What happened, Mr. Wran? Did I have some sort of fainting spell?"

He told her it was something like that.

Later, riding home in an empty elevated car, he wondered how long he would be safe from the thing. It was a purely practical problem. He had no way of knowing, but instinct told him he had satisfied the brute for some time. Would it want more when it came again? Time enough to answer that question when it arose. It might be hard, he realized, to keep out of an insane asylum. With Helen and Ronny to protect, as well as himself, he would have to be careful and tight-lipped. He began to speculate as to how many other men and women had seen the thing or things like it, and knew that mankind had once again spawned a ghost world, and that superstition once more ruled.

The elevated slowed and lurched in a familiar fashion. He looked at the roofs again, near the curve. They seemed very ordinary, as if what made them impressive had gone away for a while.

THE GIRL WITH THE HUNGRY EYES

ALL RIGHT, I'LL TELL YOU why the Girl gives me the creeps. Why I can't stand to go downtown and see the mob slavering up at her on the tower, with that pop bottle or pack of cigarettes or whatever it is beside her. Why I hate to look at magazines any more because I know she'll turn up somewhere in a brassiere or a bubble bath. Why I don't like to think of millions of Americans drinking in that poisonous half-smile. It's quite a story—more story than you're expecting.

No, I haven't suddenly developed any long-haired indignation at the evils of advertising and the national glamor-girl complex. That'd be a laugh for a man in my racket, wouldn't it? Though I think you'll agree there's something a little perverted about trying to capitalize on sex that way. But it's okay with me. And I know we've had the Face and the Body and the Look and what not else, so why shouldn't someone come along who sums it all up so completely, that we have to call her the Girl and blazon her on all the billboards from Times Square to Telegraph Hill?

But the Girl isn't like any of the others. She's unnatural. She's morbid. She's unholy.

Oh it's 1948, is it, and the sort of thing I'm hinting at went out with witchcraft? But you see I'm not altogether sure myself what I'm hinting at, beyond a certain point. There are vampires and vampires, and not all of them suck blood.

And there were the murders, if they were murders.

Besides, let me ask you this. Why, when America is obsessed with the Girl, don't we find out more about her? Why doesn't she rate a *Time* cover with a droll biography inside? Why hasn't there been a feature in *Life* or the *Post*? A Profile in *The New Yorker*? Why hasn't *Charm* or *Mademoiselle* done her career saga? Not ready for it? Nuts!

Why haven't the movies snapped her up? Why hasn't she been on *Information, Please*? Why don't we see her kissing candidates at political rallies? Why isn't she chosen queen of some sort of junk or other at a convention?

Why don't we read about her tastes and hobbies, her views of the Russian situation? Why haven't the columnists interviewed her in a kimono on the top floor of the tallest hotel in Manhattan and told us who her boyfriends are?

Finally—and this is the real killer—why hasn't she ever been drawn or painted?

Oh, no she hasn't. If you knew anything about commercial art you'd know that. Every blessed one of those pictures was worked up from a photograph. Expertly? Of course. They've got the top artists on it.

But that's how it's done.

And now I'll tell you the *why* of all that. It's because from the top to the bottom of the whole world of advertising, news, and business, there isn't a solitary soul who knows where the Girl came from, where she lives, what she does, who she is, even what her name is.

You heard me. What's more, not a single solitary soul ever *sees* her—except one poor damned photographer, who's making more money off her than he ever hoped to in his life and who's scared and miserable as hell every minute of the day.

No, I haven't the faintest idea who he is or where he has his studio. But I know there has to be such a man and I'm morally certain he feels just like I said.

Yes, I might be able to find her, if I tried. I'm not sure though—by now she probably has other safeguards. Besides, I don't want to.

Oh, I'm off my rocker, am I? That sort of thing can't happen in this Year of our Atom 1948? People can't keep out of sight that way, not even Garbo?

Well I happen to know they can, because last year I was that poor damned photographer I was telling you about. Yes, last year, in 1947, when the Girl made her first poisonous splash right here in this big little city of ours.

Yes, I knew you weren't here last year and you don't know about it. Even the Girl had to start small. But if you hunted through the files of the local newspapers, you'd find some ads, and I might be able to locate you some of the old displays—I think Lovelybelt is still using one of them. I used to have a mountain of photos myself, until I burned them.

Yes, I made my cut off her. Nothing like what that other photographer must be making, but enough so it still bought this whisky. She was funny about money. I'll tell you about that.

But first picture me in 1947. I had a fourth-floor studio in that rathole the Hauser Building, catty-corner from Ardleigh Park.

I'd been working at the Marsh-Mason studios until I'd got my bellyful of it and decided to start in for myself. The Hauser Building was crummy—I'll never forget how the stairs creaked—but it was cheap and there was a skylight.

Business was lousy. I kept making the rounds of all the advertisers and agencies, and some of them didn't object to me too much personally, but my stuff never clicked. I was pretty near broke. I was behind on my rent. Hell, I didn't even have enough money to have a girl.

It was one of those dark gray afternoons. The building was awfully quiet—even with the shortage they can't half rent the Hauser. I'd just finished developing some pix I was doing on speculation for Lovelybelt Girdles and Buford's Pool and Playground—the last a faked-up beach scene. My model had left. A Miss Leon. She was a civics teacher at one of the high schools and modeled for me on the side, just lately on speculation too. After one look at the prints, I decided that Miss Leon probably wasn't just what Lovelybelt was looking for—or my photography either. I was about to call it a day.

And then the street door slammed four stories down and there were steps on the stairs and she came in.

She was wearing a cheap, shiny black dress. Black pumps. No stockings. And except that she had a gray cloth coat over one of them, those skinny arms of hers were bare. Her arms are pretty skinny, you know, or can you see things like that any more?

And then the thin neck, the slightly gaunt, almost prim face, the tumbling mass of dark hair, and looking out from under it the hungriest eyes in the world.

That's the real reason she's plastered all over the country today, you know—those eyes. Nothing vulgar, but just the same they're looking at you with a hunger that's all sex and something more than sex. That's what everybody's been looking for since the Year One—something a little more than sex.

Well, boys, there I was, alone with the Girl, in an office that was getting shadowy, in a nearly empty building. A situation that a million male Americans have undoubtedly pictured to themselves with various lush details. How was I feeling? Scared.

I know sex can be frightening. That cold, heart-thumping when you're alone with a girl and feel you're going to touch her. But if it was sex this time, it was overlaid with something else.

At least I wasn't thinking about sex.

I remember that I took a backward step and that my hand jerked so that the photos I was looking at sailed to the floor.

There was the faintest dizzy feeling like something was being drawn out of me. Just a little bit.

That was all. Then she opened her mouth and everything was back to normal for a while.

"I see you're a photographer, mister," she said. "Could you use a model?"

Her voice wasn't very cultivated.

"I doubt it," I told her, picking up the pix. You see, I wasn't impressed. The commercial possibilities of her eyes hadn't registered on me yet, by a long shot. "What have you done?"

Well she gave me a vague sort of story and I began to check her knowledge of model agencies and studios and rates and what not and pretty soon I said to her, "Look here, you never modeled for a photographer in your life. You just walked in here cold."

Well, she admitted that was more or less so.

All along through our talk I got the idea she was feeling her way, like someone in a strange place. Not that she was uncertain of herself, or of me, but just of the general situation.

"And you think anyone can model?" I asked her pityingly.

"Sure," she said.

"Look," I said, "a photographer can waste a dozen negatives trying to get one halfway human photo of an average woman. How many do you think he'd have to waste before he got a real catchy, glamorous pix of her?"

"I think I could do it," she said.

Well, I should have kicked her out right then. Maybe I admired the cool way she stuck to her dumb little guns. Maybe I was touched by her underfed look. More likely I was feeling mean on account of the way my pix had been snubbed by everybody and I wanted to take it out on her by showing her up.

"Okay, I'm going to put you on the spot," I told her. "I'm going to try a couple of shots of you. Understand, it's strictly on spec. If somebody should ever want to use a photo of you, which is about one chance in two million, I'll pay you regular rates for your time. Not otherwise."

She gave me a smile. The first. "That's swell by me," she said.

Well, I took three or four shots, close-ups of her face since I didn't fancy her cheap dress, and at least she stood up to my sarcasm. Then I remembered I still had the Lovelybelt stuff and I guess the meanness was still working in me because I handed her a girdle and told her to go behind the screen and get into it and she did, without getting flustered as I'd expected, and since we'd gone that far I figured we might as well shoot the beach scene to round it out, and that was that.

All this time I wasn't feeling anything particular in one way or the other except every once in a while I'd get one of those faint dizzy flashes and wonder if there was something wrong with my stomach or if I could have been a bit careless with my chemicals.

Still, you know, I think the uneasiness was in me all the while.

I tossed her a card and pencil. "Write your name and address and phone," I told her, and made for the darkroom.

A little later she walked out. I didn't call any good-byes. I was irked because she hadn't fussed around or seemed anxious about her poses, or even thanked me, except for that one smile.

I finished developing the negatives, made some prints, glanced at them, decided they weren't a great deal worse than Miss Leon. On an impulse I slipped them in with the pix I was going to take on the rounds next morning.

By now I'd worked long enough so I was a bit fagged and nervous, but I didn't dare waste enough money on liquor to help that. I wasn't very hungry. I think I went to a cheap movie.

I didn't think of the Girl at all, except maybe to wonder faintly why in my present womanless state I hadn't made a pass at her. She had seemed to belong to a, well, distinctly more approachable social stratum than Miss Leon. But then of course there were all sorts of arguable reasons for my not doing that.

Next morning I made the rounds. My first step was Munsch's Brewery. They were looking for a "Munsch Girl." Papa Munsch had a sort of affection for me, though he razzed my photography. He had a good natural judgment about that, too. Fifty years ago he might have been one of the shoestring boys who made Hollywood.

Right now he was out in the plant pursuing his favorite occupation. He put down the beaded can, smacked his lips, gabbled something technical to someone about hops, wiped his fat hands on the big apron he was wearing, and grabbed my thin stack of pix.

He was about halfway through, making noises with his tongue and teeth, when he came to her. I kicked myself for even having stuck her in.

"That's her," he said. "The photography's not so hot, but that's the girl."

It was all decided. I wondered now why Papa Munsch sensed what the Girl had right away, while I didn't. I think it was because I saw her first in the flesh, if that's the right word.

At the time I just felt faint.

"Who is she?" he asked.

"One of my new models." I tried to make it casual.

"Bring her out tomorrow morning," he told me. "And your stuff. We'll photograph her here. I want to show you.

"Here, don't look so sick," he added. "Have some beer."

Well I went away telling myself it was just a fluke, so that she'd probably blow it tomorrow with her inexperience, and so on.

Just the same, when I reverently laid my next stack of pix on Mr. Fitch, of Lovelybelt's rose-colored blotter, I had hers on top.

Mr. Fitch went through the motions of being an art critic. He leaned over backward, squinted his eyes, waved his long fingers, and said, "Hmmm. What do you think, Miss Willow? Here, in this light. Of course the photograph doesn't show the bias cut. And perhaps we should use the Lovelybelt Imp instead of the Angel. Still, the girl… Come over here, Binns." More finger-waving. "I want a married man's reaction."

He couldn't hide the fact that he was hooked.

Exactly the same thing happened at Buford's Pool and Playground, except that Da Costa didn't need a married man's say-so.

"Hot stuff," he said, sucking his lips. "Oh, boy, you photographers!"

I hot-footed it back to the office and grabbed up the card I'd given to her to put down her name and address.

It was blank.

I don't mind telling you that the next five days were about the worst I ever went through, in an ordinary way. When next morning rolled around and I still hadn't got hold of her, I had to start stalling.

"She's sick," I told Papa Munsch over the phone.

"She at a hospital?" he asked me.

"Nothing that serious." I told him.

"Get her out here then. What's a little headache?"

"Sorry, I can't."

Papa Munsch got suspicious. "You really got this girl?"

"Of course I have."

"Well, I don't know. I'd think it was some New York model, except I recognized your lousy photography."

I laughed.

"Well look, you get her here tomorrow morning, you hear?"

"I'll try."

"Try nothing. You get her out here."

He didn't know half of what I tried. I went around to all the model and employment agencies. I did some slick detective work at the photographic and art studios. I used up some of my last dimes putting advertisements in all three papers. I looked at high school yearbooks and at employee photos in local house organs. I went to restaurants and drugstores, looking for waitresses, and to dime stores and department stores, looking at clerks. I watched the crowds coming out of movie theatres. I roamed the streets.

Evenings I spent quite a bit of time along Pick-up Row. Somehow that seemed the right place.

The fifth afternoon I knew I was licked. Papa Munsch's deadline—he'd given me several, but this was it—was due to run out at six o'clock. Mr. Fitch had already canceled.

I was at the studio window, looking out at Ardleigh Park.

She walked in.

I'd gone over this moment so often in my mind that I had no trouble putting on my act. Even the faint dizzy feeling didn't throw me off.

"Hello," I said, hardly looking at her.

"Hello," she said.

"Not discouraged yet?"

"No." It didn't sound uneasy or defiant. It was just a statement.

I snapped a look at my watch, got up and said curtly, "Look here, I'm going to give you a chance. There's a client of mine looking for a girl your general type. If you do a real good job you may break into the modeling business.

"We can see him this afternoon if we hurry." I said. I picked up my stuff. "Come on. And next time, if you expect favors, don't forget to leave your phone number."

"Uh, uh," she said, not moving.

"What do you mean?" I said.

"I'm not going to see any client of yours."

"The hell you aren't," I said. "You little nut, I'm giving you a break."

She shook her head slowly. "You're not fooling me, baby, you're not fooling me at all. They *want* me."

And she gave me the second smile.

At the time I thought she must have seen my newspaper ad. Now I'm not so sure.

"And now I'll tell you how we're going to work," she went on. "You aren't going to have my name or address or phone number. Nobody is. And we're going to do all the pictures right here. Just you and me."

You can imagine the roar I raised at that. I was everything—angry, sarcastic, patiently explanatory, off my nut, threatening, pleading.

I would have slapped her face off, except it was photographic capital.

In the end all I could do was phone Papa Munsch and tell him her conditions. I know I didn't have a chance, but I had to take it.

He gave me a really angry bawling out, said "no" several times and hung up.

It didn't faze her. "We'll start shooting at ten o'clock tomorrow," she said.

It was just like her, using that corny line from the movie magazines.

About midnight Papa Munsch called me up.

"I don't know what insane asylum you're renting this girl from," he said, "but I'll take her. Come around tomorrow morning and I'll try to get it through your head just how I want the pictures. And I'm glad I got you out of bed!"

After that it was a breeze. Even Mr. Fitch reconsidered and after taking two days to tell me it was quite impossible, he accepted the conditions too.

Of course you're all under the spell of the Girl, so you can't understand how much self-sacrifice it represented on Mr. Fitch's part when he agreed to forego supervising the photography of my model in the Lovelybelt Imp or Vixen or whatever it was we finally used.

Next morning she turned up on time according to her schedule, and we went to work. I'll say one thing for her, she never got tired and she never kicked at the way I fussed over shots. I got along okay except I still had the feeling of something being shoved away gently. Maybe you've felt it just a little, looking at her picture.

When we finished I found out there were still more rules. It was about the middle of the afternoon. I started down with her to get a sandwich and coffee.

"Uh uh," she said, "I'm going down alone. And look, baby, if you ever try to follow me, if you ever so much as stick your head out that window when I go, you can hire yourself another model."

You can imagine how all this crazy stuff strained my temper—and my imagination. I remember opening the window after she was gone—I waited a few minutes first—and standing there getting some fresh air and trying to figure out what could be back of it, whether she was hiding from the police, or was somebody's ruined daughter, or maybe had got the idea it was smart to be temperamental, or more likely Papa Munsch was right and she was partly nuts.

But I had my pix to finish up.

Looking back it's amazing to think how fast her magic began to take hold of the city after that.

Remembering what came after, I'm frightened of what's happening to the whole country—and maybe the world. Yesterday I read something in *Time* about the Girl's picture turning up on billboards in Egypt.

The rest of my story will help show you why I'm frightened in that big general way. But I have a theory, too, that helps explain, though it's one of those things that's beyond that "certain point." It's about the Girl. I'll give it to you in a few words.

You know how modern advertising gets everybody's mind set in the same direction, wanting the same things, imagining the same things. And you know the psychologists aren't so skeptical of telepathy as they used to be.

Add up the two ideas. Suppose the identical desires of millions of people focused on one telepathic person. Say a girl. Shaped her in their image.

Imagine her knowing the hidden-most hungers of millions of men. Imagine her seeing deeper into those hungers than the people that had them, seeing the hatred and the wish for death behind the lust. Imagine her shaping herself in that complete image, keeping herself as aloof as marble. Yet imagine the hunger she might feel in answer to their hunger.

But that's getting a long way from the facts of my story. And some of those facts are darn solid. Like money. We made money.

That was the funny thing I was going to tell you. I was afraid the Girl was going to hold me up. She really had me over a barrel, you know.

But she didn't ask for anything but the regular rates. Later on I insisted on pushing more money at her, a whole lot. But she always took it with that same contemptuous look, as if she were going to toss it down the first drain when she got outside.

Maybe she did.

At any rate, I had money. For the first time in months I had money enough to get drunk, buy new clothes, take taxicabs. I could make a play for any girl I wanted to. I only had to pick.

And so of course I had to go and pick—

But first let me tell you about Papa Munsch.

Papa Munsch wasn't the first of the boys to try to meet my model but I think he was the first to really go soft on her. I could watch the change in his eyes as he looked at her pictures. They began to get sentimental, reverent. Mama Munsch had been dead for two years.

He was smart about the way he planned it. He got me to drop some information which told him when she came to work, and then one morning he came pounding up the stairs a few minutes before.

"I've got to see her, Dave," he told me.

I argued with him, I kidded him. I explained he didn't know just how serious she was about her crazy ideas. I pointed out he was cutting both our throats. I even amazed myself by bawling him out.

He didn't take any of it in his usual way. He just kept repeating, "But, Dave, I've got to see her."

The street door slammed.

"That's her," I said, lowering my voice. "You've got to get out."

He wouldn't, so I shoved him in the darkroom. "And keep quiet," I whispered. "I'll tell her I can't work today."

I knew he'd try to look at her and probably come busting in, but there wasn't anything else I could do.

The footsteps came to the fourth floor. But she never showed at the door. I got uneasy.

"Get that bum out of there!" she yelled suddenly from beyond the door. Not very loud, but in her commonest voice.

"I'm going up to the next landing," she said, "And if that fat-bellied bum doesn't march straight down to the street, he'll never get another pix of me except spitting in his lousy beer."

Papa Munsch came out of the darkroom. He was white. He didn't look at me as he went out. He never looked at her pictures in front of me again.

That was Papa Munsch. Now it's me I'm telling about. I talked about the subject with her, I hinted, eventually I made my pass.

She lifted my hand off her as if it were a damp rag.

"Nix, baby," she said. "This is working time."

"But afterward…" I pressed.

"The rules still hold." And I got what I think was the fifth smile.

It's hard to believe, but she never budged an inch from that crazy line. I mustn't make a pass at her in the office, because our work was very important and she loved it and there mustn't be any distractions.

And I couldn't see her anywhere else, because if I tried to, I'd never snap another picture of her—and all this with more money coming in all the time and me never so stupid as to think my photography had anything to do with it.

Of course I wouldn't have been human if I hadn't made more passes. But they always got the wet-rag treatment and there weren't any more smiles.

I changed. I went sort of crazy and light-headed—only sometimes I felt my head was going to burst. And I started to talk to her all the time. About myself.

It was like being in a constant delirium that never interfered with business. I didn't pay attention to the dizzy feeling. It seemed natural.

I'd walk around and for a moment the reflector would look like a sheet of white-hot steel, or the shadows would seem like armies of moths, or the camera would be a big black coal car. But the next instant they'd come all right again.

I think sometimes I was scared to death of her. She'd seem the strangest, horriblest person in the world.

But other times…

And I talked. It didn't matter what I was doing—lighting her, posing her, fussing with props, snapping my pix—or where she was—on the platform, behind the screen, relaxing with a magazine—I kept up a steady gab.

I told her everything I knew about myself. I told her about my first girl. I told her about my brother Bob's bicycle. I told her about running away on a freight and the licking Pa gave me when I came home.

I told her about shipping to South America and the blue sky at night. I told her about Betty. I told her about my mother dying of cancer. I told her about being beaten up in a fight in an alley behind a bar. I told her about Mildred. I told her about the first picture I ever sold. I told her how Chicago looked from a sailboat. I told her about the longest drunk I was ever on. I told her about Marsh-Mason. I told her about Gwen. I told her about how I met Papa Munsch. I told her about hunting her. I told her about how I felt now.

She never paid the slightest attention to what I said. I couldn't even tell if she heard me.

It was when we were getting our first nibble from national advertisers that I decided to follow her when she went home.

Wait, I can place it better than that. Something you'll remember from the out-of-town papers—those maybe-murders I mentioned. I think there were six.

I say "maybe" because the police could never be sure they weren't heart attacks. But there's bound to be suspicion when heart attacks happen to people whose hearts have been okay, and always at night when they're alone and away from home and there's a question of what they were doing.

The six deaths created one of those "mystery poisoner" scares. And afterward there was a feeling that they hadn't really stopped, but were being continued in a less suspicious way.

That's one of the things that scares me now.

But at that time my only feeling was relief that I'd decided to follow her.

I made her work until dark one afternoon. I didn't need any excuses, we were snowed under with orders. I waited until the street door slammed, then I ran down. I was wearing rubber-soled shoes. I'd slipped on a dark coat she'd never seen me in, and a dark hat.

I stood in the doorway until I spotted her. She was walking by Ardleigh Park toward the heart of town. It was one of those warm fall nights. I followed her on the other side of the street. My idea for tonight was just to find out where she lived. That would give me a hold on her.

She stopped in front of a display window of Everly's department store, standing back from the glow.

She stood there looking in.

I remembered we'd done a big photograph of her for Everly's, to make a flat model for a lingerie display. That was what she was looking at.

At the time it seemed all right to me that she should adore herself, if that was what she was doing.

When people passed she'd turn away a little or drift back farther into the shadows.

Then a man came by alone. I couldn't see his face very well, but he looked middle-aged. He stopped and stood looking in the window.

She came out of the shadows and stepped up beside him.

How would you boys feel if you were looking at a poster of the Girl and suddenly she was there beside you, her arm linked with yours?

This fellow's reaction showed plain as day. A crazy dream had come to life for him.

They talked for a moment. Then he waved a taxi to the curb. They got in and drove off.

I got drunk that night. It was almost as if she'd known I was following her and had picked that way to hurt me. Maybe she had. Maybe this was the finish.

But the next morning she turned up at the usual time and I was back in the delirium, only now with some new angles added.

That night when I followed her she picked a spot under a street lamp, opposite one of the Munsch Girl billboards.

Now it frightens me to think of her lurking that way.

After about twenty minutes a convertible slowed down going past her, backed up, swung in to the curb. I was closer this time. I got a good look at the fellow's face. He was a little younger, about my age.

Next morning the same face looked up at me from the front page of the paper. The convertible had been found parked on a side street. He had been in it. As in the other maybe-murders, the cause of death was uncertain.

All kinds of thoughts were spinning in my head that day, but there were only two things I knew for sure.

That I'd got the first real offer from a national advertiser, and that I was going to take the Girl's arm and walk down the stairs with her when we quit work.

She didn't seem surprised. "You know what you're doing?" she said.

"I know."

She smiled. "I was wondering when you'd get around to it."

I began to feel good. I was kissing everything good-bye, but I had my arm around hers.

It was another of those warm fall evenings. We cut across into Ardleigh Park. It was dark there, but all around the sky was a sallow pink from the advertising signs.

We walked for a long time in the park. She didn't say anything and she didn't look at me, but I could see her lips twitching and after a while her hand tightened on my arm.

We stopped. We'd been walking across the grass. She dropped down and pulled me after her. She put her hands on my shoulders. I was looking down at her face. It was the faintest sallow pink from the glow in the sky. The hungry eyes were dark smudges.

I was fumbling with her blouse. She took my hand away, not like she had in the studio. "I don't want that," she said.

First I'll tell you what I did afterward. Then I'll tell you why I did it. Then I'll tell you what she said.

What I did was run away. I don't remember all of that because I was dizzy, and the pink sky was swinging against the dark trees. But after a while I staggered into the lights of the street. The next day I closed up the studio. The telephone was ringing when I locked the door and there were unopened letters on the floor. I never saw the Girl again in the flesh, if that's the right word.

I did it because I didn't want to die. I didn't want the life drawn out of me. There are vampires and vampires, and the ones that suck blood aren't the worst. If it hadn't been for the warning of those dizzy flashes, and Papa Munsch and the face in the morning paper, I'd have gone the way the others did. But I realized what I was up against while there was still time to tear myself away. I realized that wherever she came from, whatever shaped her, she's the quintessence of the horror behind the bright billboard.

She's the smile that tricks you into throwing away your money and your life. She's the eyes that lead you on and on, and then show you death. She's the creature you give everything for and never really get.

She's the being that takes everything you've got and gives nothing in return. When you yearn toward her face on the billboards, remember that. She's the lure. She's the bait. She's the Girl.

And this is what she said, "I want you. I want your high spots. I want everything that's made you happy and everything that's hurt you bad. I want your first girl. I want that shiny bicycle. I want that licking. I want that pinhole camera. I want Betty's legs. I want the blue sky filled with stars. I want your mother's death. I want your blood on the cobblestones. I want Mildred's mouth. I want the first picture you sold. I want the lights of Chicago. I want the gin. I want Gwen's hands. I want your wanting me. I want your life. Feed me, baby, feed me."

COMING ATTRACTION

THE COUPE WITH THE FISHHOOKS welded to the fender shouldered up over the curb like the nose of a nightmare. The girl in its path stood frozen, her face probably stiff with fright under her mask. For once my reflexes weren't shy. I took a fast step toward her, grabbed her elbow, yanked her back. Her black skirt swirled out.

The big coupe shot by, its turbine humming. I glimpsed three faces. Something ripped. I felt the hot exhaust on my ankles as the big coupe swerved back into the street. A thick cloud like a black flower blossomed from its jouncing rear end, while from the fishhooks flew a black shimmering rag.

"Did they get you?" I asked the girl.

She had twisted around to look where the side of her skirt was torn away. She was wearing nylon tights.

"The hooks didn't touch me," she said shakily. "I guess I'm lucky."

I heard voices around us:

"Those kids! What'll they think up next?"

"They're a menace. They ought to be arrested."

Sirens screamed at a rising pitch as two motor police, their rocket-assist jets full on, came whizzing toward us after the coupe. But the black flower had become an inky fog obscuring the whole street. The motor police switched from rocket assists to rocket brakes and swerved to a stop near the smoke cloud.

"Are you English?" the girl asked me. "You have an English accent." Her voice came shudderingly from behind the sleek black satin mask. I fancied her teeth must be chattering. Eyes that were perhaps blue searched my face from behind the black gauze covering the eyeholes of the mask.

I told her she'd guessed right.

She stood close to me. "Will you come to my place tonight?" she asked

33

rapidly. "I can't thank you now. And there's something else you can help me about."

My arm, still lightly circling her waist, felt her body trembling. I was answering the plea in that as much as in her voice when I said, "Certainly."

She gave me an address south of Inferno, an apartment number and a time. She asked me my name and I told her.

"Hey, you!"

I turned obediently to the policeman's shout. He shooed away the small clucking crowd of masked women and barefaced men. Coughing from the smoke that the black coupe had thrown out, he asked for my papers. I handed him the essential ones.

He looked at them and then at me. "British Barter? How long will you be in New York?"

Suppressing the urge to say, "For as short a time as possible." I told him I'd be here for a week or so.

"May need you as a witness," he explained. "Those kids can't use smoke on us. When they do that, we pull them in."

He seemed to think the smoke was the bad thing. "They tried to kill the lady," I pointed out.

He shook his head wisely. "They always pretend they're going to, but actually they just want to snag skirts. I've picked up rippers with as many as fifty skirt snags tacked up in their rooms. Of course, sometimes they come a little too close."

I explained that if I hadn't yanked her out of the way she'd have been hit by more than hooks. But he interrupted. "If she'd thought it was a real murder attempt, she'd have stayed here."

I looked around. It was true. She was gone.

"She was fearfully frightened," I told him.

"Who wouldn't be? Those kids would have scared old Stalin himself."

"I mean frightened of more than 'kids.' They didn't look like kids."

"What did they look like?"

I tried without much success to describe the three faces. A vague impression of viciousness and effeminacy doesn't mean much.

"Well, I could be wrong," he said finally. "Do you know the girl? Where she lives?"

"No," I half lied.

The other policeman hung up his radiophone and ambled toward us, kicking at the tendrils of dissipating smoke. The black cloud no longer hid the dingy façades with their five-year-old radiation flash burns, and I could begin to make out the distant stump of the Empire State Building, thrusting up out of Inferno like a mangled finger.

"They haven't been picked up so far," the approaching policeman grumbled. "Left smoke for five blocks, from what Ryan says."

The first policeman shook his head. "That's bad," he observed solemnly.

I was feeling a bit uneasy and ashamed. An Englishman shouldn't lie, at least not on impulse.

"They sound like nasty customers," the first policeman continued in the same grim tone. "We'll need witnesses. Looks as if you may have to stay in New York longer than you expect."

I got the point. I said, "I forgot to show you all my papers," and handed him a few others, making sure there was a five-dollar bill in among them.

When he handed them back a bit later, his voice was no longer ominous. My feelings of guilt vanished.

To cement our relationship, I chatted with the two of them about their job.

"I suppose the masks give you some trouble," I observed. "Over in England we've been reading about your new crop of masked female bandits."

"Those things get exaggerated," the first policeman assured me. "It's the men masking as women that really mix us up. But, brother, when we nab them, we jump on them with both feet."

"And you get so you can spot women almost as well as if they had naked faces," the second policeman volunteered. "You know, hands and all that."

"Especially all that," the first agreed with a chuckle. "Say, is it true that some girls don't mask over in England?"

"A number of them have picked up the fashion," I told him. "Only a few, though—the ones who always adopt the latest style, however extreme."

"They're usually masked in the British newscasts."

"I imagine it's arranged that way out of deference to American taste," I confessed. "Actually, not very many do mask."

The second policeman considered that. "Girls going down the street bare from the neck up." It was not clear whether he viewed the prospect with relish or moral distaste. Likely both.

"A few members keep trying to persuade Parliament to enact a law forbidding all masking," I continued, talking perhaps a bit too much.

The second policeman shook his head. "What an idea. You know, masks are a pretty good thing, brother. Couple of years more and I'm going to make my wife wear hers around the house."

The first policeman shrugged. "If women were to stop wearing masks, in six weeks you wouldn't know the difference. You get used to anything, if enough people do or don't do it."

I agreed, rather regretfully, and left them. I turned north on Broadway (old Tenth Avenue, I believe) and walked rapidly until I was beyond Inferno. Passing such an area of undecontaminated radioactivity always makes a person queasy. I thanked God there weren't any such in England, as yet.

The street was almost empty, though I was accosted by a couple of beggars with faces tunneled by H-bomb scars, whether real or of make-up putty I couldn't tell. A fat woman held out a baby with webbed fingers and toes. I told myself it would have been deformed anyway and that she was only capitalizing on our fear of bomb-induced mutations. Still, I gave her a seven-and-a-half-cent piece. Her mask made me feel I was paying tribute to an African fetish.

"May all your children be blessed with one head and two eyes, sir."

"Thanks," I said, shuddering, and hurried past her.

"…There's only trash behind the mask, so turn your head, stick to your task: Stay away, stay away—from—the—girls!"

This last was the end of an anti-sex song being sung by some religionists half a block from the circle-and-cross insignia of a femalist temple. They reminded me only faintly of our small tribe of British monastics. Above their heads was a jumble of billboards advertising predigested foods, wrestling instruction, radio handles and the like.

I stared at the hysterical slogans with disagreeable fascination. Since the female face and form have been banned on American signs, the very letters of the advertiser's alphabet have begun to crawl with sex—the fat-bellied, big-breasted capital B, the lascivious double O. However, I reminded myself, it is chiefly the mask that so strangely accents sex in America.

A British anthropologist has pointed out that, while it took more than five thousand years to shift the chief point of sexual interest from the hips to the breasts, the next transition, to the face, has taken less than fifty years. Comparing the American style with Moslem tradition is not valid; Moslem women are compelled to wear veils, the purpose of which is to make a husband's property private, while American women have only the compulsion of fashion and use masks to create mystery.

Theory aside, the actual origins of the trend are to be found in the anti-radiation clothing of World War III, which led to masked wrestling, now a fantastically popular sport, and that in turn led to the current female fashion. Only a wild style at first, masks quickly became as necessary as brassieres and lipsticks had been earlier in the century.

I finally realized that I was not speculating about masks in general, but about what lay behind one in particular. That's the devil of the things; you're never sure whether a girl is heightening loveliness or hiding ugliness. I pictured a cool, pretty face in which fear showed only in widened eyes.

Then I remembered her blonde hair, rich against the blackness of the satin mask. She'd told me to come at the twenty-second hour—10 P.M.

I climbed to my apartment near the British Consulate; the elevator shaft had been shoved out of plumb by an old blast, a nuisance in these tall New York buildings. Before it occurred to me that I would be going out again, I automatically tore a tab from the film strip under my shirt. I developed it just to be sure. It showed that the total radiation I'd taken that day was still within the safety limit. I'm not phobic about it, as so many people are these days, but there's no point in taking chances.

I flopped down on the daybed and stared at the silent speaker and the dark screen of the video set. As always, they made me think, somewhat bitterly, of the two great nations of the world. Mutilated by each other, yet still strong, they were crippled giants poisoning the planet with their respective dreams of an impossible equality and an impossible success.

I fretfully switched on the speaker. By luck, the newscaster was talking excitedly of the prospects of a bumper wheat crop, sown by planes across a dust bowl moistened by seeded rains. I listened carefully to the rest of the program (it was remarkably clear of Russian telejamming), but there was no further news of interest to me. And, of course, no mention of the moon, though everyone knows that America and Russia are racing to develop their primary bases into fortresses capable of mutual assault and the launching of alphabet bombs toward Earth. I myself knew perfectly well that the British electronic equipment I was helping trade for American wheat was destined for use in spaceships.

I switched off the newscast. It was growing dark, and once again I pictured a tender, frightened face behind a mask. I hadn't had a date since England. It's exceedingly difficult to become acquainted with a girl in America, where as little as a smile often can set one of them yelping for the police—to say nothing of the increasingly puritanical morality and the roving gangs that keep most women indoors after dark.

And, naturally, the masks, which are definitely not, as the Soviets claim, a last invention of capitalist degeneracy, but a sign of great psychological insecurity. The Russians have no masks, but they have their own signs of stress.

I went to the window and impatiently watched the darkness gather. I was getting very restless. After a while a ghostly violet cloud appeared to the south. My hair rose. Then I laughed. I had momentarily fancied it a radiation from the crater of the Hell-bomb, though I should instantly have known it was only the radio-induced glow in the sky over the amusement and residential area south of Inferno.

Promptly at twenty-two hours I stood before the door of my unknown girl friend's apartment. The electronic say-who-please said just that. I answered clearly, "Wysten Turner," wondering if she'd given my name to the mechanism. She evidently had, for the door opened. I walked into a small empty living room, my heart pounding a bit.

The room was expensively furnished with the latest pneumatic hassocks and sprawlers. There were some midgie books on the table. The one I picked up was the standard hard-boiled detective story in which two female murderers go gunning for each other.

The television was on. A masked girl in green was crooning a love song. Her right hand held something that blurred off into the foreground. I saw the set had a handie, which we haven't in England as yet, and curiously thrust my hand into the handie orifice beside the screen. Contrary to my expectations, it was not like slipping into a pulsing rubber glove, but rather as if the girl on the screen actually held my hand.

A door opened behind me. I jerked out my hand with as guilty a reaction as if I'd been caught peering through a keyhole.

She stood in the bedroom doorway. I think she was trembling. She was wearing a gray fur coat, white-speckled, and a gray velvet evening mask with shirred gray lace around the eyes and mouth. Her fingernails twinkled like silver.

It hadn't occurred to me that she'd expect us to go out.

"I should have told you," she said softly. Her mask veered nervously toward the books and the screen and the room's dark corners. "But I can't possibly talk to you here."

I said doubtfully, "There's a place near the Consulate…"

"I know where we can be together and talk," she said rapidly. "If you don't mind."

As we entered the elevator I said, "I'm afraid I dismissed the cab."

But the cab driver hadn't gone, for some reason of his own. He jumped out and smirkingly held the front door open for us. I told him we preferred to sit in back. He sulkily opened the rear door, slammed it after us, jumped in front and slammed the door behind him.

My companion leaned forward. "Heaven," she said.

The driver switched on the turbine and televisor.

"Why did you ask if I were a British subject?" I said, to start the conversation.

She leaned away from me, tilting her mask close to the window. "See the moon," she said in a quick, dreamy voice.

"But why, really?" I pressed, conscious of an irritation that had nothing to do with her.

"It's edging up into the purple of the sky."

"And what's your name?"

"The purple makes it look yellower."

Just then I became aware of the source of my irritation. It lay in the square of writhing light in the front of the cab beside the driver.

I don't object to ordinary wrestling matches, though they bore me, but I simply detest watching a man wrestle a woman. The fact that the bouts are generally "on the level," with the man greatly outclassed in weight and reach and the masked females young and personable, only makes them seem worse to me.

"Please turn off the screen," I requested the driver.

He shook his head without looking around. "Uh-uh, man," he said. "They've been grooming that babe for weeks for this bout with Little Zirk."

Infuriated, I reached forward, but my companion caught my arm. "Please," she whispered frightenedly, shaking her head.

I settled back, frustrated. She was closer to me now, but silent, and for a few moments I watched the heaves and contortions of the powerful masked girl and her wiry masked opponent on the screen. His frantic scrambling at her reminded me of a male spider.

I jerked around, facing my companion. "Why did those three men want to kill you?" I asked sharply.

The eyeholes of her mask faced the screen. "Because they're jealous of me," she whispered.

"Why are they jealous?"

She still didn't look at me. "Because of him."

"Who?"

She didn't answer.

I put my arm around her shoulders. "Are you afraid to tell me?" I asked. "What is the matter?" She still didn't look my way. She smelled nice.

"See here," I said laughingly, changing my tactics, "you really should tell me something about yourself. I don't even know what you look like."

I half playfully lifted my hand to the band of her neck. She gave it an astonishingly swift slap. I pulled it away in sudden pain. There were four tiny indentations on the back. From one of them a tiny bead of blood welled out as I watched. I looked at her silver fingernails and saw they were actually delicate and pointed metal caps.

"I'm dreadfully sorry," I heard her say, "but you frightened me. I thought for a moment you were going to…"

At last she turned to me. Her coat had fallen open. Her evening dress was Cretan Revival, a bodice of lace beneath and supporting the breasts without covering them.

"Don't be angry," she said, putting her arms around my neck. "You were wonderful this afternoon."

The soft gray velvet of her mask, molding itself to her cheek, pressed mine. Through the mask's lace the wet warm tip of her tongue touched my chin.

"I'm not angry," I said. "Just puzzled and anxious to help."

The cab stopped. To either side were black windows bordered by spears of broken glass. The sickly purple light showed a few ragged figures slowly moving toward us.

The driver muttered, "It's the turbine, man. We're grounded." He sat there hunched and motionless.

"Wish it had happened somewhere else."

My companion whispered, "Five dollars is the usual amount."

She looked out so shudderingly at the congregating figures that I suppressed my indignation and did as she suggested. The driver took the bill without a word. As he started up, he put his hand out the window and I heard a few coins clink on the pavement.

My companion came back into my arms, but her mask faced the television screen, where the tall girl had just pinned the convulsively kicking Little Zirk.

"I'm so frightened," she breathed.

Heaven turned out to be an equally ruinous neighborhood, but it had a club with an awning and a huge doorman uniformed like a spaceman, but in gaudy colors. In my sensuous daze I rather liked it all. We stepped out of the cab just as a drunken old woman came down the sidewalk, her mask awry. A couple ahead of us turned their heads from the half-revealed face as if from an ugly body at the beach. As we followed them in I heard the doorman say, "Get along, grandma, and cover yourself."

Inside, everything was dimness and blue glows. She had said we could talk here, but I didn't see how. Besides the inevitable chorus of sneezes and coughs (they say America is fifty per cent allergic these days), there was a band going full blast in the latest robop style, in which an electronic composing machine selects an arbitrary sequence of tones into which the musicians weave their raucous little individualities.

Most of the people were in booths. The band was behind the bar. On a small platform beside them a girl was dancing, stripped to her mask. The little cluster of men at the shadowy far end of the bar weren't looking at her.

We inspected the menu in gold script on the wall and pushed the buttons for breast of chicken, fried shrimps and two Scotches. Moments later, the serving bell tinkled. I opened the gleaming panel and took out our drinks.

The cluster of men at the bar filed off toward the door, but first they stared around the room. My companion had just thrown back her coat. Their look lingered on our booth. I noticed that there were three of them.

The band chased off the dancing girls with growls. I handed my companion a straw and we sipped our drinks.

"You wanted me to help you about something," I said. "Incidentally, I think you're lovely."

She nodded quick thanks, looked around, leaned forward. "Would it be hard for me to get to England?"

"No," I replied, a bit taken aback. "Provided you have an American passport."

"Are they difficult to get?"

"Rather," I said, surprised at her lack of information. "Your country doesn't like its nationals to travel, though it isn't quite as stringent as Russia."

"Could the British Consulate help me get a passport?"

"It's hardly their—"

"Could you?"

I realized we were being inspected. A man and two girls had paused opposite our table. The girls were tall and wolfish-looking, with spangled masks. The man stood jauntily between them like a fox on its hind legs.

My companion didn't glance at them, but she sat back. I noticed that one of the girls had a big yellow bruise on her forearm. After a moment they walked to a booth in the deep shadows.

"Know them?" I asked. She didn't reply. I finished my drink. "I'm not sure you'd like England," I said. "The austerity's altogether different from your American brand of misery."

She leaned forward again. "But I must get away," she whispered.

"Why?" I was getting impatient.

"Because I'm so frightened."

There were chimes. I opened the panel and handed her the fried shrimps. The sauce on my breast of chicken was a delicious steaming compound of almonds, soy and ginger. But something must have been wrong with the radionic oven that had thawed and heated it, for at the first bite I crunched a kernel of ice in the meat. These delicate mechanisms need constant repair and there aren't enough mechanics.

I put down my fork. "What are you really scared of?" I asked her.

For once her mask didn't waver away from my face. As I waited I could feel the fears gathering without her naming them, tiny dark shapes swarming through the curved night outside, converging on the radioactive pest spot of New York, dipping into the margins of the purple. I felt a sudden rush of sympathy, a desire to protect the girl opposite me. The warm feeling added itself to the infatuation engendered in the cab.

"Everything," she said finally.

I nodded and touched her hand.

"I'm afraid of the moon," she began, her voice going dreamy and brittle, as it had in the cab. "You can't look at it and not think of guided bombs."

"It's the same moon over England," I reminded her.

"But it's not England's moon any more. It's ours and Russia's. You're not responsible. Oh, and then," she said with a tilt of her mask, "I'm afraid of the cars and the gangs and the loneliness and Inferno. I'm afraid of the lust that undresses your face. And"—her voice hushed—"I'm afraid of the wrestlers."

"Yes?" I prompted softly after a moment.

Her mask came forward. "Do you know something about the wrestlers?" she asked rapidly. "The ones that wrestle women, I mean. They often lose, you know. And then they have to have a girl to take their frustration out on. A girl who's soft and weak and terribly frightened. They need that, to keep them men. Other men don't want them to have a girl. Other men want them just to fight women and be heroes. But they must have a girl. It's horrible for her."

I squeezed her fingers tighter, as if courage could be transmitted—granting I had any. "I think I can get you to England," I said.

Shadows crawled onto the table and stayed there. I looked up at the three men who had been at the end of the bar. They were the men I had seen in the big coupe. They wore black sweaters and close-fitting black trousers. Their faces were as expressionless as dopers. Two of them stood about me. The other loomed over the girl.

"Drift off, man," I was told. I heard the other inform the girl, "We'll wrestle a fall, sister. What shall it be? Judo, slapsie or kill-who-can?"

I stood up. There are times when an Englishman simply must be maltreated. But just then the foxlike man came gliding in like the star of a ballet. The reaction of the other three startled me. They were acutely embarrassed.

He smiled at them thinly. "You won't win my favor by tricks like this," he said.

"Don't get the wrong idea, Zirk," one of them pleaded.

"I will if it's right," he said. "She told me what you tried to do this afternoon. That won't endear you to me, either. Drift."

They backed off awkwardly. "Let's get out of here," one of them said loudly as they turned. "I know a place where they fight naked with knives."

Little Zirk laughed musically and slipped into the seat beside my companion. She shrank from him, just a little. I pushed my feet back, leaned forward.

"Who's your friend, baby?" he asked, not looking at her.

She passed the question to me with a little gesture. I told him. "British," he observed. "She's been asking you about getting out of the country? About passports?" He smiled pleasantly. "She likes to start running away. Don't you, baby?" His small hand began to stroke her wrist, the fingers bent a little, the tendons ridged, as if he were about to grab and twist.

"Look here," I said sharply. "I have to be grateful to you for ordering off those bullies, but—"

"Think nothing of it," he told me. "They're no harm except when they're behind steering wheels. A well-trained fourteen-year-old girl could cripple any one of them. Why, even Theda here, if she went in for that sort of thing…" He turned to her, shifting his hand from her wrist to her hair. He stroked it, letting the strands slip slowly through his fingers. "You know I lost tonight, baby, don't you?" he said softly.

I stood up. "Come along," I said to her. "Let's leave."

She just sat there. I couldn't even tell if she was trembling. I tried to read a message in her eyes through the mask.

"I'll take you away," I said to her. "I can do it. I really will."

He smiled at me. "She'd like to go with you," he said. "Wouldn't you, baby?"

"Will you or won't you?" I said to her. She still just sat there.

He slowly knotted his fingers in her hair.

"Listen, you little vermin," I snapped at him. "Take your hands off her."

He came up from the seat like a snake. I'm no fighter. I just know that the more scared I am, the harder and straighter I hit. This time I was lucky. But as he crumpled back I felt a slap and four stabs of pain in my cheek. I clapped my hand to it. I could feel the four gashes made by her dagger finger caps, and the warm blood oozing out from them.

She didn't look at me. She was bending over Little Zirk and cuddling her mask to his cheek and crooning, "There, there, don't feel bad, you'll be able to hurt me afterward."

There were sounds around us, but they didn't come close. I leaned forward and ripped the mask from her face.

I really don't know why I should have expected her face to be anything else. It was very pale, of course, and there weren't any cosmetics. I suppose there's no point in wearing any under a mask. The eyebrows were untidy and the lips chapped. But as for the general expression, as for the feelings crawling and wriggling across it…

Have you ever lifted a rock from damp soil? Have you ever watched the slimy white grubs?

I looked down at her, she up at me. "Yes, you're so frightened, aren't you?"

I said sarcastically. "You dread this little nightly drama, don't you? You're scared to death."

And I walked right out into the purple night, still holding my hand to my bleeding cheek. No one stopped me, not even the girl wrestlers. I wished I could tear a tab from under my shirt and test it then and there, and find I'd taken too much radiation, and so be able to ask to cross the Hudson and go down New Jersey, past the lingering radiance of the Narrows Bomb, and so on to Sandy Hook to wait for the rusty ship that would take me back over the seas to England.

A PAIL OF AIR

PA HAD SENT ME OUT to get an extra pail of air. I'd just about scooped it full and most of the warmth had leaked from my fingers when I saw the thing.

You know, at first I thought it was a young lady. Yes, a beautiful young lady's face all glowing in the dark and looking at me from the fifth floor of the opposite apartment, which hereabouts is the floor just above the white blanket of frozen air four stories thick. I'd never seen a live young lady before, except in the old magazines—Sis is just a kid and Ma is pretty sick and miserable—and it gave me such a start that I dropped the pail. Who wouldn't, knowing everyone on Earth was dead except Pa and Ma and Sis and you?

Even at that, I don't suppose I should have been surprised. We all see things now and then. Ma sees some pretty bad ones, to judge from the way she bugs her eyes at nothing and just screams and screams and huddles back against the blankets hanging around the Nest. Pa says it is natural we should react like that sometimes.

When I'd recovered the pail and could look again at the opposite apartment, I got an idea of what Ma might be feeling at those times, for I saw it wasn't a young lady at all but simply a light—a tiny light that moved stealthily from window to window, just as if one of the cruel little stars had come down out of the airless sky to investigate why the Earth had gone away from the Sun, and maybe to hunt down something to torment or terrify, now that the Earth didn't have the Sun's protection.

I tell you, the thought of it gave me the creeps. I just stood there shaking, and almost froze my feet and did frost my helmet so solid on the inside that I couldn't have seen the light even if it had come out of one of the windows to get me. Then I had the wit to go back inside.

Pretty soon I was feeling my familiar way through the thirty or so blankets and rugs and rubbery sheets Pa has got hung and braced around to slow down the escape of air from the Nest, and I wasn't quite so scared. I began to hear the tick-ticking of the clocks in the Nest and knew I was getting back into air, because there's no sound outside in the vacuum, of course. But my mind was still crawly and uneasy as I pushed through the last blankets—Pa's got them faced with aluminum foil to hold in the heat—and came into the Nest.

Let me tell you about the Nest. It's low and snug, just room for the four of us and our things. The floor is covered with thick woolly rugs. Three of the sides are blankets, and the blankets roofing it touch Pa's head. He tells me it's inside a much bigger room, but I've never seen the real walls or ceiling.

Against one of the blanket-walls is a big set of shelves, with tools and books and other stuff, and on top of it a whole row of clocks. Pa's very fussy about keeping them wound. He says we must never forget time, and without a sun or moon, that would be easy to do.

The fourth wall has blankets all over except around the fireplace, in which there is a fire that must never go out. It keeps us from freezing and does a lot more besides. One of us must always watch it. Some of the clocks are alarm and we can use them to remind us. In the early days there was only Ma to take turns with Pa—I think of that when she gets difficult—but now there's me to help, and Sis too.

It's Pa who is the chief guardian of the fire, though. I always think of him that way: a tall man sitting cross-legged, frowning anxiously at the fire, his lined face golden in its light, and every so often carefully placing on it a piece of coal from the big heap beside it. Pa tells me there used to be guardians of the fire sometimes in the very old days—vestals, he calls them—although there was unfrozen air all around then and a sun too and you didn't really need a fire.

He was sitting just that way now, though he got up quick to take the pail from me and bawl me out for loitering—he'd spotted my frozen helmet right off. That roused Ma and she joined in picking on me.

She's always trying to get the load off her feelings, Pa explains. He shut her up pretty fast. Sis let off a couple of silly squeals too.

Pa handled the pail of air in a twist of cloth. Now that it was inside the Nest, you could really feel its coldness. It just seemed to suck the heat out of everything. Even the flames cringed away from it as Pa put it down close by the fire.

Yet it's that glimmery blue-white stuff in the pail that keeps us alive. It slowly melts and vanishes and refreshes the Nest and feeds the fire. The blankets keep it from escaping too fast. Pa'd like to seal the whole place, but he can't—building's too earthquake-twisted, and besides he has to leave the chimney open for smoke. But the chimney has special things Pa calls baffles up inside it, to keep the air from getting out too quick that way. Sometimes Pa, making a joke, says it baffles him they keep on working, or work at all.

Pa says air is tiny molecules that fly away like a flash if there isn't something to stop them. We have to watch sharp not to let the air run low. Pa always keeps a big reserve supply of it in buckets behind the first blankets, along with extra coal and cans of food and bottles of vitamins and other things, such as pails of snow to melt for water. We have to go way down to the bottom floor for that stuff, which is a mean trip, and get it through a door to outside.

You see, when the Earth got cold, all the water in the air froze first and made a blanket ten feet thick or so everywhere, and then down on top of that dropped the crystals of frozen air, making another mostly white blanket sixty or seventy feet thick maybe.

Of course, all the parts of the air didn't freeze and snow down at the same time.

First to drop out was the carbon dioxide—when you're shovelling for water, you have to make sure you don't go too high and get any of that stuff mixed in, for it would put you to sleep, maybe for good, and make the fire go out. Next there's the nitrogen, which doesn't count one way or the other, though it's the biggest part of the blanket. On top of that and easy to get at, which is lucky for us, there's the oxygen that keeps us alive. It's pale blue, which helps you tell it from the nitrogen. It has to be colder for oxygen to freeze solid than nitrogen. That's why the oxygen snowed down last. Pa says we live better than kings ever did, breathing pure oxygen, but we're used to it and don't notice.

Finally, at the very top, there's a slick of liquid helium, which is funny stuff. All of these gases are in neat separate layers. Like a pussy caffay, Pa laughingly says, whatever that is.

I was busting to tell them all about what I'd seen, and so as soon as I'd ducked out of my helmet and while I was still climbing out of my suit, I cut loose. Right away Ma got nervous and began making eyes at the entry-slit in the blankets and wringing her hands together—the hand where she'd lost three fingers from frostbite inside the good one, as usual. I could tell that Pa was annoyed at me scaring her and wanted to explain it all away quickly, yet I knew he knew I wasn't fooling.

"And you watched this light for some time, son?" he asked when I finished.

I hadn't said anything about first thinking it was a young lady's face.

Somehow that part embarrassed me.

"Long enough for it to pass five windows and go to the next floor."

"And it didn't look like stray electricity or crawling liquid or starlight focused by a growing crystal, or anything like that?"

He wasn't just making up those ideas. Odd things happen in a world that's about as cold as can be, and just when you think matter would be frozen dead, it takes on a strange new life. A slimy stuff comes crawling toward the Nest, just like an animal snuffing for heat—that's the liquid helium. And once, when I was little, a bolt of lightning—not even Pa could figure where it came from—hit the nearby steeple and crawled up and down it for weeks, until the glow finally died.

"Not like anything I ever saw," I told him.

He stood for a moment frowning. Then, "I'll go out with you, and you show it to me," he said.

Ma raised a howl at the idea of being left alone, and Sis joined in, too, but Pa quieted them. We started climbing into our outside clothes—mine had been warming by the fire. Pa made them. They have triple-pane plastic headpieces that were once big double-duty transparent food cans, but they keep heat and air in and can replace the air for a little while, long enough for our trips for water and coal and food and so on.

Ma started moaning again, "I've always known there was something outside there, waiting to get us. I've felt it for years—something that's part of the cold and hates all warmth and wants to destroy the Nest. It's been watching us all this time, and now it's coming after us. It'll get you and then come for me. Don't go, Harry!"

Pa had everything on but his helmet. He knelt by the fireplace and reached in and shook the long metal rod that goes up the chimney and knocks off the ice that keeps trying to clog it. Once a week he goes up on the roof to check if it's working all right. That's our worst trip and Pa won't let me make it alone.

"Sis," Pa said quietly, "come watch the fire. Keep an eye on the air, too. If it gets low or doesn't seem to be boiling fast enough, fetch another bucket from behind the blanket. But mind your hands. Use the cloth to pick up the bucket."

Sis quit helping Ma be frightened and came over and did as she was told. Ma quieted down pretty suddenly, though her eyes were still kind of wild as she watched Pa fix on his helmet tight and pick up a pail and the two of us go out.

Pa led the way and I took hold of his belt. It's a funny thing, I'm not afraid to go by myself, but when Pa's along I always want to hold on to him. Habit, I guess, and then there's no denying that this time I was a bit scared.

You see, it's this way. We know that everything is dead out there. Pa heard the last radio voices fade away years ago, and had seen some of the last folks die who weren't as lucky or well-protected as us. So we knew that if there was something groping around out there, it couldn't be anything human or friendly.

Besides that, there's a feeling that comes with it always being night, *cold* night. Pa says there used to be some of that feeling even in the old days, but then every morning the Sun would come and chase it away. I have to take his word for that, not ever remembering the Sun as being anything more than a big star. You see, I hadn't been born when the dark star snatched us away from the Sun, and by now it's dragged us out beyond the orbit of the planet Pluto, Pa says, and taking us farther out all the time.

We can see the dark star as it crosses the sky because it blots out stars, and especially when it's outlined by the Milky Way. It's pretty big, for we're closer to it than the planet Mercury was to the Sun, Pa says, but we don't care to look at it much and Pa won't set his clocks by it.

I found myself wondering whether there mightn't be something on the dark star that wanted us, and if that was why it had captured the Earth. Just then we came to the end of the corridor and I followed Pa out on the balcony.

I don't know what the city looked like in the old days, but now it's beautiful. The starlight lets you see it pretty well—there's quite a bit of light in those steady points speckling the blackness above. (Pa says the stars used to twinkle once, but that was because there was air.) We are on a hill and the shimmery plain drops away from us and then flattens out, cut up into neat squares by the troughs that used to be streets. I sometimes make my mashed potatoes look like it, before I pour on the gravy.

Some taller buildings push up out of the feathery plain, topped by rounded caps of air crystals, like the fur hood Ma wears, only whiter. On those buildings you can see the darker squares of windows, underlined by white dashes of air crystals. Some of them are on a slant, for many of the buildings are pretty badly twisted by the quakes and all the rest that happened when the dark star captured the Earth.

Here and there a few icicles hang, water icicles from the first days of the cold, other icicles of frozen air that melted on the roofs and dropped and froze again. Sometimes one of those icicles will catch the light of a star and send it to you so brightly you think the star has swooped into the city. That was one of the things Pa had been thinking of when I told him about the light, but I had thought of it myself first and known it wasn't so.

He touched his helmet to mine so we could talk easier and he asked me to point out the windows to him. But there wasn't any light moving around inside them now, or anywhere else. To my surprise, Pa didn't bawl me out and tell me I'd been seeing things. He looked all around quite a while after filling his pail, and just as we were going inside he whipped around without warning, as if to take some peeping thing off guard.

I could feel it, too. The old peace was gone. There was something lurking out there, watching, waiting, getting ready.

Inside, he said to me, touching helmets, "If you see something like that again, son, don't tell the others. Your Ma's sort of nervous these days and we owe her all the feeling of safety we can give her. Once—it was when your sister was born—I was ready to give up and die, but your mother kept me trying. Another time she kept the fire going a whole week all by herself when I was sick. Nursed me and took care of two of you, too.

"You know that game we sometimes play, sitting in a square in the Nest, tossing a ball around? Courage is like a ball, son. A person can hold it only so long, and then he's got to toss it to someone else. When it's tossed your way, you've got to catch it and hold it tight—and hope there'll be someone else to toss it to when you get tired of being brave."

His talking to me that way made me feel grown-up and good. But it didn't wipe away the thing outside from the back of my mind—or the fact that Pa took it seriously.

It's hard to hide your feelings about such a thing. When we got back in the Nest and took off our outside clothes, Pa laughed about it all and told them it was nothing and kidded me for having such an imagination, but his words fell flat. He didn't convince Ma and Sis any more than he did me. It looked for a minute like we were all fumbling the courage-ball. Something had to be done, and almost before I knew what I was going to say, I heard myself asking Pa to tell us about the old days, and how it all happened.

He sometimes doesn't mind telling that story, and Sis and I sure like to listen to it, and he got my idea. So we were all settled around the fire in a wink, and Ma pushed up some cans to thaw for supper, and Pa began. Before he did, though, I noticed him casually get a hammer from the shelf and lay it down beside him.

It was the same old story as always—I think I could recite the main thread of it in my sleep—though Pa always puts in a new detail or two and keeps improving it in spots.

He told us how the Earth had been swinging around the Sun ever so steady and warm, and the people on it fixing to make money and wars and have a good time and get power and treat each other right or wrong, when without warning there comes charging out of space this dead star, this burned out sun, and upsets everything.

You know, I find it hard to believe in the way those people felt, any more than I can believe in the swarming number of them. Imagine people getting ready for the horrible sort of war they were cooking up. Wanting it even, or at least wishing it were over so as to end their nervousness. As if all folks didn't have to hang together and pool every bit of warmth just to keep alive. And how can they have hoped to end danger, any more than we can hope to end the cold?

Sometimes I think Pa exaggerates and makes things out too black. He's cross with us once in a while and was probably cross with all those folks. Still, some of the things I read in the old magazines sound pretty wild. He may be right.

The dark star, as Pa went on telling it, rushed in pretty fast and there wasn't much time to get ready. At the beginning they tried to keep it a secret from most people, but then the truth came out, what with the earthquakes and floods—imagine, oceans of *unfrozen* water!—and people seeing stars blotted out by something on a clear night. First off they thought it would hit the Sun, and then they thought it would hit the Earth. There was even the start of a rush to get to a place called China, because people thought the star would hit on the other side. Not that that would have helped them, they were just crazy with fear.

But then they found it wasn't going to hit either side, but was going to come very close to the Earth. Most of the other planets were on the other side of the Sun and didn't get involved. The Sun and the newcomer fought over the Earth for a little while—pulling it this way and that, in a twisty curve, like two dogs growling over a bone, Pa described it this time—and then the newcomer won and carried us off. The Sun got a consolation prize, though. At the last minute he managed to hold on to the Moon. That was the time of the monster earthquakes and floods, twenty times worse than anything before. It was also the time of the Big Swoop, as Pa calls it, when the Earth speeded up, going into a close orbit around the dark star.

I've asked Pa, wasn't the Earth yanked then, just as he has done to me sometimes, grabbing me by the collar to do it, when I've been sitting too far from the fire. But Pa says no, gravity doesn't work that way. It was like a yank, but nobody felt it. I guess it was like being yanked in a dream.

You see, the dark star was going through space faster than the Sun, and in the opposite direction, and it had to speed up the world a lot in order to take it away.

The Big Swoop didn't last long. It was over as soon as the Earth was settled down in its new orbit around the dark star. But the earthquakes and floods were terrible while it lasted, twenty times worse than anything before. Pa says that all sorts of cliffs and buildings toppled, oceans slopped over, swamps and sandy deserts gave great sliding surges that buried nearby lands. Earth's blanket of air, still up in the sky then, was stretched out and got so thin in spots that people keeled over and fainted—though of course, at the same time, they were getting knocked down by the earthquakes that went with the Big Swoop and maybe their bones broke or skulls cracked.

We've often asked Pa how people acted during that time, whether they were scared or brave or crazy or stunned, or all four, but he's sort of leery of the subject, and he was again tonight. He says he was mostly too busy to notice.

You see, Pa and some scientist friends of his had figured out part of what was going to happen—they'd known we'd get captured and our air would freeze—and they'd been working like mad to fix up a place with airtight walls and doors, and insulation against the cold, and big supplies of food and fuel and water and bottled air. But the place got smashed in the last earthquakes and all Pa's friends were killed then and in the Big Swoop. So he had to start over and throw the Nest together quick without any advantages, just using any stuff he could lay his hands on.

I guess he's telling pretty much the truth when he says he didn't have any time to keep an eye on how other folks behaved, either then or in the Big Freeze that followed—followed very quick, you know, both because the dark star was pulling us away very fast and because Earth's rotation had been slowed by the tug-of-war and the tides, so that the nights were longer.

Still, I've got an idea of some of the things that happened from the frozen folk I've seen, a few of them in other rooms in our building, others clustered around the furnaces in the basements where we go for coal.

In one of the rooms, an old man sits stiff in a chair with an arm and a leg in splints. In another, a man and woman are huddled together in a bed with heaps of covers over them. You can just see their heads peeking out, close together. And in another a beautiful young lady is sitting with a pile of wraps huddled around her, looking hopefully toward the door, as if waiting for someone who never came back with warmth and food. They're all still and stiff as statues, of course, but just like life.

Pa showed them to me once in quick winks of his flashlight, when he still had a fair supply of batteries and could afford to waste a little light. They scared me pretty bad and made my heart pound, especially the young lady.

Now, with Pa telling his story for the umpteenth time to take our minds off another scare, I got to thinking of the frozen folk again. All of a sudden I got an idea that scared me worse than anything yet. You see, I'd just remembered the face I'd thought I'd seen in the window. I'd forgotten about that on account of trying to hide it from the others.

What, I asked myself, if the frozen folk were coming to life? What if they were like the liquid helium that got a new lease on life and started crawling toward the heat just when you thought its molecules ought to freeze solid for ever? Or like the electricity that moves endlessly when it's just about as cold as that? What if the ever-growing cold, with the temperature creeping down the last few degrees to the last zero, had mysteriously wakened the frozen folk to life—not warm-blooded life, but something icy and horrible?

That was a worse idea than the one about something coming down from the dark star to get us. Or maybe, I thought, both ideas might be true. Something coming down from the dark star and making the frozen folk move, using them to do its work. That would fit with both things I'd seen—the beautiful young lady and the moving, starlight light.

The frozen folk with minds from the dark star behind their unwinking eyes, creeping, crawling, snuffing their way, following the heat to the Nest, maybe wanting the heat, but more likely hating it and wanting to chill it for ever, snuff out our fire.

I tell you, that thought gave me a very bad turn and I wanted very badly to tell the others my fears, but I remembered what Pa had said and clenched my teeth and didn't speak.

We were all sitting very still. Even the fire was burning silently. There was just the sound of Pa's voice and the clocks.

And then, from beyond the blankets, I thought I heard a tiny noise. My skin tightened all over me. Pa was telling about the early years in the Nest and had come to the place where he philosophizes. "So I asked myself then," he said, "what's the use of dragging it out for a few years? Why prolong a doomed existence of hard work and cold and loneliness? The human race is done. The Earth is done. Why not give up, I asked myself—and all of a sudden I got the answer."

Again I heard the noise, louder this time, a kind of uncertain, shuffling tread, coming closer. I couldn't breathe.

"Life's always been a business of working hard and fighting the cold," Pa was saying. "The Earth's always been a lonely place, millions of miles from the next planet. And no matter how long the human race might have lived, the end would have come some night. Those things don't matter. What matters is that life is good. It has a lovely texture, like some thick fur or the petals of flowers—you've never seen those, but you know our ice-flowers—or like the texture of flames, never twice the same. It makes everything else worth while. And that's as true for the last man as the first."

And still the steps kept shuffling closer. It seemed to me that the inmost blanket trembled and bulged a little. Just as if they were burned into my imagination, I kept seeing those peering, frozen eyes.

"So right then and there," Pa went on, and now I could tell that he heard the steps, too, and was talking loud so we maybe wouldn't hear them, "right then and there I told myself, that I was going on as if we had all eternity ahead of us. I'd have children and teach them all I could. I'd get them to read books. I'd plan for the future, try to enlarge and seal the Nest. I'd do what I could to keep everything beautiful and growing. I'd keep alive my feeling of wonder even at the cold and the dark and the distant stars."

But then the blanket actually did move and lift. And there was a bright light somewhere behind it. Pa's voice stopped and his eyes turned to the widening slit and his hand went out until it touched and gripped the handle of the hammer beside him.

In through the blanket stepped the beautiful young lady. She stood there looking at us in the strangest way, and she carried something bright and un-winking in her hand. And two other faces peered over her shoulders—men's faces, white and staring.

Well, my heart couldn't have been stopped for more than four or five beats before I realized she was wearing a suit and helmet like Pa's homemade ones, only fancier, and that the men were, too—and that the frozen folk certainly wouldn't be wearing those. Also, I noticed that the bright thing in her hand was just a kind of flashlight.

Sinking down very softly, Ma fainted.

The silence kept on while I swallowed hard a couple of times, and after that there was all sorts of jabbering and commotion.

They were simply people, you see. We hadn't been the only ones to survive; we'd just thought so, for natural enough reasons. These three people had survived, and quite a few others with them. And when we found out *how* they'd survived, Pa let out the biggest whoop of joy.

They were from Los Alamos and they were getting their heat and power from atomic energy. Just using the uranium and plutonium intended for bombs, they had enough to go on for thousands of years. They had a regular little airtight city, with airlocks and all. They even generated electric light and grew plants and animals by it. (At this Pa let out a second whoop, waking Ma from her faint.)

But if we were flabbergasted at them, they were double flabbergasted at us.

One of the men kept saying, "But it's impossible, I tell you. You can't maintain an air supply without hermetic sealing. It's simply impossible."

That was after he had got his helmet off and was using our air. Meanwhile, the young lady kept looking around at us as if we were saints, and telling us we'd done something amazing, and suddenly she broke down and cried.

They'd been scouting around for survivors, but they never expected to find any in a place like this. They had rocket ships at Los Alamos and plenty of chemical fuel. As for liquid oxygen, all you had to do was go out and shovel the air blanket at the top level. So after they'd got things going smoothly at Los Alamos, which had taken years, they'd decided to make some trips to likely places where there might be other survivors. No good trying long-distance radio signals, of course, since there was no atmosphere, no ionosphere, to carry them around the curve of the Earth. That was why all the radio signals had died out.

Well, they'd found other colonies at Argonne and Brookhaven and way around the world at Harwell and Tanna Tuva. And now they'd been giving our city a look, not really expecting to find anything. But they had an instrument that noticed the faintest heat waves and it had told them there was something warm down here, so they'd landed to investigate. Of course we hadn't heard them land, since there was no air to carry the sound, and they'd had to investigate around quite a while before finding us. Their instruments had given them a wrong steer and they'd wasted some time in the building across the street.

By now, all five adults were talking like sixty. Pa was demonstrating to the men how he worked the fire and got rid of the ice in the chimney and all that. Ma had perked up wonderfully and was showing the young lady her cooking and sewing stuff, and even asking about how the women dressed at Los Alamos. The strangers marveled at everything and praised it to the skies. I could tell from the way they wrinkled their noses that they found the Nest a bit smelly, but they never mentioned that at all and just asked bushels of questions.

In fact, there was so much talking and excitement that Pa forgot about things, and it wasn't until they were all getting groggy that he looked and found the air had all boiled away in the pail. He got another bucket of air quick from behind the blankets. Of course that started them all laughing and jabbering again. The newcomers even got a little drunk. They weren't used to so much oxygen.

Funny thing, though—I didn't do much talking at all and Sis hung on to Ma all the time and hid her face when anybody looked at her. I felt pretty uncomfortable and disturbed myself, even about the young lady. Glimpsing her outside there, I'd had all sorts of mushy thoughts, but now I was just embarrassed and scared of her, even though she tried to be nice as anything to me.

I sort of wished they'd all quit crowding the Nest and let us be alone and get our feelings straightened out.

And when the newcomers began to talk about our all going to Los Alamos, as if that were taken for granted, I could see that something of the same feeling struck Pa and Ma, too. Pa got very silent all of a sudden and

Ma kept telling the young lady, "But I wouldn't know how to act there and I haven't any clothes."

The strangers were puzzled like anything at first, but then they got the idea. As Pa kept saying, "It just doesn't seem right to let this fire go out."

Well, the strangers are gone, but they're coming back. It hasn't been decided yet just what will happen. Maybe the Nest will be kept up as what one of the strangers called a "survival school." Or maybe we will join the pioneers who are going to try to establish a new colony at the uranium mines at Great Slave Lake or in the Congo.

Of course, now that the strangers are gone, I've been thinking a lot about Los Alamos and those other tremendous colonies. I have a hankering to see them for myself.

You ask me, Pa wants to see them, too. He's been getting pretty thoughtful, watching Ma and Sis perk up.

"It's different, now that we know others are alive," he explains to me. "Your mother doesn't feel so hopeless any more. Neither do I, for that matter, not having to carry the whole responsibility for keeping the human race going, so to speak. It scares a person."

I looked around at the blanket walls and the fire and the pails of air boiling away and Ma and Sis sleeping in the warmth and the flickering light.

"It's not going to be easy to leave the Nest," I said, wanting to cry, kind of. "It's so small and there's just the four of us. I get scared at the idea of big places and a lot of strangers."

He nodded and put another piece of coal on the fire. Then he looked at the little pile and grinned suddenly and put a couple of handfuls on, just as if it was one of our birthdays or Christmas.

"You'll quickly get over that feeling, son," he said. "The trouble with the world was that it kept getting smaller and smaller, till it ended with just the Nest. Now it'll be good to start building up to a real huge world again, the way it was in the beginning."

I guess he's right. You think the beautiful young lady will wait for me till I grow up? I asked her that and she smiled to thank me and then she told me she's got a daughter almost my age and that there are lots of children at the atomic places. Imagine that.

A DESKFUL OF GIRLS

YES, I SAID GHOSTGIRLS, sexy ones. Personally I never in my life saw any ghosts except the sexy kind, though I saw enough of those I'll tell you, but only for one evening, in the dark of course, with the assistance of an eminent (I should also say notorious) psychologist. It was an interesting experience, to put it mildly, and it introduced me to an unknown field of psycho-physiology, but under no circumstances would I want to repeat it.

But ghosts are supposed to be frightening? Well, who ever said that sex isn't? It is to the neophyte, female or male, and don't let any of the latter try to kid you. For one thing, sex opens up the unconscious mind, which isn't exactly a picnic area. Sex is a force and rite that is basic, primal; and the caveman or cavewoman in each of us is a truth bigger than the jokes and cartoons about it. Sex was behind the witchcraft religion, the sabbats were sexual orgies. The witch was a sexual creature. So is the ghost. After all, what is a ghost, according to all traditional views, but the shell of a human being—an animated skin? And the skin is all sex—it's touch, the boundary, the mask of flesh.

I got that notion about skin from my eminent-notorious psychologist, Dr. Emil Slyker, the first and the last evening I met him, at the Countersign Club, though he wasn't talking about ghosts to begin with. He was pretty drunk and drawing signs in the puddle spilled from his triple martini.

He grinned at me and said, "Look here, What's-Your-Name—oh yes, Carr Mackay, Mister *Justine* himself. Well, look here, Carr, I got a deskful of girls at my office in this building and they're needing attention. Let's shoot up and have a look."

Right away my hopelessly naive imagination flashed me a vivid picture of a desk swarming inside with girls about five or six inches high. They weren't dressed—my imagination never dresses girls except for special effects after long thought—but these looked as if they had been modeled from the drawings of Heinrich Kley or Mahlon Elaine. Literal vest-pocket Venuses, saucy and active. Right now they were attempting a mass escape from the desk, using a couple of nail files for saws, and they'd already cut some trap doors between the drawers so they could circulate around. One group was improvising a blowtorch from an atomizer and lighter fluid. Another was trying to turn a key from the inside, using tweezers for a wrench. And they were tearing down and defacing small signs, big to them, which read

YOU BELONG TO DR. EMIL SLYKER.

My mind, which looks down at my imagination and refuses to associate with it, was studying Dr. Slyker and also making sure that I behaved outwardly like a worshipful fan, a would-be Devil's apprentice. This approach, helped by the alcohol, seemed to be relaxing him into the frame of mind I wanted him to have—one of boastful condescension. Slyker was a plump gut of a man with a perpetually sucking mouth, in his early fifties, fair-complexioned, blond, balding, with the power-lines around his eyes and at the corners of the nostrils. Over it all he wore the ready-for-photographers mask that is a sure sign its wearer is on the Big Time. Eyes weak, as shown by the dark glasses, but forever peering for someone to strip or cow. His hearing bad too, for that matter, as he didn't catch the barman approaching and started a little when he saw the white rag reaching out toward the spill from his drink. Emil Slyker, "doctor" courtesy of some European universities and a crust like blued steel, movie columnist, pumper of the last ounce of prestige out of that ashcan word "psychologist," psychic researcher several mysterious rumored jumps ahead of Wilhelm Reich with his orgone and Rhine with his ESP, psychological consultant to starlets blazing into stars and other ladies in the bucks, and a particularly expert disher-out of that goulash of psychoanalysis, mysticism and magic that is the *chef-d'oeuvre* of our era. *And,* I was assuming, a particularly successful blackmailer. A stinker to be taken very seriously.

My real purpose in contacting Slyker, of which I hoped he hadn't got an inkling yet, was to offer him enough money to sink a small luxury liner in exchange for a sheaf of documents he was using to blackmail Evelyn Cordew, current pick-of-the-pantheon among our sex goddesses. I was working for another film star, Jeff Crain, Evelyn's ex-husband, but not "ex" when it came to the protective urge. Jeff said that Slyker refused to bite on the direct approach, that he was so paranoid in his suspiciousness as to be psychotic, and that I would have to make friends with him first. Friends with a paranoid!

So in pursuit of this doubtful and dangerous distinction, there I was at the Countersign Club, nodding respectfully happy acquiescence to the Master's suggestion and asking tentatively, "Girls needing attention?"

He gave me his whoremaster, keeper-of-the-keys grin and said, "Sure, women need attention whatever form they're in. They're like pearls in a vault, they grow dull and fade unless they have regular contact with warm human flesh. Drink up." He gulped half of what was left of his martini—the puddle had been blotted up meantime and the black surface reburnished—and we made off without any fuss over checks or tabs; I had expected him to stick me with the former at least, but evidently I wasn't enough of an acolyte yet to be granted that honor.

It fitted that I had caught up with Emil Slyker at the Countersign Club. It is to a key club what the latter is to a top-crust bar. Strictly Big Time, set up to provide those in it with luxury, privacy and security. Especially security: I had heard that the Countersign Club bodyguarded even their sober patrons home late of an evening with or without their pickups, but I hadn't believed it until this well-dressed and doubtless well-heeled silent husky rode the elevator up the dead midnight office building with us and only turned back at Dr. Slyker's door. Of course I couldn't have got into the Countersign Club on my own—Jeff had provided me with my entree: an illustrated edition of the Marquis de Sade's *Justine*, its margins annotated by a world-famous recently deceased psychoanalyst. I had sent it in to Slyker with a note full of flowery expression of "my admiration for your work in the psycho-physiology of sex."

The door to Slyker's office was something. No glass, just a dark expanse—teak or ironwood, I guessed—with EMIL SLYKER, CONSULTING PSYCHOLOGIST burnt into it. No Yale lock, but a large keyhole with a curious silver valve that the key pressed aside. Slyker showed me the key with a deprecating smile; the gleaming castellations of its web were the most complicated I'd ever seen, its stem depicted Pasiphaë and the bull. He certainly was willing to pay for atmosphere.

There were three sounds: first the soft grating of the turning key, then the solid snap of the bolts retracting, then a faint creak from the hinges.

Open, the door showed itself four inches thick, more like that of a safe or vault, with a whole cluster of bolts that the key controlled. Just before it closed, something very odd happened: a filmy plastic sheet whipped across the bolts from the outer edge of the doorway and conformed itself to them so perfectly that I suspected static electrical attraction of some sort. Once in place it barely clouded the silvery surface of the bolts and would have taken a close look to spot. It didn't interfere in any way with the door closing or the bolts snapping back into their channels.

The Doctor sensed or took for granted my interest in the door and explained over his shoulder in the dark, "My Siegfried Line. More than one ambitious crook or inspired murderer has tried to smash or think his or her way through that door. They've had no luck. They can't. At this moment there is literally no one in the world who could come through that door without using explosives—and they'd have to be well placed. Cozy."

I privately disagreed with the last remark. Not to make a thing of it, I would have preferred to feel in a bit closer touch with the silent corridors outside, even though they held nothing but the ghosts of unhappy stenographers and neurotic dames my imagination had raised on the way up.

"Is the plastic film part of an alarm system?" I asked. The Doctor didn't answer. His back was to me. I remembered that he'd shown himself a shade deaf. But I didn't get a chance to repeat my question for just then some indirect lighting came on, although Slyker wasn't near any switch ("Our talk triggers it," he said) and the office absorbed me.

Naturally the desk was the first thing I looked for, though I felt foolish doing it. It was a big deep job with a dark soft gleam that might have been that of fine-grained wood or metal. The drawers were file size, not the shallow ones my imagination had played with, and there were three tiers of them to the right of the kneehole— space enough for a couple of life-size girls if they were doubled up according to one of the formulas for the hidden operator of Maelzel's chess-playing automaton. My imagination, which never learns, listened hard for the patter of tiny bare feet and the clatter of little tools. There wasn't even the scurry of mice, which would have done something to my nerves, I'm sure.

The office was an L with the door at the end of this leg. The walls I could see were mostly lined with books, though a few line drawings had been hung—my imagination had been right about Heinrich Kley, though I didn't recognize these pen-and-ink originals, and there were some Fuselis you won't ever see reproduced in books handled over the counter.

The desk was in the corner of the L with the components of a hi-fi spaced along the bookshelves this side of it. All I could see yet of the other leg of the L was a big surrealist armchair facing the desk but separated from it by a wide, low, bare table. I took a dislike to that armchair on first sight, though it looked extremely comfortable. Slyker had reached the desk now and had one hand on it as he turned back toward me, and I got the impression that the armchair had changed shape since I had entered the office—that it had been more like a couch to start with, although now the back was almost straight.

But the Doctor's left thumb indicated I was to sit in it and I couldn't see another chair in the place except the padded button on which he was now settling himself—one of those stenographer deals with a boxing-glove back placed to catch you low in the spine like the hand of a knowledgeable masseur. In the other leg of the L, besides the armchair, were more books, a heavy concertina blind sealing off the window, two narrow doors that I supposed were those of a closet and a lavatory, and what looked like a slightly scaled-down and windowless telephone booth until I guessed it must be an orgone box of the sort Reich had invented to restore the libido when the patient occupies it. I quickly settled myself in the chair, not to be gingerly about it. It was rather incredibly comfortable, almost as if it had adjusted its dimensions a bit at the last instant to conform to mine. The back was narrow at the base but widened and then curled in and over to almost a canopy around my head and shoulders. The seat too widened a lot toward the front, where the stubby legs were far apart. The bulky arms sprang unsupported from the back and took my own just right, though curving inwards with the barest suggestion of a hug. The leather or unfamiliar plastic was as firm and cool as young flesh and its texture was mat under my fingertips.

"An historic chair," the Doctor observed, "designed and built for me by von Helmholtz of the Bauhaus. It has been occupied by all my best mediums during their so-called trance states. It was in that chair that I established to my entire satisfaction the real existence of ectoplasm—that elaboration of the mucous membrane and occasionally the entire epidermis that is distantly analogous to the birth envelope and is the fact behind the persistent legends of the snake-shedding of filmy live skins by human beings, and which the spiritualist quacks are forever trying to fake with their fluorescent cheesecloth and doctored negatives. Orgone, the primal sexual energy?—Reich makes a persuasive case, still… But ectoplasm?—yes! Angna went into trance sitting just where you are, her entire body dusted with a special powder, the tracks and distant smudges of which later revealed the ectoplasm's movements and origin—chiefly in the genital area. The test was conclusive and led to further researches, very interesting and quite revolutionary, none of which I have published; my professional colleagues froth at the mouth, elaborating an opposite sort of foam, whenever I mix the psychic with psychoanalysis—they seem to forget that hypnotism gave Freud his start and that for a time the man was keen on cocaine. Yes indeed, an historic chair."

I naturally looked down at it and for a moment I thought I had vanished, because I couldn't see my legs. Then I realized that the upholstery had changed to a dark gray exactly matching my suit except for the ends of the arms, which merged by fine gradations into a sallow hue which blotted out my hands.

"I should have warned you that it's now upholstered in chameleon plastic," Slyker said with a grin. "It changes color to suit the sitter. The fabric was supplied me over a year ago by Henri Artois, the French dilettante chemist. So the chair has been many shades: dead black when Mrs. Fairlee—you recall the case?—came to tell me she had just put on mourning and then shot her bandleader husband, a charming Florida tan during the later experiments with Angna. It helps my patients forget themselves when they're free-associating and it amuses some people."

I wasn't one of them, but I managed a smile I hoped wasn't too sour. I told myself to stick to business—Evelyn Cordew's and Jeff Crain's business. I must forget the chair and other incidentals, and concentrate on Dr. Emil Slyker and what he was saying—for I have by no means given all of his remarks, only the more important asides. He had turned out to be the sort of conversationalist who will talk for two hours solid, then when you have barely started your reply, give you a hurt look and say, "Excuse me, but if I can get a word in edgewise—" and talk for two hours more. The liquor may have been helping, but I doubt it. When we had left the Countersign Club he had started to tell me the stories of three of his female clients—a surgeon's wife, an aging star scared by a comeback opportunity, and a college girl in trouble—and the presence of the bodyguard hadn't made him hold back on gory details.

Now, sitting at his desk and playing with the catch of a file drawer as if wondering whether to open it, he had got to the point where the surgeon's wife had arrived at the operating theater early one morning to publish her infidelities, the star had stabbed her press agent with the wardrobe mistress' scissors, and the college girl had fallen in love with her abortionist. He had the conversation-hogger's trick of keeping a half-dozen topics in the air at once and weaving back and forth between them without finishing any. And of course he was a male tantalizer. Now he whipped open the file drawer and scooped out some folders and then held them against his belly and watched me as if to ask himself, "Should I?"

After a maximum pause to build suspense he decided he should, and so I began to hear the story of Dr. Emil Slyker's girls, not the first three, of course—they had to stay frozen at their climaxes unless their folders turned up—but others.

I wouldn't be telling the truth if I didn't admit it was a let-down. Here I was expecting I don't know what from his desk and all I got was the usual glimpses into childhood's garden of father-fixation and sibling rivalry and the bed-changing *Sturm und Drang* of later adolescence. The folders seemed to hold nothing but conventional medico-psychiatric case histories, along with physical measurements and other details of appearance, unusually penetrating *precis* of each client's financial resources, occasional notes on possible psychic gifts and other extrasensory talents, and maybe some candid snapshots, judging from the way he'd sometimes pause to study appreciatively and then raise his eyebrows at me with a smile.

Yet after a while I couldn't help starting to be impressed, if only by the sheer numbers. Here was this stream, this freshet, this flood of females, young and not-so-young all thinking of themselves as girls and wearing the girl's suede mask even if they didn't still have the girl's natural face, all converging on Dr. Slyker's office with money stolen from their parents or highjacked from their married lovers, or paid when they signed the six-year contract with semiannual options, or held out on their syndicate boyfriends, or received in a lump sum in lieu of alimony, or banked for dreary years every fortnight from paychecks and then withdrawn in one grand gesture, or thrown at them by their husbands that morning like so much confetti, or, so help me, advanced them on their half-written novels. Yes, there was something very impressive about this pink stream of womankind rippling with the silver and green of cash conveyed infallibly, as if all the corridors and streets outside were concrete-walled spillways, to Dr. Slyker's office, but not to work any dynamos there except financial ones, instead to be worked over by a one-man dynamo and go foaming madly or trickling depletedly away or else stagnate excitingly for months, then: souls like black swamp water gleaming with mysterious lights.

Slyker stopped short with a harsh little laugh. "We ought to have music with this, don't you think?" he said. "I believe I've got the *Nutcracker Suite* on the spindle," and he touched one of an unobtrusive bank of buttons on his desk.

They came without the whisper of a turntable or the faintest preliminary susurrus of tape, those first evocative, rich, sensual, yet eerie chords, but they weren't the opening of any section of the *Nutcracker* I knew—and yet, damn it, they sounded as if they should be. And then they were cut off as if the tape had been snipped and I looked at Slyker and he was white and one of his hands was just coming back from the bank of buttons and the other was clutching the file folders as if they might somehow get away from him and both hands were shaking and I felt a shiver crawling down my own neck.

"Excuse me, Carr," he said slowly, breathing heavily, "but that's high-voltage music, psychically very dangerous, that I use only for special purposes. It is part of the *Nutcracker*, incidentally—the 'Ghostgirls Pavan' which Tchaikovsky suppressed completely under orders from Madam Sesostris, the Saint Petersburg clairvoyant. It was tape-recorded for me by... no, I don't know you quite well enough to tell you that. However, we will shift from tape to disk and listen to the known sections of the suite, played by the same artists."

I don't know how much this recording or the circumstances added to it, but I have never heard the "Danse Arabe" or the "Waltz of the Flowers" or the "Dance of the Flutes" so voluptuous and exquisitely menacing—those tinkling, superficially sugar-frosted bits of music that class after class of little-girl ballerinas have minced and teetered to ad nauseam, but underneath the glittering somber fancies of a thorough-going eroticist. As Slyker, guessing my thoughts, expressed it: "Tchaikovsky shows off each instrument—the flute, the throatier woodwinds, the silver chimes, the harp bubbling gold—as if he were dressing beautiful women in jewels and feathers and furs solely to arouse desire and envy in other men."

For of course we only listened to the music as background for Dr. Slyker's zigzagging, fragmentary, cream-skimming reminiscences. The stream of girls flowed on in their smart suits and flowered dresses and bouffant blouses and toreador pants, their improbable loves and unsuspected hates and incredible ambitions, the men who gave them money, the men who gave them love, the men who took both, the paralyzing trivial fears behind their wisely chic or corn-fed fresh facades, their ravishing and infuriating mannerisms, the trick of eye or lip or hair or wrist-curve or bosom-angle that was the focus of sex in each.

For Slyker could bring his girls to life very vividly, I had to grant that, as if he had more to jog his memory than case histories and notes and even photographs, as if he had the essence of each girl stoppered up in a little bottle, like perfume, and was opening them one by one to give me a whiff. Gradually I became certain that there *were* more than papers and pictures in the folders, though this revelation, like the earlier one about the desk, at first involved a let-down. Why should I get excited if Dr. Slyker filed away mementos of his clients?—even if they were keepsakes of love: lace handkerchiefs and filmy scarves, faded flowers, ribbons and bows, twenty-denier stockings, long locks of hair, gay little pins and combs, swatches of material that might have been torn from dresses, snippets of silk delicate as ghost dandelions—what difference did it make to me if he treasured this junk or it fed his sense of power or was part of his blackmail? Yet it did make a difference to me, for like the music, like the little fearful starts he'd kept giving ever since the business of the "Ghostgirls Pavan," it helped to make everything very real, as if in some more-than-ordinary sense he did have a deskful of girls. For now as he opened or closed the folders there'd often be a puff of powder, a pale little cloud as from a jogged compact, and the pieces of silk gave the impression of being larger than they could be, like a magician's colored handkerchiefs, only most of them were flesh-colored, and I began to get glimpses of what looked like X-ray photographs and artist's transparencies, maybe life-size but cunningly folded, and other slack pale things that made me think of the ultra-fine rubber masks some aging actresses are rumored to wear, and all sorts of strange little flashes and glimmers of I don't know what, except there was that aura of femininity and I found myself remembering what he'd said about fluorescent cheesecloth and I did seem to get whiffs of very individual perfume with each new folder.

He had two file drawers open now, and I could just make out the word burnt into their fronts. The word certainly looked like PRESENT, and there were two of the closed file drawers labeled what looked like PAST and FUTURE. I didn't know what sort of hocus-pocus was supposed to be furthered by those words, but along with Slyker's darting, lingering monologue they did give me the feeling that I was afloat in a river of girls from all times and places, and the illusion that there somehow was a girl in each folder became so strong that I almost wanted to say, "Come on, Emil, trot 'em out, let me look at 'em."

He must have known exactly what feelings he was building up in me, for now he stopped in the middle of a saga of a starlet married to a Negro baseball player and looked at me with his eyes open a bit too wide and said, "All right, Carr, let's quit fooling around. Down at the Countersign I told you I had a deskful of girls and I wasn't kidding—although the truth behind that assertion would get me certified by all the little headshrinkers and Viennese windbags except it would scare the pants off them first. I mentioned ectoplasm earlier, and the proof of its reality. It's exuded by most properly stimulated women in deep trance, but it's not just some dimly fluorescent froth swirling around in a dark seance chamber. It takes the form of an envelope or limp balloon, closed toward the top but open toward the bottom, weighing less than a silk stocking but duplicating the person exactly down to features and hair, following the master-plan of the body's surface buried in the genetic material of the cells. It is a real shed skin but also dimly alive, a gossamer mannequin. A breath can crumple it, a breeze can whisk it away, but under some circumstances it becomes startlingly stable and resilient, a real apparition. It's invisible and almost impalpable by day, but by night, when your eyes are properly accommodated, you can just manage to see it. Despite its fragility it's almost indestructible, except by fire, and potentially immortal. Whether generated in sleep or under hypnosis, in spontaneous or induced trance, it remains connected to the source by a thin strand I call the 'umbilicus' and it returns to the source and is absorbed back into the individual again as the trance fades. But sometimes it becomes detached and then it lingers around as a shell, still dimly alive and occasionally glimpsed, forming the very real basis for the stories of hauntings we have from all centuries and cultures— in fact, I call such shells 'ghosts.' A strong emotional shock generally accounts for a ghost becoming detached from its owner, but it can also be detached artificially. Such a ghost is remarkably docile to one who understands how to handle and cherish it—for instance, it can be folded into an incredibly small compass and tucked away in an envelope, though by daylight you wouldn't notice anything in such an envelope if you looked inside. 'Detached artificially' I said, and that's what I do here in this office, and you know what I use to do it with, Carr?" He snatched up something long and daggerlike and gleaming and held it tight in his plump hand so that it pointed at the ceiling. "Silver shears, Carr, silver for the same reason you use a silver bullet to kill a werewolf, though those words would set the little headshrinkers howling. But would they be howling from outraged scientific attitude, Carr, or from professional jealousy or simply from fear? Just the same as it's unclear why they'd be howling, only certain they would be howling, if I told them that in every fourth or fifth folder in these files I have one or more ghostgirls."

He didn't need to mention fear—I was scared enough myself now, what with him spouting this ghost guff, this spiritualism blather put far more precisely than any spiritualist would dare, this obviously firmly held and elaborately rationalized delusion, this perfect symbolization of a truly insane desire for power over women—filing them away in envelopes!—and then when he got bug-eyed and brandished those foot-long stiletto-shears… Jeff Crain had warned me Slyker was "nuts—brilliant, but completely nuts and definitely dangerous," and I hadn't believed it, hadn't really visualized myself frozen on the medium's throne, locked in ("no one without explosives") with the madman himself. It cost me a lot of effort to keep on the acolyte's mask and simper adoringly at the Master.

My attitude still seemed to be fooling him, though he was studying me in a funny way, for he went on, "All right, Carr, I'll show you the girls, or at least one, though we'll have to put out all the lights after a bit—that's why I keep the window shuttered so tightly—and wait for our eyes to accommodate. But which one should it be?—we have a large field of choice. I think since it's your first and probably your last, it should be someone out of the ordinary, don't you think, someone who's just a little bit special? Wait a second—I know." And his hand shot under the desk where it must have touched a hidden button, for a shallow drawer shot out from a place where there didn't seem to be room for one. He took from it a single fat file folder that had been stored flat and laid it on his knees.

Then he began to talk again in his reminiscing voice and damn if it wasn't so cool and knowing that it started to pull me back toward the river of girls and set me thinking that this man wasn't really crazy, only extremely eccentric, maybe the eccentricity of genius, maybe he actually had hit on a hitherto unknown phenomenon depending on the more obscure properties of mind and matter, describing it to me in whimsically florid jargon, maybe he really had discovered something in one of the blind spots of modern science-and-psychology's picture of the universe.

"Stars, Carr. Female stars. Movie queens. Royal princesses of the gray world, the ghostly chiaroscuro. Shadow empresses. They're realer than people, Carr, realer than the great actresses or casting-couch champions they start as, for they're symbols, Carr, symbols of our deepest longings and—yes—most hidden fears and secretest dreams. Each decade has several who achieve this more-than-life and less-than-life existence, but there's generally one who's the chief symbol, the top ghost, the dream who lures men along toward fulfillment and destruction. In the Twenties it was Garbo, Garbo the Free Soul—that's my name for the symbol she became; her romantic mask heralded the Great Depression. In the late Thirties and early Forties it was Bergman the Brave Liberal; her dewiness and Swedish-Modern smile helped us accept World War Two. And now it's"—he touched the bulky folder on his knees—"now it's Evelyn Cordew the Good-Hearted Bait, the gal who accepts her troublesome sexiness with a resigned shrug and a foolish little laugh, and what general catastrophe she foreshadows we don't know yet. But here she is, and in five ghost versions. Pleased, Carr?"

I was so completely taken by surprise that I couldn't say anything for a moment. Either Slyker had guessed my real purpose in contacting him, or I was faced with a sizable coincidence. I wet my lips and then just nodded.

Slyker studied me and finally grinned. "Ah," he said, "takes you aback a bit, doesn't it? I perceive that in spite of your moderate sophistication you are one of the millions of males who have wistfully contemplated desert-islanding with Delectable Evvie. A complex cultural phenomenon, Eva-Lynn Korduplewski. The child of a coal miner, educated solely in backstreet movie houses—shaped by dreams, you see, into a master dream, an empress dream-figure. A hysteric, Carr, in fact the most classic example I have ever encountered, with unequaled mediumistic capacities and also with a hyper-trophied and utterly ruthless ambition. Riddled by hypochondrias, but with more real drive than a million other avid school-girls tangled and trapped in the labyrinth of film ambitions. Dumb as they come, no rational mind at all, but with ten times Einstein's intuition—intuition enough, at least, to realize that the symbol our sex-exploiting culture craved was a girl who accepted like a happy martyr the incandescent sexuality men and Nature forced on her—and with the patience and malleability to let the feathersoft beating of the black-and-white light in a cheap cinema shape her into that symbol. I sometimes think of her as a girl in a cheap dress standing on the shoulder of a big throughway, her eyes almost blinded by the lights of an approaching bus. The bus stops and she climbs on, dragging a pet goat and breathlessly giggling explanations at the driver. The bus is Civilization.

"Everybody knows her life story, which has been put out in a surprisingly accurate form up to a point: her burlesque-line days, the embarrassingly faithful cartoon-series *Girl in a Fix* for which she posed, her bit parts, the amazingly timed success of the movies *Hydrogen Blonde* and *The Jean Harlow Saga*, her broken marriage to Jeff Crain—What was that, Carr? Oh, I thought you'd started to say something—and her hunger for the real stage and intellectual distinction and power. You can't imagine how hungry for brains and power that girl became *after* she hit the top.

"I've been part of the story of that hunger, Carr, and I pride myself that I've done more to satisfy it than all the culture-johnnies she's had on her payroll. Evelyn Cordew has learned a lot about herself right where you're sitting, and also threaded her way past two psychotic crack-ups. The trouble is that when her third loomed up she didn't come to me, she decided to put her trust in wheat germ and yogurt instead, so now she hates my guts—and perhaps her own, on that diet. She's made two attempts on my life, Carr, and had me trailed by gangsters... and by other individuals. She's talked about me to Jeff Crain, whom she still sees from time to time, and Jerry Smyslov and Nick De Grazia, telling them I've got a file of information on her burlesque days and a few of her later escapades, including some interesting photostats and the real dope on her income and her tax returns, and that I'm using it to blackmail her white. What she actually wants is her five ghosts back, and I can't give them to her because they might kill her. Yes, kill her, Carr." He flourished the shears for emphasis. "She claims that the ghosts I've taken from her have made her lose weight permanently—'look like a skeleton' are her words—and given her fits of mental blackout, a sort of psychic fading—whereas actually the ghosts have bled off from her a lot of malignant thoughts and destructive emotions, which could literally kill her (or someone!) if reabsorbed—they're drenched with death-wish. Still, I hear she actually does look a little haggard, a trifle faded, in her last film, in spite of all Hollywood's medico-cosmetic lore, so maybe she has a sort of case against me. I haven't seen the film, I suppose you have. What do you think, Carr?"

I knew I'd been overworking the hesitation and the silent flattery, so I whipped out quickly, "I'd say it was due to her anemia. It seems to me that the anemia is quite enough to account for her loss of weight and her tired look."

"Ah! You've slipped, Carr," he lashed back, pointing at me triumphantly, except that instead of the outstretched finger there were those ridiculous, horrible shears. "Her anemia is one of the things that's been kept top-secret, known only to a very few of her intimates. Even in all the half-humorous releases about her hypochondrias that's one disease that has never been mentioned. I suspected you were from her when I got your note at the Countersign Club—the handwriting squirmed with tension and secrecy—but the *Justine* amused me—that was a fairly smart dodge—and your sorcerer's apprentice act amused me too, and I happened to feel like talking. But I've been studying you all along, especially your reactions to certain test-remarks I dropped in from time to time, and now you've really slipped." His voice was loud and clear, but he was shaking and giggling at the same time and his eyes showed white all the way around the irises. He drew back the shears a little, but clenched his fingers more tightly around them in a dagger grip, as he said with a chuckle, "Our dear little Evvie has sent all types up against me, to bargain for her ghosts or try to scare or assassinate me, but this is the first time she's sent an idealistic fool. Carr, why didn't you have the sense not to meddle?"

"Look here, Dr. Slyker," I countered before he started answering for me, "it's true I have a special purpose in contacting you. I never denied it. But I don't know anything about ghosts or gangsters. I'm here on a simple, businesslike assignment from the same guy who lent me the *Justine* and who has no purpose whatever beyond protecting Evelyn Cordew. I'm representing Jeff Crain."

That was supposed to calm him. Well, he did stop shaking and his eyes stopped wandering, but only because they were going over me like twin searchlights, and the giggle went out of his voice.

"Jeff Crain! Evvie just wants to murder me, but that cinematic Hemingway, that hulking guardian of hers, that human Saint Bernard tonguing the dry crumbs of their marriage—he wants to set the T-men on me, and the boys in blue and the boys in white too. Evvie's agents I mostly kid along, even the gangsters, but for Jeff's agents I have only one answer."

The silver shears pointed straight at my chest and I could see his muscles tighten like a fat tiger's. I got ready for a spring of my own at the first movement this madman made toward me.

But the move he made was back across the desk with his free hand. I decided it was a good time to be on my feet in any case, but just as I sent my own muscles their orders I was hugged around the waist and clutched by the throat and grabbed by the wrists and ankles. By something soft but firm.

I looked down. Padded, broad, crescent-shaped clamps had sprung out of hidden traps in my chair and now held me as comfortably but firmly as a gang of competent orderlies. Even my hands were held by wide, velvet-soft cuffs that had snapped out of the bulbous arms. They were all a nondescript gray but even as I looked they began to change color to match my suit or skin, whichever they happened to border.

I wasn't scared. I was merely frightened half to death.

"Surprised, Carr? You shouldn't be." Slyker was sitting back like an amiable schoolteacher and gently wagging the shears as if they were a ruler. "Streamlined unobtrusiveness and remote control are the essence of our times, especially in medical furniture. The buttons on my desk can do more than that. Hypos might slip out—hardly hygienic, but then germs are overrated. Or electrodes for shock. You see, restraints are necessary in my business. Deep mediumistic trance can occasionally produce convulsions as violent as those of electroshock, especially when a ghost is cut. And I sometimes administer electroshock too, like any garden-variety headshrinker. Also, to be suddenly and firmly grabbed is a profound stimulus to the unconscious and often elicits closely guarded facts from difficult patients. So a means of making my patients hold still is absolutely necessary—something swift, sure, tasteful and preferably without warning. You'd be surprised, Carr, at the situations in which I've been forced to activate those restraints. This time I prodded you to see just how dangerous you were. Rather to my surprise you showed yourself ready to take physical action against me. So I pushed the button. Now we'll be able to deal comfortably with Jeff Crain's problem… and yours. But first I've a promise to keep to you. I said I would show you one of Evelyn Cordew's ghosts. It will take a little time and after a bit it will be necessary to turn out the lights."

"Dr. Slyker," I said as evenly as I could, "I—"

"Quiet! Activating a ghost for viewing involves certain risks. Silence is essential, though it will be necessary to use—very briefly— the suppressed Tchaikovsky music which I turned off so quickly earlier this evening." He busied himself with the hi-fi for a few moments. "But partly because of that it will be necessary to put away all the other folders and the four ghosts of Evvie we aren't using, and lock the file drawers. Otherwise there might be complications."

I decided to try once more. "Before you go any further, Dr. Slyker," I began, "I would really like to explain—"

He didn't say another word, merely reached back across the desk again. My eyes caught something coming over my shoulder fast and the next instant it clapped down over my mouth and nose, not quite covering my eyes, but lapping up to them—something soft and dry and clinging and faintly crinkled-feeling. I gasped and I could feel the gag sucking in, but not a bit of air came through it. That scared me seven-eighths of the rest of the way to oblivion, of course, and I froze. Then I tried a very cautious inhalation and a little air did seep through. It was wonderfully cool coming into the furnace of my lungs, that little suck of air—I felt I hadn't breathed for a week.

Slyker looked at me with a little smile. "I never say 'Quiet' twice, Carr. The foam plastic of that gag is another of Henri Artois' inventions. It consists of millions of tiny valves. As long as you breathe softly—very, very softly, Carr—they permit ample air to pass, but if you gasp or try to shout through it, they'll close up tight. A wonderfully soothing device. Compose yourself, Carr; your life depends on it."

I have never experienced such utter helplessness. I found that the slightest muscular tension, even crooking a finger, made my breathing irregular enough so that the valves started to close and I was in the fringes of suffocation. I could see and hear what was going on, but I dared not react, I hardly dared think. I had to pretend that most of my body wasn't there (the chameleon plastic helped!), only a pair of lungs working constantly but with infinite caution.

Slyker had just set the Cordew folder back in its drawer, without closing it, and started to gather up the other scattered folders, when he touched the desk again and the lights went out. I have mentioned that the place was completely sealed against light. The darkness was complete.

"Don't be alarmed, Carr," Slyker's voice came chuckling through it. "In fact, as I am sure you realize, you had better not be. I can tidy up just as handily—working by touch is one of my major skills, my sight and hearing being rather worse than appears—and even your eyes must be fully accommodated if you're to see anything at all. I repeat, don't be alarmed, Carr, least of all by ghosts."

I would never have expected it, but in spite of the spot I was in (which actually did seem to have its soothing effects), I still got a little kick—a very little one—out of thinking I was going to see some sort of secret vision of Evelyn Cordew, real in some sense or faked by a master faker. Yet at the same time, and I think beyond all my fear for myself, I felt a dispassionate disgust at the way Slyker reduced all human drives and desires to a lust for power, of which the chair imprisoning me, the "Siegfried Line" door, and the files of ghosts, real or imagined, were perfect symbols.

Among immediate worries, although I did a pretty good job of suppressing all of them, the one that nagged at me the most was that Slyker had admitted to me the inadequacy of his two major senses. I didn't think he would make that admission to someone who was going to live very long.

The black minutes dragged on. I heard from time to time the rustle of folders, but only one soft thud of a file drawer closing, so I knew he wasn't finished yet with the putting-away and locking-up job.

I concentrated the free corner of my mind—the tiny part I dared spare from breathing—on trying to hear something else, but I couldn't even catch the background noise of the city. I decided the office must be sound-proofed as well as light-sealed. Not that it mattered, since I couldn't get a signal out anyway.

Then a noise did come—a solid snap that I'd heard just once before, but knew instantly. It was the sound of the bolts in the office door retracting. There was something funny about it that took me a moment to figure out: there had been no preliminary grating of the key.

For a moment too I thought Slyker had crept noiselessly to the door, but then I realized that the rustling of folders at the desk had kept up all the time.

And the rustling of folders continued. I guessed Slyker had not noticed the door. He hadn't been exaggerating about his bad hearing.

There was the faint creaking of the hinges, once, twice—as if the door were being opened and closed—then again the solid snap of the bolts. That puzzled me, for there should have been a big flash of light from the corridor—unless the lights were all out.

I couldn't hear any sound after that, except the continued rustling of the file folders, though I listened as hard as the job of breathing let me—and in a crazy kind of way the job of cautious breathing helped my hearing, because it made me hold absolutely still yet without daring to tense up. I knew that someone was in the office with us and that Slyker didn't know it. The black moments seemed to stretch out forever, as if an edge of eternity had got hooked into our time-stream.

All of a sudden there was a *swish*, like that of a sheet being whipped through the air very fast, and a grunt of surprise from Slyker that started toward a screech and then was cut off as sharp as if he'd been gagged nose-and-mouth like me. Then there came the scuff of feet and the squeal of the castors of a chair, the sound of a struggle, not of two people struggling, but of a man struggling against restraints of some sort, a frantic confined heaving and panting. I wondered if Slyker's little lump of chair had sprouted restraints like mine, but that hardly made sense.

Then abruptly there was the whistle of breath, as if his nostrils had been uncovered, but not his mouth. He was panting through his nose. I got a mental picture of Slyker tied to his chair some way and eyeing the darkness just as I was doing.

Finally out of the darkness came a voice I knew very well because I'd heard it often enough in movie houses and from Jeff Crain's tape-recorder. It had the old familiar caress mixed with the old familiar giggle, the naiveté and the knowingness, the warm sympathy and cool-headedness, the high-school charmer and the sybil. It was Evelyn Cordew's voice, all right.

"Oh for goodness sake stop threshing around, Emmy. It won't help you shake off that sheet and it makes you look so funny. Yes, I said 'look,' Emmy—you'd be surprised at how losing five ghosts improves your eyesight, like having veils taken away from in front of them; you get more sensitive all over.

"And don't try to appeal to me by pretending to suffocate. I tucked the sheet under your nose even if I did keep your mouth covered. Couldn't bear you talking now. The sheet's called wraparound plastic—I've got my chemical friend too, though he's not Parisian. It'll be next year's number-one packaging material, he tells me. Filmy, harder to see than cellophane, but very tough. An electronic plastic, no less, positive one side, negative the other. Just touch it to something and it wraps around, touches itself, and clings like anything. Like I just had to touch it to you. To make it unwrap fast you can just shoot some electrons into it from a handy static battery—my friend's advertising copy, Emmy—and it flattens out *whang*. Give it enough electrons and it's stronger than steel.

"We used another bit of it that last way, Emmy, to get through your door. Fitted it outside, so it'd wrap itself against the bolts when your door opened. Then just now, after blacking out the corridor, we pumped electrons into it and it flattened out, pushing back all the bolts. Excuse me, dear, but you know how you love to lecture about your valved plastics and all your other little restraints, so you mustn't mind me giving a little talk about mine. And boasting about my friends too. I've got some you don't know about, Emmy. Ever heard the name Smyslov, or the Arain? Some of them cut ghosts themselves and weren't pleased to hear about you, especially the past-future angle."

There was a protesting little squeal of castors, as if Slyker were trying to move his chair.

"Don't go away, Emmy. I'm sure you know why I'm here. Yes, dear, I'm taking them all back as of now. All five. And I don't care how much death-wish they got, because I've got some ideas for that. So now 'scuse me, Emmy, while I get ready to slip into my ghosts."

There wasn't any noise then except Emil Slyker's wheezy breathing and the occasional rustle of silk and the whir of a zipper, followed by soft feathery falls.

"There we are, Emmy, all clear. Next step, my five lost sisters. Why, your little old secret drawer is open—you didn't think I knew about that, Emmy, did you? Let's see now, I don't think we'll need music for this—they know my touch; it should make them stand up and shine."

She stopped talking. After a bit I got the barest hint of light over by the desk, very uncertain at first, like a star at the limit of vision, where it keeps winking back and forth from utter absence to the barest dim existence, or like a lonely lake lit only by starlight and glimpsed through a thick forest, or as if those dancing points of light that persist even in absolute darkness and indicate only a restless retina and optic nerve had fooled me for a moment into thinking they represented something real.

But then the hint of light took definite form, though staying at the dim limit of vision and crawling back and forth as I focused on it because my eyes had no other point of reference to steady it by.

It was a dim angular band making up three edges of a rectangle, the top edge longer than the two vertical edges, while the bottom edge wasn't there. As I watched it and it became a little clearer, I saw that the bands of light were brightest toward the inside—that is, toward the rectangle they partly enclosed, where they were bordered by stark blackness—while toward the outside they faded gradually away. Then as I continued to watch I saw that the two corners were rounded while up from the top edge there projected a narrow, lesser rectangle—a small tab.

The tab made me realize that I was looking at a file folder silhouetted by something dimly glowing inside it

Then the top band darkened toward the center, as would happen if a hand were dipping into the folder, and then lightened again as if the hand were being withdrawn. Then up out of the folder, as if the invisible hand were guiding or coaxing it, swam something no brighter than the bands of light.

It was the shape of a woman, but distorted and constantly flowing, the head and arms and upper torso maintaining more of an approximation to human proportions than the lower torso and legs, which were like churning, trailing draperies or a long gauzy skirt. It was extremely dim, so I had to keep blinking my eyes, and it didn't get brighter.

It was like the figure of a woman phosphorescently painted on a long-skirted slip of the filmiest silk that had silk-stocking-like sheaths for arms and head attached—yes, and topped by some illusion of dim silver hair. And yet it was more than that. Although it looped up gracefully through the air as such a slip might when shaken out by a woman preparing to put it on, it also had a writhing life of its own.

But in spite of all the distortions, as it flowed in an arc toward the ceiling and dove downward, it was seductively beautiful and the face was recognizably that of Evvie Cordew.

It checked its dive and reversed the direction of its flow, so that for a moment it floated upright high in the air, like a filmy nightgown a woman swishes above her head before she slips into it. Then it began to settle toward the floor and I saw that there really was a woman standing under it and pulling it down over her head, though I could see her body only very dimly by the reflected glow of the ghost she was drawing down around her.

The woman on the floor shot up her hands close to her body and gave a quick wriggle and twist and ducked her head and then threw it back, as a woman does when she's getting into a tight dress, and the flowing glowing thing lost its distortions as it fitted itself around her.

Then for a moment the glow brightened a trifle as the woman and her ghost merged and I saw Evvie Cordew with her flesh gleaming by its own light—the long slim ankles, the vase-curve of hips and waist, the impudent breasts almost as you'd guess them from the bikini shots, but with larger aureoles—saw it for an instant before the ghost-light winked out like white sparks dying, and there was utter darkness again.

Utter darkness and a voice that crooned, "Oh that was like silk, Emmy, pure silk stocking all over. Do you remember when you cut it, Emmy? I'd just got my first screen credit and I'd signed the seven-year contract and I knew I was going to have the world by the tail and I felt wonderful and I suddenly got terribly dizzy for no reason and I came to you. And you straightened me out then by coaxing out and cutting away my happiness. You told me it would be a little like giving blood, and it was. That was my first ghost, Emmy, but only the first."

My eyes, recovering swiftly from the brighter glow of the ghost returning to its sources, again made out the three glowing sides of the file folder. And again there swam up out of it a crazily churning phosphorescent woman trailing gauzy streamers. The face was recognizably Evvie's, but constantly distorting, now one eye big as an orange then small as a pea, the lips twisting in impossible smiles and grimaces, the brow shrinking to that of a pinhead or swelling to that of a Mongolian idiot, like a face reflected from a plate-glass window running with water. As it came down over the real Evelyn's face there was a moment when the two were together but didn't merge, like the faces of twins in such a flooded window. Then, as if a squeegee had been wiped down it, the single face came bright and clear, and just as the darkness returned she caressed her lips with her tongue.

And I heard her say, "That one was like hot velvet, Emmy, smooth but with a burn in it. You took it two days after the sneak preview of *Hydrogen Blonde*, when we had the little party to celebrate after the big party, and the current Miss America was there and I showed her what a really valuable body looked like.

That was when I realized that I'd hit the top and it hadn't changed me into a goddess or anything. I still had the same ignorances as before and the same awkwardnesses for the cameramen and cutters to hide—only they were worse because I was in the center of the show window—and I was going to have to fight for the rest of my life to keep my body like it was and then I was going to start to die, wrinkle by wrinkle, lose my juice cell by cell, like anybody else."

The third ghost arched toward the ceiling and down, waves of phosphorescence flickering it all the time. The slender arms undulated like pale serpents and the hands, the finger- and thumb-tips gently pressed together, were like the inquisitive heads of serpents—until the fingers spread so the hands resembled five-tongued creeping puddles of phosphorescent ink. Then into them as if into shoulder-length ivory silk gloves came the solid fingers and arms. For a bit the hands, first part to be merged, were brightest of the whole figure and I watched them help fit each other on and then sweep symmetrically down brow and cheeks and chin, fitting the face, with a little sidewise dip of the ring fingers as they smoothed in the eyes. Then they swept up and back and raked through both heads of hair, mixing them. This ghost's hair was very dark and, mingling, it toned down Evelyn's blonde a little.

"That one felt slimy, Emmy, like the top crawled off of a swamp. Remember, I'd just teased the boys into fighting over me at the Troc. Jeff hurt Lester worse than they let out and even old Sammy got a black eye. I'd just discovered that when you get to the top you have all the ordinary pleasures the boobs yearn for all their lives, and they don't mean anything, and you have to work and scheme every minute to get the pleasures beyond pleasure that you've got to have to keep your life from going dry."

The fourth ghost rose toward the ceiling like a diver paddling up from the depths. Then, as if the whole room were filled with its kind of water, it seemed to surface at the ceiling and jackknife there and plunge down again with a little swoop and then reverse direction again and hover for a moment over the real Evelyn's head and then sink slowly down around her like a diver drowning. This time I watched the bright hands cupping the ghost's breasts around her own as if she were putting on a luminescent net brassiere. Then the ghost's filminess shrank suddenly to tighten over her torso like a cheap cotton dress in a cloudburst.

As the glow died to darkness a fourth time, Evelyn said softly, "Ah but that was cool, Emmy. I'm shivering. I'd just come back from my first location work in Europe and was sick to get at Broadway, and before you cut it you made me relive the yacht party where I overheard Ricco and the author laughing at how I'd messed up my first legitimate play reading, and we swam in the moonlight and Monica almost drowned. That was when I realized that nobody, even the bottom boobs in the audience, really respected you because you were their sex queen. They respected the little female boob in the seat beside them more than they did you. Because you were just something on the screen that they could handle as they pleased inside their minds. With the top folk, the Big Timers, it wasn't any better. To them you were just a challenge, a prize, something to show off to other men to drive them nuts, but never something to love. Well, that's four, Emmy, and four and one makes all."

The last ghost rose whirling and billowing like a silk robe in the wind, like a crazy photomontage, like a surrealist painting done in a barely visible wash of pale flesh tones on a black canvas, or rather like an endless series of such surrealist paintings, each distortion melting into the next—trailing behind it a gauzy wake of draperies, which I realized was the way ghosts were always pictured and described. I watched the draperies bunch as Evelyn pulled them down around her, and then they suddenly whipped tight against her thighs, like a skirt in a strong wind or like nylon clinging in the cold. The final glow was a little stronger, as if there were more life in the shining woman than there had been at first.

"Ah that was like the brush of wings, Emmy, like feathers in the wind. You cut it after the party in Sammy's plane to celebrate me being the top money star in the industry. I bothered the pilot because I wanted him to smash us in a dive. That was when I realized I was just property—something for men to make money out of (and me to make money, too, out of me), from the star who married me to prop his box-office rating to the sticks theater owner who hoped I'd sell a few extra tickets. I found that my deepest love—it was once for you, Emmy—was just something for a man to capitalize on. That any man, no matter how sweet or strong, could in the end never be anything but a pimp. Like you, Emmy."

Just darkness for a while then, darkness and silence, broken only by the faint rustling of clothing. Finally her voice again: "So now I got my pictures back, Emmy. All the original negatives, you might say, for you can't make prints of them or second negatives—I don't think. Or is there a way of making prints of them, Emmy—duplicate women? It's not worth letting you answer—you'd be bound to say yes to scare me.

"What do we do with you now, Emmy? I know what you'd do to me if you had the chance, for you've done it already. You've kept parts of me—no, five real *me's*—tucked away in envelopes for a long time, something to take out and look at or run through your hand or twist around a finger or crumple in a ball, whenever you felt bored on a long afternoon or an endless night. Or maybe show off to special friends or even give other girls to wear—you didn't think I knew about that trick, did you, Emmy?—I hope I poisoned them, I hope I made them burn! Remember, Emmy, I'm full of death-wish now, five ghosts of it. Yes, Emmy, what do we do with you now?"

Then, for the first time since the ghosts had shown, I heard the sound of Dr. Slyker's breath whistling through his nose and the muffled grunts and creakings as he lurched against the clinging sheet.

"Makes you think, doesn't it, Emmy? I wish I'd asked my ghosts what to do with you when I had the chance—I wish I'd known how to ask them. They'd have been the ones to decide. Now they're too mixed in.

"We'll let the other girls decide—the other ghosts. How many dozen are there, Emmy? How many hundred? I'll trust their judgment. Do your ghosts love you, Emmy?"

I heard the click of her heels followed by soft rushes ending in thuds—the file drawers being yanked open. Slyker got noisier.

"You don't think they love you, Emmy? Or they do but their way of showing affection won't be exactly comfortable, or safe? We'll see."

The heels clicked again for a few steps.

"And now, music. The fourth button, Emmy?"

There came again those sensual, spectral chords that opened the "Ghost-girls Pavan," and this time they led gradually into a music that seemed to twirl and spin, very slowly and with a lazy grace, the music of space, the music of free fall. It made easier the slow breathing that meant life to me. I became aware of dim fountains. Each file drawer was outlined by a phosphorescent glow shooting upward.

Over the edge of one drawer a pale hand flowed. It slipped back, but there was another, and another. The music strengthened, though spinning still more lazily, and out of the phosphorescence-edged parallelogram of the file drawers there began to pour, swiftly now, pale streams of womankind. Ever-changing faces that were gossamer masks of madness, drunkenness, desire and hate; arms like a flood of serpents; bodies that writhed, convulsed, yet flowed like milk by moonlight.

They swirled out in a circle like slender clouds in a ring, a spinning circle that dipped close to me, inquisitively, a hundred strangely slitted eyes seeming to peer.

The spinning forms brightened. By their light I began to see Dr. Slyker, the lower part of his face tight with the transparent plastic, only the nostrils flaring and the bulging eyes switching their gaze about, his arms tight to his sides.

The first spiral of the ring speeded up and began to tighten around his head and neck. He was beginning to twirl slowly on his tiny chair, as if he were a fly caught in the middle of a web and being spun in a cocoon by the spider. His face was alternately obscured and illuminated by the bright smoky forms swinging past it. It looked as if he was being strangled by his own cigarette smoke in a film run backwards.

His face began to darken as the glowing circle tightened against him.

Once more there was utter darkness.

Then a whirring click and a tiny shower of sparks, three times repeated, then a tiny blue flame. It moved and stopped and moved, leaving behind it more silent tiny flames, yellow ones. They grew. Evelyn was systematically setting fire to the files.

I knew it might be curtains for me, but I shouted—it came out as a kind of hiccup—and my breath was instantly cut off as the valves in the gag closed.

But Evelyn turned. She had been bending close over Emil's chest and the light from the growing flames highlighted her smile. Through the dark red mist that was closing in on my vision I saw the flames begin to leap from one drawer after another. There was a sudden low roar, like film or acetate shavings burning.

Suddenly Evelyn reached across the desk and touched a button. As I started to red out, I realized that the gag was off, the clamps were loose.

I floundered to my feet, pain stabbing my numbed muscles. The room was full of flickering brightness under a dirty cloud bulging from the ceiling. Evelyn had jerked the transparent sheet off Slyker and was crumpling it up. He started to fall forward, very slowly. Looking at me she said, "Tell Jeff he's dead."

But before Slyker hit the floor, she was out the door. I took a step toward Slyker, felt the stinging heat of the flames. My legs were like shaky stilts as I made for the door. As I steadied myself on the jamb I took a last look back, then lurched on.

There wasn't a light in the corridor. The glow of the flames behind me helped a little.

The top of the elevator was dropping out of sight as I reached the shaft. I took the stairs. It was a painful descent. As I trotted out of the building—it was the best speed I could manage—I heard sirens coming. Evelyn must have put in a call—or one of her "friends," though not even Jeff Crain was able to tell me more about them: who her chemist was and who were the Arain—it's an old word for spider, but that leads nowhere. I don't even know how she knew I was working for Jeff; Evelyn Cordew is harder than ever to see and I haven't tried. I don't believe even Jeff's seen her; though I've sometimes wondered if I wasn't used as a cat's paw.

I'm keeping out of it—just as I left it to the firemen to discover Dr. Emil Slyker "suffocated by smoke" from a fire in his "weird" private office, a fire which it was reported did little more than char the furniture and burn the contents of his files and the tapes of his hi-fi.

I think a little more was burned. When I looked back the last time I saw the Doctor lying in a strait jacket of pale flames. It may have been scattered papers or the electronic plastic. I think it was ghostgirls burning.

SPACE-TIME FOR SPRINGERS

GUMMITCH WAS A SUPERKITTEN, as he knew very well, with an I.Q. of about 160. Of course, he didn't talk. But everybody knows that I.Q. tests based on language ability are very one-sided. Besides, he would talk as soon as they started setting a place for him at table and pouring him coffee. Ashurbanipal and Cleopatra ate horsemeat from pans on the floor and they didn't talk. Baby dined in his crib on milk from a bottle and he didn't talk. Sissy sat at table but they didn't pour her coffee and she didn't talk—not one word. Father and Mother (whom Gummitch had nicknamed Old Horsemeat and Kitty-Come-Here) sat at table and poured each other coffee and they *did* talk. Q.E.D.

Meanwhile, he would get by very well on thought projection and intuitive understanding of all human speech—not even to mention cat patois, which almost any civilized animal could play by ear. The dramatic monologues and Socratic dialogues, the quiz and panel-show appearances, the felidological expedition to darkest Africa (where he would uncover the real truth behind lions and tigers), the exploration of the outer planets—all these could wait. The same went for the books for which he was ceaselessly accumulating material: *The Encyclopedia of Odors, Anthropofeline Psychology, Invisible Signs and Secret Wonders, Space-Time for Springers, Slit Eyes Look at Life*, et cetera. For the present it was enough to live existence to the hilt and soak up knowledge, missing no experience proper to his age level—to rush about with tail aflame.

So to all outward appearances Gummitch was just a vividly normal kitten, as shown by the succession of nicknames he bore along the magic path that led from blue-eyed infancy toward puberty: Little One, Squawker, Portly, Bumble (for purring not clumsiness), Old Starved-to-Death, Fierso, Loverboy (affection not sex), Spook and Catnik. Of these only the last perhaps requires further explanation: the Russians had just sent Muttnik up after Sputnik, so that when one evening Gummitch streaked three times across the firmament of the living room floor in the same direction, past the fixed stars of the humans and the comparatively slow-moving heavenly bodies of the two older cats, and Kitty-Come-Here quoted the line from Keats:

> Then felt I like some watcher of the skies
> When a new planet swims into his ken;

it was inevitable that Old Horsemeat would say, "Ah—Catnik!"

The new name lasted all of three days, to be replaced by Gummitch, which showed signs of becoming permanent. The little cat was on the verge of truly growing up, at least so Gummitch overheard Old Horsemeat comment to Kitty-Come-Here. A few short weeks, Old Horsemeat said, and Gummitch's fiery flesh would harden, his slim neck thicken, the electricity vanish from everything but his fur, and all his delightful kittenish qualities rapidly give way to the earthbound single-mindedness of a tom. They'd be lucky, Old Horsemeat concluded, if he didn't turn completely surly like Ashurbanipal.

Gummitch listened to these predictions with gay unconcern and with secret amusement from his vantage point of superior knowledge, in the same spirit that he accepted so many phases of his outwardly conventional existence: the murderous sidelong looks he got from Ashurbanipal and Cleopatra as he devoured his own horsemeat from his own little tin pan, because they sometimes were given canned catfood but he never; the stark idiocy of Baby, who didn't know the difference between a live cat and a stuffed teddy bear and who tried to cover up his ignorance by making goo-goo noises and poking indiscriminately at all eyes; the far more serious—because cleverly hidden—maliciousness of Sissy, who had to be watched out for warily— especially when you were alone—and whose retarded—even warped —development, Gummitch knew, was Old Horsemeat and Kitty-Come-Here's deepest, most secret, worry (more of Sissy and her evil ways soon); the limited intellect of Kitty-Come-Here, who despite the amounts of coffee she drank was quite as featherbrained as kittens are supposed to be and who firmly believed, for example, that kittens operated in the same space-time as other beings—that to get from *here* to *there* they had to cross the space *between*—and similar fallacies; the mental stodginess of even Old Horsemeat, who although he understood quite a bit of the secret doctrine and talked intelligently to Gummitch when they were alone, nevertheless suffered from the limitations of his status—a rather nice old god but a maddeningly slow-witted one.

But Gummitch could easily forgive all this massed inadequacy and down-right brutishness in his felino-human household, because he was aware that he alone knew the real truth about himself and about other kittens and babies as well, the truth which was hidden from weaker minds, the truth that was as intrinsically incredible as the germ theory of disease or the origin of the whole great universe in the explosion of a single atom.

As a baby kitten Gummitch had believed that Old Horsemeat's two hands were hairless kittens permanently attached to the ends of Old Horsemeat's arms but having an independent life of their own. How he had hated and loved those two five-legged sallow monsters, his first playmates, comforters and battle-opponents!

Well, even that fantastic discarded notion was but a trifling fancy compared to the real truth about himself!

The forehead of Zeus split open to give birth to Minerva. Gummitch had been born from the waist-fold of a dirty old terrycloth bathrobe, Old Horsemeat's basic garment. The kitten was intuitively certain of it and had proved it to himself as well as any Descartes or Aristotle. In a kitten-size tuck of that ancient bathrobe the atoms of his body had gathered and quickened into life. His earliest memories were of snoozing wrapped in terrycloth, warmed by Old Horsemeat's heat. Old Horsemeat and Kitty-Come-Here were his true parents. The other theory of his origin, the one he heard Old Horsemeat and Kitty-Come-Here recount from time to time—that he had been the only surviving kitten of a litter abandoned next door, that he had had the shakes from vitamin deficiency and lost the tip of his tail and the hair on his paws and had to be nursed back to life and health with warm yellowish milk-and-vitamins fed from an eyedropper—that other theory was just one of those rationalizations with which mysterious nature cloaks the birth of heroes, perhaps wisely veiling the truth from minds unable to bear it, a rationalization as false as Kitty-Come-Here and Old Horsemeat's touching belief that Sissy and Baby were their children rather than the cubs of Ashurbanipal and Cleopatra.

The day that Gummitch had discovered by pure intuition the secret of his birth he had been filled with a wild instant excitement. He had only kept it from tearing him to pieces by rushing out to the kitchen and striking and devouring a fried scallop, torturing it fiendishly first for twenty minutes.

And the secret of his birth was only the beginning. His intellectual faculties aroused, Gummitch had two days later intuited a further and greater secret: since he was the child of humans he would, upon reaching this matura-tion date of which Old Horsemeat had spoken, turn not into a sullen tom but into a godlike human youth with reddish golden hair the color of his present fur. He would be poured coffee; and he would instantly be able to talk, probably in all languages. While Sissy (how clear it was now!) would at approximately the same time shrink and fur out into a sharp-clawed and vicious she-cat dark as her hair, sex and self-love her only concerns, fit harem-mate for Cleopatra, concubine to Ashurbanipal.

Exactly the same was true, Gummitch realized at once, for all kittens and babies, all humans and cats, wherever they might dwell. Metamorphosis was as much a part of the fabric of their lives as it was of the insects'. It was also the basic fact underlying all legends of werewolves, vampires and witches' familiars.

If you just rid your mind of preconceived notions, Gummitch told himself, it was all very logical. Babies were stupid, fumbling, vindictive creatures without reason or speech. What more natural than that they should grow up into mute, sullen, selfish beasts bent only on rapine and reproduction? While kittens were quick, sensitive, subtle, supremely alive. What other destiny were they possibly fitted for except to become the deft, word-speaking, book-writing, music-making, meat-getting-and-dispensing masters of the world? To dwell on the physical differences, to point out that kittens and men, babies and cats, are rather unlike in appearance and size, would be to miss the forest for the trees—very much as if an entomologist should proclaim metamorphosis a myth because his microscope failed to discover the wings of a butterfly in a caterpillar's slime or a golden beetle in a grub.

Nevertheless it was such a mind-staggering truth, Gummitch realized at the same time, that it was easy to understand why humans, cats, babies and perhaps most kittens were quite unaware of it. How to safely explain to a butterfly that he was once a hairy crawler, or to a dull larva that he will one day be a walking jewel? No, in such situations the delicate minds of man- and feline-kind are guarded by a merciful mass amnesia, such as Velikovsky has explained prevents us from recalling that in historical times the Earth was catastrophically bumped by the planet Venus operating in the manner of a comet before settling down (with a cosmic sigh of relief, surely!) into its present orbit.

This conclusion was confirmed when Gummitch in the first fever of illumination tried to communicate his great insight to others. He told it in cat patois, as well as that limited jargon permitted, to Ashurbanipal and Cleopatra and even, on the off chance, to Sissy and Baby. They showed no interest whatever, except that Sissy took advantage of his unguarded preoccupation to stab him with a fork.

Later, alone with Old Horsemeat, he projected the great new thoughts, staring with solemn yellow eyes at the old god, but the latter grew markedly nervous and even showed signs of real fear, so Gummitch desisted.

("You'd have sworn he was trying to put across something as deep as the Einstein theory or the doctrine of original sin," Old Horsemeat later told Kitty-Come-Here.) But Gummitch was a man now in all but form, the kitten reminded himself after these failures, and it was part of his destiny to shoulder secrets alone when necessary. He wondered if the general amnesia would affect him when he metamorphosed. There was no sure answer to this question, but he hoped not—and sometimes felt that there was reason for his hopes. Perhaps he would be the first true kitten-man, speaking from a wisdom that had no locked doors in it.

Once he was tempted to speed up the process by the use of drugs. Left alone in the kitchen, he sprang onto the table and started to lap up the black puddle in the bottom of Old Horsemeat's coffee cup. It tasted foul and poisonous and he withdrew with a little snarl, frightened as well as revolted. The dark beverage would not work its tongue-loosening magic, he realized, except at the proper time and with the proper ceremonies. Incantations might be necessary as well. Certainly unlawful tasting was highly dangerous.

The futility of expecting coffee to work any wonders by itself was further demonstrated to Gummitch when Kitty-Come-Here, wordlessly badgered by Sissy, gave a few spoonfuls to the little girl, liberally lacing it first with milk and sugar. Of course Gummitch knew by now that Sissy was destined shortly to turn into a cat and that no amount of coffee would ever make her talk, but it was nevertheless instructive to see how she spat out the first mouthful, drooling a lot of saliva after it, and dashed the cup and its contents at the chest of Kitty-Come-Here.

Gummitch continued to feel a great deal of sympathy for his parents in their worries about Sissy and he longed for the day when he would metamorphose and be able as an acknowledged man-child truly to console them. It was heartbreaking to see how they each tried to coax the little girl to talk, always attempting it while the other was absent, how they seized on each accidentally wordlike note in the few sounds she uttered and repeated it back to her hopefully, how they were more and more possessed by fears not so much of her retarded (they thought) development as of her increasingly obvious maliciousness, which was directed chiefly at Baby... though the two cats and Gummitch bore their share. Once she had caught Baby alone in his crib and used the sharp corner of a block to dot Baby's large-domed lightly downed head with triangular red marks. Kitty-Come-Here had discovered her doing it, but the woman's first action had been to rub Baby's head to obliterate the marks so that Old Horsemeat wouldn't see them. That was the night Kitty-Come-Here hid the abnormal psychology books.

Gummitch understood very well that Kitty-Come-Here and Old Horsemeat, honestly believing themselves to be Sissy's parents, felt just as deeply about her as if they actually were and he did what little he could under the present circumstances to help them. He had recently come to feel a quite independent affection for Baby—the miserable little proto-cat was so completely stupid and defenseless—and so he unofficially constituted himself the creature's guardian, taking his naps behind the door of the nursery and dashing about noisily whenever Sissy showed up. In any case he realized that as a potentially adult member of a felino-human household he had his natural responsibilities.

Accepting responsibilities was as much a part of a kitten's life, Gummitch told himself, as shouldering unsharable intuitions and secrets, the number of which continued to grow from day to day.

There was, for instance, the Affair of the Squirrel Mirror.

Gummitch had early solved the mystery of ordinary mirrors and of the creatures that appeared in them.

A little observation and sniffing and one attempt to get behind the heavy wall-job in the living room had convinced him that mirror beings were insubstantial or at least hermetically sealed into their other world, probably creatures of pure spirit, harmless imitative ghosts—including the silent Gummitch Double who touched paws with him so softly yet so coldly.

Just the same, Gummitch had let his imagination play with what would happen if one day, while looking into the mirror world, he should let loose his grip on his spirit and let it slip into the Gummitch Double while the other's spirit slipped into his body—if, in short, he should change places with the scentless ghost kitten. Being doomed to a life consisting wholly of imitation and completely lacking in opportunities to show initiative—except for the behind-the-scenes judgment and speed needed in rushing from one mirror to another to keep up with the real Gummitch—would be sickeningly dull, Gummitch decided, and he resolved to keep a tight hold on his spirit at all times in the vicinity of mirrors.

But that isn't telling about the Squirrel Mirror. One morning Gummitch was peering out the front bedroom window that overlooked the roof of the porch. Gummitch had already classified windows as semi-mirrors having two kinds of space on the other side: the mirror world and that harsh region filled with mysterious and dangerously organized-sounding noises called the outer world, into which grownup humans reluctantly ventured at intervals, donning special garments for the purpose and shouting loud farewells that were meant to be reassuring but achieved just the opposite effect. The coexistence of two kinds of space presented no paradox to the kitten who carried in his mind the twenty-seven-chapter outline of *Space-Time for Springers*—indeed, it constituted one of the minor themes of the book.

This morning the bedroom was dark and the outer world was dull and sunless, so the mirror world was unusually difficult to see. Gummitch was just lifting his face toward it, nose twitching, his front paws on the sill, when what should rear up on the other side, exactly in the space that the Gummitch Double normally occupied, but a dirty brown, narrow-visaged image with savagely low forehead, dark evil walleyes, and a huge jaw filled with shovel-like teeth.

Gummitch was enormously startled and hideously frightened. He felt his grip on his spirit go limp, and without volition he teleported himself three yards to the rear, making use of that faculty for cutting corners in space-time, traveling by space-warp in fact, which was one of his powers that Kitty-Come-Here refused to believe in and that even Old Horsemeat accepted only on faith.

Then, not losing a moment, he picked himself up by his furry seat, swung himself around, dashed downstairs at top speed, sprang to the top of the sofa, and stared for several seconds at the Gummitch Double in the wall-mirror—not relaxing a muscle strand until he was completely convinced that he was still himself and had not been transformed into the nasty brown apparition that had confronted him in the bedroom window.

"Now what do you suppose brought that on?" Old Horsemeat asked Kitty-Come-Here.

Later Gummitch learned that what he had seen had been a squirrel, a savage, nut-hunting being belonging wholly to the outer world (except for forays into attics) and not at all to the mirror one. Nevertheless he kept a vivid memory of his profound momentary conviction that the squirrel had taken the Gummitch Double's place and been about to take his own. He shuddered to think what would have happened if the squirrel had been actively interested in trading spirits with him. Apparently mirrors and mirror-situations, just as he had always feared, were highly conducive to spirit transfers. He filed the information away in the memory cabinet reserved for dangerous, exciting and possibly useful information, such as plans for climbing straight up glass (diamond-tipped claws!) and flying higher than the trees.

These days his thought cabinets were beginning to feel filled to bursting and he could hardly wait for the moment when the true rich taste of coffee, lawfully drunk, would permit him to speak.

He pictured the scene in detail: the family gathered in conclave at the kitchen table, Ashurbanipal and Cleopatra respectfully watching from floor level, himself sitting erect on chair with paws (or would they be hands?) lightly touching his cup of thin china, while Old Horsemeat poured the thin black steaming stream. He knew the Great Transformation must be close at hand.

At the same time he knew that the other critical situation in the household was worsening swiftly. Sissy, he realized now, was far older than Baby and should long ago have undergone her own somewhat less glamorous though equally necessary transformation (the first tin of raw horsemeat could hardly be as exciting as the first cup of coffee). Her time was long overdue. Gummitch found increasing horror in this mute vampirish being inhabiting the body of a rapidly growing girl, though inwardly equipped to be nothing but a most bloodthirsty she-cat. How dreadful to think of Old Horsemeat and Kitty-Come-Here having to care all their lives for such a monster! Gummitch told himself that if any opportunity for alleviating his parents' misery should ever present itself to him, he would not hesitate for an instant.

Then one night, when the sense of Change was so burstingly strong in him that he knew tomorrow must be the Day, but when the house was also exceptionally unquiet with boards creaking and snapping, taps adrip, and curtains mysteriously rustling at closed windows (so that it was clear that the many spirit worlds including the mirror one must be pressing very close), the opportunity came to Gummitch.

Kitty-Come-Here and Old Horsemeat had fallen into especially sound, drugged sleeps, the former with a bad cold, the latter with one unhappy highball too many (Gummitch knew he had been brooding about Sissy). Baby slept too, though with uneasy whimperings and joggings—moonlight shone full on his crib past a window shade which had whirringly rolled itself up without human or feline agency. Gummitch kept vigil under the crib, with eyes closed but with wildly excited mind pressing outward to every boundary of the house and even stretching here and there into the outer world. On this night of all nights sleep was unthinkable.

Then suddenly he became aware of footsteps, footsteps so soft they must, he thought, be Cleopatra's. No, softer than that, so soft they might be those of the Gummitch Double escaped from the mirror world at last and padding up toward him through the darkened halls. A ribbon of fur rose along his spine.

Then into the nursery Sissy came prowling. She looked slim as an Egyptian princess in her long, thin, yellow nightgown and as sure of herself, but the cat was very strong in her tonight, from the flat intent eyes to the dainty canine teeth slightly bared—one look at her now would have sent Kitty-Come-Here running for the telephone number she kept hidden, the telephone number of the special doctor—and Gummitch realized he was witnessing a monstrous suspension of natural law in that this being should be able to exist for a moment without growing fur and changing round pupils for slit eyes.

He retreated to the darkest corner of the room, suppressing a snarl.

Sissy approached the crib and leaned over Baby in the moonlight, keeping her shadow off him. For a while she gloated. Then she began softly to scratch his cheek with a long hatpin she carried, keeping away from his eye, but just barely. Baby awoke and saw her and Baby didn't cry. Sissy continued to scratch, always a little more deeply. The moonlight glittered on the jeweled end of the pin.

Gummitch knew he faced a horror that could not be countered by running about or even spitting and screeching. Only magic could fight so obviously supernatural a manifestation. And this was also no time to think of consequences, no matter how clearly and bitterly etched they might appear to a mind intensely awake.

He sprang up onto the other side of the crib, not uttering a sound, and fixed his golden eyes on Sissy's in the moonlight. Then he moved forward straight at her evil face, stepping slowly, not swiftly, using his extraordinary knowledge of the properties of space *to walk straight through her hand and arm as they flailed the hatpin at him.* When his nose-tip finally paused a fraction of an inch from hers his eyes had not blinked once, and she could not look away. Then he unhesitatingly flung his spirit into her like a fistful of flaming arrows and he worked the Mirror Magic.

Sissy's moonlit face, feline and terrified, was in a sense the last thing that Gummitch, the real Gummitch-kitten, ever saw in this world. For the next instant he felt himself enfolded by the foul black blinding cloud of Sissy's spirit, which his own had displaced. At the same time he heard the little girl scream, very loudly but even more distinctly, "*Mommy!*"

That cry might have brought Kitty-Come-Here out of her grave, let alone from sleep merely deep or drugged. Within seconds she was in the nursery, closely followed by Old Horsemeat, and she had caught up Sissy in her arms and the little girl was articulating the wonderful word again and again, and miraculously following it with the command—there could be no doubt, Old Horsemeat heard it too—"Hold me tight!"

Then Baby finally dared to cry. The scratches on his cheek came to attention and Gummitch, as he had known must happen, was banished to the basement amid cries of horror and loathing chiefly from Kitty-Come-Here.

The little cat did not mind. No basement would be one-tenth as dark as Sissy's spirit that now enshrouded him for always, hiding all the file drawers and the labels on all the folders, blotting out forever even the imagining of the scene of first coffee-drinking and first speech.

In a last intuition, before the animal blackness closed in utterly, Gummitch realized that the spirit, alas, is not the same thing as the consciousness and that one may lose—sacrifice—the first and still be burdened with the second.

Old Horsemeat had seen the hatpin (and hid it quickly from Kitty-Come-Here) and so he knew that the situation was not what it seemed and that Gummitch was at the very least being made into a sort of scapegoat. He was quite apologetic when he brought the tin pans of food to the basement during the period of the little cat's exile. It was a comfort to Gummitch, albeit a small one. Gummitch told himself, in his new black halting manner of thinking, that after all a cat's best friend is his man.

From that night Sissy never turned back in her development. Within two months she had made three years' progress in speaking. She became an outstandingly bright, light-footed, high-spirited little girl. Although she never told anyone this, the moonlit nursery and Gummitch's magnified face were her first memories. Everything before that was inky blackness. She was always very nice to Gummitch in a careful sort of way. She could never stand to play the game "Owl Eyes." After a few weeks Kitty-Come-Here forgot her fears and Gummitch once again had the run of the house. But by then the transformation Old Horsemeat had always warned about had fully taken place. Gummitch was a kitten no longer but an almost burly tom. In him it took the psychological form not of sullenness or surliness but an extreme dignity. He seemed at times rather like an old pirate brooding on treasures he would never live to dig up, shores of adventure he would never reach. And sometimes when you looked into his yellow eyes you felt that he had in him all the materials for the book *Slit Eyes Look at Life*—three or four volumes at least—although he would never write it. And that was natural when you come to think of it, for as Gummitch knew very well, bitterly well indeed, his fate was to be the only kitten in the world that did not grow up to be a man.

ILL MET IN LANKHMAR

SILENT AS SPECTERS, THE TALL AND THE FAT THIEF edged past the dead, noose-strangled watch-leopard, out the thick, lock-picked door of Jengao the Gem Merchant, and strolled east on Cash Street through the thin black night-smog of Lankhmar.

East on Cash it had to be, for west at Cash and Silver was a police post with unbribed guardsmen restlessly grounding and rattling their pikes.

But tall, tight-lipped Slevyas, master thief candidate, and fat, darting-eyed Fissif, thief second class, with a rating of talented in double-dealing, were not in the least worried. Everything was proceeding according to plan. Each carried thonged in his pouch a smaller pouch of jewels of the first water only, for Jengao, now breathing stentoriously inside and senseless from the slugging he'd suffered, must be allowed, nay, nursed and encouraged to build up his business again and so ripen it for another plucking. Almost the first law of the Thieves' Guild was never to kill the hen that laid eggs with a ruby in the yolk.

The two thieves also had the relief of knowing that they were going straight home now, not to a wife, Arath forbid!—or to parents and children, all gods forfend!— but to Thieves' House, headquarters and barracks of the almighty Guild, which was father to them both and mother too, though no woman was allowed inside its ever-open portal on Cheap Street.

In addition there was the comforting knowledge that although each was armed only with his regulation silver-hilted thief's knife, they were nevertheless most strongly convoyed by three reliable and lethal bravoes hired for the evening from the Slayers' Brotherhood, one moving well ahead of them as point, the other two well behind as rear guard and chief striking force.

And if all that were not enough to make Slevyas and Fissif feel safe and serene, there danced along soundlessly beside them in the shadow of the north curb a small, malformed or at any rate somewhat large-headed shape that might have been a very small dog, a somewhat undersized cat, or a very big rat.

True, this last guard was not an absolutely unalloyed reassurance. Fissif strained upward to whisper softly in Slevyas' long-lobed ear, "Damned if I like being dogged by that familiar of Hristomilo, no matter what security he's supposed to afford us. Bad enough that Krovas did employ or let himself be cowed into employing a sorcerer of most dubious, if dire, reputation and aspect, but that—"

"Shut your trap!" Slevyas hissed still more softly.

Fissif obeyed with a shrug and employed himself in darting his gaze this way and that, but chiefly ahead.

Some distance in that direction, in fact just short of Gold Street, Cash was bridged by an enclosed second-story passageway connecting the two buildings which made up the premises of the famous stone-masons and sculptors Rokkermas and Slaarg. The firm's buildings themselves were fronted by very shallow porticoes supported by unnecessarily large pillars of varied shape and decoration, advertisements more than structural members.

From just beyond the bridge came two low, brief whistles, a signal from the point bravo that he had inspected that area for ambushes and discovered nothing suspicious and that Gold Street was clear.

Fissif was by no means entirely satisfied by the safety signal. To tell the truth, the fat thief rather enjoyed being apprehensive and even fearful, at least up to a point. So he scanned most closely through the thin, sooty smog the frontages and overhangs of Rokkermas and Slaarg.

On this side the bridge was pierced by four small windows, between which were three large niches in which stood—another advertisement—three life-size plaster statues, somewhat eroded by years of weather and dyed varyingly tones of dark gray by as many years of smog. Approaching Jengao's before the burglary, Fissif had noted them. Now it seemed to him that the statue to the right had indefinably changed. It was that of a man of medium height wearing cloak and hood, who gazed down with crossed arms and brooding aspect. No, not indefinably quite—the statue was a more uniform dark gray now, he fancied, cloak, hood, and face; it seemed somewhat sharper featured, less eroded; and he would almost swear it had grown shorter!

Just below the niches, moreover, there was a scattering of gray and raw white rubble which he didn't recall having been there earlier. He strained to remember if during the excitement of the burglary, the unsleeping watch-corner of his mind had recorded a distant crash, and now he believed it had. His quick imagination pictured the possibility of a hole behind each statue, through which it might be given a strong push and so tumbled onto passersby, himself and Slevyas specifically, the right-hand statue having been crashed to test the device and then replaced with a near twin.

He would keep close watch on all the statues as he and Slevyas walked under. It would be easy to dodge if he saw one start to overbalance. Should he yank Slevyas out of harm's way when that happened? It was something to think about.

His restless attention fixed next on the porticoes and pillars. The latter, thick and almost three yards tall, were placed at irregular intervals as well as being irregularly shaped and fluted, for Rokkermas and Slaarg were most modern and emphasized the unfinished look, randomness, and the unexpected.

Nevertheless it seemed to Fissif that there was an intensification of unexpectedness, specifically that there was one more pillar under the porticoes than when he had last passed by. He couldn't be sure which pillar was the newcomer, but he was almost certain there was one.

The enclosed bridge was close now. Fissif glanced up at the right-hand statue and noted other differences from the one he'd recalled. Although shorter, it seemed to hold itself more strainingly erect, while the frown carved in its dark gray face was not so much one of philosophic brooding as sneering contempt, self-conscious cleverness, and conceit.

Still, none of the three statues toppled forward as he and Slevyas walked under the bridge. However, something else happened to Fissif at that moment.

One of the pillars winked at him.

The Gray Mouser turned round in the right-hand niche, leaped up and caught hold of the cornice, silently vaulted to the flat roof, and crossed it precisely in time to see the two thieves emerge below.

Without hesitation he leaped forward and down, his body straight as a crossbow bolt, the soles of his ratskin boots aimed at the shorter thief's fat-buried shoulder blades, though leading him a little to allow for the yard he'd walk while the Mouser hurtled toward him.

In the instant that he leaped, the tall thief glanced up overshoulder and whipped out a knife, though making no move to push or pull Fissif out of the way of the human projectile speeding toward him.

More swiftly than one would have thought he could manage, Fissif whirled round then and thinly screamed, "Slivikin!"

The ratskin boots took him high in the belly. It was like landing on a big cushion. Writhing aside from Slevyas' thrust, the Mouser somersaulted forward, and as the fat thief's skull hit a cobble with a dull *bong* he came to his feet with dirk in hand, ready to take on the tall one.

But there was no need. Slevyas, his eyes glazed, was toppling too.

One of the pillars had sprung forward, trailing a voluminous robe. A big hood had fallen back from a youthful face and long-haired head. Brawny arms had emerged from the long, loose sleeves that had been the pillar's topmost section. While the big fist ending one of the arms had dealt Slevyas a shrewd knockout punch on the chin.

Fafhrd and the Gray Mouser faced each other across the two thieves sprawled senseless. They were poised for attack, yet for the moment neither moved.

Fafhrd said, "Our motives for being here seem identical."

"Seem? Surely must be!" the Mouser answered curtly, fiercely eyeing this potential new foe, who was taller by a head than the tall thief.

"You said?"

"I said, 'Seem? Surely must be!'"

"How civilized of you!" Fafhrd commented in pleased tones.

"Civilized?" the Mouser demanded suspiciously, gripping his dirk tighter.

"To care, in the eye of action, exactly what's said," Fafhrd explained. Without letting the Mouser out of his vision, he glanced down. His gaze traveled from the pouch of one fallen thief to that of the other. Then he looked up at the Mouser with a broad, ingenuous smile.

"Fifty-fifty?" he suggested.

The Mouser hesitated, sheathed his dirk, and rapped out, "A deal!" He knelt abruptly, his fingers on the drawstrings of Fissif's pouch. "Loot you Slivikin," he directed.

It was natural to suppose that the fat thief had been crying his companion's name at the end.

Without looking up from where he knelt, Fafhrd remarked, "That... ferret they had with them. Where did it go?"

"Ferret?" the Mouser answered briefly. "It was a marmoset!"

"Marmoset," Fafhrd mused. "That's a small tropical monkey, isn't it? Well, might have been—I've never been south—but I got the impression that—"

The silent, two-pronged rush which almost overwhelmed them at that instant really surprised neither of them. Each had unconsciously been expecting it.

The three bravoes racing down upon them in concerted attack, all with swords poised to thrust, had assumed that the two highjackers would be armed at most with knives and as timid in weapons-combat as the general run of thieves and counter-thieves. So it was they who were thrown into confusion when with the lightning speed of youth the Mouser and Fafhrd sprang up, whipped out fearsomely long swords, and faced them back to back.

The Mouser made a very small parry in carte so that the thrust of the bravo from the east went past his left side by only a hair's breadth. He instantly riposted. His adversary, desperately springing back, parried in turn in carte. Hardly slowing, the tip of the Mouser's long, slim sword dropped under that parry with the delicacy of a princess curtsying and then leapt forward and a little upward and went between two scales of the bravo's armored jerkin and between his ribs and through his heart and out his back as if all were angel food cake.

Meanwhile Fafhrd, facing the two bravoes from the west, swept aside their low thrusts with somewhat larger, down-sweeping parries in seconde and low prime, then flipped up his sword, as long as the Mouser's but heavier, so that it slashed through the neck of his right-hand adversary, half decapitating him. Then dropping back a swift step, he readied a thrust for the other.

But there was no need. A narrow ribbon of bloodied steel, followed by a gray glove and arm, flashed past him from behind and transfixed the last bravo with the identical thrust the Mouser had used on the first.

The two young men wiped their swords. Fafhrd brushed the palm of his open right hand down his robe and held it out. The Mouser pulled off his right-hand gray glove and shook it. Without word exchanged, they knelt and finished looting the two unconscious thieves, securing the small bags of jewels. With an oily towel and then a dry one, the Mouser sketchily wiped from his face the greasy ash-soot mixture which had darkened it.

Then, after only a questioning eye-twitch east on the Mouser's part and a nod from Fafhrd, they swiftly walked on in the direction Slevyas and Fissif and their escort had been going.

After reconnoitering Gold Street, they crossed it and continued east on Cash at Fafhrd's gestured proposal.

"My woman's at the Golden Lamprey," he explained.

"Let's pick her up and take her home to meet my girl," the Mouser suggested.

"Home?" Fafhrd inquired politely.

"Dim Lane," the Mouser volunteered.

"Silver Eel?"

"Behind it. We'll have some drinks."

"I'll pick up a jug. Never have too much juice."

"True. I'll let you."

Fafhrd stopped, again wiped right hand on robe, and held it out. "Name's Fafhrd."

Again the Mouser shook it. "Gray Mouser," he said a touch defiantly, as if challenging anyone to laugh at the sobriquet.

"Gray Mouser, eh?" Fafhrd remarked. "Well, you killed yourself a couple of rats tonight."

"That I did." The Mouser's chest swelled and he threw back his head. Then with a comic twitch of his nose and a sidewise half-grin he admitted, "You'd have got your second man easily enough. I stole him from you to demonstrate my speed. Besides, I was excited."

Fafhrd chuckled. "You're telling me? How do you suppose I was feeling?"

Once more the Mouser found himself grinning. What the deuce did this big fellow have that kept him from putting on his usual sneers?

Fafhrd was asking himself a similar question. All his life he'd mistrusted small men, knowing his height awakened their instant jealousy. But this clever little chap was somehow an exception. He prayed to Kos that Vlana would like him.

On the northeast corner of Cash and Whore a slow-burning torch shaded by a broad, gilded spiral cast a cone of light up into the thickening black night-smog and another cone down on the cobbles before the tavern door. Out of the shadows into the second cone stepped Vlana, handsome in a narrow black velvet dress and red stockings, her only ornaments a silver-hilted dagger in a silver sheath and a silver-worked black pouch, both on a plain black belt.

Fafhrd introduced the Gray Mouser, who behaved with an almost fawning courtesy. Vlana studied him boldly, then gave him a tentative smile.

Fafhrd opened under the torch the small pouch he'd taken off the tall thief. Vlana looked down into it. She put her arms around Fafhrd, hugged him tight and kissed him soundly. Then she thrust the jewels into the pouch on her belt.

When that was done, he said, "Look, I'm going to buy a jug. You tell her what happened, Mouser."

When he came out of the Golden Lamprey he was carrying four jugs in the crook of his left arm and wiping his lips on the back of his right hand. Vlana frowned. He grinned at her. The Mouser smacked his lips at the jugs. They continued east on Cash. Fafhrd realized that the frown was for more than the jugs and the prospect of stupidly drunken male revelry. The Mouser tactfully walked ahead.

When his figure was little more than a blob in the thickening smog, Vlana whispered harshly, "You had two members of the Thieves' Guild knocked out cold and you didn't cut their throats?"

"We slew three bravoes," Fafhrd protested by way of excuse.

"My quarrel is not with the Slayers' Brotherhood, but that abominable guild. You swore to me that whenever you had the chance—"

"Vlana! I couldn't have the Gray Mouser thinking I was an amateur counter-thief consumed by hysteria and blood lust."

"Well, he told me that *he'd* have slit their throats in a wink, if he'd known I wanted it that way."

"He was only playing up to you from courtesy."

"Perhaps and perhaps not. But you knew and you didn't—"

"Vlana, shut up!"

Her frown became a rageful glare, then suddenly she laughed widely, smiled twitchingly as if she were about to cry, mastered herself and smiled more lovingly. "Pardon me, darling," she said. "Sometimes you must think I'm going mad and sometimes I believe I am."

"Well, don't," he told her shortly. "Think of the jewels we've won instead. And behave yourself with our new friends. Get some wine inside you and relax. I mean to enjoy myself tonight. I've earned it."

She nodded and clutched his arm in agreement and for comfort and sanity. They hurried to catch up with the dim figure ahead.

The Mouser, turning left, led them a half square north on Cheap Street to where a narrower way went east again. The black mist in it looked solid.

"Dim Lane," the Mouser explained.

Vlana said, "Dim's too weak—too *transparent* a word for it tonight," with an uneven laugh in which there were still traces of hysteria and which ended in a fit of strangled coughing.

She gasped out, "Damn Lankhmar's night-smog! What a hell of a city!"

"It's the nearness here of the Great Salt Marsh," Fafhrd explained.

And he did indeed have part of the answer. Lying low betwixt the Marsh, the Inner Sea, the River Hlal, and the southern grain fields watered by canals fed by the Hlal, Lankhmar with its innumerable smokes was the prey of fogs and sooty smogs.

About halfway to Carter Street, a tavern on the north side of the lane emerged from the murk. A gape-jawed serpentine shape of pale metal crested with soot hung high for a sign. Beneath it they passed a door curtained with begrimed leather, the slit in which spilled out noise, pulsing torchlight, and the reek of liquor.

Just beyond the Silver Eel the Mouser led them through an inky passageway outside the tavern's east wall. They had to go single file, feeling their way along rough, slimily bemisted brick.

"Mind the puddle," the Mouser warned. "It's deep as the Outer Sea."

The passageway widened. Reflected torchlight filtering down through the dark mist allowed them to make out only the most general shape of their surroundings. Crowding close to the back of the Silver Eel rose a dismal, rickety building of darkened brick and blackened, ancient wood. From the fourth-story attic under the ragged-guttered roof, faint lines of yellow light shone around and through three tightly latticed windows. Beyond was a narrow alley.

"Bones Alley," the Mouser told them.

By now Vlana and Fafhrd could see a long, narrow wooden outside stairway, steep yet sagging and without a rail, leading up to the lighted attic. The Mouser relieved Fafhrd of the jugs and went up it quite swiftly.

"Follow me when I've reached the top," he called back. "I think it'll take your weight, Fafhrd, but best one of you at a time."

Fafhrd gently pushed Vlana ahead. She mounted to the Mouser where he now stood in an open doorway, from which streamed yellow light that died swiftly in the night-smog. He was lightly resting a hand on a big, empty, wrought-iron lamp-hook firmly set in a stone section of the outside wall. He bowed aside, and she went in.

Fafhrd followed, placing his feet as close as he could to the wall, his hands ready to grab for support. The whole stairs creaked ominously and each step gave a little as he shifted his weight onto it. Near the top, one step gave way with the muted crack of half-rotted wood. Gently as he could, he sprawled himself hand and knee on as many steps as he could get, to distribute his weight, and cursed sulphurously.

"Don't fret, the jugs are safe," the Mouser called down gayly.

Fafhrd crawled the rest of the way and did not get to his feet until he was inside the doorway. When he had done so, he almost gasped with surprise.

It was like rubbing the verdigris from a cheap brass ring and revealing a rainbow-fired diamond of the first water. Rich drapes, some twinkling with embroidery of silver and gold, covered the walls except where the shuttered windows were—and the shutters of those were gilded. Similar but darker fabrics hid the low ceiling, making a gorgeous canopy in which the flecks of gold and silver were like stars. Scattered about were plump cushions and low tables, on which burned a multitude of candles. On shelves against the walls was neatly stacked like small logs a vast reserve of candles, numerous scrolls, jugs, bottles, and enameled boxes. In a large fireplace was set a small metal stove, neatly blacked, with an ornate firepot. Also set beside the stove was a tidy pyramid of thin, resinous torches with frayed ends—fire-kindlers and other pyramids of small, short logs and gleamingly black coal.

On a low dais by the fireplace was a couch covered with cloth of gold. On it sat a thin, pale-faced, delicately handsome girl clad in a dress of thick violet silk worked with silver and belted with a silver chain. Silver pins headed with amethysts held in place her high-piled black hair. Round her shoulders was drawn a wrap of snow-white serpent fur. She was leaning forward with uneasy-seeming graciousness and extending a narrow white hand which shook a little to Vlana, who knelt before her and now gently took the proffered hand and bowed her head over it, her own glossy, straight, dark-brown hair making a canopy, and pressed its back to her lips.

Fafhrd was happy to see his woman playing up properly to this definitely odd, though delightful situation. Then looking at Vlana's long, red-stockinged leg stretched far behind her as she knelt on the other, he noted that the floor was everywhere strewn—to the point of double, treble, and quadruple overlaps—with thick-piled, close-woven, many-hued rugs of the finest quality imported from the Eastern Lands. Before he knew it, his thumb had shot toward the Gray Mouser.

"You're the Rug Robber!" he proclaimed. "You're the Carpet Crimp!—and the Candle Corsair too!" he continued, referring to two series of unsolved thefts which had been on the lips of all Lankhmar when he and Vlana had arrived a moon ago.

The Mouser shrugged impassive-faced at Fafhrd, then suddenly grinned, his slitted eyes a-twinkle, and broke into an impromptu dance which carried him whirling and jigging around the room and left him behind Fafhrd, where he deftly reached down the hooded and long-sleeved huge robe from the latter's stooping shoulders, shook it out, carefully folded it, and set it on a pillow.

The girl in violet nervously patted with her free hand the cloth of gold beside her, and Vlana seated herself there, carefully not too close, and the two women spoke together in low voices, Vlana taking the lead.

The Mouser took off his own gray, hooded cloak and laid it beside Fafhrd's. Then they unbelted their swords, and the Mouser set them atop folded robe and cloak.

Without those weapons and bulking garments, the two men looked suddenly like youths, both with clear, close-shaven faces, both slender despite the swelling muscles of Fafhrd's arms and calves, he with long red-gold hair falling down his back and about his shoulders, the Mouser with dark hair cut in bangs, the one in brown leather tunic worked with copper wire, the other in jerkin of coarsely woven gray silk.

They smiled at each other. The feeling each had of having turned boy all at once made their smiles embarrassed. The Mouser cleared his throat and, bowing a little, but looking still at Fafhrd, extended a loosely spread-fingered arm toward the golden couch and said with a preliminary stammer, though otherwise smoothly enough, "Fafhrd, my good friend, permit me to introduce you to my princess. Ivrian, my dear, receive Fafhrd graciously if you please, for tonight he and I fought back to back against three and we conquered."

Fafhrd advanced, stooping a little, the crown of his red-gold hair brushing the be-starred canopy, and knelt before Ivrian exactly as Vlana had. The slender hand extended to him looked steady now, but was still quiveringly a-tremble, he discovered as soon as he touched it. He handled it as if it were silk woven of the white spider's gossamer, barely brushing it with his lips, and still felt nervous as he mumbled some compliments.

He did not sense that the Mouser was quite as nervous as he, if not more so, praying hard that Ivrian would not overdo her princess part and snub their guests, or collapse in trembling or tears, for Fafhrd and Vlana were literally the first beings that he had brought into the luxurious nest he had created for his aristocratic beloved—save the two love birds that twittered in a silver cage hanging to the other side of the fireplace from the dais.

Despite his shrewdness and cynicism, it never occurred to the Mouser that it was chiefly his charming but preposterous coddling of Ivrian that was making her doll-like.

But now as Ivrian smiled at last, the Mouser relaxed with relief, fetched two silver cups and two silver mugs, carefully selected a bottle of violet wine, then with a grin at Fafhrd uncorked instead one of the jugs the Northerner had brought, and near-brimmed the four gleaming vessels and served them all four.

With no trace of stammer this time, he toasted, "To my greatest theft to date in Lankhmar, which willy-nilly I must share fifty-fifty with—" He couldn't resist the sudden impulse "—with this great, long-haired, barbarian lout here!" And he downed a quarter of his mug of pleasantly burning wine fortified with brandy.

Fafhrd quaffed off half of his, then toasted back, "To the most boastful and finical little civilized chap I've ever deigned to share loot with," quaffed off the rest, and with a great smile that showed white teeth, held out his empty mug.

The Mouser gave him a refill, topped off his own, then set that down to go to Ivrian and pour into her lap from their small pouch the gems he'd filched from Fissif. They gleamed in their new, enviable location like a small puddle of rainbow-hued quicksilver.

Ivrian jerked back a-tremble, almost spilling them, but Vlana gently caught her arm, steadying it. At Ivrian's direction, Vlana fetched a blue-enameled box inlaid with silver, and the two of them transferred the jewels from Ivrian's lap into its blue velvet interior. Then they chatted on.

As he worked through his second mug in smaller gulps, Fafhrd relaxed and began to get a deeper feeling of his surroundings. The dazzling wonder of the first glimpse of this throne room in a slum faded, and he began to note the ricketiness and rot under the grand overlay.

Black, rotten wood showed here and there between the drapes and loosed its sick, ancient stinks.

The whole floor sagged under the rugs, as much as a span at the center of the room. Threads of night-smog were coming through the shutters, making evanescent black arabesques against the gilt. The stones of the large fireplace had been scrubbed and varnished, yet most of the mortar was gone from between them; some sagged, others were missing altogether.

The Mouser had been building a fire there in the stove. Now he pushed in all the way the yellow-flaring kindler he'd lit from the fire-pot, hooked the little black door shut over the mounting flames, and turned back into the room. As if he'd read Fafhrd's mind, he took up several cones of incense, set their peaks a-smolder at the fire-pot, and placed them about the room in gleaming, shallow brass bowls. Then he stuffed silken rags in the widest shutter-cracks, took up his silver mug again, and for a moment gave Fafhrd a very hard look.

Next moment he was smiling and lifting his mug to Fafhrd, who was doing the same. Need of refills brought them close together. Hardly moving his lips, the Mouser explained, "Ivrian's father was a duke. I slew him. A most cruel man, cruel to his daughter too, yet a duke, so that Ivrian is wholly unused to fending for herself. I pride myself that I maintain her in grander state than her father did with all his servants."

Fafhrd nodded and said amiably, "Surely you've thieved together a charming little palace."

From the couch Vlana called in her husky contralto, "Gray Mouser, your Princess would hear an account of tonight's adventure. And might we have more wine?"

Ivrian called, "Yes, please, Mouser."

The Mouser looked to Fafhrd for the go-ahead, got the nod, and launched into his story. But first he served the girls wine. There wasn't enough for their cups, so he opened another jug and after a moment of thought uncorked all three, setting one by the couch, one by Fafhrd where he sprawled now on the pillowy carpet, and reserving one for himself. Ivrian looked apprehensive at this signal of heavy drinking ahead, Vlana cynical.

The Mouser told the tale of counter-thievery well, acting it out in part, and with only the most artistic of embellishments—the ferret-marmoset before escaping ran up his body and tried to scratch out his eyes—and he was interrupted only twice.

When he said, "And so with a whish and a snick I bared Scalpel —" Fafhrd remarked, "Oh, so you've nicknamed your sword as well as yourself?"

The Mouser drew himself up. "Yes, and I call my dirk Cat's Claw. Any objections? Seem childish to you?"

"Not at all. I call my own sword Graywand. Pray continue."

And when he mentioned the beastie of uncertain nature that had gamboled along with the thieves (and attacked his eyes!), Ivrian paled and said with a shudder, "Mouser! That sounds like a witch's familiar!"

"Wizard's," Vlana corrected. "Those gutless Guild-villains have no truck with women, except as fee'd or forced vehicles for their lust. But Krovas, their current king, is noted for taking *all* precautions, and might well have a warlock in his service."

"That seems most likely; it harrows me with dread," the Mouser agreed with ominous gaze and sinister voice, eagerly accepting any and all atmospheric enhancements of his performance.

When he was done, the girls, eyes flashing and fond, toasted him and Fafhrd for their cunning and bravery. The Mouser bowed and eye-twinklingly smiled about, then sprawled him down with a weary sigh, wiping his forehead with a silken cloth and downing a large drink.

After asking Vlana's leave, Fafhrd told the adventurous tale of their escape from Cold Corner—he from his clan, she from an acting troupe—and of their progress to Lankhmar, where they lodged now in an actors' tenement near the Plaza of Dark Delights. Ivrian hugged herself to Vlana and shivered large-eyed at the witchy parts of his tale.

The only proper matter he omitted from his account was Vlana's fixed intent to get a monstrous revenge on the Thieves' Guild for torturing to death her accomplices and harrying her out of Lankhmar when she'd tried freelance thieving in the city before they met. Nor of course did he mention his own promise—foolish, he thought now—to help her in this bloody business.

After he'd done and got his applause, he found his throat dry despite his skald's training, but when he sought to wet it, he discovered that his mug was empty and his jug too, though he didn't feel in the least drunk—he had talked all the liquor out of him, he told himself, a little of the stuff escaping in each glowing word he'd spoken.

The Mouser was in like plight and not drunk either—though inclined to pause mysteriously and peer toward infinity before answering question or making remark. This time he suggested, after a particularly long infinity-gaze, that Fafhrd accompany him to the Eel while he purchased a fresh supply.

"But we've a lot of wine left in *our* jug," Ivrian protested. "Or at least a little," she amended. It did sound empty when Vlana shook it. "Besides, you've wine of all sorts here."

"Not this sort, dearest, and first rule is never mix 'em," the Mouser explained, wagging a finger. "That way lies unhealth, aye, and madness."

"My dear," Vlana said, sympathetically patting her wrist, "at some time in any good party all the men who are really men simply have to go out. It's extremely stupid, but it's their nature and can't be dodged, believe me."

"But, Mouser, I'm scared. Fafhrd's tale frightened me. So did yours—I'll hear that familiar a-scratch at the shutters when you're gone, I know I will!"

"Darlingest," the Mouser said with a small hiccup, "there is all the Inner Sea, all the Land of the Eight Cities, and to boot all the Trollstep Mountains in their sky-scraping grandeur between you and Fafhrd's Cold Corner and its silly sorcerers. As for familiars, pish!—they've never in the world been anything but the loathy, all-too-natural pets of stinking old women and womanish old men."

Vlana said merrily, "Let the sillies go, my dear. 'Twill give us chance for a private chat, during which we'll take 'em apart from wine-fumy head to restless foot."

So Ivrian let herself be persuaded, and the Mouser and Fafhrd slipped off, quickly shutting the door behind them to keep out the night-smog, and the girls heard their light steps down the stairs.

Waiting for the four jugs to be brought up from the Eel's cellar, the two newly met comrades ordered a mug each of the same fortified wine, or one near enough, and ensconced themselves at the least noisy end of the long serving counter in the tumultuous tavern. The Mouser deftly kicked a rat that thrust black head and shoulders from his hole.

After each had enthusiastically complimented the other on his girl, Fafhrd said diffidently, "Just between ourselves, do you think there might be anything to your sweet Ivrian's notion that the small dark creature with Slivikin and the other Guild-thief was a wizard's familiar, or at any rate the cunning pet of a sorcerer, trained to act as go-between and report disasters to his master or to Krovas?"

The Mouser laughed lightly. "You're building bugbears—formless baby ones unlicked by logic—out of nothing, dear barbarian brother, if I may say so. How could that vermin make useful report? I don't believe in animals that talk—except for parrots and such birds, which only… parrot.

"Ho, there, you back of the counter! Where are my jugs? Rats eaten the boy who went for them days ago? Or he simply starved to death while on his cellar quest? Well, tell him to get a swifter move on and brim us again!

"No, Fafhrd, even granting the beastie to be directly or indirectly a creature of Krovas, and that it raced back to Thieves' House after our affray, what would that tell them there? Only that something had gone wrong with the burglary at Jengao's."

Fafhrd frowned and muttered stubbornly, "The furry slinker might, nevertheless, somehow convey our appearances to the Guild masters, and they might recognize us and come after us and attack us in our homes."

"My dear friend," the Mouser said condolingly, "once more begging your indulgence, I fear this potent wine is addling your wits. If the Guild knew our looks or where we lodge, they'd have been nastily on our necks days, weeks, nay, months ago. Or conceivably you don't know that their penalty for freelance thieving within the walls of Lankhmar is nothing less than death, after torture, if happily that can be achieved."

"I know all about that, and my plight is worse even than yours," Fafhrd retorted, and after pledging the Mouser to secrecy, told him the tale of Vlana's vendetta against the Guild and her deadly serious dreams of an all-encompassing revenge.

During his story the four jugs came up from the cellar, but the Mouser only ordered that their earthenware mugs be refilled.

Fafhrd finished, "And so, in consequence of a promise given by an infatuated and unschooled boy in a southern angle of the Cold Waste, I find myself now as a sober—well, at other times—man being constantly asked to make war on a power as great as that of Lankhmar's overlord, for as you may know, the Guild has locals in all other cities and major towns of this land. I love Vlana dearly and she is an experienced thief herself, but on this one topic she has a kink in her brains, a hard knot neither logic nor persuasion can even begin to loosen."

"Certes t'would be insanity to assault the Guild direct, your wisdom's perfect there," the Mouser commented. "If you cannot break your most handsome girl of this mad notion, or coax her from it, then you must stoutly refuse e'en her least request in that direction."

"Certes I must," Fafhrd agreed with great emphasis and conviction. "I'd be an idiot taking on the Guild. Of course, if they should catch me, they'd kill me in any case for freelancing and highjacking. But wantonly to assault the Guild direct, kill one Guild-thief needlessly—lunacy entire!"

"You'd not only be a drunken, drooling idiot, you'd questionless be stinking in three nights at most from that emperor of diseases, Death. Malicious attacks on her person, blows directed at the organization, the Guild requites tenfold what she does other rule-breaking, freelancing included. So, no least giving-in to Vlana in this one matter."

"Agreed!" Fafhrd said loudly, shaking the Mouser's iron-thewed hand in a near crusher grip.

"And now we should be getting back to the girls," the Mouser said.

"After one more drink while we settle the score. Ho, boy!"

"Suits."

Vlana and Ivrian, deep in excited talk, both started at the pounding rush of footsteps up the stairs. Racing behemoths could hardly have made more noise. The creaking and groaning were prodigious, and there were the crashes of two treads breaking. The door flew open and their two men rushed in through a great mushroom top of night-smog which was neatly sliced off its black stem by the slam of the door.

"I told you we'd be back in a wink," the Mouser cried gayly to Ivrian, while Fafhrd strode forward, unmindful of the creaking floor, crying, "Dearest heart, I've missed you sorely," and caught up Vlana despite her voiced protests and pushings-off and kissed and hugged her soundly before setting her back on the couch again.

Oddly, it was Ivrian who appeared to be angry at Fafhrd then, rather than Vlana, who was smiling fondly if somewhat dazedly.

"Fafhrd, sir," she said boldly, her little fists set on her narrow hips, her tapered chin held high, her dark eyes blazing, "my beloved Vlana has been telling me about the unspeakably atrocious things the Thieves' Guild did to her and to her dearest friends. Pardon my frank speaking to one I've only met, but I think it quite unmanly of you to refuse her the just revenge she desires and fully deserves. And that goes for you too, Mouser, who boasted to Vlana of what you would have done had you but known, all the while intending only empty ingratiation. You who in like case did not scruple to slay my very own father!"

It was clear to Fafhrd that while he and the Gray Mouser had idly boozed in the Eel, Vlana had been giving Ivrian a doubtless empurpled account of her grievances against the Guild and playing mercilessly on the naive girl's bookish, romantic sympathies and high concept of knightly honor. It was also clear to him that Ivrian was more than a little drunk. A three-quarters empty flask of violet wine of far Kiraay sat on the low table next the couch.

Yet he could think of nothing to do but spread his big hands helplessly and bow his head, more than the low ceiling made necessary, under Ivrian's glare, now reinforced by that of Vlana. After all, they *were* in the right. He *had* promised.

So it was the Mouser who first tried to rebut. "Come now, pet," he cried lightly as he danced about the room, silk-stuffing more cracks against the thickening night-smog and stirring up and feeding the fire in the stove, "and you too, beauteous Lady Vlana. For the past month Fafhrd has by his highjackings been hitting the Guild-thieves where it hurts them most—in their purses a-dangle between their legs. Come, drink we up all." Under his handling, one of the new jugs came uncorked with a pop, and he darted about brimming silver cups and mugs.

"A merchant's revenge!" Ivrian retorted with scorn, not one whit appeased, but rather enangered anew. "At the least you and Fafhrd must bring Vlana the head of Krovas!"

"What would she *do* with it? What *good* would it be except to spot the carpets?" the Mouser plaintively inquired, while Fafhrd, gathering his wits at last and going down on one knee, said slowly, "Most respected Lady Ivrian, it is true I solemnly promised my beloved Vlana I would help her in her revenge, but if Mouser and I should bring Vlana the head of Krovas, she and I would have to flee Lankhmar on the instant, every man's hand against us. While you infallibly would lose this fairyland Mouser has created for love of you and be forced to do likewise, be with him a beggar on the run for the rest of your natural lives."

While Fafhrd spoke, Ivrian snatched up her new-filled cup and drained it. Now she stood up straight as a soldier, her pale face flushed, and said scathingly, *"You count the cost!* You speak to me of *things—"* She waved at the many-hued splendor around her, "—of mere property, however costly—when *honor* is at stake. You gave Vlana *your word.* Oh, is knighthood wholly dead?"

Fafhrd could only shrug again and writhe inside and gulp a little easement from his silver mug.

In a master stroke, Vlana tried gently to draw Ivrian down to her golden seat again. "Softly, dearest," she pled. "You have spoken nobly for me and my cause, and believe me, I am most grateful. Your words revived in me great, fine feelings dead these many years. But of us here, only you are truly an aristocrat attuned to the highest proprieties. We other three are naught but thieves. Is it any wonder some of us put safety above honor and word-keeping, and most prudently avoid risking our lives? Yes, we are three thieves and I am outvoted. So please speak no more of honor and rash, dauntless bravery, but sit you down and—"

"You mean they're both *afraid* to challenge the Thieves' Guild, don't you?" Ivrian said, eyes wide and face twisted by loathing. "I always thought my Mouser was a nobleman first and a thief second. Thieving's nothing. My father lived by cruel thievery done on rich wayfarers and neighbors less powerful than he, yet he was an aristocrat. Oh, you're *cowards,* both of you! *Poltroons!"* she finished, turning her eyes flashing with cold scorn first on the Mouser, then on Fafhrd.

The latter could stand it no longer. He sprang to his feet, face flushed, fists clenched at his sides, quite unmindful of his down-clattered mug and the ominous creak his sudden action drew from the sagging floor.

"I am not a coward!" he cried. "I'll dare Thieves' House and fetch you Krovas' head and toss it with blood a-drip at Vlana's feet. I swear that by my sword Graywand here at my side!"

He slapped his left hip, found nothing there but his tunic, and had to content himself with pointing tremble-armed at his belt and scabbarded sword where they lay atop his neatly folded robe—and then picking up, refilling splashily, and draining his mug.

The Gray Mouser began to laugh in high, delighted, tuneful peals. All stared at him. He came dancing up beside Fafhrd, and still smiling widely, asked, "*Why not?* Who speaks of fearing the Guild-thieves? Who becomes upset at the prospect of this ridiculously easy exploit, when all of us know that all of them, even Krovas and his ruling clique, are but pygmies in mind and skill compared to me or Fafhrd here? A wondrously simple, foolproof scheme has just occurred to me for penetrating Thieves' House, every closet and cranny. Stout Fafhrd and I will put it into effect at once. Are you with me, Northerner?"

"Of course I am," Fafhrd responded gruffly, at the same time frantically wondering what madness had gripped the little fellow.

"Give me a few heartbeats to gather needed props, and we're off!" the Mouser cried. He snatched from shelf and unfolded a stout sack, then raced about, thrusting into it coiled ropes, bandage rolls, rags, jars of ointment and unction and unguent, and other oddments.

"But you can't go *tonight*," Ivrian protested, suddenly grown pale and uncertain-voiced. "You're both… in no condition to."

"You're both *drunk*," Vlana said harshly. "Silly drunk—and that way you'll get naught in Thieves' House but your deaths. Fafhrd! Control yourself!"

"Oh, no," Fafhrd told her as he buckled on his sword. "You wanted the head of Krovas heaved at your feet in a great splatter of blood, and that's what you're going to get, like it or not!"

"Softly, Fafhrd," the Mouser interjected, coming to a sudden stop and drawing tight the sack's mouth by its strings. "And softly you too, Lady Vlana, and my dear princess. Tonight I intend but a scouting expedition. No risks run, only the information gained needful for planning our murderous strike tomorrow or the day after. So no head-choppings whatsoever tonight, Fafhrd, you hear me? Whatever may hap, hist's the word. And don your hooded robe."

Fafhrd shrugged, nodded, and obeyed.

Ivrian seemed somewhat relieved. Vlana too, though she said, "Just the same you're both drunk."

"All to the good!" the Mouser assured her with a mad smile. "Drink may slow a man's sword-arm and soften his blows a bit, but it sets his wits ablaze and fires his imagination, and those are the qualities we'll need tonight."

Vlana eyed him dubiously.

Under cover of this confab Fafhrd made quietly yet swiftly to fill once more his and the Mouser's mugs, but Vlana noted it and gave him such a glare that he set down mugs and uncorked jug so swiftly his robe swirled.

The Mouser shouldered his sack and drew open the door. With a casual wave at the girls, but no word spoken, Fafhrd stepped out on the tiny porch. The night-smog had grown so thick he was almost lost to view. The Mouser waved four fingers at Ivrian, then followed Fafhrd.

"Good fortune go with you," Vlana called heartily.

"Oh, be careful, Mouser," Ivrian gasped.

The Mouser, his figure slight against the loom of Fafhrd's, silently drew shut the door.

Their arms automatically gone around each other, the girls waited for the inevitable creaking and groaning of the stairs. It delayed and delayed. The night-smog that had entered the room dissipated and still the silence was unbroken.

"What can they be doing out there?" Ivrian whispered. "Plotting their course?"

Vlana impatiently shook her head, then disentangled herself, tiptoed to the door, opened it, descended softly a few steps, which creaked most dolefully, then returned, shutting the door behind her.

"They're gone," she said in wonder.

"I'm frightened!" Ivrian breathed and sped across the room to embrace the taller girl.

Vlana hugged her tight, then disengaged an arm to shoot the door's three heavy bolts.

In Bones Alley the Mouser returned to his pouch the knotted line by which they'd descended from the lamp hook. He suggested, "How about stopping at the Silver Eel?"

"You mean and just *tell* the girls we've been to Thieves' House?" Fafhrd asked.

"Oh, no," the Mouser protested. "But you missed your stirrup cup upstairs—and so did I."

With a crafty smile Fafhrd drew from his robe two full jugs.

"Palmed 'em, as 'twere, when I set down the mugs. Vlana sees a lot, but not all."

"You're a prudent, far-sighted fellow," the Mouser said admiringly. "I'm proud to call you comrade."

Each uncorked and drank a hearty slug. Then the Mouser led them west, they veering and stumbling only a little, and then north into an even narrower and more noisome alley.

"Plague Court," the Mouser said.

After several preliminary peepings and peerings, they staggered swiftly across wide, empty Crafts Street and into Plague Court again. For a wonder it was growing a little lighter. Looking upward, they saw stars. Yet there was no wind blowing from the north. The air was deathly still.

In their drunken preoccupation with the project at hand and mere locomotion, they did not look behind them. There the night-smog was thicker than ever. A high-circling nighthawk would have seen the stuff converging from all sections of Lankhmar in swift-moving black rivers and rivulets, heaping, eddying, swirling, dark and reeking essence of Lankhmar from its branding irons, braziers, bonfires, kitchen fires and warmth fires, kilns, forges, breweries, distilleries, junk and garbage fires innumerable, sweating alchemists' and sorcerers' dens, crematoriums, charcoal burners' turfed mounds, all those and many more... converging purposefully on Dim Lane and particularly on the Silver Eel and the rickety house behind it. The closer to that center it got, the more substantial the smog became, eddy-strands and swirl-tatters tearing off and clinging like black cobwebs to rough stone corners and scraggly surfaced brick.

But the Mouser and Fafhrd merely exclaimed in mild, muted amazement at the stars and cautiously zigzagging across the Street of the Thinkers, called Atheist Avenue by moralists, continued up Plague Court until it forked.

The Mouser chose the left branch, which trended northwest.

"Death Alley."

After a curve and recurve, Cheap Street swung into sight about thirty paces ahead. The Mouser stopped at once and lightly threw his arm against Fafhrd's chest.

Clearly in view across Cheap Street was the wide, low, open doorway of Thieves' House, framed by grimy stone blocks. There led up to it two steps hollowed by the treadings of centuries. Orange-yellow light spilled out from bracketed torches inside.

There was no porter or guard in sight, not even a watchdog on a chain. The effect was ominous.

"Now how do we get into the damn place?" Fafhrd demanded in a hoarse whisper. "That doorway stinks of traps."

The Mouser answered, scornful at last, "Why, we'll walk straight through that doorway you fear." He frowned. "Tap and hobble, rather. Come on, while I prepare us."

As he drew the skeptically grimacing Fafhrd back down Death Alley until all Cheap Street was again cut off from view, he explained, "We'll pretend to be beggars, members of *their* guild, which is but a branch of the Thieves' Guild and reports in to the Begggarmasters at Thieves' House. We'll be new members, who've gone out by day, so it'll not be expected that the Night Beggarmaster will know our looks."

"But we don't look like beggars," Fafhrd protested. "Beggars have awful sores and limbs all a-twist or lacking altogether."

"That's just what I'm going to take care of now," the Mouser chuckled, drawing Scalpel. Ignoring Fafhrd's backward step and wary glance, the Mouser gazed puzzledly at the long tapering strip of steel he'd bared, then with a happy nod unclipped from his belt Scalpel's scabbard furbished with ratskin, sheathed the sword and swiftly wrapped it up, hilt and all, spirally, with the wide ribbon of a bandage roll dug from his sack.

"There!" he said, knotting the bandage ends. "Now I've a tapping cane."

"What's that?" Fafhrd demanded. "And why?"

The Mouser laid a flimsy black rag across his own eyes and tied it fast behind his head.

"Because I'll be blind, that's why." He took a few shuffling steps, tapping the cobbles ahead with wrapped sword—gripping it by the quillons, or cross guard, so that the grip and pommel were up his sleeve—and groping ahead with his other hand. "That look all right to you?" he asked Fafhrd as he turned back. "Feels perfect to me. Bat-blind!—eh? Oh, don't fret, Fafhrd—the rag's but gauze. I can see through it—fairly well. Besides, I don't have to convince anyone inside Thieves' House I'm actually blind. Most Guild-beggars fake it, as you must know. Now what to do with you? Can't have you blind also—too obvious, might wake suspicion." He uncorked his jug and sucked inspiration. Fafhrd copied this action, on principle.

The Mouser smacked his lips and said, "I've got it! Fafhrd, stand on your right leg and double up your left behind you at the knee. Hold!—don't fall on me! Avaunt! But steady yourself by my shoulder. That's right. Now get that left foot higher. We'll disguise your sword like mine, for a crutch cane—it's thicker and'll look just right. You can also steady yourself with your other hand on my shoulder as you hop—the halt leading the blind. But higher with that left foot! No, it just doesn't come off—I'll have to rope it. But first unclip your scabbard."

Soon the Mouser had Graywand and its scabbard in the same state as Scalpel and was tying Fafhrd's left ankle to his thigh, drawing the rope cruelly tight, though Fafhrd's wine-numbed nerves hardly registered it. Balancing himself with his steel-cored crutch cane as the Mouser worked, he swigged from his jug and pondered deeply.

Brilliant as the Mouser's plan undoubtedly was, there did seem to be drawbacks to it.

"Mouser," he said, "I don't know as I like having our swords tied up, so we can't draw 'em in emergency."

"We can still use 'em as clubs," the Mouser countered, his breath hissing between his teeth as he drew the last knot hard. "Besides, we'll have our knives. Say, pull your belt around until your knife is behind your back, so your robe will hide it sure. I'll do the same with Cat's Claw. Beggars don't carry weapons, at least in view. Stop drinking now, you've had enough. I myself need only a couple swallows more to reach my finest pitch."

"And I don't know as I like going hobbled into that den of cutthroats. I can hop amazingly fast, it's true, but not as fast as I can run. Is it really wise, think you?"

"You can slash yourself loose in an instant," the Mouser hissed with a touch of impatience and anger. "Aren't you willing to make the least sacrifice for art's sake?"

"Oh, very well," Fafhrd said, draining his jug and tossing it aside. "Yes, of course I am."

"Your complexion's too hale," the Mouser said, inspecting him critically. He touched up Fafhrd's features and hands with pale gray grease paint, then added wrinkles with dark. "And your garb's too tidy." He scooped dirt from between the cobbles and smeared it on Fafhrd's robe, then tried to put a rip in it, but the material resisted. He shrugged and tucked his lightened sack under his belt.

"So's yours," Fafhrd observed, and crouching on his right leg got a good handful of muck himself. Heaving himself up with a mighty effort, he wiped the stuff off on the Mouser's cloak and grey silken jerkin too.

The small man cursed, but, "Dramatic consistency," Fafhrd reminded him. "Now come on, while our fires and our stinks are still high." And grasping hold of the Mouser's shoulder, he propelled himself rapidly toward Cheap Street, setting his bandaged sword between cobbles well ahead and taking mighty hops.

"Slow down, idiot," the Mouser cried softly, shuffling along with the speed almost of a skater to keep up, while tapping his (sword) cane like mad. "A cripple's supposed to be *feeble*—that's what draws the sympathy."

Fafhrd nodded wisely and slowed somewhat. The ominous empty doorway slid again into view. The Mouser tilted his jug to get the last of his wine, swallowed awhile, then choked sputteringly. Fafhrd snatched and drained the jug, then tossed it overshoulder to shatter noisily.

They hop-shuffled across Cheap Street and without pause up the two worn steps and through the doorway, past the exceptionally thick wall. Ahead was a long, straight, high-ceilinged corridor ending in a stairs and with doors spilling light at intervals and wallset torches adding their flare, but empty all its length.

They had just got through the doorway when cold steel chilled the neck and pricked a shoulder of each of them. From just above, two voices commanded in unison, "Halt!"

Although fired—and fuddled—by fortified wine, they each had wit enough to freeze and then very cautiously look upward.

Two gaunt, scarred, exceptionally ugly faces, each topped by a gaudy scarf binding back hair, looked down at them from a big, deep niche just above the doorway. Two bent, gnarly arms thrust down the swords that still pricked them.

"Gone out with the noon beggar-batch, eh?" one of them observed. "Well, you'd better have a high take to justify your tardy return. The Night Beggarmaster's on a Whore Street furlough. Report above to Krovas. Gods, you stink! Better clean up first, or Krovas will have you bathed in live steam. Begone!"

The Mouser and Fafhrd shuffled and hobbled forward at their most authentic. One niche-guard cried after them, "Relax, boys! You don't have to put it on here."

"Practice makes perfect," the Mouser called back in a quavering voice. Fafhrd's fingerends dug his shoulder warningly. They moved along somewhat more naturally, so far as Fafhrd's tied-up leg allowed. Truly, thought Fafhrd, Kos of the Dooms seemed to be leading him direct to Krovas and perhaps head-chopping *would* be the order of the night. And now he and the Mouser began to hear voices, mostly curt and clipped ones, and other noises.

They passed some doorways they'd liked to have paused at, yet the most they dared do was slow down a bit more.

Very interesting were some of those activities. In one room young boys were being trained to pick pouches and slit purses. They'd approach from behind an instructor, and if he heard scuff of bare foot or felt touch of dipping hand—or, worst, heard clunk of dropped leaden mock-coin—that boy would be thwacked.

In a second room, older student thieves were doing laboratory work in lock picking. One group was being lectured by a grimy-handed graybeard, who was taking apart a most complex lock piece by weighty piece.

In a third, thieves were eating at long tables. The odors were tempting, even to men full of booze. The Guild did well by its members.

In a fourth, the floor was padded in part and instruction was going on in slipping, dodging, ducking, tumbling, tripping, and otherwise foiling pursuit. A voice like a sergeant-major's rasped, "Nah, nah, nah! You couldn't give your crippled grandmother the slip. I said duck, not genuflect to holy Aarth. Now this time—"

By that time the Mouser and Fafhrd were halfway up the end stairs, Fafhrd vaulting somewhat laboriously as he grasped curving banister and swaddled sword.

The second floor duplicated the first, but was as luxurious as the other had been bare. Down the long corridor lamps and filigreed incense pots pendent from the ceiling alternated, diffusing a mild light and spicy smell. The walls were richly draped, the floor thick-carpeted. Yet this corridor was empty too and, moreover, *completely* silent. After a glance at each other, they started off boldly.

The first door, wide open, showed an untenanted room full of racks of garments, rich and plain, spotless and filthy, also wig stands, shelves of beards and such. A disguising room, clearly.

The Mouser darted in and out to snatch up a large green flask from the nearest table. He unstoppered and sniffed it. A rotten-sweet gardenia-reek contended with the nose-sting of spirits of wine. The Mouser sloshed his and Fafhrd's fronts with this dubious perfume.

"Antidote to muck," he explained with the pomp of a physician, stoppering the flask. "Don't want to be parboiled by Krovas. No, no, no."

Two figures appeared at the far end of the corridor and came toward them. The Mouser hid the flask under his cloak, holding it between elbow and side, and he and Fafhrd continued boldly onward.

The next three doorways they passed were shut by heavy doors. As they neared the fifth, the two approaching figures, coming up arm-in-arm, became distinct. Their clothing was that of noblemen, but their faces those of thieves. They were frowning with indignation and suspicion, too, at the Mouser and Fafhrd.

Just then, from somewhere between the two man-pairs, a voice began to speak words in a strange tongue, using the rapid monotone priests employ in a routine service, or some sorcerers in their incantations.

The two richly clad thieves slowed at the seventh doorway and looked in. Their progress ceased altogether. Their necks strained, their eyes widened. They paled. Then of a sudden they hastened onward, almost running, and by-passed Fafhrd and the Mouser as if they were furniture. The incantatory voice drummed on without missing a beat.

The fifth doorway was shut, but the sixth was open. The Mouser peeked in with one eye, his nose brushing the jamb. Then he stepped forward and gazed inside with entranced expression, pushing the black rag up onto his forehead for better vision. Fafhrd joined him.

It was large room, empty so far as could be told of human and animal life, but filled with most interesting things. From knee-height up, the entire far wall was a map of the city of Lankhmar. Every building and street seemed depicted, down to the meanest hovel and narrowest court. There were signs of recent erasure and redrawing at many spots, and here and there little colored hieroglyphs of mysterious import.

The floor was marble, the ceiling blue as lapis lazuli. The side walls were thickly hung, the one with all manner of thieves' tools, from a huge, thick, pry-bar that looked as if it could unseat the universe, to a rod so slim it might be an elf-queen's wand and seemingly designed to telescope out and fish from a distance for precious gauds on milady's spindle-legged, ivory-topped vanity table. The other wall had padlocked to it all sorts of quaint, gold-gleaming and jewel-flashing objects, evidently mementos chosen for their oddity from the spoils of memorable burglaries, from a female mask of thin gold, breathlessly beautiful in its features and contours but thickly set with rubies simulating the spots of the pox in its fever stage, to a knife whose blade was wedge-shaped diamonds set side by side and this diamond cutting-edge looking razor-sharp.

In the center of the room was a bare round table of ebony and ivory squares. About it were set seven straight-backed but well-padded chairs, the one facing the map and away from the Mouser and Fafhrd being higher backed and wider armed than the others—a chief's chair, likely that of Krovas.

The Mouser tiptoed forward, irresistibly drawn, but Fafhrd's left hand clamped down on his shoulder.

Scowling his disapproval, the Northerner brushed down the black rag over the Mouser's eyes again and with his crutch-hand thumbed ahead, then set off in that direction in most carefully calculated, silent hops. With a shrug of disappointment the Mouser followed.

As soon as they had turned away from the doorway, a neatly black-bearded, crop-haired head came like a serpent's around the side of the highest-backed chair and gazed after them from deep-sunken yet glinting eyes. Next a snake-supple, long hand followed the head out, crossed thin lips with ophidian forefinger for silence, and then finger-beckoned the two pairs of dark-tunicked men who were standing to either side of the doorway, their backs to the corridor wall, each of the four gripping a curvy knife in one hand and a dark leather, lead-weighted bludgeon in the other.

When Fafhrd was halfway to the seventh doorway, from which the monotonous yet sinister recitation continued to well, there shot out through it a slender, whey-faced youth, his narrow hands clapped over his mouth, under terror-wide eyes, as if to shut in screams or vomit, and with a broom clamped in an armpit, so that he seemed a bit like a young warlock about to take to the air. He dashed past Fafhrd and the Mouser and away, his racing footsteps sounding rapid-dull on the carpeting and hollow-sharp on the stairs before dying away.

Fafhrd gazed back at the Mouser with a grimace and shrug, then squatting one-legged until the knee of his bound-up leg touched the floor, advanced half his face past the doorjamb. After a bit, without otherwise changing position, he beckoned the Mouser to approach. The latter slowly thrust half his face past the jamb, just above Fafhrd's.

What they saw was a room somewhat smaller than that of the great map and lit by central lamps that burnt blue-white instead of customary yellow. The floor was marble, darkly colorful and complexly whorled. The dark walls were hung with astrological and anthropomantic charts and instruments of magic and shelved with cryptically labeled porcelain jars and also with vitreous flasks and glass pipes of the oddest shapes, some filled with colored fluids, but many gleamingly empty. At the foot of the walls, where the shadows were thickest, broken and discarded stuff was irregularly heaped, as if swept out of the way and forgot, and here and there opened a large rathole.

In the center of the room and brightly illuminated by contrast was a long table with thick top and many stout legs. The Mouser thought fleetingly of a centipede and then of the bar at the Eel, for the table top was densely stained and scarred by many a spilt elixir and many a deep black burn by fire or acid or both.

In the midst of the table an alembic was working. The lamp's flame—deep blue, this one—kept a-boil in the large crystal cucurbit a dark, viscid fluid with here and there diamond glints. From out of the thick, seething stuff, strands of a darker vapor streamed upward to crowd through the cucurbit's narrow mouth and stain—oddly, with bright scarlet—the transparent head and then, dead black now, flow down the narrow pipe from the head into a spherical crystal receiver, larger even than the cucurbit, and there curl and weave about like so many coils of living black cord—an endless, skinny, ebon serpent.

Behind the left end of the table stood a tall, yet hunchbacked man in black robe and hood, which shadowed more than hid a face of which the most prominent features were a long, thick, pointed nose with out-jutting, almost chinless mouth. His complexion was sallow-gray like sandy clay. A short-haired, bristly, gray beard grew high on his wide cheeks. From under a receding forehead and bushy gray brows, wide-set eyes looked intently down at an age-browned scroll, which his disgustingly small clubhands, knuckles big, short backs gray-bristled, ceaselessly unrolled and rolled up again. The only move his eyes ever made, besides the short side-to-side one as he read the lines he was rapidly intoning, was an occasional glance at the alembic.

On the other end of the table, beady eyes darting from the sorcerer to the alembic and back again, crouched a small black beast, the first glimpse of which made Fafhrd dig fingers painfully into the Mouser's shoulder and the latter almost gasp, but not from the pain. It was most like a rat, yet it had a higher forehead and closer-set eyes, while its forepaws, which it constantly rubbed together in what seemed restless glee, looked like tiny copies of the sorcerer's clubhands.

Simultaneously yet independently, Fafhrd and the Mouser each became certain it was the beast which had gutter-escorted Slivikin and his mate, then fled, and each recalled what Ivrian had said about a witch's familiar and Vlana about the likelihood of Krovas employing a warlock.

The tempo of the incantation quickened; the blue-white flames brightened and hissed audibly; the fluid in the cucurbit grew thick as lava; great bubbles formed and loudly broke; the black rope in the receiver writhed like a nest of snakes; there was an increasing sense of invisible presences; the supernatural tension grew almost unendurable, and Fafhrd and the Mouser were hard put to keep silent the open-mouthed gapes by which they now breathed, and each feared his heartbeat could be heard yards away.

Abruptly the incantation peaked and broke off, like a drum struck very hard, then instantly silenced by palm and fingers outspread against the head. With a bright flash and dull explosion, cracks innumerable appeared in the cucurbit; its crystal became white and opaque, yet it did not shatter or drip. The head lifted a span, hung there, fell back. While two black nooses appeared among the coils in the receiver and suddenly narrowed until there were only two big black knots.

The sorcerer grinned, let the end of the parchment roll up with a snap, and shifted his gaze from the receiver to his familiar, while the latter chittered shrilly and bounded up and down in rapture.

"Silence, Slivikin! Comes now *your* time to race and strain and sweat," the sorcerer cried, speaking pidgin Lankhmarese now, but so rapidly and in so squeakingly high-pitched a voice that Fafhrd and the Mouser could barely follow him. They did, however, both realize they had been completely mistaken as to the identity of Slivikin. In the moment of disaster, the fat thief had called to the witch-beast for help rather than to his human comrade.

"Yes, master," Slivikin squeaked back no less clearly, in an instant revising the Mouser's opinions about talking animals. He continued in the same fife-like, fawning tones, "Harkening in obedience, Hristomilo."

Hristomilo ordered in whiplash pipings, "To your appointed work! See to it you summon an ample sufficiency of feasters!—I want the bodies stripped to skeletons, so the bruises of the enchanted smog and all evidence of death by suffocation will be vanished utterly. But forget not the loot! On your mission, now—depart!"

Slivikin, who at every command had bobbed his head in manner reminiscent of his bouncing, now squealed, "I'll see it done!" and gray lightning-like, leaped a long leap to the floor and down an inky rathole.

Hristomilo, rubbing together his disgusting clubhands much as Slivikin had his, cried chucklingly, "What Slevyas lost, my magic has re-won!"

Fafhrd and the Mouser drew back out of the doorway, partly for fear of being seen, partly in revulsion from what they had seen and heard, and in poignant if useless pity for Slevyas, whoever he might be, and for the other unknown victims of the rat-like and conceivably rat-related sorcerer's death-spells, poor strangers already dead and due to have their flesh eaten from their bones.

Fafhrd wrested the green bottle from the Mouser and, though almost gagging on the rotten flowery reek, gulped a large, stinging mouthful. The Mouser couldn't quite bring himself to do the same, but was comforted by the spirits of wine he inhaled.

Then he saw, beyond Fafhrd, standing before the doorway to the map room, a richly clad man with gold-hilted knife jewel-scabbarded at his side. His sunken-eyed face was prematurely wrinkled by responsibility, overwork, and authority, and framed by neatly cropped black hair and beard. Smiling, he silently beckoned them with a serpentine gesture.

The Mouser and Fafhrd obeyed, the latter returning the green bottle to the former, who recapped it and thrust it under his left elbow with well-concealed irritation.

Each guessed their summoner was Krovas, the Guild's Grandmaster. Once again Fafhrd marveled, as he hobbledehoyed along, reeling and belching, how Kos or the Fates were guiding him to his target tonight. The Mouser, more alert and more apprehensive too, was reminding himself that they had been directed by the niche-guards to report to Krovas, so that the situation, if not developing quite in accord with his own misty plans, was still not deviating disastrously.

Yet not even his alertness, nor Fafhrd's primeval instincts, gave them forewarning as they followed Krovas into the map room.

Two steps inside, each of them was shoulder-grabbed and bludgeon-menaced by a pair of ruffians further armed with knives tucked in their belts.

"All secure, Grandmaster," one of the ruffians rapped out.

Krovas swung the highest-backed chair around and sat down, eyeing them coolly.

"What brings two stinking, drunken beggar-guildsmen into the top-restricted precincts of the masters?" he asked quietly.

The Mouser felt the sweat of relief bead his forehead. The disguises he had brilliantly conceived were still working, taking in even the head man, though he had spotted Fafhrd's tipsiness. Resuming his blind-man manner, he quavered, "We were directed by the guard above the Cheap Street door to report to you in person, great Krovas, the Night Beggarmaster being on furlough for reasons of sexual hygiene. Tonight we've made good haul!" And fumbling in his purse, ignoring as far as possible the tightened grip on his shoulders, he brought out a golden coin and displayed it tremble-handed.

"Spare me your inexpert acting," Krovas said sharply. "I'm not one of your marks. And take that rag off your eyes."

The Mouser obeyed and stood to attention again insofar as his pinion-ing would permit, and smiling the more seeming carefree because of his reawakening uncertainties. Conceivably he wasn't doing quite as brilliantly as he'd thought.

Krovas leaned forward and said placidly yet piercingly, "Granted you were so ordered, why were you spying into a room beyond this one when I spotted you?"

"We saw brave thieves flee from that room," the Mouser answered pat. "Fearing that some danger threatened the Guild, my comrade and I inves-tigated, ready to scotch it."

"But what we saw and heard only perplexed us, great sir," Fafhrd ap-pended quite smoothly.

"I didn't ask you, sot. Speak when you're spoken to," Krovas snapped at him. Then, to the Mouser, "You're an overweening rogue, most presumptu-ous for your rank. Beggars claim to protect thieves indeed! I'm of a mind to have you both flogged for your spying, and again for your drunkenness, aye, and once more for your lies."

In a flash the Mouser decided that further insolence—and lying, too—rather than fawning, was what the situation required. "I am a most presumptuous rogue indeed, sir," he said smugly. Then he set his face sol-emn. "But now I see the time has come when I must speak darkest truth entire. The Day Beggarmaster suspects a plot against your own life, sir, by one of your highest and closest lieutenants—one you trust so well you'd not believe it, sir. He told us that! So he set me and my comrade secretly to guard you and sniff out the verminous villain."

"More and clumsier lies!" Krovas snarled, but the Mouser saw his face grow pale. The Grandmaster half rose from his seat. "Which lieutenant?"

The Mouser grinned and relaxed. His two captors gazed sidewise at him curiously, loosing their grip a little. Fafhrd's pair seemed likewise intrigued.

The Mouser then asked coolly, "Are you questioning me as a trusty spy or a pinioned liar? If the latter, I'll not insult you with one more word."

Krovas' face darkened. "Boy!" he called. Through the curtains of an inner doorway, a youth with the dark complexion of a Kleshite and clad only in a black loincloth sprang to kneel before Krovas, who ordered, "Summon first my sorcerer, next the thieves Slevyas and Fissif," whereupon the dark youth dashed into the corridor.

Krovas hesitated a moment in thought, then shot a hand toward Fafhrd. "What do you know of this, drunkard? Do you support your mate's crazy tale?"

Fafhrd merely sneered his face and folded his arms, the still-slack grip of his captors permitting it, his sword-crutch hanging against his body from his lightly gripping hand. Then he scowled as there came a sudden shooting pain in his numbed, bound-up left leg, which he had forgotten.

Krovas raised a clenched fist and himself wholly from his chair, in prelude to some fearsome command—likely that Fafhrd and the Mouser be tortured, but at that moment Hristomilo came gliding into the room, his feet presumably taking swift, but very short steps—at any rate his black robe hung undisturbed to the marble floor despite his slithering speed.

There was a shock at his entrance. All eyes in the map room followed him, breaths were held, and the Mouser and Fafhrd felt the horny hands that gripped them shake just a little. Even Krovas' tense expression became also guardedly uneasy.

Outwardly oblivious to this reaction to his appearance, Hristomilo, smiling thin-lipped, halted close to one side of Krovas' chair and inclined his hood-shadowed rodent face in the ghost of a bow.

Krovas asked sharply yet nervously, gesturing toward the Mouser and Fafhrd, "Do you know these two?"

Hristomilo nodded decisively. "They just now peered a befuddled eye each at me," he said, "whilst I was about that business we spoke of. I'd have shooed them off, reported them, save such action would have broken my spell, put my words out of time with the alembic's workings. The one's a Northerner, the other's features have a southern cast—from Tovilyis or near, most like. Both younger than their now-looks. Freelance bravoes, I'd judge 'em, the sort the Brotherhood hires as extras when they get at once several big guard and escort jobs. Clumsily disguised now, of course, as beggars."

Fafhrd by yawning, the Mouser by pitying headshake tried to convey that all this was so much poor guesswork. The Mouser even added a warning glare, brief as lightning, to suggest to Krovas that the conspiring lieutenant might be the Grandmaster's own sorcerer.

"That's all I can tell you without reading their minds," Hristomilo concluded. "Shall I fetch my lights and mirrors?"

"Not yet." Krovas faced the Mouser and said, "Now speak truth, or have it magicked from you and then be whipped to death. Which of my lieutenants were you set to spy on by the Day Beggarmaster? But you're lying about that commission, I believe?"

"Oh, no," the Mouser denied it guilelessly. "We reported our every act to the Day Beggarmaster and he approved them, told us to spy our best and gather every scrap of fact and rumor we could about the conspiracy."

"And he told me not a word about it!" Krovas rapped out. "If true, I'll have Bannat's head for this! But you're lying, aren't you?"

As the Mouser gazed with wounded eyes at Krovas, a portly man limped past the doorway with help of a gilded staff. He moved with silence and aplomb.

But Krovas saw him. "Night Beggarmaster!" he called sharply. The limping man stopped, turned, came crippling majestically through the door. Krovas stabbed a finger at the Mouser, then Fafhrd. "Do you know these two, Flim?"

The Night Beggarmaster unhurriedly studied each for a space, then shook his head with its turban of cloth of gold. "Never seen either before. What are they? Fink beggars?"

"But Flim wouldn't know us," the Mouser explained desperately, feeling everything collapsing in on him and Fafhrd. "All our contacts were with Bannat alone."

Flim said quietly, "Bannat's been abed with the swamp ague this past ten-day. Meanwhile I have been Day Beggarmaster as well as Night."

At that moment Slevyas and Fissif came hurrying in behind Flim. The tall thief bore on his jaw a bluish lump. The fat thief's head was bandaged above his darting eyes. He pointed quickly at Fafhrd and the Mouser and cried, "There are the two that slugged us, took our Jengao loot, and slew our escort."

The Mouser lifted his elbow and the green bottle crashed to shards at his feet on the hard marble. Gardenia-reek sprang swiftly through the air.

But more swiftly still the Mouser, shaking off the careless hold of his startled guards, sprang toward Krovas, clubbing his wrapped-up sword.

With startling speed Flim thrust out his gilded staff, tripping the Mouser, who went heels over head, midway seeking to change his involuntary somersault into a voluntary one.

Meanwhile Fafhrd lurched heavily against his left-hand captor, at the same time swinging bandaged Graywand strongly upward to strike his right-hand captor under the jaw. Regaining his one-legged balance with a mighty contortion, he hopped for the loot-wall behind him.

Slevyas made for the wall of thieves' tools, and with a muscle-cracking effort wrenched the great pry-bar from its padlocked ring. Scrambling to his feet after a poor landing in front of Krovas chair, the Mouser found it empty and the Thief King in a half-crouch behind it, gold-hilted dagger drawn, deep-sunk eyes coldly battle-wild. Spinning around, he saw Fafhrd's guards on the floor, the one sprawled senseless, the other starting to scramble up, while the great Northerner, his back against the wall of weird jewelry, menaced the whole room with wrapped-up Graywand and with his long knife, jerked from its scabbard behind him.

Likewise drawing Cat's Claw, the Mouser cried in trumpet-voice of battle, "Stand aside, all! He's gone mad! I'll hamstring his good leg for you!" And racing through the press and between his own two guards, who still appeared to hold him in some awe, he launched himself with flashing dirk at Fafhrd, praying that the Northerner, drunk now with battle as well as wine and poisonous perfume, would recognize him and guess his stratagem.

Graywand slashed well above his ducking head. His new friend not only guessed, but was playing up—and not just missing by accident, the Mouser hoped. Stooping low by the wall, he cut the lashings on Fafhrd's left leg. Graywand and Fafhrd's long knife continued to spare him. Springing up, he headed for the corridor, crying overshoulder to Fafhrd, "Come on!"

Hristomilo stood well out of his way, quietly observing. Fissif scuttled toward safety. Krovas stayed behind his chair, shouting, "Stop them! Head them off!"

The three remaining ruffian guards, at last beginning to recover their fighting-wits, gathered to oppose the Mouser. But menacing them with swift feints of his dirk, he slowed them and darted between—and then just in the nick of time knocked aside with a downsweep of wrapped-up Scalpel Flim's gilded staff, thrust once again to trip him.

All this gave Slevyas time to return from the tools-wall and aim at the Mouser a great swinging blow with the massive pry-bar. But even as that blow started, a very long, bandaged and scabbarded sword on a very long arm thrust over the Mouser's shoulder and solidly and heavily poked Slevyas high on the chest, jolting him backwards, so that the pry-bar's swing was short and sang past harmlessly.

Then the Mouser found himself in the corridor and Fafhrd beside him, though for some weird reason still only hopping. The Mouser pointed toward the stairs. Fafhrd nodded, but delayed to reach high, still on one leg only, and rip off the nearest wall a dozen yards of heavy drapes, which he threw across the corridor to baffle pursuit.

They reached the stairs and started up the next flight, the Mouser in advance. There were cries behind, some muffled.

"Stop hopping, Fafhrd!" the Mouser ordered querulously. "You've got two legs again."

"Yes, and the other's still dead," Fafhrd complained. "Ahh! Now feeling begins to return to it."

A thrown knife whished between them and dully clinked as it hit the wall point-first and stone powder flew. Then they were around the bend.

Two more empty corridors, two more curving flights, and then they saw above them on the last landing a stout ladder mounting to a dark, square hole in the roof. A thief with hair bound back by a colorful handkerchief—it appeared to be the door guards' identification—menaced the Mouser with drawn sword, but when he saw that there were two of them, both charging him determinedly with shining knives and strange staves or clubs, he turned and ran down the last empty corridor.

The Mouser, followed closely by Fafhrd, rapidly mounted the ladder and vaulted up through the hatch into the star-crusted night.

He found himself near the unrailed edge of a slate roof which slanted enough to have made it look most fearsome to a novice roof-walker, but safe as houses to a veteran.

Turning back at a bumping sound, he saw Fafhrd prudently hoisting the ladder. Just as he got it free, a knife flashed up close past him out of the hatch.

It clattered down near them and slid off the roof. The Mouser loped south across the slates and was halfway from the hatch to that end of the roof when the faint chink came of the knife striking the cobbles of Murder Alley.

Fafhrd followed more slowly, in part perhaps from a lesser experience of roofs, in part because he still limped a bit to favor his left leg, and in part because he was carrying the heavy ladder balanced on his right shoulder.

"We won't need that," the Mouser called back.

Without hesitation Fafhrd heaved it joyously over the edge. By the time it crashed in Murder Alley, the Mouser was leaping down two yards and across a gap of one to the next roof, of opposite and lesser pitch. Fafhrd landed beside him.

The Mouser led them at almost a run through a sooty forest of chimneys, chimney pots, ventilators with tails that made them always face the wind, black-legged cisterns, hatch covers, bird houses, and pigeon traps across five roofs, until they reached the Street of the Thinkers at a point where it was crossed by a roofed passageway much like the one at Rokkermas and Slaarg's.

While they crossed it at a crouching lope, something hissed close past them and clattered ahead. As they leaped down from the roof of the bridge, three more somethings hissed over their heads to clatter beyond. One rebounded from a square chimney almost to the Mouser's feet. He picked it up, expecting a stone, and was surprised by the greater weight of a leaden ball big as two doubled-up fingers.

"They," he said, jerking thumb overshoulder, "lost no time in getting slingers on the roof. When roused, they're good."

Southeast then through another black chimney-forest toward a point on Cheap Street where upper stories overhung the street so much on either side that it would be easy to leap the gap. During this roof-traverse, an advancing front of night-smog, dense enough to make them cough and wheeze, engulfed them and for perhaps sixty heartbeats the Mouser had to slow to a shuffle and feel his way, Fafhrd's hand on his shoulder. Just short of Cheap Street they came abruptly and completely out of the smog and saw the stars again, while the black front rolled off northward behind them.

"Now what the devil was that?" Fafhrd asked and the Mouser shrugged.

A nighthawk would have seen a vast thick hoop of black night-smog blowing out in all directions from a center near the Silver Eel. East of Cheap Street the two comrades soon made their way to the ground, landing back in Plague Court.

Then at last they looked at each other and their trammeled swords and their filthy faces and clothing made dirtier still by roof-soot, and they laughed and laughed and laughed, Fafhrd roaring still as he bent over to massage his left leg above and below knee. This hooting self-mockery continued while they unwrapped their swords—the Mouser as if his were a surprise package—and clipped their scabbards once more to their belts. Their exertions had burnt out of them the last mote and atomy of strong wine and even stronger stenchful perfume, but they felt no desire whatever for more drink, only the urge to get home and eat hugely and guzzle hot, bitter gahveh, and tell their lovely girls at length the tale of their mad adventure.

They loped on side by side.

Free of night-smog and drizzled with starlight, their cramped surroundings seemed much less stinking and oppressive than when they had set out. Even Bones Alley had a freshness to it.

They hastened up the long, creaking, broken-treaded stairs with an easy carefulness, and when they were both on the porch, the Mouser shoved at the door to open it with surprise-swiftness.

It did not budge.

"Bolted," he said to Fafhrd shortly. He noted now there was hardly any light at all coming through the cracks around the door, nor had any been noticeable through the lattices—at most, a faint orange-red glow. Then with sentimental grin and in fond voice in which only the ghost of uneasiness lurked, he said, "They've gone to sleep, the unworrying wenches!" He knocked loudly thrice and then cupping his lips called softly at the door crack, "Hola, Ivrian! I'm home safe. Hail, Vlana! Your man's done you proud, felling Guild-thieves innumerable with one foot tied behind his back!"

There was no sound whatever from inside—that is, if one discounted a rustling so faint it was impossible to be sure of it.

Fafhrd was wrinkling his nostrils. "I smell vermin."

The Mouser banged on the door again. Still no response.

Fafhrd motioned him out of the way, hunching his big shoulder to crash the portal.

The Mouser shook his head and with a deft tap, slide, and a tug removed a brick that a moment before had looked to be a firm-set part of the wall beside the door. He reached in all his arm. There was the scrape of a bolt being withdrawn, then another, then a third. He swiftly recovered his arm and the door swung fully inward at touch.

But neither he nor Fafhrd rushed in at once, as both had intended to, for the indefinable scent of danger and the unknown came puffing out along with an increased reek of filthy beast and a slight, sickening sweet scent that though female was no decent female perfume.

They could see the room faintly by the orange glow coming from the small oblong of the open door of the little, well-blacked stove. Yet the oblong did not sit properly upright but was unnaturally a-tilt—clearly the stove had been half overset and now leaned against a side wall of the fireplace, its small door fallen open in that direction.

By itself alone, that unnatural angle conveyed the entire impact of a universe overturned.

The orange glow showed the carpets oddly rucked up with here and there ragged black circles a palm's breadth across, the neatly stacked candles scattered about below their shelves along with some of the jars and enameled boxes, and—above all—two black, low, irregular, longish heaps, the one by the fireplace, the other half on the golden couch, half at its foot.

From each heap there stared at the Mouser and Fafhrd innumerable pairs of tiny, rather widely set, furnace-red eyes.

On the thickly carpeted floor on the other side of the fireplace was a silver cobweb—a fallen silver cage, but no love birds sang from it.

There was the faint scrape of metal as Fafhrd made sure Graywand was loose in his scabbard.

As if that tiny sound had beforehand been chosen as the signal for attack, each instantly whipped out sword and they advanced side by side into the room, warily at first, testing the floor with each step.

At the screech of the swords being drawn, the tiny furnace-red eyes had winked and shifted restlessly, and now with the two men's approach they swiftly scattered pattering, pair by red pair, each pair at the forward end of a small, low, slender, hairless-tailed black body, and each making for one of the black circles in the rugs, where they vanished.

Indubitably the black circles were ratholes newly gnawed up through the floor and rugs, while the red-eyed creatures were black rats.

Fafhrd and the Mouser sprang forward, slashing and chopping at them in a frenzy, cursing and human-snarling besides.

They sundered few. The rats fled with preternatural swiftness, most of them disappearing down holes near the walls and the fireplace.

Also Fafhrd's first frantic chop went through the floor and on his third step, with an ominous crack and splintering, his leg plunged through the floor to his hip. The Mouser darted past him, unmindful of further crackings.

Fafhrd heaved out his trapped leg, not even noting the splinter-scratches it got and as unmindful as the Mouser of the continuing creakings. The rats were gone. He lunged after his comrade, who had thrust a bunch of kindlers into the stove, to make more light.

The horror was that, although the rats were all gone, the two longish heaps remained, although considerably diminished and, as now shown clearly by the yellow flames leaping from the tilted black door, changed in hue—no longer were the heaps red-beaded black, but a mixture of gleaming black and dark brown, a sickening purple-blue, violet and velvet black and snow-serpent white, and the reds of stockings and blood and bloody flesh and bone.

Although hands and feet had been gnawed bone-naked, and bodies tunneled heart-deep, the two faces had been spared. But that was not good, for they were the parts purple-blue from death by strangulation, lips drawn back, eyes bulging, all features contorted in agony. Only the black and very dark brown hair gleamed unchanged—that and the white, white teeth.

As each man stared down at his love, unable to look away despite the waves of horror and grief and rage washing higher and higher in him, each saw a tiny black strand uncurl from the black depression ringing each throat and drift off, dissipating, toward the open door behind them—two strands of night-smog.

With a crescendo of crackings the floor sagged three spans more in the center before arriving at a new temporary stability.

Edges of centrally tortured minds noted details: That Vlana's silver-hilted dagger skewered to the floor a rat, which, likely enough, overeager had approached too closely before the night-smog had done its magic work. That her belt and pouch were gone. That the blue-enameled box inlaid with silver, in which Ivrian had put the Mouser's share of the highjacked jewels, was gone too.

The Mouser and Fafhrd lifted to each other white, drawn faces which were quite mad, yet completely joined in understanding and purpose. No need for Fafhrd to explain why he stripped off his robe and hood, or why he jerked up Vlana's dagger, snapped the rat off it with a wrist-flick, and thrust it in his belt. No need for the Mouser to tell why he searched out a half-dozen jars of oil and after smashing three of them in front of the flaming stove, paused, thought, and stuck the other three in the sack at his waist, adding to them the remaining kindlers and the fire-pot, brimmed with red coals, its top lashed down tight.

Then, still without word exchanged, the Mouser reached into the fireplace and without a wince at the burning metal's touch, deliberately tipped the flaming stove forward, so that it fell door-down on oil-soaked rugs. Yellow flames sprang up around him.

They turned and raced for the door. With louder crackings than any before, the floor collapsed. They desperately scrambled their way up a steep hill of sliding carpets and reached door and porch just before all behind them gave way and the flaming rugs and stove and all the firewood and candles and the golden couch and all the little tables and boxes and jars—and the unthinkably mutilated bodies of their first loves—cascaded into the dry, dusty, cobweb-choked room below, and the great flames of a cleansing or at least obliterating cremation began to flare upward.

They plunged down the stairs, which tore away from the wall and collapsed in the dark as they reached the ground. They had to fight their way over the wreckage to get to Bones Alley.

By then flames were darting their bright lizard-tongues out of the shuttered attic windows and the boarded-up ones in the story just below. By the time they reached Plague Court, running side by side at top speed, the Silver Eel's fire alarm was clanging cacophonously behind them.

They were still sprinting when they took the Death Alley fork. Then the Mouser grappled Fafhrd and forced him to a halt. The big man struck out, cursing insanely, and only desisted—his white face still a lunatic's—when the Mouser cried panting, "Only ten heartbeats to arm us!"

He pulled the sack from his belt and keeping tight hold of its neck, crashed it on the cobbles—hard enough to smash not only the bottles of oil, but also the fire-pot, for the sack was soon flaming at its base.

Then he drew gleaming Scalpel and Fafhrd Graywand, and they raced on, the Mouser swinging his sack in a great circle beside him to fan its flames. It was a veritable ball of fire burning his left hand as they dashed across Cheap Street and into Thieves' House, and the Mouser, leaping high, swung it up into the great niche above the doorway and let go of it.

The niche-guards screeched in surprise and pain at the fiery invader of their hidey-hole.

Student thieves poured out of the doors ahead at the screeching and foot-pounding, and then poured back as they saw the fierce point of flames and the two demon-faced on-comers brandishing their long, shining swords.

One skinny little apprentice—he could hardly have been ten years old—lingered too long. Graywand thrust him pitilessly through, as his big eyes bulged and his small mouth gaped in horror and plea to Fafhrd for mercy.

Now from ahead of them there came a weird, wailing call, hollow and hair-raising, and doors began to thud shut instead of spewing forth the armed guards Fafhrd and the Mouser prayed would appear to be skewered by their swords. Also, despite the long, bracketed torches looking newly renewed, the corridor was darkening.

The reason for this last became clear as they plunged up the stairs. Strands of night-smog appeared in the stairwell, materializing from nothing, or the air.

The strands grew longer and more tangible. They touched and clung nastily. In the corridor above they were forming from wall to wall and from ceiling to floor, like a gigantic cobweb, and were becoming so substantial that the Mouser and Fafhrd had to slash them to get through, or so their two maniac minds believed. The black web muffled a little a repetition of the eerie, wailing call, which came from the seventh door ahead and this time ended in a gleeful chittering and cackling as insane as the emotions of the two attackers.

Here, too, doors were thudding shut. In an ephemeral flash of rationality, it occurred to the Mouser that it was not he and Fafhrd the thieves feared, for they had not been seen yet, but rather Hristomilo and his magic, even though working in defense of Thieves' House.

Even the map room, whence counterattack would most likely erupt, was closed off by a huge oaken, iron-studded door.

They were now twice slashing the black, clinging, rope-thick spiderweb for every single step they drove themselves forward. While midway between the map and magic rooms, there was forming on the inky web, ghostly at first but swiftly growing more substantial, a black spider as big as a wolf.

The Mouser slashed heavy cobweb before it, dropped back two steps, then hurled himself at it in a high leap. Scalpel thrust through it, striking amidst its eight new-formed jet eyes, and it collapsed like a daggered bladder, loosing a vile stink.

Then he and Fafhrd were looking into the magic room, the alchemist's chamber. It was much as they had seen it before, except some things were doubled, or multiplied even further.

On the long table two blue-boiled cucurbits bubbled and roiled, their heads shooting out a solid, writhing rope more swiftly than moves the black swamp-cobra, which can run down a man—and not into twin receivers, but into the open air of the room (if any of the air in Thieves' House could have been called open then) to weave a barrier between their swords and Hristomilo, who once more stood tall though hunchbacked over his sorcerous, brown parchment, though this time his exultant gaze was chiefly fixed on Fafhrd and the Mouser, with only an occasional downward glance at the text of the spell he drummingly intoned.

While at the other end of the table, in web-free space, there bounced not only Slivikin, but also a huge rat matching him in size in all members except the head.

From the ratholes at the foot of the walls, red eyes glittered and gleamed in pairs.

With a bellow of rage Fafhrd began slashing at the black barrier, but the ropes were replaced from the cucurbit heads as swiftly as he sliced them, while the cut ends, instead of drooping slackly, now began to strain hungrily toward him like constrictive snakes or strangle-vines.

He suddenly shifted Graywand to his left hand, drew his long knife and hurled it at the sorcerer. Flashing toward its mark, it cut through three strands, was deflected and slowed by a fourth and fifth, almost halted by a sixth, and ended hanging futilely in the curled grip of a seventh.

Hristomilo laughed cacklingly and grinned, showing his huge upper incisors, while Slivikin chittered in ecstasy and bounded the higher.

The Mouser hurled Cat's Claw with no better result—worse, indeed, since his action gave two darting smog-strands time to curl hamperingly around his sword-hand and stranglingly around his neck. Black rats came racing out of the big holes at the cluttered base of the walls.

Meanwhile other strands snaked around Fafhrd's ankles, knees and left arm, almost toppling him. But even as he fought for balance, he jerked Vlana's dagger from his belt and raised it over his shoulder, its silver hilt glowing, its blade brown with dried rat's-blood.

The grin left Hristomilo's face as he saw it. The sorcerer screamed strangely and importuningly then, and drew back from his parchment and the table, and raised clawed clubhands to ward off doom.

Vlana's dagger sped unimpeded through the black web—its strands even seemed to part for it—and betwixt the sorcerer's warding hands, to bury itself to the hilt in his right eye.

He screamed thinly in dire agony and clawed at his face.

The black web writhed as if in death spasm.

The cucurbits shattered as one, spilling their lava on the scarred table, putting out the blue flames even as the thick wood of the table began to smoke a little at the lava's edge. Lava dropped with *plops* on the dark marble floor.

With a faint, final scream Hristomilo pitched forward, hands clutched to his eyes above his jutting nose, silver dagger-hilt protruding between his fingers.

The web grew faint, like wet ink washed with a gush of clear water.

The Mouser raced forward and transfixed Slivikin and the huge rat with one thrust of Scalpel before the beasts knew what was happening. They too died swiftly with thin screams, while all the other rats turned tail and fled back down their holes swift almost as black lightning.

Then the last trace of night-smog or sorcery-smoke vanished, and Fafhrd and the Mouser found themselves standing alone with three dead bodies amidst a profound silence that seemed to fill not only this room but all Thieves' House. Even the cucurbit-lava had ceased to move, was hardening, and the wood of the table no longer smoked.

Their madness was gone and all their rage, too—vented to the last red atomy and glutted to more than satiety. They had no more urge to kill Krovas or any other thieves than to swat flies. With horrified inner-eye Fafhrd saw the pitiful face of the child-thief he'd skewered in his lunatic anger.

Only their grief remained with them, diminished not one whit, but rather growing greater—that and an ever more swiftly growing revulsion from all that was around them: the dead, the disordered magic room, all Thieves' House, all of the city of Lankhmar to its last stinking alleyway.

With a hiss of disgust the Mouser jerked Scalpel from the rodent cadavers, wiped it on the nearest cloth, and returned it to its scabbard. Fafhrd likewise sketchily cleansed and sheathed Graywand. Then the two men picked up their knife and dirk from where they'd dropped to the floor when the web had dematerialized, though neither glanced at Vlana's dagger where it was buried. But on the sorcerer's table they did notice Vlana's black velvet, silver-worked pouch and belt, and Ivrian's blue-enameled box inlaid with silver. These they took.

With no more word than they had exchanged back at the Mouser's burnt nest behind the Eel, but with a continuing sense of their unity of purpose, their identity of intent, and of their comradeship, they made their way with shoulders bowed and with slow, weary steps which only very gradually quickened out of the magic room and down the thick-carpeted corridor, past the map room's wide door now barred with oak and iron, and past all the other shut, silent doors, down the echoing stairs, their footsteps speeding a little; down the bare-floored lower corridor past its closed, quiet doors, their footsteps resounding loudly no matter how softly they sought to tread; under the deserted, black-scorched guard-niche, and so out into Cheap

Street, turning left and north because that was the nearest way to the Street of the Gods, and there turning right and east—not a waking soul in the wide street except for one skinny, bent-backed apprentice lad unhappily swabbing the flagstones in front of a wine shop in the dim pink light beginning to seep from the east, although there were many forms asleep, a-snore and a-dream in the gutters and under the dark porticoes—yes, turning right and east down the Street of the Gods, for that way was the Marsh Gate, leading to Causey Road across the Great Salt Marsh; and the Marsh Gate was the nearest way out of the great and glamorous city that was now loathsome to them, a city of beloved, unfaceable ghosts—indeed, not to be endured for one more stabbing, leaden heartbeat than was necessary.

FOUR GHOSTS IN HAMLET

ACTORS ARE A SUPERSTITIOUS LOT, probably because chance plays a big part in the success of a production of a company or merely an actor—and because we're still a little closer than other people to the gypsies in the way we live and think. For instance, it's bad luck to have peacock feathers on stage or say the last line of a play at rehearsals or whistle in the dressing room (the one nearest the door gets fired) or sing God Save the Sovereign on a railway train. (A Canadian company got wrecked that way.)

Shakespearean actors are no exceptions. They simply travel a few extra superstitions, such as the one which forbids reciting the lines of the Three Witches, or anything from *Macbeth,* for that matter, except at performances, rehearsals, and on other legitimate occasions. This might be a good rule for outsiders too—then there wouldn't be the endless flood of books with titles taken from the text of *Macbeth*—you know, *Brief Candle, Tomorrow and Tomorrow, The Sound and the Fury, A Poor Player, All Our Yesterdays,* and those are all just from one brief soliloquy.

And our company, the Governor's company, has a rule against the Ghost in *Hamlet* dropping his greenish cheesecloth veil over his helmet-framed face until the very moment he makes each of his entrances. Hamlet's dead father mustn't stand veiled in the darkness of the wings.

This last superstition commemorates something which happened not too long ago, an actual ghost story. Sometimes I think it's the greatest ghost story in the world—though certainly not from my way of telling it, which is gossipy and poor, but from the wonder blazing at its core.

It's not only a true tale of the supernatural, but also very much a story about people, for after all—and before everything else—ghosts are people.

The ghostly part of the story first showed itself in the tritest way imaginable:

131

three of our actresses (meaning practically all the ladies in a Shakespearean company) took to having sessions with a Ouija board in the hour before curtain time and sometimes even during a performance when they had long offstage waits, and they became so wrapped up in it and conceited about it and they squeaked so excitedly at the revelations which the planchette spelled out—and three or four times almost missed entrances because of it—that if the Governor weren't such a tolerant commander-in-chief, he would have forbidden them to bring the board to the theater. I'm sure he was tempted to and might have, except that Props pointed out to him that our three ladies probably wouldn't enjoy Ouija sessions one bit in the privacy of a hotel room, that much of the fun in operating a Ouija board is in having a half-exasperated, half-intrigued floating audience, and that when all's done the basic business of all ladies is glamour, whether of personal charm or of actual witchcraft, since the word means both.

Props—that is, our property man, Billy Simpson—was fascinated by their obsession, as he is by any new thing that comes along, and might very well have broken our Shakespearean taboo by quoting the Three Witches about them, except that Props has no flair for Shakespearean speech at all, no dramatic ability whatsoever, in fact he's the one person in our company who never acts even a bit part or carries a mute spear on stage, though he has other talents which make up for this deficiency—he can throw together a papier-mâché bust of Pompey in two hours, or turn out a wooden prop dagger all silvery-bladed and hilt-gilded, or fix a zipper, and that's not all.

As for myself, I was very irked at the ridiculous alphabet board, since it seemed to occupy most of Monica Singleton's spare time and satisfy all her hunger for thrills.

I'd been trying to promote a romance with her—a long touring season becomes deadly and cold without some sort of heart-tickle—and for a while I'd made progress. But after Ouija came along, I became a ridiculous Guildenstern mooning after an unattainable unseeing Ophelia—which were the parts I and she actually played in *Hamlet*.

I cursed the idiot board with its childish corner-pictures of grinning suns and smirking moons and windblown spirits, and I further alienated Monica by asking her why wasn't it called a Nenein or No-No board (Ninny board!) instead of a Yes-Yes board? Was that, I inquired, because all spiritualists are forever accentuating the positive and behaving like a pack of fawning yes-men?—yes, we're here; yes, we're your uncle Harry; yes, we're happy on this plane; yes, we have a doctor among us who'll diagnose that pain in your chest; and so on.

Monica wouldn't speak to me for a week after that.

I would have been even more depressed except that Props pointed out to me that no flesh-and-blood man can compete with ghosts in a girl's affections, since ghosts being imaginary have all the charms and perfections a girl can dream of, but that all girls eventually tire of ghosts, or if their minds don't, their bodies do. This eventually did happen, thank goodness, in the case of myself and Monica, though not until we'd had a grisly, mind-wrenching experience—a night of terrors before the nights of love.

So Ouija flourished and the Governor and the rest of us put up with it one way or another, until there came that three-night-stand in Wolverton, when its dismal uncanny old theater tempted our three Ouija-women to ask the board who was the ghost haunting the spooky place and the swooping planchette spelled out the name S-H-A-K-E-S-P-E-A-R-E…

But I am getting ahead of my story. I haven't introduced our company except for Monica, Props, and the Governor—and I haven't identified the last of those three.

We call Gilbert Usher the Governor out of sheer respect and affection. He's about the last of the old actor-managers. He hasn't the name of Gielgud or Olivier or Evans or Richardson, but he's spent most of a lifetime keeping Shakespeare alive, spreading that magical a-religious gospel in the more remote counties and the Dominions and the United States, like Benson once did. Our other actors aren't names at all—I refuse to tell you mine!—but with the exception of myself they're good troupers, or if they don't become that the first season, they drop out. Gruelingly long seasons, much uncomfortable traveling, and small profits are our destiny.

This particular season had got to that familiar point where the plays are playing smoothly and everyone's a bit tireder than he realizes and the restlessness sets in. Robert Dennis, our juvenile, was writing a novel of theatrical life (he said) mornings at the hotel—up at seven to slave at it, our Robert claimed. Poor old Guthrie Boyd had started to drink again, and drink quite too much, after an abstemious two months which had astonished everyone.

Francis Farley Scott, our leading man, had started to drop hints that he was going to organize a Shakespearean repertory company of his own next year and he began to have conspiratorial conversations with Gertrude Grainger, our leading lady, and to draw us furtively aside one by one to make us hypothetical offers, no exact salary named. F. F. is as old as the Governor—who is our star, of course—and he has no talents at all except for self-infatuation and a somewhat grandiose yet impressive fashion of acting. He's portly like an opera tenor and quite bald and he travels with an assortment of thirty toupees, ranging from red to black shot with silver, which he alternates with shameless abandon —they're for wear offstage, not on. It doesn't matter to him that the company knows all about his multi-colored artificial toppings, for we're part of his world of illusion, and he's firmly convinced that the stage-struck local ladies he squires about never notice, or at any rate mind the deception. He once gave me a lecture on the subtleties of suiting the color of your hair to the lady you're trying to fascinate—her own age, hair color, and so on.

Every year F. F. plots to start a company of his own—it's a regular midseason routine with him—and every year it comes to nothing, for he's as lazy and impractical as he is vain. Yet F. F. believes he could play any part in Shakespeare or all of them at once in a pinch; perhaps the only F. F. Scott Company which would really satisfy him would be one in which he would be the only actor—a Shakespearean monologue; in fact, the one respect in which F. F. is not lazy is in his eagerness to double as many parts as possible in any single play.

F. F.'s yearly plots never bother the Governor a bit—he keeps waiting wistfully for F. F. to fix him with a hypnotic eye and in a hoarse whisper ask *him* to join the Scott company.

And I of course was hoping that now at last Monica Singleton would stop trying to be the most exquisite ingenue that ever came tripping Shakespeare's way (rehearsing her parts even in her sleep, I guessed, though I was miles from being in a position to know that for certain) and begin to take note and not just advantage of my devoted attentions.

But then old Sybil Jameson bought the Ouija board and Gertrude Grainger dragooned an unwilling Monica into placing her fingertips on the planchette along with theirs "just for a lark." Next day Gertrude announced to several of us in a hushed voice that Monica had the most amazing undeveloped mediumistic talent she'd ever encountered, and from then on the girl was a Ouija-addict. Poor tight-drawn Monica, I suppose she had to explode out of her self-imposed Shakespearean discipline somehow, and it was just too bad it had to be the board instead of me. Though come to think of it, I shouldn't have felt quite so resentful of the board, for she might have exploded with Robert Dennis, which would have been infinitely worse, though we were never quite sure of Robert's sex. For that matter I wasn't sure of Gertrude's and suffered agonies of uncertain jealousy when she captured my beloved. I was obsessed with the vision of Gertrude's bold knees pressing Monica's under the Ouija board, though with Sybil's bony ones for chaperones, fortunately.

Francis Farley Scott, who was jealous too because this new toy had taken Gertrude's mind off their annual plottings, said rather spitefully that Monica must be one of those grabby girls who have to take command of whatever they get their fingers on, whether it's a man or a planchette, but Props told me he'd bet anything that Gertrude and Sybil had "followed' Monica's first random finger movements like the skillfulest dancers guiding a partner while seeming to yield, in order to coax her into the business and make sure of their third.

Sometimes I thought that F. F. was right and sometimes Props and sometimes I thought that Monica had a genuine supernatural talent, though I don't ordinarily believe in such things, and that last really frightened me, for such a person might give up live men for ghosts forever. She was such a sensitive, subtle, wraith-cheeked girl and she could get so keyed up and when she touched the planchette her eyes got such an empty look, as if her mind had traveled down into her fingertips or out to the ends of time and space. And once the three of them gave me a character reading from the board which embarrassed me with its accuracy. The same thing happened to several other people in the company. Of course, as Props pointed out, actors can be pretty good character analysts whenever they stop being egomaniacs.

After reading characters and foretelling the future for several weeks, our Three Weird Sisters got interested in reincarnation and began asking the board and then telling us what famous or infamous people we'd been in past lives. Gertrude Grainger had been Queen Boadicea, I wasn't surprised to hear. Sybil Jameson had been Cassandra. While Monica was once mad Queen Joanna of Castile and more recently a prize hysterical patient of Janet at the Sâlpetrière—touches which irritated and frightened me more than they should have. Billy Simpson—Props—had been an Egyptian silversmith under Queen Hatshepsut and later a servant of Samuel Pepys; he heard this with a delighted chuckle. Guthrie Boyd had been the Emperor Claudius and Robert Dennis had been Caligula. For some reason I had been both John Wilkes Booth and Lambert Simnel, which irritated me considerably, for I saw no romance but only neurosis in assassinating an American president and dying in a burning barn, or impersonating the Earl of Warwick, pretending unsuccessfully to the British throne, being pardoned for it—of all things! —and spending the rest of my life as a scullion in the kitchen of Henry VII and his son. The fact that both Booth and Simnel had been actors of a sort—a poor sort—naturally irritated me the more. Only much later did Monica confess to me that the board had probably made those decisions because I had had such a "tragic, dangerous, defeated look"—a revelation which surprised and flattered me.

Francis Farley Scott was flattered too, to hear he'd once been Henry VIII— he fancied all those wives and he wore his golden blond toupee after the show that night—until Gertrude and Sybil and Monica announced that the Governor was a reincarnation of no less than William Shakespeare himself. That made F. F. so jealous that he instantly sat down at the prop table, grabbed up a quill pen, and did an impromptu rendering of Shakespeare composing Hamlet's "To be or not to be" soliloquy. It was an effective performance, though with considerably more frowning and eye-rolling and trying of lines for sound than I imagine Willy S. himself used originally, and when F. F. finished, even the Governor, who'd been standing unobserved in the shadows beside Props, applauded with the latter.

Governor kidded the pants off the idea of himself as Shakespeare. He said that if Willy S. were ever reincarnated it ought to be as a world-famous dramatist who was secretly in his spare time the world's greatest scientist and philosopher and left clues to his identity in his mathematical equations —that way he'd get his own back at Bacon, or rather the Baconians.

Yet I suppose if you had to pick someone for a reincarnation of Shakespeare, Gilbert Usher wouldn't be a bad choice. Insofar as a star and director ever can be, the Governor is gentle and self-effacing—as Shakespeare himself must have been, or else there would never have arisen that ridiculous Bacon-Oxford-Marlowe-Elizabeth-take-your-pick-who-wrote-Shakespeare controversy. And the Governor has a sweet melancholy about him, though he's handsomer and despite his years more athletic than one imagines Shakespeare being. And he's generous to a fault, especially where old actors who've done brave fine things in the past are concerned.

This season his mistake in that last direction had been in hiring Guthrie Boyd to play some of the more difficult older leading roles, including a couple F. F. usually handles: Brutus, Othello, and besides those Duncan in *Macbeth*, Kent in *King Lear*, and the Ghost in *Hamlet*.

Guthrie was a bellowing hard-drinking bear of an actor, who'd been a Shakespearean star in Australia and successfully smuggled some of his reputation west—he learned to moderate his bellowing, while his emotions were always simple and sincere, though explosive—and finally even spent some years in Hollywood. But there his drinking caught up with him, probably because of the stupid film parts he got, and he failed six times over. His wife divorced him. His children cut themselves off. He married a starlet and she divorced him. He dropped out of sight.

Then after several years the Governor ran into him. He'd been rusticating in Canada with a stubborn teetotal admirer. He was only a shadow of his former self, but there was some substance to the shadow—and he wasn't drinking. The Governor decided to take a chance on him—although the company manager Harry Grossman was dead set against it—and during rehearsals and the first month or so of performances it was wonderful to see how old Guthrie Boyd came back, exactly as if Shakespeare were a restorative medicine.

It may be stuffy or sentimental of me to say so, but you know, I think

Shakespeare's good for people. I don't know of an actor, except myself, whose character hasn't been strengthened and his vision widened and charity quickened by working in the plays. I've heard that before Gilbert Usher became a Shakespearean, he was a more ruthlessly ambitious and critical man, not without malice, but the plays mellowed him, as they've mellowed Props's philosophy and given him a zest for life.

Because of his contact with Shakespeare, Robert Dennis is a less strident and pettish swish (if he is one), Gertrude Grainger's outbursts of cold rage have an undercurrent of queenly make-believe, and even Francis Farley Scott's grubby little seductions are probably kinder and less insultingly illusionary.

In fact I sometimes think that what civilized serenity the British people possess, and small but real ability to smile at themselves, is chiefly due to their good luck in having had William Shakespeare born one of their company.

But I was telling how Guthrie Boyd performed very capably those first weeks, against the expectations of most of us, so that we almost quit holding our breaths—or sniffing at his. His Brutus was workmanlike, his Kent quite fine—that bluff rough honest part suited him well—and he regularly got admiring notices for his Ghost in *Hamlet*. I think his years of living death as a drinking alcoholic had given him an understanding of loneliness and frozen abilities and despair that he put to good use—probably unconsciously—in interpreting that small role.

He was really a most impressive figure in the part, even just visually. The Ghost's basic costume is simple enough—a big all-enveloping cloak that brushes the ground-cloth, a big dull helmet with the tiniest battery light inside its peak to throw a faint green glow on the Ghost's features, and over the helmet a veil of greenish cheesecloth that registers as mist to the audience. He wears a suit of stage armor under the cloak, but that's not important and at a pinch he can do without it, for his cloak can cover his entire body.

The Ghost doesn't switch on his helmet-light until he makes his entrance, for fear of it being glimpsed by an edge of the audience, and nowadays because of that superstition or rule I told you about, he doesn't drop the cheesecloth veil until the last second either, but when Guthrie Boyd was playing the part that rule didn't exist and I have a vivid recollection of him standing in the wings, waiting to go on, a big bearish inscrutable figure about as solid and unsupernatural as a bushy seven-foot evergreen covered by a gray tarpaulin. But then when Guthrie would switch on the tiny light and stride smoothly and silently on stage and its hollow distant tormented voice boom out, there'd be a terrific shivery thrill, even for us backstage, as if we were listening to words that really had traveled across black windy infinite gulfs from the Afterworld or the Other Side.

At any rate Guthrie was a great ghost, and adequate or a bit better than that in most of his other parts—for those first nondrinking weeks. He seemed very cheerful on the whole, modestly buoyed up by his comeback, though sometimes something empty and dead would stare for a moment out of his eyes—the old drinking alcoholic wondering what all this fatiguing sober nonsense was about. He was especially looking forward to our three-night-stand at Wolverton, although that was still two months in the future. The reason was that both his children—married and with families now, of course—lived and worked at Wolverton and I'm sure he set great store on proving to them in person his rehabilitation, figuring it would lead to a reconciliation and so on.

But then came his first performance as Othello. (The Governor, although the star, always played Iago—an equal role, though not the title one.) Guthrie was almost too old for Othello, of course, and besides that, his health wasn't good—the drinking years had taken their toll of his stamina and the work of rehearsals and of first nights in eight different plays after years away from the theater had exhausted him. But somehow the old volcano inside him got seething again and he gave a magnificent performance. Next morning the papers raved about him and one review rated him even better than the Governor.

That did it, unfortunately. The glory of his triumph was too much for him. The next night—Othello again—he was drunk as a skunk. He remembered most of his lines—though the Governor had to throw him about every sixth one out of the side of his mouth—but he weaved and wobbled, he planked a big hand on the shoulder of every other character he addressed to keep from falling over, and he even forgot to put in his false teeth the first two acts, so that his voice was mushy. To cap that, he started really to strangle Gertrude Grainger in the last scene, until that rather brawny Desdemona, unseen by the audience, gave him a knee in the gut; then, after stabbing himself, he flung the prop dagger high in the flies so that it came down with two lazy twists and piercing the ground-cloth buried its blunt point deep in the soft wood of the stage floor not three feet from Monica, who plays Iago's wife Emilia and so was lying dead on the stage at that point in the drama, murdered by her villainous husband—and might have been dead for real if the dagger had followed a slightly different trajectory.

Since a third performance of *Othello* was billed for the following night, the Governor had no choice but to replace Guthrie with Francis Farley Scott, who did a good job (for him) of covering up his satisfaction at getting his old role back. F. F., always a plushy and lascivious-eyed Moor, also did a good job with the part, coming in that way without even a brush-up rehearsal, so that one critic, catching the first and third shows, marveled how we could change big roles at will, thinking we'd done it solely to demonstrate our virtuosity.

Of course the Governor read the riot act to Guthrie and carried him off to a doctor, who without being prompted threw a big scare into him about his drinking and his heart, so that he just might have recovered from his lapse, except that two nights later we did *Julius Caesar* and Guthrie, instead of being satisfied with being workmanlike, decided to recoup himself with a really rousing performance. So he bellowed and groaned and bugged his eyes as I suppose he had done in his palmiest Australian days. His optimistic self-satisfaction between scenes was frightening to behold. Not too terrible a performance, truly, but the critics all panned him and one of them said, "Guthrie Boyd played Brutus —a bunch of vocal cords wrapped up in a toga."

That tied up the package and knotted it tight. Thereafter Guthrie was medium pie-eyed from morning to night—and often more than medium. The Governor had to yank him out of Brutus too (F. F. again replacing), but being the Governor he didn't sack him. He put him into a couple of bit parts—Montano and the Soothsayer—in *Othello* and *Caesar* and let him keep on at the others and he gave me and Joe Rubens and sometimes Props the job of keeping an eye on the poor old sot and making sure he got to the theater by the half hour and if possible not too plastered. Often he played the Ghost or the Doge of Venice in his street clothes under cloak or scarlet robe, but he played them. And many were the nights Joe and I made the rounds of half the local bars before we corralled him. The Governor sometimes refers to Joe Rubens and me in mild derision as "the American element" in his company, but just the same he depends on us quite a bit; and I certainly don't mind being one of his trouble-shooters—it's a joy to serve him.

All this may seem to contradict my statement about our getting to the point, about this time, where the plays were playing smoothly and the monotony setting in. But it doesn't really. There's always something going wrong in a theatrical company—anything else would be abnormal; just as the Samoans say no party is a success until somebody's dropped a plate or spilled a drink or tickled the wrong woman.

Besides, once Guthrie had got Othello and Brutus off his neck, he didn't do too badly. The little parts and even Kent he could play passably whether drunk or sober. King Duncan, for instance, and the Doge in *The Merchant* are easy to play drunk because the actor always has a couple of attendants to either side of him, who can guide his steps if he weaves and even hold him up if necessary—which can turn out to be an effective dramatic touch, registering as the infirmity of extreme age.

And somehow Guthrie continued to give that same masterful performance as the Ghost and get occasional notices for it. In fact Sybil Jameson insisted he was a shade better in the Ghost now that he was invariably drunk; which could have been true. And he still talked about the three-night-stand coming up in Wolverton, though now as often with gloomy apprehension as with proud fatherly anticipation.

Well, the three-night-stand eventually came. We arrived at Wolverton on a non-playing evening. To the surprise of most of us, but especially Guthrie, his son and daughter were there at the station to welcome him with their respective spouses and all their kids and numerous in-laws and a great gaggle of friends. Their cries of greeting when they spotted him were almost an organized cheer and I looked around for a brass band to strike up.

I found out later that Sybil Jameson, who knew them, had been sending them all his favorable notices, so that they were eager as weasels to be reconciled with him and show him off as blatantly as possible.

When he saw his children's and grandchildren's faces and realized the cries were for him, old Guthrie got red in the face and beamed like the sun, and they closed in around him and carried him off in triumph for an evening of celebrations.

Next day I heard from Sybil, whom they'd carried off with him, that everything had gone beautifully. He'd drunk like a fish, but kept marvelous control, so that no one but she noticed, and the warmth of the reconciliation of Guthrie to everyone, complete strangers included, had been wonderful to behold. Guthrie's son-in-law, a pugnacious chap, had got angry when he'd heard Guthrie wasn't to play Brutus the third night, and he declared that Gilbert Usher must be jealous of his magnificent father-in-law. Everything was forgiven twenty times over. They'd even tried to put old Sybil to bed with Guthrie, figuring romantically, as people will about actors, that she must be his mistress. All this was very fine, and of course wonderful for Guthrie, and for Sybil too in a fashion, yet I suppose the unconstrained nightlong bash, after two months of uninterrupted semi-controlled drunkenness, was just about the worst thing anybody could have done to the old boy's sodden body and laboring heart.

Meanwhile on that first evening I accompanied Joe Rubens and Props to the theater we were playing at Wolverton to make sure the scenery got stacked right and the costume trunks were all safely arrived and stowed. Joe is our stage manager besides doing rough or Hebraic parts like Caliban and Tubal—he was a professional boxer in his youth and got his nose smashed crooked. Once I started to take boxing lessons from him, figuring an actor should know everything, but during the third lesson I walked into a gentle right cross and although it didn't exactly stun me there were bells ringing faintly in my head for six hours afterwards and I lived in a world of faery and that was the end of my fistic career. Joe is actually a most versatile actor—for instance, he understudies the Governor in Macbeth, Lear, Iago, and of course Shylock—though his brutal moon-face is against him, especially when his make-up doesn't include a beard. But he dotes on being genial and in the States he often gets a job by day playing Santa Claus in big department stores during the month before Christmas.

The Monarch was a cavernous old place, very grimy backstage, but with a great warren of dirty little dressing rooms and even a property room shaped like an L stage left. Its empty shelves were thick with dust.

There hadn't been a show in the Monarch for over a year, I saw from the yellowing sheets thumbtacked to the callboard as I tore them off and replaced them with a simple black-crayoned HAMLET: TONIGHT AT 8:30.

Then I noticed, by the cold inadequate working lights, a couple of tiny dark shapes dropping down from the flies and gliding around in wide swift circles—out into the house too, since the curtain was up. Bats, I realized with a little start—the Monarch was really halfway through the lich gate. The bats would fit very nicely with *Macbeth*, I told myself, but not so well with *The Merchant of Venice*, while with *Hamlet* they should neither help nor hinder, provided they didn't descend in nightfighter squadrons; it would be nice if they stuck to the Ghost scenes.

I'm sure the Governor had decided we'd open at Wolverton with *Hamlet* so that Guthrie would have the best chance of being a hit in his children's home city.

Billy Simpson, shoving his properties table into place just in front of the dismal L of the prop room, observed cheerfully, "It's a proper haunted house. The girls'll find some rare ghosts here, I'll wager, if they work their board."

Which turned out to be far truer than he realized at the time—I think.

"Bruce!" Joe Rubens called to me. "We better buy a couple of rat traps and set them out. There's something scuttling back of the drops."

But when I entered the Monarch next night, well before the hour, by the creaky thick metal stage door, the place had been swept and tidied a bit. With the ground-cloth down and the *Hamlet* set up, it didn't look too terrible, even though the curtain was still unlowered, dimly showing the house and its curves of empty seats and the two faint green exit lights with no one but myself to look at them.

There was a little pool of light around the callboard stage right, and another glow the other side of the stage beyond the wings, and lines of light showing around the edges of the door of the second dressing room, next to the star's.

I started across the dark stage, sliding my shoes softly so as not to trip over a cable or stage-screw and brace, and right away I got the magic electric feeling I often do in an empty theater the night of a show. Only this time there was something additional, something that started a shiver crawling down my neck. It wasn't, I think, the thought of the bats which might now be swooping around me unseen, skirling their inaudibly shrill trumpet calls, or even of the rats which *might* be watching sequin-eyed from behind trunks and flats, although not an hour ago Joe had told me that the traps he'd actually procured and set last night had been empty today.

No, it was more as if all of Shakespeare's characters were invisibly there around me—all the infinite possibilities of the theater. I imagined Rosalind and Falstaff and Prospero standing arm-in-arm watching me with different smiles. And Caliban grinning down from where he silently swung in the flies. And side by side, but unsmiling and not arm-in-arm: Macbeth and Iago and Dick the Three Eyes—Richard III. And all the rest of Shakespeare's myriad-minded good-evil crew.

I passed through the wings opposite and there in the second pool of light Billy Simpson sat behind his table with the properties for *Hamlet* set out on it: the skulls, the foils, the lantern, the purses, the parchmenty letters, Ophelia's flowers, and all the rest. It was odd Props having everything ready quite so early and a bit odd too that he should be alone, for Props has the un-actorish habit of making friends with all sorts of locals, such as policemen and porters and flower women and newsboys and shopkeepers and tramps who claim they're indigent actors, and even inviting them backstage with him—a fracture of rules which the Governor allows since Props is such a sensible chap. He has a great liking for people, especially low people, Props has, and for all the humble details of life. He'd make a good writer, I'd think, except for his utter lack of dramatic flair and story-skill—a sort of prosiness that goes with his profession.

And now he was sitting at his table, his stooped shoulders almost inside the doorless entry to the empty-shelfed prop room—no point in using it for a three-night-stand—and he was gazing at me quizzically. He has a big forehead—the light was on that—and a tapering chin—that was in shadow—and rather large eyes, which were betwixt the light and the dark. Sitting there like that, he seemed to me for a moment (mostly because of the outspread props, I guess) like the midnight Master of the Show in *The Rubaiyat* round whom all the rest of us move like shadow shapes.

Usually he has a quick greeting for anyone, but tonight he was silent, and that added to the illusion.

"Props," I said, "this theater's got a supernatural smell."

His expression didn't change at that, but he solemnly sniffed the air in several little whiffles adding up to one big inhalation, and as he did so he threw his head back, bringing his weakish chin into the light and shattering the illusion.

"Dust," he said after a moment. "Dust and old plush and scenery water-paint and sweat and drains and gelatin and greasepaint and powder and a breath of whisky. But the supernatural... no, I can't smell that. Unless..." And he sniffed again, but shook his head.

I chuckled at his materialism—although that touch about whisky did seem fanciful, since I hadn't been drinking and Props never does and Guthrie Boyd was nowhere in evidence. Props has a mind like a notebook for sensory details—and for the minutia of human habits too. It was Props, for instance, who told me about the actual notebook in which John McCarthy (who would be playing Fortinbras and the Player King in a couple of hours) jots down the exact number of hours he sleeps each night and keeps totting them up, so he knows when he'll have to start sleeping extra hours to average the full nine he thinks he must get each night to keep from dying.

It was also Props who pointed out to me that F. F. is much more careless gumming his offstage toupees to his head than his theater wigs—a studied carelessness, like that in tying a bowtie, he assured me; it indicated, he said, a touch of contempt for the whole offstage world.

Props isn't *only* a detail-worm, but it's perhaps because he is one that he has sympathy for all human hopes and frailties, even the most trivial, like my selfish infatuation with Monica.

Now I said to him, "I didn't mean an actual smell, Billy. But back there just now I got the feeling anything might happen tonight."

He nodded slowly and solemnly. With anyone but Props I'd have wondered if he weren't a little drunk. Then he said, "You were on a stage. You know, the science-fiction writers are missing a bet there. We've got time machines right now. Theaters. Theaters are time machines and spaceships too. They take people on trips through the future and the past and the elsewhere and the might-have-been—yes, and if it's done well enough, give them glimpses of Heaven and Hell."

I nodded back at him. Such grotesque fancies are the closest Props ever comes to escaping from prosiness.

I said, "Well, let's hope Guthrie gets aboard the spaceship before the curtain up-jets. Tonight we're depending on his children having the sense to deliver him here intact. Which from what Sybil says about them is not to be taken for granted."

Props stared at me owlishly and slowly shook his head. "Guthrie got here about ten minutes ago," he said, "and looking no drunker than usual."

"That's a relief," I told him, meaning it.

"The girls are having a Ouija session," he went on, as if he were determined to account for all of us from moment to moment. "They smelt the supernatural here, just as you did, and they're asking the board to name the culprit." Then he stooped so that he looked almost hunchbacked and he felt for something under the table.

I nodded. I'd guessed the Ouija part from the lines of light showing around the door of Gertrude Grainger's dressing room.

Props straightened up and he had a pint bottle of whisky in his hand. I don't think a loaded revolver would have dumbfounded me as much. He unscrewed the top.

"There's the Governor coming in," he said tranquilly, hearing the stage door creak and evidently some footsteps my own ears missed. "That's seven of us in the theater before the hour."

He took a big slow swallow of whisky and recapped the bottle, as naturally as if it were a nightly action. I goggled at him without comment. What he was doing was simply unheard of—for Billy Simpson.

At that moment there was a sharp scream and a clatter of thin wood and something twangy and metallic falling and a scurry of footsteps. Our previous words must have cocked a trigger in me, for I was at Gertrude Grainger's dressing-room door as fast as I could sprint—no worry this time about tripping over cables or braces in the dark.

I yanked the door open and there by the bright light of the bulbs framing the mirror were Gertrude and Sybil sitting close together with the Ouija board face down on the floor in front of them along with a flimsy wire-backed chair, overturned. While pressing back into Gertrude's costumes hanging on the rack across the little room, almost as if she wanted to hide behind them like bedclothes, was Monica pale and staring-eyed. She didn't seem to recognize me. The dark-green heavily brocaded costume Gertrude wears as the Queen in *Hamlet*, into which Monica was chiefly pressing herself, accentuated her pallor. All three of them were in their street clothes.

I went to Monica and put an arm around her and gripped her hand. It was cold as ice. She was standing rigidly.

While I was doing that Gertrude stood up and explained in rather haughty tones what I told you earlier: about them asking the board who the ghost was haunting the Monarch tonight and the planchette spelling out S-H-A-K-E-S-P-E-A-R-E...

"I don't know why it startled you so, dear," she ended crossly, speaking to Monica. "It's very natural his spirit should attend performances of his plays."

I felt the slim body I clasped relax a little. That relieved me. I was selfishly pleased at having got an arm around it, even under such public and unamorous circumstances, while at the same time my silly mind was thinking that if Props had been lying to me about Guthrie Boyd having come in no more drunken than usual (this new Props who drank straight whisky in the theater could lie too, I supposed), why then we could certainly use William Shakespeare tonight, since the Ghost in *Hamlet* is the one part in all his plays Shakespeare himself is supposed to have acted on the stage.

"I don't know why myself now," Monica suddenly answered from beside me, shaking her head as if to clear it. She became aware of me at last, started to pull away, then let my arm stay around her.

The next voice that spoke was the Governor's. He was standing in the doorway, smiling faintly, with Props peering around his shoulder. Props would be as tall as the Governor if he ever straightened up, but his stoop takes almost a foot off his height.

The Governor said softly, a comic light in his eyes, "I think we should be content to bring Shakespeare's plays to life, without trying for their author. It's hard enough on the nerves just to *act* Shakespeare."

He stepped forward with one of his swift, naturally graceful movements and kneeling on one knee he picked up the fallen board and planchette. "At all events I'll take these in charge for tonight. Feeling better now, Miss Singleton?" he asked as he straightened and stepped back.

"Yes, quite all right," she answered flusteredly, disengaging my arm and pulling away from me rather too quickly.

He nodded. Gertrude Grainger was staring at him coldly, as if about to say something scathing, but she didn't. Sybil Jameson was looking at the floor. She seemed embarrassed, yet puzzled too.

I followed the Governor out of the dressing room and told him, in case Props hadn't, about Guthrie Boyd coming to the theater early. My momentary doubt of Props's honesty seemed plain silly to me now, although his taking that drink remained an astonishing riddle.

Props confirmed me about Guthrie coming in, though his manner was a touch abstracted.

The Governor nodded his thanks for the news, then twitched a nostril and frowned. I was sure he'd caught a whiff of alcohol and didn't know to which of us two to attribute it—or perhaps even to one of the ladies, or to an earlier passage of Guthrie this way.

He said to me, "Would you come into my dressing room for a bit, Bruce?"

I followed him, thinking he'd picked me for the drinker and wondering how to answer—best perhaps simply silently accept the fatherly lecture—but when he'd turned on the lights and I'd shut the door, his first question was, "You're attracted to Miss Singleton, aren't you, Bruce?"

When I nodded abruptly, swallowing my morsel of surprise, he went on softly but emphatically, "Then why don't you quit hovering and playing Galahad and really go after her? Ordinarily I must appear to frown on affairs in the company, but in this case it would be the best way I know of to break up those Ouija sessions, which are obviously harming the girl."

I managed to grin and tell him I'd be happy to obey his instructions—and do it entirely on my own initiative too.

He grinned back and started to toss the Ouija board on his couch, but instead put it and the planchette carefully down on the end of his long dressing table and put a second question to me.

"What do you think of some of this stuff they're getting over the board, Bruce?"

I said, "Well, that last one gave me a shiver, all right—I suppose because…" and I told him about sensing the presence of Shakespeare's characters in the dark. I finished, "But of course the whole idea is nonsense," and I grinned.

He didn't grin back.

I continued impulsively, "There was one idea they had a few weeks back that impressed me, though it didn't seem to impress you. I hope you won't think I'm trying to butter you up, Mr. Usher. I mean the idea of you being a reincarnation of William Shakespeare."

He laughed delightedly and said, "Clearly you don't yet know the difference between a player and a playwright, Bruce. Shakespeare striding about romantically with head thrown back?—and twirling a sword and shaping his body and voice to every feeling handed him? Oh no! I'll grant he might have played the Ghost—it's a part within the scope of an average writer's talents, requiring nothing more than that he stand still and sound off sepulchrally."

He paused and smiled and went on. "No, there's only one person in this company who might be Shakespeare come again, and that's Billy Simpson. Yes, I mean Props. He's a great listener and he knows how to put himself in touch with everyone and then he's got that rat-trap mind for every hue and scent and sound of life, inside or out the mind. And he's very analytic. Oh, I know he's got no poetic talent, but surely Shakespeare wouldn't have that in *every* reincarnation. I'd think he'd need about a dozen lives in which to gather material for every one in which he gave it dramatic form. Don't you find something very poignant in the idea of a mute inglorious Shakespeare spending whole humble lifetimes collecting the necessary stuff for one great dramatic burst? Think about it some day."

I was doing that already and finding it a fascinating fantasy. It crystallized so perfectly the feeling I'd got seeing Billy Simpson behind his property table. And then Props did have a high-foreheaded poet-schoolmaster's face like that given Shakespeare in the posthumous engravings and woodcuts and portraits. Why, even their initials were the same. It made *me* feel strange.

Then the Governor put his third question to me.

"He's drinking tonight, isn't he? I mean Props, not Guthrie."

I didn't say anything, but my face must have answered for me at least to such a student of expressions as the Governor—for he smiled and said, "You needn't worry. I wouldn't be angry with him. In fact, the only other time I know of that Props drank spirits by himself in the theater, I had a great deal to thank him for." His lean face grew thoughtful. "It was long before your time, in fact it was the first season I took out a company of my own. I had barely enough money to pay the printer for the three-sheets and get the first-night curtain up. After that it was touch and go for months. Then in mid-season we had a run of bad luck—a two-night heavy fog in one city, an influenza scare in another, Harvey Wilkins' Shakespearean troupe two weeks ahead of us in a third. And when in the next town we played, it turned out the advance sale was very light—because my name was un-known there and the theater an unpopular one—I realized I'd have to pay off the company while there was still money enough to get them home, if not the scenery.

"That night I caught Props swigging, but I hadn't the heart to chide him for it—in fact I don't think I'd have blamed anyone, except perhaps myself, for getting drunk that night. But then during the performance the actors and even the union stagehands we travel began coming to my dressing room by ones and twos and telling me they'd be happy to work without salary for another three weeks, if I thought that might give us a chance of recouping. Well, of course I grabbed at their offers and we got a spell of brisk pleasant weather and we hit a couple of places starved for Shakespeare, and things worked out, even to paying all the back salary owed before the season was ended.

"Later on I discovered it was Props who had put them all up to doing it."

Gilbert Usher looked up at me and one of his eyes was wet and his lips were working just a little. "I couldn't have done it myself," he said, "for I wasn't a popular man with my company that first season—I'd been riding everyone much too hard and with nasty sarcasms—and I hadn't yet learned how to ask anyone for help when I really needed it. But Billy Simpson did what I couldn't, though he had to nerve himself for it with spirits. He's quick enough with his tongue in ordinary circumstances, as you know, particularly when he's being the friendly listener, but apparently when something very special is required of him, he must drink himself to the proper pitch. I'm wondering…"

His voice trailed off and then he straightened up before his mirror and started to unknot his tie and he said to me briskly, "Better get dressed now, Bruce. And then look in on Guthrie, will you?"

My mind was churning some rather strange thoughts as I hurried up the iron stairs to the dressing room I shared with Robert Dennis. I got on my Guildenstern make-up and costume, finishing just as Robert arrived; as Laertes, Robert makes a late entrance and so needn't hurry to the theater on *Hamlet* nights. Also, although we don't make a point of it, he and I spend as little time together in the dressing room as we can.

Before going down I looked into Guthrie Boyd's. He wasn't there, but the lights were on and the essentials of the Ghost's costume weren't in sight—impossible to miss that big helmet!—so I assumed he'd gone down ahead of me.

It was almost the half hour. The house lights were on, the curtain down, more stage lights on too, and quite a few of us about. I noticed that Props was back in the chair behind his table and not looking particularly different from any other night—perhaps the drink had been a once-only aberration and not some symptom of a crisis in the company.

I didn't make a point of hunting for Guthrie. When he gets costumed early he generally stands back in a dark corner somewhere, wanting to be alone—perchance to sip, aye, there's the rub!—or visits with Sybil in her dressing room.

I spotted Monica sitting on a trunk by the switchboard, where backstage was brightest lit at the moment. She looked ethereal yet springlike in her blonde Ophelia wig and first costume, a pale green one. Recalling my happy promise to the Governor, I bounced up beside her and asked her straight out about the Ouija business, pleased to have something to the point besides the plays to talk with her about—and really not worrying as much about her nerves as I suppose I should have.

She was in a very odd mood, both agitated and abstracted, her gaze going back and forth between distant and near and very distant. My questions didn't disturb her at all, in fact I got the feeling she welcomed them, yet she genuinely didn't seem able to tell me much about why she'd been so frightened at the last name the board had spelled. She told me that she actually did get into a sort of dream state when she worked the board and that she'd screamed before she'd quite comprehended what had shocked her so; then her mind had blacked out for a few seconds, she thought.

"One thing though, Bruce," she said. "I'm not going to work the board any more, at least when the three of us are alone like that."

"That sounds like a wise idea," I agreed, trying not to let the extreme heartiness of my agreement show through.

She stopped peering around as if for some figure to appear that wasn't in the play and didn't belong backstage, and she laid her hand on mine and said, "Thanks for coming so quickly when I went idiot and screamed."

I was about to improve this opportunity by telling her that the reason I'd come so quickly was that she was so much in my mind, but just then Joe Rubens came hurrying up with the Governor behind him in his Hamlet black to tell me that neither Guthrie Boyd nor his Ghost costume was to be found anywhere in the theater.

What's more, Joe had got the phone numbers of Guthrie's son and daughter from Sybil and rung them up. The one phone hadn't answered, while on the other a female voice—presumably a maid's—had informed him that everyone had gone to see Guthrie Boyd in *Hamlet.*

Joe was already wearing his cumbrous chain-mail armor for Marcellus—woven cord silvered—so I knew I was elected. I ran upstairs and in the space of time it took Robert Dennis to guess my mission and advise me to try the dingiest bars first and have a drink or two myself in them, I'd put on my hat, overcoat, and wristwatch and left him.

So garbed and as usual nervous about people looking at my ankles, I sallied forth to comb the nearby bars of Wolverton. I consoled myself with the thought that if I found Hamlet's father's ghost drinking his way through them, no one would ever spare a glance for my own costume.

Almost on the stroke of curtain I returned, no longer giving a damn what anyone thought about my ankles. I hadn't found Guthrie or spoken to a soul who'd seen a large male imbiber—most likely of Irish whisky—in great-cloak and antique armor, with perhaps some ghostly green light cascading down his face.

Beyond the curtain the overture was fading to its sinister close and the backstage lights were all down, but there was an angry hushed-voice dispute going on stage left, where the Ghost makes all his entrances and exits. Skipping across the dim stage in front of the blue-lit battlements of Elsinore—I still in my hat and overcoat—I found the Governor and Joe Rubens and with them John McCarthy all ready to go on as the Ghost in his Fortinbras armor with a dark cloak and some green gauze over it.

But alongside them was Francis Farley Scott in a very similar getup—no armor, but a big enough cloak to hide his King costume and a rather more impressive helmet than John's.

They were all very dim in the midnight glow leaking back from the dimmed-down blue floods. The five of us were the only people I could see on this side of the stage.

F. F. was arguing vehemently that he must be allowed to double the Ghost with King Claudius because he knew the part better than John and because—this was the important thing—he could imitate Guthrie's voice perfectly enough to deceive his children and perhaps save their illusions about him. Sybil had looked through the curtain hole and seen them and all of their yesterday crowd, with new recruits besides, occupying all of the second, third, and fourth rows center, chattering with excitement and beaming with anticipation. Harry Grossman had confirmed this from the front of the house.

I could tell that the Governor was vastly irked at F. F. and at the same time touched by the last part of his argument. It was exactly the sort of sentimental heroic rationalization with which F. F. cloaked his insatiable yearnings for personal glory. Very likely he believed it himself.

John McCarthy was simply ready to do what the Governor asked him. He's an actor untroubled by inward urgencies—except things like keeping a record of the hours he sleeps and each penny he spends—though with a natural facility for portraying on stage emotions which he doesn't feel one iota.

The Governor shut up F. F. with a gesture and got ready to make his decision, but just then I saw that there was a sixth person on this side of the stage.

Standing in the second wings beyond our group was a dark figure like a tarpaulined Christmas tree topped by a big helmet of unmistakable general shape despite its veiling. I grabbed the Governor's arm and pointed at it silently. He smothered a large curse and strode up to it and rasped, "Guthrie, you old Son of a B! Can you go on?" The figure gave an affirmative grunt.

Joe Rubens grimaced at me as if to say "Show business!" and grabbed a spear from the prop table and hurried back across the stage for his entrance as Marcellus just before the curtain lifted and the first nervous, superbly atmospheric lines of the play rang out, loud at first, but then going low with unspoken apprehension.

"Who's there?"

"Nay, answer me; stand, and unfold yourself."

"Long live the king!"

"Bernardo?"

"He."

"You come most carefully upon your hour."

"'Tis now struck twelve; get thee to bed, Francisco."

"For this relief much thanks; 'tis bitter cold and I am sick at heart."

"Have you had quiet guard?"

"Not a mouse stirring."

With a resigned shrug, John McCarthy simply sat down. F. F. did the same, though *his* gesture was clench-fisted and exasperated. For a moment it seemed to me very comic that two Ghosts in *Hamlet* should be sitting in the wings, watching a third perform. I unbuttoned my overcoat and slung it over my left arm.

The Ghost's first two appearances are entirely silent ones. He merely goes on stage, shows himself to the soldiers, and comes off again. Nevertheless there was a determined little ripple of hand-clapping from the audience—the second, third, and fourth rows center greeting their patriarchal hero, it seemed likely. Guthrie didn't fall down at any rate and he walked reasonably straight—an achievement perhaps rating applause, if anyone out there knew the degree of intoxication Guthrie was probably burdened with at this moment—a cask-bellied Old Man of the Sea on his back.

The only thing out of normal was that he had forgot to turn on the little green light in the peak of his helmet—an omission which hardly mattered, certainly not on this first appearance. I hurried up to him when he came off and told him about it in a whisper as he moved off toward a dark backstage corner. I got in reply, through the inscrutable green veil, an exhalation of whisky and three affirmative grunts: one, that he knew it; two, that the light was working; three, that he'd remember to turn it on next time.

Then the scene had ended and I darted across the stage as they changed to the room-of-state set. I wanted to get rid of my overcoat. Joe Rubens grabbed me and told me about Guthrie's green light not being on and I told him that was all taken care of.

"Where the hell was he all the time we were hunting for him?" Joe asked me.

"I don't know," I answered.

By that time the second scene was playing, with F. F., his Ghost-coverings shed, playing the King as well as he always does (it's about his best part) and Gertrude Grainger looking very regal beside him as the Queen, her namesake, while there was another flurry of applause, more scattered this time, for the Governor in his black doublet and tights beginning about his seven hundredth performance of Shakespeare's longest and meatiest role.

Monica was still sitting on the trunk by the switchboard, looking paler than ever under her make-up, it seemed to me, and I folded my overcoat and silently persuaded her to use it as a cushion. I sat beside her and she took my hand and we watched the play from the wings.

After a while I whispered to her, giving her hand a little squeeze, "Feeling better now?"

She shook her head. Then leaning toward me, her mouth close to my ear, she whispered rapidly and unevenly, as if she just had to tell someone, "Bruce, I'm frightened. There's something in the theater. I don't think that was Guthrie playing the Ghost."

I whispered back, "Sure it was. I talked with him."

"Did you see his face?" she asked.

"No, but I smelled his breath," I told her and explained to her about him forgetting to turn on the green light. I continued, "Francis and John were both ready to go on as the Ghost, though, until Guthrie turned up. Maybe you glimpsed one of them before the play started and that gave you the idea it wasn't Guthrie."

Sybil Jameson in her Player costume looked around at me warningly. I was letting my whispering get too loud.

Monica put her mouth so close that her lips for an instant brushed my ear and she mouse-whispered, "I don't mean another *person* playing the Ghost—not that exactly. Bruce, there's *something* in the theater."

"You've got to forget that Ouija nonsense," I told her sharply. "And buck up now," I added, for the curtain had just gone down on Scene Two and it was time for her to get on stage for her scene with Laertes and Polonius.

I waited until she was launched into it, speaking her lines brightly enough, and then I carefully crossed the stage behind the backdrop. I was sure there was no more than nerves and imagination to her notions, though they'd raised shivers on me, but just the same I wanted to speak to Guthrie again and see his face.

When I'd completed my slow trip (you have to move rather slowly, so the drop won't ripple or bulge), I was dumbfounded to find myself witnessing the identical backstage scene that had been going on when I'd got back from my tour of the bars. Only now there was a lot more light because the scene being played on stage was a bright one. And Props was there behind his table, watching everything like the spectator he basically is. But beyond him were Francis Farley Scott and John McCarthy in their improvised Ghost costumes again, and the Governor and Joe with them, and all of them carrying on that furious lip-reader's argument, now doubly hushed.

I didn't have to wait to get close to them to know that Guthrie must have disappeared again. As I made my way toward them, watching their silent antics, my silly mind became almost hysterical with the thought that Guthrie had at last discovered that invisible hole every genuine alcoholic wishes he had, into which he could decorously disappear and drink during the times between his absolutely necessary appearances in the real world.

As I neared them, Donald Fryer (our Horatio) came from behind me, having made the trip behind the backdrop faster than I had, to tell the Governor in hushed gasps that Guthrie wasn't in any of the dressing rooms or anywhere else stage right.

Just at that moment the bright scene ended, the curtain came down, the drapes before which Ophelia and the others had been playing swung back to reveal again the battlements of Elsinore, and the lighting shifted back to the midnight blue of the first scene, so that for the moment it was hard to see at all. I heard the Governor say decisively, "*You* play the Ghost," his voice receding as he and Joe and Don hurried across the stage to be in place for their proper entrance. Seconds later there came the dull soft hiss of the main curtain opening and I heard the Governor's taut resonant voice saying, "The air bites shrewdly; it is very cold," and Don responding as Horatio with, "It is a nipping and an eager air."

By that time I could see again well enough—see Francis Farley Scott and John McCarthy moving side by side toward the back wing through which the Ghost enters. They were still arguing in whispers. The explanation was clear enough: each thought the Governor had pointed at him in the sudden darkness—or possibly in F. F.'s case was pretending he so thought. For a moment the comic side of my mind, grown a bit hysterical by now, almost collapsed me with the thought of twin Ghosts entering the stage side by side. Then once again, history still repeating itself, I saw beyond them that other bulkier figure with the unmistakable shrouded helmet. They must have seen it too for they stopped dead just before my hands touched a shoulder of each of them. I circled quickly past them and reached out my hands to put them lightly on the third figure's shoulders, intending to whisper, "Guthrie, are you okay?" It was a very stupid thing for one actor to do to another—startling him just before his entrance—but I was made thoughtless by the memory of Monica's fears and by the rather frantic riddle of where Guthrie could possibly have been hiding.

But just then Horatio gasped, "Look, my lord, it comes," and Guthrie moved out of my light grasp onto the stage without so much as turning his head—and leaving me shaking because where I'd touched the rough buckram-braced fabric of the Ghost's cloak I'd felt only a kind of insubstantiality beneath instead of Guthrie's broad shoulders.

I quickly told myself that was because Guthrie's cloak had stood out from his shoulders and his back as he had moved. I had to tell myself something like that. I turned around. John McCarthy and F. F. were standing in front of the dark prop table and by now my nerves were in such a state that their paired forms gave me another start. But I tiptoed after them into the downstage wings and watched the scene from there.

The Governor was still on his knees with his sword held hilt up like a cross doing the long speech that begins, "Angels and ministers of grace defend us!" And of course the Ghost had his cloak drawn around him so you couldn't see what was under it—and the little green light still wasn't lit in his helmet. Tonight the absence of that theatric touch made him a more frightening figure—certainly to me, who wanted so much to see Guthrie's ravaged old face and be reassured by it. Though there was still enough comedy left in the ragged edges of my thoughts that I could imagine Guthrie's pugnacious son-in-law whispering angrily to those around him that Gilbert Usher was so jealous of his great father-in-law that he wouldn't let him show his face on the stage.

Then came the transition to the following scene where the Ghost has led Hamlet off alone with him—just a five-second complete darkening of the stage while a scrim is dropped—and at last the Ghost spoke those first lines of "Mark me" and "My hour is almost come, When I to sulphurous and tormenting flames Must render up myself."

If any of us had any worries about the Ghost blowing up on his lines or slurring them drunkenly, they were taken care of now. Those lines were delivered with the greatest authority and effect. And I was almost certain that it was Guthrie's rightful voice—at least I was at first—but doing an even better job than the good one he had always done of getting the effect of distance and otherworldliness and hopeless alienation from all life on Earth. The theater became silent as death, yet at the same time I could imagine the soft pounding of a thousand hearts, thousands of shivers crawling—and I *knew* that Francis Farley Scott, whose shoulder was pressed against mine, was trembling.

Each word the Ghost spoke was like a ghost itself, mounting the air and hanging poised for an impossible extra instant before it faded towards eternity.

Those great lines came: "I am thy father's spirit; Doomed for a certain term to walk the night…" and just at that moment the idea came to me that Guthrie Boyd might be dead, that he might have died and be lying unnoticed somewhere between his children's home and the theater—no matter what Props had said or the rest of us had seen—and that his ghost might have come to give a last performance. And on the heels of that shivery impossibility came the thought that similar and perhaps even eerier ideas must be frightening Monica. I knew I had to go to her.

So while the Ghost's words swooped and soared in the dark—marvelous black-plumed birds—I again made that nervous cross behind the backdrop.

Everyone stage right was standing as frozen and absorbed—motionless loomings—as I'd left John and F. F. I spotted Monica at once. She'd moved forward from the switchboard and was standing, crouched a little, by the big floodlight that throws some dimmed blue on the backdrop and across the back of the stage. I went to her just as the Ghost was beginning his exit stage left, moving backward along the edge of the light from the flood, but not quite in it, and reciting more lonely and eerily than I'd ever heard them before, those memorable last lines:

> "Fare thee well at once!
> "The glow-worm shows the matin to be near,
> "And 'gins to pale his uneffectual fire;
> "Adieu, adieu! Hamlet, remember me."

One second passed, then another, and then there came two unexpected bursts of sound at the same identical instant: Monica screamed and a thunderous applause started out front, touched off by Guthrie's people, of course, but this time swiftly spreading to all the rest of the audience.

I imagine it was the biggest hand the Ghost ever got in the history of the theater. In fact, I never heard of him getting a hand before. It certainly was a most inappropriate place to clap, however much the performance deserved it. It broke the atmosphere and the thread of the scene.

Also, it drowned out Monica's scream, so that only I and a few of those behind me heard it.

At first I thought I'd made her scream, by touching her as I had Guthrie, suddenly, like an idiot, from behind. But instead of shrinking or dodging away she turned and clung to me, and kept clinging too even after I'd drawn her back and Gertrude Grainger and Sybil Jameson had closed in to comfort her and hush her gasping sobs and try to draw her away from me.

By this time the applause was through and Governor and Don and Joe were taking up the broken scene and knitting together its finish as best they could, while the floods came up little by little, changing to rosy, to indicate dawn breaking over Elsinore.

Then Monica mastered herself and told us in quick whispers what had made her scream. The Ghost, she said, had moved for a moment into the edge of the blue floodlight, and she had seen for a moment through his veil, and what she had seen had been a face like Shakespeare's. Just that and no more. Except that at the moment when she told us—later she became less certain—she was sure it was Shakespeare himself and no one else.

I discovered then that when you hear something like that you don't exclaim or get outwardly excited. Or even inwardly, exactly. It rather shuts you up. I know I felt at the same time extreme awe and a renewed irritation at the Ouija board. I was deeply moved, yet at the same time pettishly irked, as if some vast adult creature had disordered the toy world of my universe.

It seemed to hit Sybil and even Gertrude the same way. For the moment we were shy about the whole thing, and so, in her way, was Monica, and so were the few others who had overheard in part or all what Monica had said.

I knew we were going to cross the stage in a few more seconds when the curtain came down on that scene, ending the first act, and stage lights came up. At least I knew that I was going across. Yet I wasn't looking forward to it.

When the curtain did come down—with another round of applause from out front—and we started across, Monica beside me with my arm still tight around her, there came a choked-off male cry of horror from ahead to shock and hurry us. I think about a dozen of us got stage left about the same time, including of course the Governor and the others who had been on stage.

F. F. and Props were standing inside the doorway to the empty prop room and looking down into the hidden part of the L. Even from the side, they both looked pretty sick. Then F. F. knelt down and almost went out of view, while Props hunched over him with his natural stoop.

As we craned around Props for a look—myself among the first, just beside the Governor, we saw something that told us right away that this Ghost wasn't ever going to be able to answer that curtain call they were still fitfully clapping for out front, although the house lights must be up by now for the first intermission.

Guthrie Boyd was lying on his back in his street clothes. His face looked gray, the eyes staring straight up. While swirled beside him lay the Ghost's cloak and veil and the helmet and an empty fifth of whiskey.

Between the two conflicting shocks of Monica's revelation and the body in the prop room, my mind was in a useless state. And from her helpless incredulous expression I knew Monica felt the same. I tried to put things together and they wouldn't fit anywhere.

F. F. looked up at us over his shoulder. "He's not breathing," he said. "I think he's gone." Just the same he started loosing Boyd's tie and shirt and pillowing his head on the cloak. He handed the whisky bottle back to us through several hands and Joe Rubens got rid of it.

The Governor sent out front for a doctor and within two minutes Harry Grossman was bringing us one from the audience who'd left his seat number and bag at the box office. He was a small man—Guthrie would have made two of him—and a bit awestruck, I could see, though holding himself with greater professional dignity because of that, as we made way for him and then crowded in behind.

He confirmed F. F.'s diagnosis by standing up quickly after kneeling only for a few seconds where F. F. had. Then he said hurriedly to the Governor, as if the words were being surprised out of him against his professional caution, "Mr. Usher, if I hadn't heard this man giving that great performance just now, I'd think he'd been dead for an hour or more."

He spoke low and not all of us heard him, but I did and so did Monica, and there was Shock Three to go along with the other two, raising in my mind for an instant the grisly picture of Guthrie Boyd's spirit, or some other entity, willing his dead body to go through with that last performance. Once again I unsuccessfully tried to fumble together the parts of this night's mystery.

The little doctor looked around at us slowly and puzzledly. He said, "I take it he just wore the cloak over his street clothes?" He paused. Then, "He *did* play the Ghost?" he asked us.

The Governor and several others nodded, but some of us didn't at once and I think F. F. gave him a rather peculiar look, for the doctor cleared his throat and said, "I'll have to examine this man as quickly as possible in a better place and light. Is there—?" The Governor suggested the couch in his dressing room and the doctor designated Joe Rubens and John McCarthy and Francis Farley Scott to carry the body. He passed over the Governor, perhaps out of awe, but Hamlet helped just the same, his black garb most fitting.

It was odd the doctor picked the older men—I think he did it for dignity. And it was odder still that he should have picked two ghosts to help carry a third, though he couldn't have known that.

As the designated ones moved forward, the doctor said, "Please stand back, the rest of you."

It was then that the very little thing happened which made all the pieces of this night's mystery fall into place—for me, that is, and for Monica too, judging from the way her hand trembled in and then tightened around mine. We'd been given the key to what had happened. I won't tell you what it was until I've knit together the ends of this story.

The second act was delayed perhaps a minute, but after that we kept to schedule, giving a better performance than usual—I never knew the Graveyard Scene to carry so much feeling, or the bit with Yorick's skull to be so poignant.

Just before I made my own first entrance, Joe Rubens snatched off my street hat—I'd had it on all this while—and I played all of Guildenstern wearing a wristwatch, though I don't imagine anyone noticed.

F. F. played the Ghost as an offstage voice when he makes his final brief appearance in the Closet Scene. He used Guthrie's voice to do it, imitating him very well. It struck me afterwards as ghoulish—but right.

Well before the play ended, the doctor had decided he could say that

Guthrie had died of a heart seizure, not mentioning the alcoholism. The minute the curtain came down on the last act, Harry Grossman informed Guthrie's son and daughter and brought them backstage. They were much moved, though hardly deeply smitten, seeing they'd been out of touch with the old boy for a decade. However, they quickly saw it was a Grand and Solemn Occasion and behaved accordingly, especially Guthrie's pugnacious son-in-law.

Next morning the two Wolverton papers had headlines about it and Guthrie got his biggest notices ever in the Ghost. The strangeness of the event carried the item around the world—a six-line filler, capturing the mind for a second or two, about how a once-famous actor had died immediately after giving a performance as the Ghost in *Hamlet,* though in some versions, of course, it became Hamlet's Ghost.

The funeral came on the afternoon of the third day, just before our last performance in Wolverton, and the whole company attended along with Guthrie's children's crowd and many other Wolvertonians. Old Sybil broke down and sobbed.

Yet to be a bit callous, it was a neat thing that Guthrie died where he did, for it saved us the trouble of having to send for relatives and probably take care of the funeral ourselves. And it did give old Guthrie a grand finish, with everyone outside the company thinking him a hero-martyr to the motto The Show Must Go On. And of course we knew too that in a deeper sense he'd really been that.

We shifted around in our parts and doubled some to fill the little gaps Guthrie had left in the plays, so that the Governor didn't have to hire another actor at once. For me, and I think for Monica, the rest of the season was very sweet. Gertrude and Sybil carried on with the Ouija sessions alone.

And now I must tell you about the very little thing which gave myself and Monica a satisfying solution to the mystery of what had happened that night.

You'll have realized that it involved Props. Afterwards I asked him straight out about it and he shyly told me that he really couldn't help me there. He'd had this unaccountable devilish compulsion to get drunk and his mind had blanked out entirely from well before the performance until he found himself standing with F. F. over Guthrie's body at the end of the first act. He didn't remember the Ouija-scare or a word of what he'd said to me about theaters and time machines—or so he always insisted.

F. F. told us that after the Ghost's last exit he'd seen him—very vaguely in the dimness—lurch across backstage into the empty prop room and that he and Props had found Guthrie lying there at the end of the scene. I think the queer look F. F.—the old reality-fuddling rogue!—gave the doctor was to hint to him that *he* had played the Ghost, though that wasn't something I could ask him about.

But the very little thing—When they were picking up Guthrie's body and the doctor told the rest of us to stand back, Props turned as he obeyed and straightened his shoulders and looked directly at Monica and myself, or rather a little over our heads. He appeared compassionate yet smilingly serene as always and for a moment transfigured, as if he were the eternal observer of the stage of life and this little tragedy were only part of an infinitely vaster, endlessly interesting pattern.

I realized at that instant that Props could have done it, that he'd very effectively guarded the doorway to the empty prop room during our searches, that the Ghost's costume could be put on or off in seconds (though Props's shoulders wouldn't fill the cloak like Guthrie's), and that I'd never once before or during the play seen him and the Ghost at the same time. Yes, Guthrie had arrived a few minutes before me... and died... and Props, nerved to it by drink, had covered for him.

While Monica, as she told me later, knew at once that here was the great-browed face she'd glimpsed for a moment through the greenish gauze.

Clearly there had been four ghosts in *Hamlet* that night—John McCarthy, Francis Farley Scott, Guthrie Boyd, and the fourth who had really played the role. Mentally blacked out or not, knowing the lines from the many times he'd listened to *Hamlet* performed in this life, or from buried memories of times he'd taken the role in the days of Queen Elizabeth the First, Billy (or Willy) Simpson, or simply Willy S., had played the Ghost, a good trouper responding automatically to an emergency.

GONNA ROLL THE BONES

S UDDENLY JOE SLATTERMILL KNEW FOR SURE he'd have to get out quick or else blow his top and knock out with the shrapnel of his skull the props and patches holding up his decaying home, that was like a house of big wooden and plaster and wallpaper cards except for the huge fireplace and ovens and chimney across the kitchen from him. Those were stone-solid enough, though. The fireplace was chin-high, at least twice that long, and filled from end to end with roaring flames. Above were the square doors of the ovens in a row—his Wife baked for part of their living. Above the ovens was the wall-long mantelpiece, too high for his Mother to reach or Mr. Guts to jump any more, set with all sorts of ancestral curios, but any of them that weren't stone or glass or china had been so dried and darkened by decades of heat that they looked like nothing but shrunken human heads and black golf balls. At one end were clustered his Wife's square gin bottles. Above the mantelpiece hung one old chromo, so high and so darkened by soot and grease that you couldn't tell whether the swirls and fat cigar shape were a whaleback steamer plowing through a hurricane or a spaceship plunging through a storm of light-driven dust motes.

As soon as Joe curled his toes inside his boots, his Mother knew what he was up to. "Going bumming," she mumbled with conviction. "Pants pockets full of cartwheels of house money, too, to spend on sin." And she went back to munching the long shreds she stripped fumblingly with her right hand off the turkey carcass set close to the terrible heat, her left hand ready to fend off Mr. Guts, who stared at her yellow-eyed, gaunt-flanked, with long mangy tail a-twitch. In her dirty dress, streaky as the turkey's sides, Joe's Mother looked like a bent brown bag and her fingers were lumpy twigs.

Joe's Wife knew as soon or sooner, for she smiled thin-eyed at him over her shoulder from where she towered at the centermost oven. Before she closed its door, Joe glimpsed that she was baking two long, flat, narrow, fluted loaves and one high, round-domed one. She was thin as death and disease in her violet wrapper. Without looking, she reached out a yard-long, skinny arm for the nearest gin bottle and downed a warm slug and smiled again. And without a word spoken, Joe knew she'd said, "You're going out and gamble and get drunk and lay a floozy and come home and beat me and go to jail for it," and he had a flash of the last time he'd been in the dark gritty cell and she'd come by moonlight, which showed the green and yellow lumps on her narrow skull where he'd hit her, to whisper to him through the tiny window in back and slip him a half pint through the bars.

And Joe knew for certain that this time it would be that bad and worse, but just the same he heaved up himself and his heavy, muffledly clanking pockets and shuffled straight to the door, muttering, "Guess I'll roll the bones, up the pike a stretch and back," swinging his bent, knobby-elbowed arms like paddlewheels to make a little joke about his words.

When he'd stepped outside, he held the door open a hand's breadth behind him for several seconds. When he finally closed it, a feeling of deep misery struck him. Earlier years, Mr. Guts would have come streaking along to seek fights and females on the roofs and fences, but now the big tom was content to stay home and hiss by the fire and snatch for turkey and dodge a broom, quarreling and comforting with two housebound women. Nothing had followed Joe to the door but his Mother's chomping and her gasping breaths and the clink of the gin bottle going back on the mantel and the creaking of the floor boards under his feet.

The night was up-side-down deep among the frosty stars. A few of them seemed to move, like the white-hot jets of spaceships. Down below it looked as if the whole town of Ironmine had blown or buttoned out the light and gone to sleep, leaving the streets and spaces to the equally unseen breezes and ghosts. But Joe was still in the hemisphere of the musty dry odor of the worm-eaten carpentry behind him, and as he felt and heard the dry grass of the lawn brush his calves, it occurred to him that something deep down inside him had for years been planning things so that he and the house and his Wife and Mother and Mr. Guts would all come to an end together. Why the kitchen heat hadn't touched off the tindery place ages ago was a physical miracle.

Hunching his shoulders, Joe stepped out, not up the pike, but down the dirt road that led past Cypress Hollow Cemetery to Night Town.

The breezes were gentle, but unusually restless and variable tonight, like leprechaun squalls. Beyond the drunken, whitewashed cemetery fence dim in the starlight, they rustled the scraggly trees of Cypress Hollow and made it seem they were stroking their beards of Spanish moss. Joe sensed that the ghosts were just as restless as the breezes, uncertain where and whom to haunt, or whether to take the night off, drifting together in sorrowfully lecherous companionship. While among the trees the red-green vampire lights pulsed faintly and irregularly, like sick fireflies or a plague-stricken space fleet. The feeling of deep misery stuck with Joe and deepened and he was tempted to turn aside and curl up in any convenient tomb or around some half-toppled head board and cheat his Wife and the other three behind him out of a shared doom. He thought: Gonna roll the bones, gonna roll 'em up and go to sleep. But while he was deciding, he got past the sagged-open gate and the rest of the delirious fence and Shantyville too.

At first Night Town seemed dead as the rest of Ironmine, but then he noticed a faint glow, sick as the vampire lights but more feverish, and with it a jumping music, tiny at first as a jazz for jitterbugging ants. He stepped along the springy sidewalk, wistfully remembering the days when the spring was all in his own legs and he'd bound into a fight like a bobcat or a Martian sand-spider. God, it had been years now since he had fought a real fight, or felt *the power*. Gradually the midget music got raucous as a bunny-hug for grizzly bears and loud as a polka for elephants, while the glow became a riot of gas flares and flambeaux and corpse-blue mercury tubes and jiggling pink neon ones that all jeered at the stars where the spaceships roved. Next thing, he was facing a three-story false front flaring everywhere like a devil's rainbow, with a pale blue topping of St. Elmo's fire. There were wide swinging doors in the center of it, spilling light above and below. Above the doorway, golden calcium light scrawled over and over again, with wild curlicues and flourishes, "The Boneyard," while a fiendish red kept printing out, "Gambling."

So the new place they'd all been talking about for so long had opened at last! For the first time that night, Joe Slattermill felt a stirring of real life in him and the faintest caress of excitement.

Gonna roll the bones, he thought.

He dusted off his blue-green work clothes with big, careless swipes and slapped his pockets to hear the clank. Then he threw back his shoulders and grinned his lips sneeringly and pushed through the swinging doors as if giving a foe the straight-armed heel of his palm.

Inside, The Boneyard seemed to cover the area of a township and the bar looked as long as the railroad tracks. Round pools of light on the green poker tables alternated with hourglass shapes of exciting gloom, through which drink-girls and change-girls moved like white-legged witches. By the jazz stand in the distance, belly dancers made *their* white hourglass shapes. The gamblers were thick and hunched down as mushrooms, all bald from agonizing over the fall of a card or a die or the dive of an ivory ball, while the Scarlet Women were like fields of poinsettia.

The calls of the croupiers and the slaps of dealt cards were as softly yet fatefully staccato as the rustle and beat of the jazz drums. Every tight-locked atom of the place was controlledly jumping. Even the dust motes jigged tensely in the cones of light.

Joe's excitement climbed and he felt sift through him, like a breeze that heralds a gale, the faintest breath of a confidence which he knew could become a tornado. All thoughts of his house and Wife and Mother dropped out of his mind, while Mr. Guts remained only as a crazy young tom walking stiff-legged around the rim of his consciousness. Joe's own leg muscles twitched in sympathy and he felt them grow supplely strong.

He coolly and searchingly looked the place over, his hand going out like it didn't belong to him to separate a drink from a passing, gently bobbing tray. Finally his gaze settled on what he judged to be the Number One Crap Table. All the Big Mushrooms seemed to be there, bald as the rest but standing tall as toadstools. Then through a gap in them Joe saw on the other side of the table a figure still taller, but dressed in a long dark coat with collar turned up and a dark slouch hat pulled low, so that only a triangle of white face showed. A suspicion and a hope rose in Joe and he headed straight for the gap in the Big Mushrooms.

As he got nearer, the white-legged and shiny-topped drifters eddying out of his way, his suspicion received confirmation after confirmation and his hope budded and swelled. Back from one end of the table was the fattest man he'd ever seen, with a long cigar and a silver vest and a gold tie clasp at least eight inches wide that just said in thick script, "Mr. Bones." Back a little from the other end was the nakedest change-girl yet and the only one he'd seen whose tray, slung from her bare shoulders and indenting her belly just below her breasts, was stacked with gold in gloaming little towers and with jet-black chips. While the dice-girl, skinnier and taller and longer armed than his Wife even, didn't seem to be wearing much but a pair of long white gloves. She was all right if you went for the type that isn't much more than pale skin over bones with breasts like china doorknobs.

Beside each gambler was a high round table for his chips. The one by the gap was empty. Snapping his fingers at the nearest silver change-girl, Joe traded all his greasy dollars for an equal number of pale chips and tweaked her left nipple for luck. She playfully snapped her teeth toward his fingers.

Not hurrying but not wasting any time, he advanced and carelessly dropped his modest stacks on the empty table and took his place in the gap. He noted that the second Big Mushroom on his right had the dice. His heart but no other part of him gave an extra jump. Then he steadily lifted his eyes and looked straight across the table.

The coat was a shimmering elegant pillar of black satin with jet buttons, the upturned collar of fine dull plush black as the darkest cellar, as was the slouch hat with down-turned brim and a band of only a thin braid of black horsehair. The arms of the coat were long, lesser satin pillars, ending in slim, long-fingered hands that moved swiftly when they did, but held each position of rest with a statue's poise.

Joe still couldn't see much of the face except for smooth lower forehead with never a bead or trickle of sweat, the eyebrows were like straight snippets of the hat's braid and gaunt, aristocratic cheeks and narrow but somewhat flat nose. The complexion of the face wasn't as white as Joe had first judged. There was a faint touch of brown in it, like ivory that's just begun to age, or Venusian soapstone. Another glance at the hands confirmed this.

Behind the man in black was a knot of just about the flashiest and nastiest customers, male or female, Joe had ever seen. He knew from one look that each bediamonded, pomaded bully had a belly gun beneath the flap of his flowered vest and a blackjack in his hip pocket, and each snake-eyed sporting-girl a stiletto in her garter and a pearl-handled silver-plated derringer under the sequined silk in the hollow between her jutting breasts.

Yet at the same time Joe knew they were just trimmings.

It was the man in black, their master, who was the deadly one, the kind of man you know at a glance you couldn't touch and live. If without asking you merely laid a finger on his sleeve, no matter how lightly and respectfully, an ivory hand would move faster than thought and you'd be stabbed or shot. Or maybe just the touch would kill you, as if every black article of his clothing were charged from his ivory skin outward with a high-voltage, high-amperage ivory electricity. Joe looked at the shadowed face again and decided he wouldn't care to try it.

For it was the eyes that were the most impressive feature.

All great gamblers have dark-shadowed deep-set eyes. But this one's eyes were sunk so deep you couldn't even be sure you were getting a gleam of them. They were inscrutability incarnate. They were unfathomable. They were like black holes.

But all this didn't disappoint Joe one bit, though it did terrify him considerably. On the contrary, it made him exult. His first suspicion was completely confirmed and his hope spread into full flower.

This must be one of those really big gamblers who hit Ironmine only once a decade at most, come from the Big City on one of the river boats that ranged the watery dark like luxurious comets, spouting long thick tails of sparks from their sequoia-tall stacks with top foliage of curvy-snipped sheet iron. Or like silver space-liners with dozens of jewel-flamed jets, their portholes a-twinkle like ranks of marshaled asteroids.

For that matter, maybe some of those really big gamblers actually came from other planets where the nighttime pace was hotter and the sporting life a delirium of risk and delight.

Yes, this was the kind of man Joe had always yearned to pit his skill against. He felt *the power* begin to tingle in his rock-still fingers, just a little.

Joe lowered his gaze to the crap table. It was almost as wide as a man is tall, at least twice as long, unusually deep, and lined with black, not green, felt, so that it looked like a giant's coffin. There was something familiar about its shape which he couldn't place. Its bottom, though not its sides or ends, had a twinkling iridescence, as if it had been lightly sprinkled with very tiny diamonds. As Joe lowered his gaze all the way and looked directly down, his eyes barely over the table, he got the crazy notion that it went down all the way through the world, so that the diamonds were the stars on the other side, visible despite the sunlight there, just as Joe was always able to see the stars by day up the shaft of the mine he worked in, and so that if a cleaned-out gambler, dizzy with defeat, toppled forward into it, he'd fall forever, toward the bottommost bottom, be it Hell or some black galaxy. Joe's thoughts swirled and he felt the cold, hard-fingered clutch of fear at his crotch. Someone was crooning beside him, "Come on. Big Dick."

Then the dice, which had meanwhile passed to the Big Mushroom immediately on his right, came to rest near the table's center, contradicting and wiping out Joe's vision. But instantly there was another oddity to absorb him. The ivory dice were large and unusually round-cornered with dark red spots that gleamed like real rubies, but the spots were arranged in such a way that each face looked like a miniature skull. For instance, the seven thrown just now, by which the Big Mushroom to his right had lost his point, which had been ten, consisted of a two with the spots evenly spaced toward one side, like eyes, instead of toward opposite corners, and of a five with the same red eye-spots but also a central red nose and two spots close together below that to make teeth.

The long, skinny, white-gloved arm of the dice-girl snaked out like an albino cobra and scooped up the dice and whisked them onto the rim of the table right in front of Joe. He inhaled silently, picked up a single chip from his table and started to lay it beside the dice, then realized that wasn't the way things were done here, and put it back. He would have liked to examine the chip more closely, though. It was curiously lightweight and pale tan, about the color of cream with a shot of coffee in it, and it had embossed on its surface a symbol he could feel, though not see. He didn't know what the symbol was, that would have taken more feeling. Yet its touch had been very good, setting *the power* tingling full blast in his shooting hand.

Joe looked casually yet swiftly at the faces around the table, not missing the Big Gambler across from him, and said quietly, "Roll a penny," meaning of course one pale chip, or a dollar.

There was a hiss of indignation from all the Big Mushrooms and the moonface of big-bellied Mr. Bones grew purple as he started forward to summon his bouncers.

The Big Gambler raised a black-satined forearm and sculptured hand, palm down. Instantly Mr. Bones froze and the hissing stopped faster than that of a meteor prick in self-sealing space steel. Then in a whispery, cultured voice, without the faintest hint of derision, the man in black said, "Get on him, gamblers."

Here, Joe thought, was a final confirmation of his suspicion, had it been needed. The really great gamblers were always perfect gentlemen and generous to the poor.

With only the tiny, respectful hint of a guffaw, one of the Big Mushrooms called to Joe, "You're faded."

Joe picked up the ruby-featured dice.

Now ever since he had first caught two eggs on one plate, won all the marbles in Ironmine, and juggled six alphabet blocks so they finally fell in a row on the rug spelling "Mother," Joe Slattermill had been almost incredibly deft at precision throwing. In the mine he could carom a rock off a wall of ore to crack a rat's skull fifty feet away in the dark and he sometimes amused himself by tossing little fragments of rock back into the holes from which they had fallen, so that they stuck there, perfectly fitted in, for at least a second. Sometimes, by fast tossing, he could fit seven or eight fragments into the hole from which they had fallen, like putting together a puzzle block. If he could ever have got into space, Joe would undoubtedly have been able to pilot six Moon-skimmers at once and do figure eights through Saturn's rings blindfold.

Now the only real difference between precision-tossing rocks or alphabet blocks and dice is that you have to bounce the latter off the end wall of a crap table, and that just made it a more interesting test of skill for Joe.

Rattling the dice now, he felt *the power* in his fingers and palm as never before.

He made a swift low roll, so that the bones ended up exactly in front of the white-gloved dice-girl. His natural seven was made up, as he'd intended, of a four and a three. In red-spot features they were like the five, except that both had only one tooth and the three no nose. Sort of baby-faced skulls. He had won a penny—that is, a dollar.

"Roll two cents," said Joe Slattermill.

This time, for variety, he made his natural with an eleven.

The six was like the five, except it had three teeth, the best-looking skull of the lot.

"Roll a nickel less one."

Two big Mushrooms divided that bet with a covert smirk at each other. Now Joe rolled a three and an ace. His point was four.

The ace, with its single spot off center toward a side, still somehow looked like a skull—maybe of a Lilliputian Cyclops. He took a while making his point, once absent-mindedly rolling three successive tens the hard way. He wanted to watch the dice-girl scoop up the cubes. Each time it seemed to him that her snake-swift fingers went under the dice while they were still flat on the felt. Finally he decided it couldn't be an illusion. Although the dice couldn't penetrate the felt, her white-gloved fingers somehow could, dipping in a flash through the black, diamond-sparkling material as if it weren't there.

Right away the thought of a crap-table-size hole through the earth came back to Joe. This would mean that the dice were rolling and lying on a perfectly transparent flat surface, impenetrable for them but nothing else. Or maybe it was only the dice-girl's hands that could penetrate the surface, which would turn into a mere fantasy Joe's earlier vision of a cleaned-out gambler taking the Big Dive down that dreadful shaft, which made the deepest mine a mere pin dent. Joe decided he had to know which was true. Unless absolutely unavoidable, he didn't want to take the chance of being troubled by vertigo at some crucial stage of the game.

He made a few more meaningless throws, from time to time crooning for realism, "Come on. Little Joe." Finally he settled on his plan. When he did at last make his point the hard way, with two twos—he caromed the dice off the far corner so that they landed exactly in front of him. Then, after a minimum pause for his throw to be seen by the table, he shot his left hand down under the cubes, just a flicker ahead of the dice-girl's strike, and snatched them up.

Wow! Joe had never had a harder time in his life making his face and manner conceal what his body felt, not even when the wasp had stung him on the neck just as he had been for the first time putting his hand under the skirt of his prudish, fickle, demanding Wife-to-be. His fingers and the back of his hand were in as much agony as if he'd stuck them into a blast furnace. No wonder the dice-girl wore white gloves. They must be asbestos. And a good thing he hadn't used his shooting hand, he thought as he ruefully watched the blisters rise.

He remembered he'd been taught in school what Twenty-Mile Mine also demonstrated: that the earth was fearfully hot under its crust. The crap-table-size hole must pipe up that heat, so that any gambler taking the Big Dive would fry before he'd fallen a furlong and come out less than a cinder in China.

As if his blistered hand weren't bad enough, the Big Mushrooms were all hissing at him again and Mr. Bones had purpled once more and was opening his melon-size mouth to shout for his bouncers.

Once again a lift of the Big Gambler's hand saved Joe.

The whispery, gentle voice called, "Tell him, Mr. Bones."

The latter roared toward Joe, "No gambler may pick up the dice he or any other gambler has shot. Only my dice-girl may do that. Rule of the house!"

Joe snapped Mr. Bones the barest nod. He said coolly, "Rolling a dime less two," and when that still peewee bet was covered, he shot Phoebe for his point and then fooled around for quite a while, throwing anything but a five or a seven, until the throbbing in his left hand should fade and all his nerves feel rock-solid again. There had never been the slightest alteration in *the power* in his right hand; he felt that strong as ever, or stronger.

Midway of this interlude, the Big Gambler bowed slightly but respectfully toward Joe, hooding those unfathomable eye sockets, before turning around to take a long black cigarette from his prettiest and evilest-looking sporting-girl. Courtesy in the smallest matters, Joe thought, another mark of the master devotee of games of chance. The Big Gambler sure had himself a flash crew, all right, though in idly looking them over again as he rolled, Joe noted one bummer toward the back who didn't fit in—a raggedy-elegant chap with the elflocked hair and staring eyes and TB-spotted cheeks of a poet.

As he watched the smoke trickling up from under the black slouch hat, he decided that either the lights across the table had dimmed or else the Big Gambler's complexion was yet a shade darker than he'd thought at first. Or it might even be—wild fantasy—that the Big Gambler's skin was slowly darkening tonight, like a meerschaum pipe being smoked a mile a second. That was almost funny to think of—there was enough heat in this place, all right, to darken meerschaum, as Joe knew from sad experience, but so far as he was aware it was all under the table.

None of Joe's thoughts, either familiar or admiring, about the Big Gambler decreased in the slightest degree his certainty of the supreme menace of the man in black and his conviction that it would be death to touch him. And if any doubts had stirred in Joe's mind, they would have been squelched by the chilling incident which next occurred.

The Big Gambler had just taken into his arms his prettiest-evilest sporting-girl and was running an aristocratic hand across her haunch with perfect gentility, when the poet chap, green-eyed from jealousy and lovesickness, came leaping forward like a wildcat and aimed a long gleaming dagger at the black satin back.

Joe couldn't see how the blow could miss, but without taking his genteel right hand off the sporting-girl's plush rear end, the Big Gambler shot out his left arm like a steel spring straightening. Joe couldn't tell whether he stabbed the poet chap in the throat, or judo-chopped him there, or gave him the Martian double-finger, or just touched him, but anyhow the fellow stopped as dead as if he'd been shot by a silent elephant gun or an invisible ray pistol and he slammed down on the floor. A couple of darkies came running up to drag off the body and nobody paid the least attention, such episodes apparently being taken for granted at The Boneyard.

It gave Joe quite a turn and he almost shot Phoebe before he intended to.

But by now the waves of pain had stopped running up his left arm and his nerves were like metal-wrapped new guitar strings, so three rolls later he shot a five, making his point, and set in to clean out the table.

He rolled nine successive naturals, seven sevens and two elevens, pyramiding his first wager of a single chip to a stake of over four thousand dollars. None of the Big Mushrooms had dropped out yet, but some of them were beginning to look worried and a couple were sweating. The Big Gambler still hadn't covered any part of Joe's bets, but he seemed to be following the play with interest from the cavernous depths of his eye sockets.

Then Joe got a devilish thought. Nobody could beat him tonight, he knew, but if he held onto the dice until the table was cleaned out, he'd never get a chance to see the Big Gambler exercise *his* skill, and he was truly curious about that. Besides, he thought, he ought to return courtesy for courtesy and have a crack at being a gentleman himself.

"Pulling out forty-one dollars less a nickel," he announced. "Rolling a penny."

This time there wasn't any hissing and Mr. Bones's moonface didn't cloud over. But Joe was conscious that the Big Gambler was staring at him disappointedly, or sorrowfully, or maybe just speculatively.

Joe immediately crapped out by throwing boxcars, rather pleased to see the two best-looking tiny skulls grinning ruby-toothed side by side, and the dice passed to the Big Mushroom on his left.

"Knew when his streak was over," he heard another Big Mushroom mutter with grudging admiration.

The play worked rather rapidly around the table, nobody getting very hot and the stakes never more than medium high. "Shoot a fin." "Rolling a sawbuck." "An Andrew Jackson." "Rolling thirty bucks." Now and then Joe covered part of a bet, winning more than he lost. He had over seven thousand dollars, real money, before the bones got around to the Big Gambler.

That one held the dice for a long moment on his statue-steady palm while he looked at them reflectively, though not the hint of a furrow appeared in his almost brownish forehead down which never a bead of sweat trickled. He murmured. "Rolling a double sawbuck," and when he had been faded, he closed his fingers, lightly rattled the cubes—the sound was like big seeds inside a small gourd only half dry—and negligently cast the dice toward the end of the table.

It was a throw like none Joe had ever seen before at any crap table. The dice traveled flat through the air without turning over, struck the exact juncture of the table's end and bottom, and stopped there dead, showing a natural seven.

Joe was distinctly disappointed. On one of his own throws he was used to calculating something like, "Launch three-up, five north, two and a half rolls in the air, hit on the six-five-three corner, three-quarter roll and a one-quarter side-twist right, hit end on the one-two edge, one-half reverse role and three-quarter side-twist left, land on five face, roll over twice, come up two," and that would be for just one of the dice, and a really commonplace throw, without extra bounces.

By comparison, the technique of the Big Gambler had been ridiculously, abysmally, horrifyingly simple. Joe could have duplicated it with the greatest ease, of course. It was no more than an elementary form of his old pastime of throwing fallen rocks back into their holes. But Joe had never once thought of pulling such a babyish trick at the crap table. It would make the whole thing too easy and destroy the beauty of the game.

Another reason Joe had never used the trick was that he'd never dreamed he'd be able to get away with it. By all the rules he'd ever heard of, it was a most questionable throw. There was the possibility that one or the other die hadn't completely reached the end of the table or lay a wee bit cocked against the end. Besides, he reminded himself, weren't both dice supposed to rebound off the end, if only for a fraction of an inch?

However, as far as Joe's very sharp eyes could see, both dice lay perfectly flat and sprang up against the end wall. Moreover, everyone else at the table seemed to accept the throw, the dice-girl had scooped up the cubes, and the Big Mushrooms who had faded the man in black were paying off. As far as the rebound business went, well, The Boneyard appeared to put a slightly different interpretation on that rule, and Joe believed in never questioning House Rules except in dire extremity—both his Mother and Wife had long since taught him it was the least troublesome way. Besides, there hadn't been any of his own money riding on that roll.

In a voice like wind through Cypress Hollow or on Mars, the Big Gambler announced, "Roll a century." It was the biggest bet yet tonight, ten thousand dollars, and the way the Big Gambler said it made it seem something more than that.

A hush fell on The Boneyard, they put the mutes on the jazz horns, the croupiers' calls became more confidential, the cards fell softlier, even the roulette balls seemed to be trying to make less noise as they rattled into their cells. The crowd around the Number One Crap Table quietly thickened. The Big Gambler's flash boys and girls formed a double semicircle around him, ensuring him lots of elbow room.

That century bet, Joe realized, was thirty bucks more than his own entire pile. Three or four of the Big Mushrooms had to signal each other before they'd agreed how to fade it.

The Big Gambler shot another natural seven with exactly the same flat, stop-dead throw.

He bet another century and did it again.

And again.

And again.

Joe was getting mighty concerned and pretty indignant too. It seemed unjust that the Big Gambler should be winning such huge bets with such machinelike, utterly unromantic rolls. Why, you couldn't even call them rolls, the dice never turned over an iota, in the air or after. It was the sort of thing you'd expect from a robot, and a very dully programed robot at that. Joe hadn't risked any of his own chips fading the Big Gambler, of course, but if things went on like this he'd have to. Two of the Big Mushrooms had already retired sweatingly from the table, confessing defeat, and no one had taken their places. Pretty soon there'd be a bet the remaining Big Mushrooms couldn't entirely cover between them, and then he'd have to risk some of his own chips or else pull out of the game himself—and he couldn't do that, not with *the power* surging in his right hand like chained lightning.

Joe waited and waited for someone else to question one of the Big Gambler's shots, but no one did. He realized that, despite his efforts to look imperturbable, his face was slowly reddening.

With a little lift of his left hand, the Big Gambler stopped the dice-girl as she was about to snatch at the cubes. The eyes that were like black wells directed themselves at Joe, who forced himself to look back into them steadily. He still couldn't catch the faintest gleam in them. All at once he felt the lightest touch-on-neck of a dreadful suspicion.

With the utmost civility and amiability, the Big Gambler whispered, "I believe that the fine shooter across from me has doubts about the validity of my last throw, though he is too much of a gentleman to voice them.

Lottie, the card test."

The wraith-tall, ivory dice-girl plucked a playing card from below the table and with a venomous flash of her little white teeth spun it low across the table through the air at Joe. He caught the whirling pasteboard and examined it briefly. It was the thinnest, stiffest, flattest, shiniest playing card Joe had ever handled. It was also the Joker, if that meant anything. He spun it back lazily into her hand and she slid it very gently, letting it descend by its own weight, down the end wall against which the two dice lay. It came to rest in the tiny hollow their rounded edges made against the black felt. She deftly moved it about without force, demonstrating that there was no space between either of the cubes and the table's end at any point.

"Satisfied?" the Big Gambler asked. Rather against his will Joe nodded. The Big Gambler bowed to him. The dice-girl smirked her short, thin lips and drew herself up, flaunting her white-china-doorknob breasts at Joe.

Casually, almost with an air of boredom, the Big Gambler returned to his routine of shooting a century and making a natural seven. The Big Mushrooms wilted fast and one by one tottered away from the table. A particularly pink-faced Toadstool was brought extra cash by a gasping runner, but it was no help, he only lost the additional centuries. While the stacks of pale and black chips beside the Big Gambler grew skyscraper-tall.

Joe got more and more furious and frightened. He watched like a hawk or spy satellite the dice nesting against the end wall, but never could spot justification for calling for another card test, or nerve himself to question the House Rules at this late date. It was maddening, in fact insanitizing, to know that if only he could get the cubes once more he could shoot circles around that black pillar of sporting aristocracy. He damned himself a googolplex of ways for the idiotic, conceited, suicidal impulse that had led him to let go of the bones when he'd had them.

To make matters worse, the Big Gambler had taken to gazing steadily at Joe with those eyes like coal mines. Now he made three rolls running without even glancing at the dice or the end wall, as far as Joe could tell. Why, he was getting as bad as Joe's Wife or Mother—watching, watching, watching Joe.

But the constant staring of those eyes that were not eyes was mostly throwing a terrific scare into him. Supernatural terror added itself to his certainty of the deadliness of the Big Gambler. Just who, Joe kept asking himself, had he got into a game with tonight? There was curiosity and there was dread—a dreadful curiosity as strong as his desire to get the bones and win. His hair rose and he was all over goose bumps, though *the power* was still pulsing in his hand like a braked locomotive or a rocket wanting to lift from the pad.

At the same time the Big Gambler stayed just that—a black satin-coated, slouch-halted elegance, suave, courtly, lethal. In fact, almost the worst thing about the spot Joe found himself in was that, after admiring the Big Gambler's perfect sportsmanship all night, he must now be disenchanted by his machinelike throwing and try to catch him out on any technicality he could.

The remorseless mowing down of the Big Mushrooms went on. The empty spaces outnumbered the Toadstools. Soon there were only three left.

The Boneyard had grown still as Cypress Hollow or the Moon. The jazz had stopped and the gay laughter and the shuffle of feet and the squeak of goosed girls and the clink of drinks and coins. Everybody seemed to be gathered around the Number One Crap Table, rank on silent rank.

Joe was racked by watchfulness, sense of injustice, self-contempt, wild hopes, curiosity and dread. Especially the last two.

The complexion of the Big Gambler, as much as you could see of it, continued to darken. For one wild moment Joe found himself wondering if he'd got into a game with a nigger, maybe a witchcraft-drenched Voodoo Man whose white make-up was wearing off.

Pretty soon there came a century wager which the two remaining Big Mushrooms couldn't fade between them. Joe had to make up a sawbuck from his miserably tiny pile or get out of the game. After a moment's agonizing hesitation, he did the former.

And lost his ten.

The two Big Mushrooms reeled back into the hushed crowd.

Pit-black eyes bored into Joe. A whisper: "Rolling your pile."

Joe felt well up in him the shameful impulse to confess himself licked and run home. At least his six thousand dollars would make a hit with his Wife and Ma.

But he just couldn't bear to think of the crowd's laughter, or the thought of living with himself knowing that he'd had a final chance, however slim, to challenge the Big Gambler and passed it up.

He nodded.

The Big Gambler shot. Joe leaned out over and down the table, forgetting his vertigo, as he followed the throw with eagle or space-telescope eyes.

"Satisfied?"

Joe knew he ought to say, "Yes," and slink off with head held as high as he could manage. It was the gentlemanly thing to do. But then he reminded himself that he wasn't a gentleman, but just a dirty, working-stiff miner with a talent for precision hurling.

He also knew it was probably very dangerous for him to say anything but, "Yes," surrounded as he was by enemies and strangers. But then he asked himself what right had he, a miserable, mortal, homebound failure, to worry about danger.

Besides, one of the ruby-grinning dice looked just the tiniest hair out of line with the other.

It was the biggest effort yet of Joe's life, but he swallowed and managed to say, "No. Lottie, the card test."

The dice-girl fairly snarled and reared up and back as if she were going to spit in his eyes, and Joe had a feeling her spit was cobra venom. But the Big Gambler lifted a finger at her in reproof and she skimmed the card at Joe, yet so low and viciously that it disappeared under the black felt for an instant before flying up into Joe's hand.

It was hot to the touch and singed a pale brown all over, though otherwise unimpaired. Joe gulped and spun it back high.

Sneering poisoned daggers at him, Lottie let it glide down the end wall… and after a moment's hesitation, it slithered behind the die Joe had suspected.

A bow and then the whisper: "You have sharp eyes, sir. Undoubtedly that die failed to reach the wall. My sincerest apologies and… your dice, sir."

Seeing the cubes sitting on the black rim in front of him almost gave Joe apoplexy. All the feelings racking him, including his curiosity, rose to an almost unbelievable pitch of intensity, and when he'd said, "Rolling my pile," and the Big Gambler had replied, "You're faded," he yielded to an uncontrollable impulse and cast the two dice straight at the Big Gambler's ungleaming, midnight eyes.

They went right through into the Big Gambler's skull and bounced around inside there, rattling like big seeds in a big gourd not quite yet dry.

Throwing out a hand, palm back, to either side, to indicate that none of his boys or girls or anyone else must make a reprisal on Joe, the Big Gambler dryly gargled the two cubical bones, then spat them out so that they landed in the center of the table, the one die flat, the other leaning against it.

"Cocked dice, sir," he whispered as graciously as if no indignity whatever had been done him. "Roll again."

Joe shook the dice reflectively, getting over the shock.

After a little bit he decided that though he could now guess the Big Gambler's real name, he'd still give him a run for his money.

A little corner of Joe's mind wondered how a live skeleton hung together. Did the bones still have gristle and thews, were they wired, was it done with force-fields, or was each bone a calcium magnet clinging to the next? This tying in somehow with the generation of the deadly ivory electricity.

In the great hush of The Boneyard, someone cleared his throat, a Scarlet

Woman tittered hysterically, a coin fell from the nakedest change-girl's tray with a golden clink and rolled musically across the floor.

"Silence," the Big Gambler commanded and in a movement almost too fast to follow whipped a hand inside the bosom of his coat and out to the crap table's rim in front of him. A short-barreled silver revolver lay softly gleaming there. "Next creature, from the humblest nigger night-girl to… you, Mr. Bones, who utters a sound while my worthy opponent rolls, gets a bullet in the head."

Joe gave him a courtly bow back, it felt funny, and then decided to start his run with a natural seven made up of an ace and a six. He rolled and this time the Big Gambler, judging from the movements of his skull, closely followed the course of the cubes with his eyes that weren't there.

The dice landed, rolled over, and lay still. Incredulously, Joe realized that for the first time in his crap-shooting life he'd made a mistake. Or else there was a power in the Big Gambler's gaze greater than that in his own right hand. The six cube had come down okay, but the ace had taken an extra half-roll and come down six too.

"End of the game," Mr. Bones boomed sepulchrally.

The Big Gambler raised a brown skeletal hand. "Not necessarily," he whispered. His black eyepits aimed themselves at Joe like the mouths of siege guns. "Joe Slattermill, you still have something of value to wager, if you wish. Your life."

At that a giggling and a hysterical tittering and a guffawing and a braying and a shrieking burst uncontrollably out of the whole Boneyard. Mr. Bones summed up the sentiments when he bellowed over the rest of the racket, "Now what use or value is there in the life of a bummer like Joe Slattermill? Not two cents, ordinary money."

The Big Gambler laid a hand on the revolver gleaming before him and all the laughter died.

"I have a use for it," the Big Gambler whispered. "Joe Slattermill, on my part I will venture all my winnings of tonight, and throw in the world and everything in it for a side bet. You will wager your life, and on the side your soul. Your turn to roll the dice. What's your pleasure?"

Joe Slattermill quailed, but then the drama of the situation took hold of him. He thought it over and realized he certainly wasn't going to give up being stage center in a spectacle like this to go home broke to his Wife and Mother and decaying house and the dispirited Mr. Guts. Maybe, he told himself encouragingly, there wasn't a power in the Big Gambler's gaze, maybe Joe had just made his one and only crap-shooting error. Besides, he was more inclined to accept Mr. Bones's assessment of the value of his life than the Big Gambler's.

"It's a bet," he said.

"Lottie, give him the dice."

Joe concentrated his mind as never before, *the power*, tingled triumphantly in his hand, and he made his throw.

The dice never hit the felt. They went swooping down, then up, in a crazy curve far out over the end of the table, and then came streaking back like tiny red-glinting meteors toward the face of the Big Gambler, where they suddenly nested and hung in his black eye sockets, each with their single red gleam of an ace showing.

Snake eyes.

The whisper, as those red-glinting dice-eyes stared mockingly at him: "Joe Slattermill, you've crapped out."

Using thumb and middle finger—or bone rather—of either hand, the Big Gambler removed the dice from his eye sockets and dropped them in Lottie's white-gloved hand.

"Yes, you've crapped out, Joe Slattermill," he went on tranquilly. "And now you can shoot yourself," he touched the silver gun, "or cut your throat," he whipped a gold-handled bowie knife out of his coat and laid it beside the revolver, "or poison yourself," the two weapons were joined by a small black bottle with white skull and crossbones on it, "or Miss Flossie here can kiss you to death."

He drew forward beside him his prettiest, evilest-looking sporting-girl. She preened herself and flounced her short violet skirt and gave Joe a provocative, hungry look, lifting her carmine upper lip to show her long white canines.

"Or else," the Big Gambler added, nodding significantly toward the black-bottomed crap table, "you can take the Big Dive."

Joe said evenly, "I'll take the Big Dive."

He put his right foot on his empty chip table, his left on the black rim, fell forward... and suddenly kicking off from the rim, launched himself in a tiger spring straight across the crap table at the Big Gambler's throat, solacing himself with the thought that certainly the poet chap hadn't seemed to suffer long.

As he flashed across the exact center of the table he got an instant photograph of what really lay below, but his brain had no time to develop that snapshot, for the next instant he was plowing into the Big Gambler.

Stiffened brown palm edge caught him in the temple with a lightninglike judo chop... and the brown fingers or bones flew all apart like puff paste. Joe's left hand went through the Big Gambler's chest as if there were nothing there but black satin coat, while his right hand, straight-armedly clawing at the slouch-hatted skull, crunched it to pieces. Next instant Joe was sprawled on the floor with some black clothes and brown fragments.

He was on his feet in a flash and snatching at the Big Gambler's tall stacks. He had time for one left-handed grab. He couldn't see any gold or silver or any black chips, so he stuffed his left pants pocket with a handful of the pale chips and ran.

Then the whole population of The Boneyard was on him and after him. Teeth, knives and brass knuckles flashed. He was punched, clawed, kicked, tripped and stamped on with spike heels. A gold-plated trumpet with a bloodshot-eyed black face behind it bopped him on the head. He got a white flash of the golden dice-girl and made a grab for her, but she got away. Someone tried to mash a lighted cigar in his eye.

Lottie, writhing and flailing like a white boa constrictor, almost got a simultaneous strangle hold and scissors on him. From a squat wide-mouth bottle Flossie, snarling like a feline fiend, threw what smelt like acid past his face. Mr. Bones peppered shots around him from the silver revolver. He was stabbed at, gouged, rabbit-punched, scrag-mauled, slugged, kneed, bitten, bearhugged, butted, beaten and had his toes trampled.

But somehow none of the blows or grabs had much force. It was like fighting ghosts. In the end it turned out that the whole population of The Boneyard, working together, had just a little more strength than Joe. He felt himself being lifted by a multitude of hands and pitched out through the swinging doors so that he thudded down on his rear end on the board sidewalk. Even that didn't hurt much. It was more like a kick of encouragement.

He took a deep breath and felt himself over and worked his bones. He didn't seem to have suffered any serious damage. He stood up and looked around. The Boneyard was dark and silent as the grave, or the planet Pluto, or all the rest of Ironmine. As his eyes got accustomed to the starlight and occasional roving spaceship-gleam, he saw a padlocked sheet-iron door where the swinging ones had been.

He found he was chewing on something crusty that he'd somehow carried in his right hand all the way through the final fracas. Mighty tasty, like the bread his Wife baked for best customers. At that instant his brain developed the photograph it had taken when he had glanced down as he flashed across the center of the crap table. It was a thin wall of flames moving sideways across the table and just beyond the flames the faces of his Wife, Mother, and Mr. Guts, all looking very surprised. He realized that what he was chewing was a fragment of the Big Gambler's skull, and he remembered the shape of the three loaves his Wife had started to bake when he left the house. And he understood the magic she'd made to let him get a little ways away and feel half a man, and then come diving home with his fingers burned.

He spat out what was in his mouth and pegged the rest of the bit of giant-popover skull across the street.

He fished in his left pocket. Most of the pale poker chips had been mashed in the fight, but he found a whole one and explored its surface with his fingertips. The symbol embossed on it was a cross. He lifted it to his lips and took a bite. It tasted delicate, but delicious. He ate it and felt his strength revive. He patted his bulging left pocket. At least he'd start out well provisioned.

Then he turned and headed straight for home, but he took the long way, around the world.

THE INNER CIRCLES

A FTER THE SUPPER DISHES were done there was a general movement from the Adler kitchen to the Adler living room.

It was led by Gottfried Helmuth Adler, commonly known as Gott. He was thinking how they should be coming from a dining room, yes, with colored maids, not from a kitchen. In a large brandy snifter he was carrying what had been left in the shaker from the martinis, a colorless elixir weakened by melted ice yet somewhat stronger than his wife was supposed to know. This monster drink was a regular part of Gott's carefully thought-out program for getting safely through the end of the day.

"After the seventeenth hour of creation God got sneaky," Gott Adler once put it to himself.

He sat down in his leather-upholstered easy chair, flipped open Plutarch's *Lives* left-handed, glanced down through the lower halves of his executive bifocals at the paragraph in the biography of Caesar he'd been reading before dinner, then, without moving his head, looked through the upper halves back toward the kitchen.

After Gott came Jane Adler, his wife. She sat down at her drawing table, where pad, pencils, knife, art gum, distemper paints, water, brushes, and rags were laid out neatly.

Then came little Heinie Adler, wearing a spaceman's transparent helmet with a large hole in the top for ventilation. He went and stood beside this arrangement of objects: first a long wooden box about knee-high with a smaller box on top and propped against the latter a toy control panel of blue and silver plastic, on which only one lever moved at all; next, facing the panel, a child's wooden chair; then back of the chair another long wooden box lined up with the first.

"Good-by Mama, good-by Papa," Heinie called. "I'm going to take a trip in my spaceship."

"Be back in time for bed," his mother said.

"Hot jets!" murmured his father.

Heinie got in, touched the control panel twice, and then sat motionless in the little wooden chair, looking straight ahead.

A fourth person came into the living room from the kitchen—the Man in the Black Flannel Suit. He moved with the sick jerkiness and had the slack putty-gray features of a figure of the imagination that hasn't been fully developed. (There was a fifth person in the house, but even Gott didn't know about him yet.)

The Man in the Black Flannel Suit made a stiff gesture at Gott and gaped his mouth to talk to him, but the latter silently writhed his lips in a "Not yet, you fool!" and nodded curtly toward the sofa opposite his easy chair.

"Gott," Jane said, hovering a pencil over the pad, "you've lately taken to acting as if you were talking to someone who isn't there."

"I have, my dear?" her husband replied with a smile as he turned a page, but not lifting his face from his book. "Well, talking to oneself is the sovereign guard against madness."

"I thought it worked the other way," Jane said.

"No," Gott informed her.

Jane wondered what she should draw and saw she had very faintly sketched on a small scale the outlines of a child, done in sticks-and-blobs like Paul Klee or kindergarten art. She could do another "Children's Clubhouse," she supposed, but where should she put it this time?

The old electric clock with brass fittings that stood on the mantel began to wheeze shrilly, "Mystery, mystery, mystery, mystery." It struck Jane as a good omen for her picture. She smiled.

Gott took a slow pull from his goblet and felt the scentless vodka bite just enough and his skin shiver and the room waver pleasantly for a moment with shadows chasing across it. Then he swung the pupils of his eyes upward and looked across at the Man in the Black Flannel Suit, noting with approval that he was sitting rigidly on the sofa. Gott conducted his side of the following conversation without making a sound or parting his lips more than a quarter of an inch, just flaring his nostrils from time to time.

BLACK FLANNEL: Now if I may have your attention for a space, Mr. Adler—

GOTT: Speak when you're spoken to! Remember, I created you.

BLACK FLANNEL: I respect your belief. Have you been getting any messages?

GOTT: The number 6669 turned up three times today in orders and estimates. I received an airmail advertisement beginning "Are you ready for big success?" though the rest of the ad didn't signify. As I opened the envelope the minute hand of my desk clock was pointing at the faceless statue of Mercury on the Commerce Building. When I was leaving the office my secretary droned at me, "A representative of the Inner Circle will call on you tonight," though when I questioned her, she claimed that she'd said, "Was the letter to Innes-Burkel and Company all right?" Because she is aware of my deafness, I could hardly challenge her. In any case she sounded sincere. If those were messages from the Inner Circle, I received them. But seriously I doubt the existence of that clandestine organization. Other explanations seem to me more likely—for instance, that I am developing a psychosis. I do not believe in the Inner Circle.

BLACK FLANNEL (smiling shrewdly—his features have grown tightly handsome though his complexion is still putty gray): Psychosis is for weak minds. Look, Mr. Adler, you believe in the Mafia, the FBI, and the Communist Underground. You believe in upper-echelon control groups in unions and business and fraternal organizations. You know the workings of big companies. You are familiar with industrial and political espionage. You are not wholly unacquainted with the secret fellowships of munitions manufacturers, financiers, dope addicts and procurers and pornography connoisseurs and the brotherhoods and sisterhoods of sexual deviates and enthusiasts. Why do you boggle at the Inner Circle?

GOTT (coolly): I do not wholly believe in all of those other organizations. And the Inner Circle still seems to me more of a wish-dream than the rest. Besides, you may want me to believe in the Inner Circle in order at a later date to convict me of insanity.

BLACK FLANNEL (drawing a black briefcase from behind his legs and unzipping it on his knees): Then you do not wish to hear about the Inner Circle?

GOTT (inscrutably): I will listen for the present. Hush!

Heinie was calling out excitedly, "I'm in the stars, Papa! They're so close they burn!" He said nothing more and continued to stare straight ahead.

"Don't touch them," Jane warned without looking around. Her pencil made a few faint five-pointed stars. The Children's Clubhouse would be on a boundary of space, she decided—put it in a tree on the edge of the Old Ravine. She said, "Gott, what do you suppose Heinie sees out there besides stars?"

"Bug-eyed angels, probably," her husband answered, smiling again but still not taking his head out of his book.

BLACK FLANNEL (consulting a sheet of crackling black paper he has slipped from his briefcase, though as far as Gott can see there is no printing, typing, writing, or symbols of any sort in any color ink on the black bond):

The Inner Circle is the world's secret elite, operating behind and above all figureheads, workhorses, wealthy dolts, and those talented exhibitionists we name genius. The Inner Circle has existed *sub rose niger* for thousands of years. It controls human life. It is the repository of all great abilities, and the key to all ultimate delights.

GOTT *(tolerantly)*: You make it sound plausible enough. Everyone half believes in such a cryptic power gang, going back to Sumeria.

BLACK FLANNEL: The membership is small and very select. As you are aware, I am a kind of talent scout for the group. Qualifications for admission *(he slips a second sheet of black bond from his briefcase)* include a proven great skill in achieving and wielding power over men and women, an amoral zest for all of life, a seasoned blend of ruthlessness and reliability, plus wide knowledge and lightning wit.

GOTT *(contemptuously)*: Is that all?

BLACK FLANNEL *(flatly)*: Yes. Initiation is binding for life—and for the afterlife: one of our mottos is Ferdinand's dying cry in *The Duchess of Malfi*. "I will vault credit and affect high pleasures after death." The penalty for revealing organizational secrets is not death alone but extinction—all memory of the person is erased from public and private history; his name is removed from records; all knowledge of and feeling for him is deleted from the minds of his wives, mistresses, and children: it is as if he had never existed. That, by the by, is a good example of the powers of the Inner Circle. It may interest you to know, Mr. Adler, that as a result of the retaliatory activities of the Inner Circle, the names of three British kings have been expunged from history. Those who have suffered a like fate include two popes, seven movie stars, a brilliant Flemish artist superior to Rembrandt... *(As he spins out an apparently interminable listing, the Fifth Person creeps in on hands and knees from the kitchen. Gott cannot see him at first, as the sofa is between Gott's chair and the kitchen door. The Fifth Person is the Black Jester, who looks rather like a caricature of Gott but has the same putty complexion as the Man in the Black Flannel Suit. The Black Jester wears skin-tight clothing of that color, silver-embroidered boots and gloves, and a black hood edged with silver bells that do not tinkle. He carries a scepter topped with a small death's-head that wears a black hood like his own edged with tinier silver bells, soundless as the larger ones.)*

THE BLACK JESTER *(suddenly rearing up like a cobra from behind the sofa and speaking to the Man in the Black Flannel Suit over the latter's shoulder)*: Ho! So you're still teasing his rickety hopes with that shit about the Inner Circle? Good sport, brother!—you play your fish skillfully.

GOTT *(immensely startled, but controlling himself with some courage)*: Who are you? How dare you bring your brabblement into my court?

THE BLACK JESTER: Listen to the old cock crow innocent! As if he didn't know he'd himself created both of us, time and again, to stave off boredom, madness, or suicide.

GOTT *(firmly):* I never created *you.*

THE BLACK JESTER: Oh, yes, you did, old cock. Truly your mind has never birthed anything but twins—for every good, a bad; for every breath, a fart; and for every white, a black.

GOTT *(flares his nostrils and glares a death-spell which hums toward the newcomer like a lazy invisible bee).*

THE BLACK JESTER *(pales and staggers backward as the death-spell strikes, but shakes it off with an effort and glares back murderously at Gott):* Old cock-father, I'm beginning to hate you at last.

Just then the refrigerator motor went on in the kitchen, and its loud rapid rocking sound seemed to Jane to be a voice saying, "Watch your children, they're in danger. Watch your children, they're in danger."

"I'm no ladybug," Jane retorted tartly in her thoughts, irked at the worrisome interruption now that her pencil was rapidly developing the outlines of the Clubhouse in the Tree with the moon risen across the ravine between clouds in the late afternoon sky. Nevertheless she looked at Heinie. He hadn't moved. She could see how the plastic helmet was open at neck and top, but it made her think of suffocation just the same.

"Heinie, are you still in the stars?" she asked.

"No, now I'm landing on a moon," he called back. "Don't talk to me, Mama, I've got to watch the road."

Jane at once wanted to imagine what roads in space might look like, but the refrigerator motor had said "children," not "child," and she knew that the language of machinery is studded with tropes. She looked at Gott. He was curled comfortably over his book, and as she watched, he turned a page and touched his lips to the martini water. Nevertheless, she decided to test him.

"Gott, do you think this family is getting too ingrown?" she said. "We used to have more people around."

"Oh, I think we have quite a few as it is," he replied, looking up at the empty sofa, beyond it, and then around at her expectantly, as if ready to join in any conversation she cared to start. But she simply smiled at him and returned relieved to her thoughts and her picture. He smiled back and bowed his head again to his book.

BLACK FLANNEL *(ignoring the Black Jester):* My chief purpose in coming here tonight, Mr. Adler, is to inform you that the Inner Circle has begun a serious study of your qualifications for membership.

THE BLACK JESTER: At *his* age? After *his* failures? Now we curtsy forward toward the Big Lie!

BLACK FLANNEL (*in a pained voice*): Really! (*Then once more to Gott*) Point One: you have gained for yourself the reputation of a man of strong patriotism, deep company loyalty, and realistic self-interest, sternly contemptuous of all youthful idealism and rebelliousness. Point Two: you have cultivated constructive hatreds in your business life, deliberately knifing colleagues when you could, but allying yourself to those on the rise. Point Three and most important: you have gone some distance toward creating the master illusion of a man who has secret sources of information, secret new techniques for thinking more swiftly and acting more decisively than others, secret superior connections and contacts—in short, a dark new strength which all others envy even as they cringe from it.

THE BLACK JESTER (*in a kind of counterpoint as he advances around the sofa*): But he's come down in the world since he lost his big job. National Motors was at least a step in the right direction, but Hagbolt-Vincent has no company planes, no company apartments, no company shooting lodges, no company call girls! Besides, he drinks too much. The Inner Circle is not for drunks on the downgrade.

BLACK FLANNEL: Please! You're spoiling things.

THE BLACK JESTER: *He's* spoiled. (*Closing in on Gott.*) Just look at him now. Eyes that need crutches for near and far. Ears that mishear the simplest remark.

GOTT: Keep off me, I tell you.

THE BLACK JESTER (*ignoring the warning*): Fat belly, flaccid sex, swollen ankles. And a mouthful of stinking cavities!—did you know he hasn't dared visit his dentist for five years? Here, open up and show them! (*Thrusts black-gloved hand toward Gott's face.*)

Gott, provoked beyond endurance, snarled aloud, "Keep off, damn you!" and shot out the heavy book in his left hand and snapped it shut on the Black Jester's nose. Both black figures collapsed instantly.

Jane lifted her pencil a foot from the pad, turned quickly, and demanded, "My God, Gott, what was that?"

"Only a winter fly, my dear," he told her soothingly. "One of the fat ones that hide in December and breed all the black clouds of spring." He found his place in Plutarch and dipped his face close to study both pages and the trough between them. He looked around slyly at Jane and said, "I didn't squish her."

The chair in the spaceship rutched. Jane asked, "What is it, Heinie?"

"A meteor exploded, Mama. I'm all right. I'm out in space again, in the middle of the road."

Jane was impressed by the time it had taken the sound of Gott's book clapping shut to reach the spaceship. She began lightly to sketch blob-children in swings hanging from high limbs in the Tree, swinging far out over the ravine into the stars.

Gott took a pull of martini water, but he felt lonely and impotent. He peeped over the edge of his Plutarch at the darkness below the sofa and grinned with new hope as he saw the huge flat blob of black putty the Jester and Flannel had collapsed into. *I'm on a black kick,* he thought, *why black?*—choosing to forget that he had first started to sculpt figures of the imagination from the star-specked blackness that pulsed under his eyelids while he lay in the dark abed: tiny black heads like wrinkled peas on which any three points of light made two eyes and a mouth. He'd come a long way since then. Now with strong rays from his eyes he rolled all the black putty he could see into a woman-long bolster and hoisted it onto the sofa. The bolster helped with blind sensuous hitching movements, especially where it bent at the middle. When it was lying full length on the sofa he began with cruel strength to sculpt it into the figure of a high-breasted exaggeratedly sexual girl.

Jane found she'd sketched some flies into the picture, buzzing around the swingers. She rubbed them out and put in more stars instead. But there would be flies in the ravine, she told herself, because people dumped garbage down the other side; so she drew one large fly in the lower left-hand corner of the picture. He could be the observer. She said to herself firmly, *No black clouds of spring in this picture* and changed them to hints of Roads in Space.

Gott finished the Black Girl with two twisting tweaks to point her nipples. Her waist was barely thick enough not to suggest an actual wasp or a giant amazon ant. Then he gulped martini water and leaned forward just a little and silently but very strongly blew the breath of life into her across the eight feet of living-room air between them.

The phrase "black clouds of spring" made Jane think of dead hopes and drowned talents. She said out loud, "I wish you'd start writing in the evenings again, Gott. Then I wouldn't feel so guilty."

"These days, my dear, I'm just a dull businessman, happy to relax in the heart of his family. There's not an atom of art in me," Gott informed her with quiet conviction, watching the Black Girl quiver and writhe as the creativity-wind from his lips hit her. With a sharp twinge of fear it occurred to him that the edges of the wind might leak over to Jane and Heinie, distorting them like heat shimmers, changing them nastily. Heinie especially was sitting so still in his little chair light-years away. Gott wanted to call to him, but he couldn't think of the right bit of spaceman's lingo.

THE BLACK GIRL (*sitting up and dropping her hand coquettishly to her crotch):* He-he! Now ain't this something, Mr. Adler! First time you've ever had me in your home.

GOTT *(eyeing her savagely over Plutarch):* Shut up!

THE BLACK GIRL *(unperturbed):* Before this it was only when you were away on trips or, once or twice lately, at the office.

GOTT *(flaring his nostrils):* Shut up, I say! You're less than dirt.

THE BLACK GIRL *(smirking):* But I'm interesting dirt, ain't I? You want we should do it in front of her? I could come over and flow inside your clothes and—

GOTT: One more word and I uncreate you! I'll tear you apart like a boiled crow. I'll squunch you back to putty.

THE BLACK GIRL *(still serene, preening her nakedness):* Yes, and you'll enjoy every red-hot second of it, won't you?

Affronted beyond bearing, Gott sent chopping rays at her over the Plutarch parapet, but at that instant a black figure, thin as a spider, shot up behind the sofa and reaching over the Black Girl's shoulder brushed aside the chopping rays with one flick of a whiplike arm. Grown from the black putty Gott had overlooked under the sofa, the figure was that of an old conjure woman, stick-thin with limbs like wires and breasts like dangling ropes, face that was a pack of spearheads with black ostrich plumes a-quiver above it.

THE BLACK CRONE *(in a whistling voice like a hungry wind):* Injure one of the girls, Mr. Adler, and I'll castrate you, I'll shrivel you with spells. You'll never be able to call them up again, no matter how far a trip you go on, or even pleasure your wife.

GOTT *(frightened, but not showing it):* Keep your arms and legs on, Mother. Flossie and I were only teasing each other. Vicious play is a specialty of your house, isn't it?

With a deep groaning cry the furnace fan switched on in the basement and began to say over and over again in a low rapid rumble, "Oh, my God, my God, my God. Demons, demons, demons, demons." Jane heard the warning very clearly, but she didn't want to lose the glow of her feelings. She asked, "Are you all right out there in space, Heinie?" and thought he nodded "Yes." She began to color the Clubhouse in the Tree—blue roof, red walls, a little like Chagall.

THE BLACK CRONE *(continuing a tirade):* Understand this, Mr. Adler, you don't own us, we own you. Because you gotta have the girls to live, you're the girls' slave.

THE BLACK GIRL: He-he! Shall I call Susie and Belle? They've never been here either, and they'd enjoy this.

THE BLACK CRONE: Later, if he's humble. You understand me, Slave?

If I tell you have your wife cook dinner for the girls or wash their feet or watch you snuggle with them, then you gotta do it. And your boy gotta run our errands. Come over here now and sit by Flossie while I brand you with dry ice.

Gott quaked, for the Crone's arms were lengthening toward him like snakes, and he began to sweat, and he murmured, "God in Heaven," and the smell of fear went out of him to the walls—millions of thinking molecules.

A cold wind blew over the fence of Heinie's space road and the stars wavered and then fled before it like diamond leaves.

Jane caught the murmur and the fear-whiff too, but she was coloring the Clubhouse windows a warm rich yellow; so what she said in a rather loud, rapt, happy voice was: "I think Heaven is like a children's clubhouse. The only people there are the ones you remember from childhood—either because you were in childhood with them or they told you about their childhood honestly. The *real* people."

At the word *real* the Black Crone and the Black Girl strangled and began to bend and melt like a thin candle and a thicker one over a roaring fire.

Heinie turned his spaceship around and began to drive it bravely homeward through the unspeckled dark, following the ghostly white line that marked the center of the road. He thought of himself as the cat they'd had. Papa had told him stories of the cat coming back—from downtown, from Pittsburgh, from Los Angeles, from the moon. Cats could do that. He was the cat coming back.

Jane put down her brush and took up her pencil once more. She'd noticed that the two children swinging out farthest weren't attached yet to their swings. She started to hook them up, then hesitated. Wasn't it all right for some of the children to go sailing out to the stars? Wouldn't it be nice for some evening world—maybe the late-afternoon moon—to have a shower of babies? She wished a plane would crawl over the roof of the house and drone out an answer to her question. She didn't like to have to do all the wondering by herself. It made her feel guilty.

"Gott," she said, "why don't you at least finish the last story you were writing? The one about the Elephants' Graveyard." Then she wished she hadn't mentioned it, because it was an idea that had scared Heinie.

"Someday," her husband murmured, Jane thought.

Gott felt weak with relief, though he was forgetting why. Balancing his head carefully over his book, he drained the next to the last of the martini water. It always got stronger toward the bottom. He looked at the page through the lower halves of his executive bifocals and for a moment the word "Caesar" came up in letters an inch high, each jet serif showing its tatters and the white paper its ridgy fibers. Then, still never moving his head, he looked through the upper halves and saw the long thick blob of dull black putty on the wavering blue couch and automatically gathered the putty together and with thumb-and-palm rays swiftly shaped the Old Philosopher in the Black Toga, always an easy figure to sculpt since he was never finished, but rough-hewn in the style of Rodin or Daumier. It was always good to finish up an evening with the Old Philosopher.

The white line in space tried to fade. Heinie steered his ship closer to it. He remembered that in spite of Papa's stories, the cat had never come back.

Jane held her pencil poised over the detached children swinging out from the Clubhouse. One of them had a leg kicked over the moon.

THE PHILOSOPHER (*adjusting his craggy toga and yawning*): The topic for tonight's symposium is that vast container of all, the Void.

GOTT (*condescendingly*): The Void? That's interesting. Lately I've wished to merge with it. Life wearies me.

A smiling dull black skull, as crudely shaped as the Philosopher, looked over the latter's shoulder and then rose higher on a rickety black bone framework.

DEATH (*quietly, to Gott*): Really?

GOTT (*greatly shaken, but keeping up a front*): I *am* on a black kick tonight. Can't even do a white skeleton. Disintegrate, you two. You bore me almost as much as life.

DEATH: Really? If you did not cling to life like a limpet, you would have crashed your car, to give your wife and son the insurance, when National Motors fired you. You planned to do that. Remember?

GOTT (*with hysterical coolness*): Maybe I should have cast you in brass or aluminum. Then you'd at least have brightened things up. But it's too late now. Disintegrate quickly and don't leave any scraps around.

DEATH: Much too late. Yes, you planned to crash your car and doubly indemnify your dear ones. You had the spot picked, but your courage failed you.

GOTT (*blustering*): I'll have you know I am not only Gottfried but also Helmuth—Hell's Courage Adler!

THE PHILOSOPHER (*confused but trying to keep in the conversation*): A most swashbuckling sobriquet.

DEATH: Hell's courage failed you on the edge of the ravine. (*Pointing at Gott a three-fingered thumbless hand like a black winter branch.*) Do you wish to die now?

GOTT (*blacking out visually*): Cowards die many times. (*Draining the last of the martini water in absolute darkness.*) The valiant taste death once. Caesar.

DEATH (*a voice in darkness*): Coward. Yet you summoned me and even though you fashioned me poorly, I am indeed Death—and there are others besides yourself who take long trips. Even longer ones. Trips in the Void.

THE PHILOSOPHER (*another voice*): Ah, yes, the Void. Imprimis—

DEATH: Silence.

In the great obedient silence Gott heard the unhurried click of Death's feet as he stepped from behind the sofa across the bare floor toward Heinie's spaceship. Gott reached up in the dark and clung to his hand.

Jane heard the slow clicks too. They were the kitchen clock ticking out, "Now. Now. Now. Now. Now."

Suddenly Heinie called out, "The line's gone. Papa, Mama, I'm lost."

Jane said sharply, "No, you're not, Heinie. Come out of space at once."

"I'm not in space now. I'm in the Cats' Graveyard."

Jane told herself it was insane to feel suddenly so frightened. "Come back from wherever you are, Heinie," she said calmly. "It's time for bed."

"I'm lost, Papa," Heinie cried. "I can't hear Mama any more."

"Listen to your mother, Son," Gott said thickly, groping in the blackness for other words.

"All the Mamas and Papas in the world are dying," Heinie wailed.

Then the words came to Gott, and when he spoke his voice flowed. "Are your atomic generators turning over, Heinie? Is your space-warp lever free?"

"Yes, Papa, but the line's gone."

"Forget it. I've got a fix on you through subspace and I'll coach you home. Swing her two units to the right and three up. Fire when I give the signal. Are you ready?"

"Yes, Papa."

"Roger. Three, two, one, fire and away! Dodge that comet! Swing left around that planet! Never mind the big dust cloud! Home on the third beacon. Now! Now! Now!"

Gott had dropped his Plutarch and come lurching blindly across the room, and as he uttered the last *Now!* the darkness cleared, and he caught Heinie up from his space-chair and staggered with him against Jane and steadied himself there without upsetting her paints, and she accused him laughingly, "You beefed up the martini water again," and Heinie pulled off his helmet and crowed, "Make a big hug," and they clung to each other and looked down at the half-colored picture where a children's clubhouse sat in a tree over a deep ravine and blob children swung out from it against the cool pearly moon and the winding roads in space and the next to the last child hooked onto his swing with one hand and with the other caught the last child of all, while from the picture's lower left-hand corner a fat, black fly looked on enviously.

Searching with his eyes as the room swung toward equilibrium, Gottfried Helmuth Adler saw Death peering at him through the crack between the hinges of the open kitchen door.

Laboriously, half passing out again, Gott sneered his face at him.

AMERICA THE BEAUTIFUL

I AM RETURNING TO ENGLAND. I am shorthanding this, July 5, 2000, aboard the Dallas-London rocket as it arches silently out of the diffused violet daylight of the stratosphere into the eternally star-spangled purpling night of the ionosphere.

I have refused the semester instructorship in poetry at UTD, which would have munificently padded my honorarium for delivering the Lanier Lectures and made me for four months second only to the Poet in Residence.

And I am almost certain that I have lost Emily, although we plan to meet in London in a fortnight if she can wangle the stopover on her way to take up her Peace Corps command in Niger.

I am not leaving America because of the threat of a big war. I believe that this new threat, like all the rest, is only another move, even if a long and menacing queen's move, in the game of world politics, while the little wars go endlessly on in Chad, Czechoslovakia, Sumatra, Siam, Baluchistan, and Bolivia as America and the Communist League firm their power boundaries.

And I am certainly not leaving America because of any harassment as a satellitic neutral and possible spy. There may have been surveillance of my actions and lectures, but if so it was as impalpable as the checks they must have made on me in England before granting me visiting clearance. The U.S. intelligence agencies have become almost incredibly deft in handling such things. And I was entertained in America more than royally—I was made to feel at home by a family with a great talent for just that.

No, I am leaving because of the shadows. The shadows everywhere in America, but which I saw most clearly in Professor Grissim's serene and lovely home. The shadows which would irresistibly have gathered behind my instructor's lectern, precisely as I was learning to dress with an even trimmer and darker reserve while I was a guest at the Grissims' and even to shower more frequently. The shadows which revealed themselves to me deepest of all around Emily Grissim, and which I could do nothing to dispel.

I think that you, or at least I, can see the shadows in America more readily these days because of the very clean air there. Judging only from what I saw with my own eyes in Texas, the Americans have completely licked their smog problem. Their gently curving freeways purr with fast electric cars, like sleek and disciplined silver cats. Almost half the nation's power comes from atomic reactors, while the remaining coal-burning plants loose back into the air at most a slight shimmer of heat. Even the streams and rivers run blue and unsmirched again, while marine life is returning to the eastern Great Lakes. In brief, America is beautiful, for with the cleanliness, now greater than that of the Dutch, has come a refinement in taste, so that all buildings are gracefully shaped and disposed, while advertisements, though molding minds more surely than ever, are restrained and almost finically inoffensive.

The purity of the atmosphere was strikingly brought to my notice when I debarked at Dallas rocketport and found the Grissims waiting for me outdoors, downwind of the landing area. They made a striking group, all of them tall, as they stood poised yet familiarly together: the professor with his grizzled hair still close-trimmed in military fashion, for he had served almost as long as a line officer and in space services as he had now as a university physicist; his slim, white-haired wife; Emily, like her mother in the classic high-waisted, long-skirted Directoire style currently fashionable; and her brother Jack, in his dress pale grays with sergeant's stripes, on furlough from Siam.

Their subdued dress and easy attitudes reminded me of a patrician Roman's toga dropping in precise though seemingly accidental folds. The outworn cliché about America being Rome to England's Greece came irritatingly to my mind.

Introductions were made by the professor, who had met my father at Oxford and later seen much of him during the occupation of Britain throughout the Three Years' Alert. I was surprised to find their diction almost the same as my own. We strolled to their electric station wagon, the doors of which opened silently at our approach.

I should have been pleased by the simple beauty of the Grissims, as by that of the suburban landscape through which we now sped, especially since my poetry is that of the Romantic Revival, which looks back to Keats and Shelley more even than to Shakespeare. Instead, it rubbed me the wrong way. I became uneasy and within ten minutes found myself beginning to talk bawdy and make nasty little digs at America.

They accepted my rudeness in such an unshocked, urbane fashion, demonstrating that they understood though did not always agree with me, and they went to such trouble to assure me that not all America was like this, there were still many ugly stretches, that I soon felt myself a fool and shut up. It was I who was the crass Roman, I told myself, or even barbarian.

Thereafter Emily and her mother kept the conversation going easily and soon coaxed me back into it, with the effect of smoothing the grumbling and owlish young British poet's ruffled feathers.

The modest one story, shaded by slow-shedding silvery eucalyptus and mutated chaparral, which was all that showed of the Grissim home, opened to receive our fumeless vehicle. I was accompanied to my bedroom-and-study, served refreshments, and left there to polish up my first lecture. The scene in the view window was so faithfully transmitted from the pickup above, the air fresher if possible than that outdoors, that I found it hard to keep in mind I was well underground.

It was at dinner that evening, when my hosts made such a nicely concerted effort to soothe my nervousness over my initial lecture, and largely succeeded, that I first began truly to like and even respect the Grissims.

It was at the same instant, in that pearly dining room, that I first became aware of the shadows around them.

Physical shadows? Hardly, though at times they really seemed that. I recall thinking, my mind still chiefly on my lecture, something like, *These good people are so wedded to the way of war, the perpetual little wars and the threat of the big one, and have been so successful in masking the signs of its strains in themselves, that they have almost forgotten that those strains are there. And they love their home and country, and the security of their taut way of life, so deeply that they have become unaware of the depth of that devotion.*

My lecture went off well that night. The audience was large, respectful, and seemingly even attentive. The number of African and Mexican faces gave the lie to what I'd been told about integration being a sham in America. I should have been pleased, and I temporarily was, at the long, mutedly drumming applause I was given and at the many intelligent, flattering comments I received afterward. And I should have stopped seeing the shadows then, but I didn't.

Next morning Emily toured me around city and countryside on a long silvery scooter, I riding pillion behind her. I remember the easy though faintly formal way in which she drew my arms around her waist and laid her hand for a moment on one of mine, meanwhile smiling cryptically overshoulder. Besides that smile, I remember a charming Spanish-American graveyard in pastel stucco, the towering Kennedy shrine, the bubbling, iridescent tubes of algae farming converging toward the horizon, and rockets taking off in the distance with their bright, smokeless exhausts. Emily was almost as unaffected as a British girl and infinitely more competent, in a grand style. That one day the shadows vanished altogether.

They returned at evening when after dinner we gathered in the living room for our first wholly unhurried and relaxed conversation, my lectures being spaced out in a leisurely—to Americans, not to me—one day in two schedule.

We sat in a comfortable arc before the wide fireplace, where resinous woods burned yellow and orange. Occasionally Jack would put on another log. From time to time, a light shower of soot dropped back from the precipitron in the chimney, the tiny particles as they fell flaring into brief white points of light, like stars.

A little to my surprise, the Grissims drank as heavily as the English, though they carried their liquor very well. Emily was the exception to this family pattern, contenting herself with a little sherry and three long, slim reefers, which she drew from an elegant foil package covered with gold script and Lissajous curves, and which she inhaled sippingly, her lips rapidly shuddering with a very faint, low, trilling sound.

Professor Grissim set the pattern by deprecating the reasons for America's domestic achievements, which I had led off by admitting were far greater than I'd expected. They weren't due to any peculiar American drive, he said, and certainly not to any superior moral fiber, but simply to technology and computerized civilization given their full head and unstinting support. The powerful sweep of those two almost mathematical forces had automatically solved such problems as overpopulation, by effortless and aesthetic contraception, and stagnant or warped brain potential, by unlimited semiautomated education and psychiatry—just as on a smaller scale the drug problem had largely been resolved by the legalization of marijuana and peyote, following the simple principle of restricting only the sale of quickly addictive chemicals and those provably damaging to nervous tissue— "Control the poisons, but let each person learn to control his intoxicants, especially now that we have metabolic rectifiers for the congenitally alcoholic."

I was also told that American extremism, both of the right and left, which had seemed such a big thing in mid-century, had largely withered away or at least been muted by the great surge of the same forces which were making America ever more beautiful and prosperous. Cities were no longer warrens of discontent. Peace marches and Minutemen rallies alike, culminating in the late sixties, had thereafter steadily declined.

While impressed, I did not fall into line, but tried to point out some black holes in this glowing picture. Indeed, feeling at home with the Grissims now and having learned that nothing I could say would shock them into anger and confusion, I was able to be myself fully and to reveal frankly my anti-American ideas, though of course more politely and, I hoped, more tellingly than yesterday—it seemed an age ago—driving from the rocketport.

In particular, I argued that many or most Americans were motivated by a subtle, even sophisticated puritanism, which made them feel that the world was not safe unless they were its moral arbiters, and that this puritanism was ultimately based on the same swollen concern about property and money—industry, in its moral sense—that one found in the Swiss and Scottish Presbyterians and most of the early Protestants.

"You're puritans with a great deal of style and restraint and wide vision," I said. "Yet you're puritans just the same, even though your puritanism is light-years away from that of the Massachusetts theocrats and the harsh rule Calvin tried to impose on Geneva. In fact," I added incautiously, "your puritanism is not so much North European as Roman."

Smiles crinkled briefly at that and I kicked myself for having myself introduced into the conversation that hackneyed comparison.

At this point Emily animatedly yet coolly took up the argument for America, pointing out the nation's growing tolerance and aestheticism, historically distinguishing Puritanism from Calvinism, and also reminding me that the Chinese and Russians were far more puritanical than any other peoples on the globe—and not in a sophisticated or subtle way either.

I fought back, as by citing the different impression I'd got of the Russians during my visits in the Soviet Union and by relaying the reports of close colleagues who had spent time in China. But on the whole Emily had the best of me. And this was only partly due to the fact that the longer I sparred with her verbally, the less concerned I became to win my argument, and the more to break her calm and elicit some sharp emotional reaction from her, to see that pale skin flush, to make those reefer-serene eyes blaze with anger. But I wasn't successful there either.

At one point Jack came to her aid, mildly demonstrating for American broad-mindedness by describing to us some of the pleasure cities of southern Asia he'd visited on R&R.

"Bangkok's a dismal place now, of course," he began by admitting, "with the Com-g'rillas raiding up to and even into it, and full of fenced-off bombed and booby-trapped areas. Very much like the old descriptions of Saigon in the sixties. As you walk down the potholed streets, you listen for the insect hum of a wandering antipersonnel missile seeking human heat, or the faint flap-flap of an infiltrator coming down on a whirligig parachute. You brace your thoughts against the psychedelic strike of a mind-bomb. Out of the black alley ahead there may charge a fifty-foot steel centipede, the remote-controlled sort we use for jungle fighting, captured by the enemy and jiggered to renegade.

"But most of old Bangkok's attractive features—and the entrepreneurs and girls and other entertainers that go with them—have been transferred en masse to Kandy and Trincomalee in Ceylon." And he went on to describe the gaily orgiastic lounges and bars, the fresh pastel colors, the spicy foods and subtly potent drinks, the clean little laughing harlots supporting their families well during the ten years of their working life between fifteen and twenty-five, the gilded temples, the slim dancers with movements stylized as their black eyebrows, the priests robed in orange and yellow.

I tried to fault him in my mind for being patronizing, but without much success.

"Buddhism's an attractive way of life," he finished, "except that it doesn't know how to wage war. But if you're looking only for nirvana, I guess you don't need to know that." For an instant his tough face grew bleak, as if he could do with a spot of nirvana himself, and the shadows gathered around him and the others more thickly.

During the following off-lecture evenings we kept up our fireplace talks and Emily and I returned more than once to our debate over puritanism, while the rest listened to us with faint, benevolent smiles, that at times seemed almost knowing. She regularly defeated me.

Then on the sixth night she delivered her crowning argument, or celebrated her victory, or perhaps merely followed an impulse. I had just settled myself in bed when the indirect lightning of my "doorbell" flooded the room with brief flashes, coming at three-second intervals, of a rather ghastly white light. Blinking, I fumbled on the bedside table for the remote control of the room's appliances, including tri-V and door, and thumbed the button for the latter.

The door moved aside and there, silhouetted against the faint glow of the hall, was the dark figure of Emily, like a living shadow. She kept her finger, however, on the button long enough for two more silent flashes to illuminate her briefly. She was wearing a narrow kimono—Jack's newest gift, she later told me—and her platinum hair, combed straight down like an unrippling waterfall, almost exactly matched the silvery, pale gray silk. Without quite overdoing it, she had made up her face somewhat like a temple dancer's—pale powder, almost white; narrow slanting brows, almost black; green eye-shadow with a pinch of silvery glitter; and the not-quite-jarring sensual note of crimson lips.

She did not come into my room, but after a pause during which I sat up jerkily and she became again a shadow, she beckoned to me.

I snatched up my dressing gown and followed her as she moved noiselessly down the hall. My throat was dry and constricted, my heart was pounding a little, with apprehension as well as excitement. I realized that despite my near week with the Grissims, a part of my mind was still thinking of the professor and his wife as a strait-laced colonel and his lady from a century ago, when so many retired army officers lived in villas around San Antonio, as they do now too around the Dallas-Ft. Worth metropolitan area.

Emily's bedroom was not the austere silver cell or self-shrine I had sometimes imagined, especially when she was scoring a point against me, but an almost cluttered museum-workshop of present interests and personal memorabilia. She'd even kept her kindergarten study-machine, her first CO^2 pistol, and a hockey stick, along with mementos from her college days and her Peace Corps tours. But those I noticed much later. Now pale golden light from a rising full moon, coming through the great view window, brimmed the room. I had just enough of my wits left to recall that the real moon was new, so that this must be a tape of some past night. I never even thought of the Communist and American forts up there, with their bombs earmarked for Earth. Then, standing straight and tall and looking me full in the eyes, like some Amazonian athlete, or Phryne before her judges, Emily let her kimono glide down from her shoulders.

In the act of love she was energetic, but tender. No, the word is courteous, I think. I very happily shed a week of tensions and uncertainties and self-inflicted humiliations.

"You still think I'm a puritan, don't you?" she softly asked me afterward, smiling at me sideways with the smeared remains of her crimson mouth, her gray eyes enigmatic blurs of shadow.

"Yes, I do," I told her forthrightly. "The puritan playing the hetaera, but still the puritan."

She answered lazily, "I think you like to play the Hun raping the vestal virgin."

That made me talk dirty to her. She listened attentively—almost famishedly, I thought, for a bit—but her final comment was "You do that very well, dear," just before using her lips to stop mine, which would otherwise have sulphurously cursed her insufferable poise.

Next morning I started to write a poem about her but got lost in analysis and speculation. Tried too soon, I thought.

Although they were as gracious and friendly as ever, I got the impression that the other Grissims had quickly become aware of the change in Emily's and my relationship. Perhaps it was that they showed a slight extra fondness toward me. I don't know how they guessed—Emily was as cool as always in front of them, while I kept trying to play myself, as before. Perhaps it was that the argument about puritanism was never resumed.

Two evenings afterward the talk came around to Jack's and Emily's elder brother Jeff, who had fallen during the Great Retreat from Jammu and Kashmir to Baluchistan. It was mentioned that during his last furlough they had been putting up an exchange instructor from Yugoslavia, a highly talented young sculptress. I gathered that she and Jeff had been quite close.

"I'm glad Jeff knew her love," Emily's mother said calmly, a tear behind her voice, though not on her cheeks. "I'm very glad he had that." The professor unobtrusively put his hand on hers.

I fancied that this remark was directed at me and was her way of giving her blessing to Emily's and my affair. I was touched and at the same time irritated—and also irritated at myself for feeling irritated. Her remark had brought back the shadows, which darkened further when Jack said a touch grimly and for once with a soldier's callousness, though grinning at me to remove any possible offense, "Remember not to board any more lady artists or professors, Mother, at least when I'm on leave. Bad luck."

By now I was distinctly bothered by my poetry block. The last lectures were going swimmingly and I ought to have been feeling creative, but I wasn't. Or rather, I was feeling creative but I couldn't create. I had also begun to notice the way I was fitting myself to the Grissim family—muting myself, despite all the easiness among us. I couldn't help wondering if there weren't a connection between the two things. I had received the instructorship offer, but was delaying my final answer.

After we made love together that night—under a sinking crescent moon, the real night this time, repeated from above—I told Emily about my first trouble only. She pressed my hand. "Never stop writing poetry, dear," she said. "America needs poetry. This family—"

That broken sentence was as close as we ever got to talking about marriage. Emily immediately recovered herself with an uncharacteristically ribald "Cheer up. I don't even charge a poem for admission."

Instead of responding to that cue, I worried my subject. "I should be able to write poetry here," I said. "America is beautiful, the great golden apple of the Hesperides, hanging in the west like the setting sun. But there's a worm in the core of that apple, a great scaly black dragon."

When Emily didn't ask a question, I went on, "I remember an advertisement. 'Join all your little debts into one big debt.' Of course, they didn't put it so baldly, they made it sound wonderful. But you Americans are like that. You've collected all your angers into one big anger. You've removed your angers from things at home—where you seem to have solved your problems very well, I must admit—and directed those angers at the Communist League. Or instead of angers, I could say fears. Same thing."

Emily still didn't comment, so I continued, "Take the basic neurotic.

He sets up a program of perfection for himself—a thousand obligations, a thousand ambitions. As long as he works his program, fulfilling those obligations and ambitions, he does very well. In fact, he's apt to seem like a genius of achievement to those around him, as America does to me. But there's one big problem he always keeps out of his program and buries deep in his unconscious—the question of who he really is and what he really wants—and in the end it always throws him."

Then at last Emily said, speaking softly at first, "There's something I should tell you, dear. Although I talk a lot of it from the top of my mind, deep down I loathe discussing politics and international relations. As my old colonel used to tell me, 'It doesn't matter much which side you fight on, Emily, so long as you have the courage to stand up and be counted. You pledge your life, your fortune, and your sacred honor, and you live up to that pledge!' And now, dear, I want to sleep."

Crouching on the edge of her bed before returning to my room, and listening to her breathing regularize itself, I thought, "Yes, you're looking for nirvana too. Like Jack." But I didn't wake her to say it, or any of the other things that were boiling up in my brain.

Yet the things I left unsaid must have stayed and worked in my mind, for at our next fireside talk—four pleasant Americans, one Englishman with only one more lecture to go—I found myself launched into a rather long account of the academic Russian family I stayed with while delivering the Pushkin Lectures in Leningrad, where the smog and the minorities problems have been licked too. I stressed the Rosanovs' gentility, their friendliness, the tolerance and sophistication which had replaced the old rigid insistence on *kulturny* behavior, and also the faint melancholy underlying and somehow vitiating all they said. In short, I did everything I knew to underline their similarity to the Grissims. I ended by saying "Professor Grissim, the first night we talked, you said America's achievement had been due almost entirely to the sweep of science, technology, and computerized civilization. The people of the Communist League believe that too—in fact, they made their declaration of faith earlier than America."

"It's very strange," he mused, nodding. "So like, yet so unlike. Almost as if the chemical atoms of the East were subtly different from those of the West. The very electrons—"

"Professor, you don't actually think—"

"Of course not. A metaphor only."

But whatever he thought, I don't believe he felt it only as a metaphor.

Emily said sharply to me, "You left out one more similarity, the most important. That they hate the Enemy with all their hearts and will never trust or understand him."

I couldn't find an honest and complete answer to that, though I tried.

The next day I made one more attempt to turn my feelings into poetry, dark poetry, and I failed. I made my refusal of the instructorship final, confirmed my reservation on the Dallas-London rocket for day after tomorrow, and delivered the last of the Lanier Lectures.

The Fourth of July was a quiet day. Emily took me on a repeat of our first scooter jaunt, but although I relished the wind on my face and our conversation was passably jolly and tender, the magic was gone. I could hardly see America's beauty for the shadows my mind projected on it.

Our fireside conversation that night was as brightly banal. Midway we all went outside to watch the fireworks. It was a starry night, very clear of course, and the fireworks seemed vastly remote—transitory extra starfields of pink and green and amber. Their faint cracks and booms sounded infinitely distant, and needless to say, there was not a ribbon or whiff of chemical smoke. I was reminded of my last night in Leningrad with the Rosanovs after the Pushkin Lectures. We'd all strolled down the Kirovskiy Prospekt to the Bolshaya Neva, and across its glimmering waters watched the Vladivostok mail rocket take off from the Field of Mars up its ringed electric catapult far taller than the Eiffel Tower. That had been on a May Day.

Later that night I went for the first time by myself to Emily's door and pressed its light-button. I was afraid she wouldn't stop by for me and I needed her. She was in a taut and high-strung mood, unwilling to talk in much more than monosyllables, yet unable to keep still, pacing like a restless feline. She wanted to play in the view window the tape of a real battle in Bolivia with the original sounds too, muted down. I vetoed that and we settled for an authentic forest fire recorded in Alaska.

Sex and catastrophe fit. With the wild red light pulsing and flaring in the bedroom, casting huge wild shadows, and with the fire's muted roar and hurricane crackle and explosions filling our ears, we made love with a fierce and desperate urgency that seemed almost—I am eternally grateful for the memory—as if it would last forever. Sex and a psychedelic trip also have their meeting point.

Afterward I slept like a sated tiger. Emily waited until dawn to wake me and shoo me back to my bedroom.

Next day all the Grissims saw me off. As we strolled from the silver station wagon to the landing area, Emily and I dropped a little behind. She stopped, hooked her arms around me, and kissed me with a devouring ferocity. The others walked on, too well-bred ever to look back. The next moment she was her cool self again, sipping a reefer.

Now the rocketship is arching down. The stars are paling. There is a faint whistling as the air molecules of the stratosphere begin to carom off the titanium skin. We had only one flap, midway of freefall section of the trip, when we briefly accelerated and then decelerated to match, perhaps in order to miss a spy satellite or one of the atomic-headed watchdog rockets eternally circling the globe. The direction comes, "Secure seat harnesses."

I just don't know. Maybe I should have gone to America drunk as Dylan Thomas, but purposefully, bellowing my beliefs like the word or the thunderbolts of God. Maybe then I could have fought the shadows. No...

I hope Emily makes it to London. Perhaps there, against a very different background, with shadows of a different sort...

In a few more seconds the great jet will begin to brake, thrusting its hygienic, aseptic exhaust of helium down into the filthy cancerous London smog, and I will be home.

BAZAAR OF THE BIZARRE

THE STRANGE STARS OF THE WORLD OF NEHWON glinted
thickly above the black-roofed city of Lankhmar, where swords clink
almost as often as coins. For once there was no fog.

In the Plaza of Dark Delights, which lies seven blocks south of the Marsh
Gate and extends from the Fountain of Dark Abundance to the Shrine of
the Black Virgin, the shop-lights glinted upward no more brightly than
the stars glinted down. For there the vendors of drugs and the peddlers
of curiosa and the hawkers of assignations light their stalls and crouching
places with foxfire, glowworms, and firepots with tiny single windows, and
they conduct their business almost as silently as the stars conduct theirs.

There are plenty of raucous spots a-glare with torches in nocturnal
Lankhmar, but by immemorial tradition soft whispers and a pleasant
dimness are rule in the Plaza of Dark Delights. Philosophers often go there
solely to meditate, students to dream, and fanatic-eyed theologians to spin
like spiders abstruse new theories of the Devil and of the other dark forces
ruling the universe. And if any of these find a little illicit fun by the way,
their theories and dreams and theologies and demonologies are undoubtedly the better for it.

Tonight, however, there was a glaring exception to the darkness rule.
From a low doorway with a trefoil arch new-struck through an ancient
wall, light spilled into the Plaza. Rising above the horizon of the pavement
like some monstrous moon a-shine with the ray of a murderous sun, the
new doorway dimmed almost to extinction the stars of the other merchants
of mystery.

Eerie and unearthly objects for sale spilled out of the doorway a little way
with the light, while beside the doorway crouched an avid-faced figure clad
in garments never before seen on land or sea... in the World of Nehwon.

He wore a hat like a small red pail, baggy trousers, and outlandish red boots with upturned toes. His eyes were as predatory as a hawk's, but his smile as cynically and lasciviously cajoling as an ancient satyr's.

Now and again he sprang up and pranced about, sweeping and resweeping with a rough long broom the flagstones as if to clean a path for the entry of some fantastic emperor, and he often paused in his dance to bow low and loutingly, but always with upglancing eyes, to the crowd gathering in the darkness across from the doorway and to swing his hand from them toward the interior of the new shop in a gesture of invitation at once servile and sinister.

No one of the crowd had yet plucked up courage to step forward into the glare and enter the shop, or even inspect the rarities set out so carelessly yet temptingly before it. But the number of fascinated peerers increased momently. There were mutterings of censure at the dazzling new method of merchandising—the infraction of the Plaza's custom of darkness—but on the whole the complaints were outweighed by the gasps and murmurings of wonder, admiration, and curiosity kindling ever hotter.

The Gray Mouser slipped into the Plaza at the Fountain end as silently as if he had come to slit a throat or spy on the spies of the Overlord. His rat-skin moccasins were soundless. His sword Scalpel in its mouse-skin sheath did not swish ever so faintly against either his tunic or cloak, both of gray silk curiously coarse of weave. While the glances he shot about him from under his gray silk hood half thrown back were freighted with menace and a freezing sense of superiority.

Inwardly the Mouser was feeling very much like a schoolboy—a schoolboy in dread of rebuke and a crushing assignment of homework. For in the Mouser's pouch of rat-skin was a note scrawled in dark brown squid-ink on silvery fish-skin by Sheelba of the Eyeless Face, inviting the Mouser to be at this spot at this time.

Sheelba was the Mouser's supernatural tutor and—when the whim struck Sheelba—guardian, and it never did to ignore his invitations, for Sheelba had eyes to track down the unsociable though he did not carry them between his cheeks and forehead.

But the tasks Sheelba would set the Mouser at times like these were apt to be peculiarly onerous and even noisome—such as procuring nine white cats with never a black hair among them, or stealing five copies of the same book of magic runes from five widely separated sorcerous libraries or obtaining specimens of the dung of four kings living or dead—so the Mouser had come early, to get the bad news as soon as possible, and he had come alone, for he certainly did not want his comrade Fafhrd to stand snickering by while Sheelba delivered his little wizardly homilies to a dutiful Mouser…

and perchance thought of extra assignments.

Sheelba's note, invisibly graven somewhere inside the Mouser's skull, read merely, *When the star Akul bedizens the Spire of Rhan, be you by the Fountain of Dark Abundance,* and the note was signed only with the little featureless oval which is Sheelba's sigil.

The Mouser glided now through the darkness to the Fountain, which was a squat black pillar from the rough rounded top of which a single black drop welled and dripped every twenty elephant's heartbeats.

The Mouser stood beside the Fountain and, extending a bent hand, measured the altitude of the green star Akul. It had still to drop down the sky seven finger-widths more before it would touch the needle-point of the slim star-silhouetted distant minaret of Rhan.

The Mouser crouched doubled-up by the black pillar and then vaulted lightly atop it to see if that would make any great difference in Akul's altitude. It did not.

He scanned the nearby darkness for motionless figures ... especially that of one robed and cowled like a monk—cowled so deeply that one might wonder how he saw to walk. There were no figures at all.

The Mouser's mood changed. If Sheelba chose not to come courteously beforehand, why he could be boorish too! He strode off to investigate the new bright arch-doored shop, of whose infractious glow he had become inquisitively aware at least a block before he had entered the Plaza of Dark Delights.

Fafhrd the Northerner opened one wine-heavy eye and without moving his head scanned half the small firelit room in which he slept naked. He shut that eye, opened the other, and scanned the other half.

There was no sign of the Mouser anywhere. So far so good! If his luck held, he would be able to get through tonight's embarrassing business without being jeered at by the small gray rogue.

He drew from under his stubbly cheek a square of violet serpent-hide pocked with tiny pores so that when he held it between his eyes and the dancing fire it made stars. Studied for a time, these stars spelled out obscurely the message: *When Rhan-dagger stabs the darkness in Akul-heart, seek you the Source of the Black Drops.*

Drawn boldly across the prick-holes in an orange-brown like dried blood—in fact spanning the violet square—was one of the sigils of Ningauble of the Seven Eyes.

Fafhrd had no difficulty in interpreting the Source of the Black Drops as the Fountain of Dark Abundance. He had become wearily familiar with such cryptic poetic language during his boyhood as a scholar of the singing skalds.

Ningauble stood to Fafhrd very much as Sheelba stood to the Mouser except that the Seven-Eyed One was a somewhat more pretentious arch-image, whose taste in the thaumaturgical tasks he set Fafhrd ran in larger directions such as the slaying of dragons, the sinking of four-masted magic ships, and the kidnapping of ogre-guarded enchanted queens.

Also, Ningauble was given to quiet realistic boasting, especially about the grandeur of his vast cavern-home, whose stony serpent-twisting back corridors led, he often averred, to all spots in space and time—provided Ningauble instructed one beforehand exactly how to step those rocky crook'd low-ceilinged passageways.

Fafhrd was driven by no great desire to learn Ningauble's formulas and enchantments, as the Mouser was driven to learn Sheelba's, but the Septinocular One had enough holds on the Northerner, based on the latter's weaknesses and past misdeeds, so that Fafhrd had always to listen patiently to Ningauble's wizardly admonishments and vaunting sorcerous chit-chat—but *not,* if humanly or inhumanly possible, while the Gray Mouser was present to snigger and grin.

Meanwhile, Fafhrd, standing before the fire, had been whipping, slapping, and belting various garments and weapons and ornaments onto his huge brawny body with its generous stretches of thick short curling red-gold hairs. When he opened the outer door and, also booted and helmeted now, glanced down the darkling alleyway preparatory to leaving and noted only the hunch-backed chestnut vendor a-squat by his brazier at the next corner, one would have sworn that when he did stride forth toward the Plaza of Dark Delights it would be with the clankings and thunderous tread of a siege-tower approaching a thick-walled city.

Instead the lynx-eared old chestnut vendor, who was also a spy of the Overlord, had to swallow down his heart when it came sliding crookedly up his throat as Fafhrd rushed past him, tall as a pine tree, swift as the wind, and silent as a ghost.

The Mouser elbowed aside two gawkers with shrewd taps on the floating rib and strode across the dark flagstones toward the garishly bright shop with its doorway like an up-ended heart. It occurred to him they must have had masons working like fiends to have cut and plastered that archway so swiftly. He had been past here this afternoon and noted nothing but blank wall.

The outlandish porter with the red cylinder hat and twisty red shoe-toes came frisking out to the Mouser with his broom and then went curtsying back as he reswept a path for this first customer with many an obsequious bow and smirk.

But the Mouser's visage was set in an expression of grim and all-skeptical disdain. He paused at the heaping of objects in front of the door and scanned it with disapproval. He drew Scalpel from its thin gray sheath and with the top of the long blade flipped back the cover on the topmost of a pile of musty books. Without going any closer he briefly scanned the first page, shook his head, rapidly turned a half-dozen more pages with Scalpel's tip, using the sword as if it were a teacher's wand to point out words here and there—because they were ill-chosen, to judge from his expression—and then abruptly closed the book with another sword-flip.

Next he used Scalpel's tip to lift a red cloth hanging from a table behind the books and peer under it suspiciously, to rap contemptuously a glass jar with a human head floating in it, to touch disparagingly several other objects and to waggle reprovingly at a foot-chained owl which hooted at him solemnly from its high perch.

He sheathed Scalpel and turned toward the porter with a sour, lifted-eyebrow look which said—nay, shouted—plainly, "Is *this* all you have to offer? Is this garbage your excuse for defiling the Dark Plaza with glare?"

Actually the Mouser was mightily interested by every least item which he had glimpsed. The book, incidentally, had been in a script which he not only did not understand, but did not even recognize.

Three things were very clear to the Mouser: first, that this stuff offered here for sale did not come from anywhere in the World of Nehwon, no, not even from Nehwon's farthest outback; second, that all this stuff was, in some way which he could not yet define, extremely dangerous; third, that all this stuff was monstrously fascinating and that he, the Mouser, did not intend to stir from this place until he had personally scanned, studied, and, if need be, tested every last intriguing item and scrap.

At the Mouser's sour grimace, the porter went into a convulsion of wheedling and fawning caperings, seemingly torn between a desire to kiss the Mouser's foot and to point out with flamboyant caressing gestures every object in his shop.

He ended by bowing so low that his chin brushed the pavement, sweeping an ape-long arm toward the interior of the shop, and gibbering in atrocious Lankhmarese, "Every object to pleasure the flesh and senses and imagination of man. Wonders undreamed. Very cheap, very cheap! Yours for a penny! The Bazaar of the Bizarre. Please to inspect, oh king!"

The Mouser yawned a very long yawn with the back of his hand to his mouth, next he looked around him again with the weary, patient, worldly smile of a duke who knows he must put up with many boredoms to encourage business in his demesne, finally he shrugged faintly and entered the shop.

Behind him the porter went into a jigging delirium of glee and began to resweep the flagstones like a man maddened with delight.

Inside, the first thing the Mouser saw was a stack of slim books bound in gold-lined fine-grained red and violet leather.

The second was a rack of gleaming lenses and slim brass tubes calling to be peered through.

The third was a slim dark-haired girl smiling at him mysteriously from a gold-barred cage that swung from the ceiling.

Beyond that cage hung others with bars of silver and strange green, ruby, orange, ultramarine, and purple metals.

Fafhrd saw the Mouser vanish into the shop just as his left hand touched the rough chill pate of the Fountain of Dark Abundance and as Akul poised precisely on Rhan-top as if it were that needle-spire's green-lensed pinnacle-lantern.

He might have followed the Mouser, he might have done no such thing, he certainly would have pondered the briefly glimpsed event, but just then there came from behind him a long low "Hssssst!"

Fafhrd turned like a giant dancer and his longsword Graywand came out of its sheath swiftly and rather more silently than a snake emerges from its hole.

Ten arm-lengths behind him, in the mouth of an alleyway darker than the Dark Plaza would have been without its new commercial moon, Fafhrd dimly made out two robed and deeply cowled figures poised side by side.

One cowl held darkness absolute. Even the face of a Negro of Klesh might have been expected to shoot ghostly bronzy gleams. But here there were none.

In the other cowl there nested seven very faint pale greenish glows. They moved about restlessly, sometimes circling each other, swinging mazily. Sometimes one of the seven horizontally oval gleams would grow a little brighter, seemingly as it moved forward toward the mouth of the cowl—or a little darker, as it drew back.

Fafhrd sheathed Graywand and advanced toward the figures. Still facing him, they retreated slowly and silently down the alley.

Fafhrd followed as they receded. He felt a stirring of interest... and of other feelings. To meet his own supernatural mentor alone might be only a bore and a mild nervous strain; but it would be hard for anyone entirely to repress a shiver of awe at encountering at one and the same time both Ningauble of the Seven Eyes and Sheelba of the Eyeless Face.

Moreover, that those two bitter wizardly rivals should have joined forces, that they should apparently be operating together in amity... Something of great note must be a-foot! There was no doubting that.

The Mouser meantime was experiencing the snuggest, most mind-teasing, most exotic enjoyments imaginable. The sleekly leather-bound gold-stamped books turned out to contain scripts stranger far than that in the book whose pages he had flipped outside—scripts that looked like skeletal beasts, cloud swirls, and twisty-branched bushes and trees—but for a wonder he could read them all without the least difficulty.

The books dealt in the fullest detail with such matters as the private life of devils, the secret histories of murderous cults, and —these were illustrated—the proper dueling techniques to employ against sword-armed demons and the erotic tricks of lamias, succubi, bacchantes, and hamadryads.

The lenses and brass tubes, some of the latter of which were as fantastically crooked as if they were periscopes for seeing over the walls and through the barred windows of other universes, showed at first only delightful jeweled patterns, but after a bit the Mouser was able to see through them into all sorts of interesting places: the treasure-rooms of dead kings, the bedchambers of living queens, council-crypts of rebel angels, and the closets in which the gods hid plans for worlds too frighteningly fantastic to risk creating.

As for the quaintly clad slim girls in their playfully widely-barred cages, well, they were pleasant pillows on which to rest eyes momentarily fatigued by book-scanning and tube-peering.

Ever and anon one of the girls would whistle softly at the Mouser and then point cajolingly or imploringly or with languorous hintings at a jeweled crank set in the wall whereby her cage, suspended on a gleaming chain running through gleaming pulleys, could be lowered to the floor.

At these invitations the Mouser would smile with a bland amorousness and nod and softly wave a hand from the finger-hinge as if to whisper, "Later… later. Be patient."

After all, girls had a way of blotting out all lesser, but not thereby despicable, delights. Girls were for dessert.

Ningauble and Sheelba receded down the dark alleyway with Fafhrd following them until the latter lost patience and, somewhat conquering his unwilling awe, called out nervously, "Well, are you going to keep on fleeing me backwards until we all pitch into the Great Salt Marsh? What do you want of me? What's it all about?"

But the two cowled figures had already stopped, as he could perceive by the starlight and the glow of a few high windows, and now it seemed to Fafhrd that they had stopped a moment before he had called out. A typical sorcerers' trick for making one feel awkward! He gnawed his lip in the darkness. It was ever thus!

"Oh My Gentle Son…" Ningauble began in his most sugary-priestly tones, the dim puffs of his seven eyes now hanging in his cowl as steadily and glowing as mildly as the Pleiades seen late on a summer night through a greenish mist rising from a lake freighted with blue vitriol and corrosive gas of salt.

"I asked what it's all about!" Fafhrd interrupted harshly. Already convicted of impatience, he might as well go the whole hog.

"Let me put it as a hypothetical case," Ningauble replied imperturbably. "Let us suppose, My Gentle Son, that there is a man in a universe and that a most evil force comes to this universe from another universe, or perhaps from a congeries of universes, and that this man is a brave man who wants to defend his universe and who counts his life as a trifle and that moreover he has to counsel him a very wise and prudent and public-spirited uncle who knows all about these matters which I have been hypothecating—"

"The Devourers menace Lankhmar!" Sheelba rapped out in a voice as harsh as a tree cracking and so suddenly that Fafhrd almost started—and for all we know, Ningauble too.

Fafhrd waited a moment to avoid giving false impressions and then switched his gaze to Sheelba. His eyes had been growing accustomed to the darkness and he saw much more now than he had seen at the alley's mouth, yet he still saw not one jot more than absolute blackness inside Sheelba's cowl.

"Who are the Devourers?" he asked.

It was Ningauble, however, who replied, "The Devourers are the most accomplished merchants in all the many universes—so accomplished, indeed, that they sell only trash. There is a deep necessity in this, for the Devourers must occupy all their cunning in perfecting their methods of selling and so have not an instant to spare in considering the worth of what they sell—indeed, they dare not concern themselves with such matters for a moment, for fear of losing their golden touch—and yet such are their skills that their wares are utterly irresistible, indeed the finest wares in all the many universes—if you follow me?"

Fafhrd looked hopefully toward Sheelba, but since the latter did not this time interrupt with some pithy summation, he nodded to Ningauble.

Ningauble continued, his seven eyes beginning to weave a bit, judging from the movements of the seven green glows, "As you might readily deduce, the Devourers possess all the mightiest magics garnered from the many universes, whilst their assault groups are led by the most aggressive wizards imaginable, supremely skilled in all methods of battling, whether it be with the wits, or the feelings, or with the beweaponed body.

"The method of the Devourers is to set up shop in a new world and first entice the bravest and the most adventuresome and the supplest-minded of its people—who have so much imagination that with just a touch of suggestion they themselves do most of the work of selling themselves.

"When these are safely ensnared, the Devourers proceed to deal with the remainder of the population: meaning simply that they sell and sell and sell!—sell trash and take good money and even finer things in exchange."

Ningauble sighed windily and a shade piously. "All this is very bad, My Gentle Son," he continued, his eye-glows weaving hypnotically in his cowl, "but natural enough in universes administered by such gods as we have— natural enough and perhaps endurable. However—" he paused "—there is worse to come! The Devourers want not only the patronage of all beings in all universes, but—doubtless because they are afraid someone will some-day raise the ever-unpleasant question of the true worth of things—they want all their customers reduced to a state of slavish and submissive *sug-gestibility,* so that they are fit for nothing whatever but to gawk at and buy the trash the Devourers offer for sale. This means of course that eventually the Devourers' customers will have nothing wherewith to pay the Devourers for their trash, but the Devourers do not seem to be concerned with this eventuality. Perhaps they feel that there is always a new universe to exploit. And perhaps there is!"

"Monstrous!" Fafhrd commented. "But what do the Devourers gain from all these furious commercial sorties, all this mad merchandising? What do they really want?"

Ningauble replied, "The Devourers want only to amass cash and to raise little ones like themselves to amass more cash and they want to compete with each other at cash-amassing. (Is that coincidentally a city, do you think, Fafhrd? Cashamash?) And the Devourers want to brood about their great service to the many universes—it is their claim that servile customers make the most obedient subjects for the gods—and to complain about how the work of amassing cash tortures their minds and upsets their digestions. Be-yond this, each of the Devourers also secretly collects and hides away forever, to delight no eyes but his own, all the finest objects and thoughts created by true men and women (and true wizards and true demons) and bought by the Devourers at bankruptcy prices and paid for with trash or—this is their ultimate preference—with nothing at all."

"Monstrous indeed!" Fafhrd repeated. "Merchants are ever an evil mystery and these sound the worst. But what has all this to do with me?"

"Oh My Gentle Son," Ningauble responded, the piety in his voice now tinged with a certain clement disappointment, "you force me once again to resort to hypothecating. Let us return to the supposition of this brave man whose whole universe is direly menaced and who counts his life a trifle and to the related supposition of this brave man's wise uncle, whose advice the brave man invariably follows—"

"The Devourers have set up shop in the Plaza of Dark Delights!" Sheelba interjected so abruptly and in such iron-harsh syllables that this time Fafhrd actually did start. "You must obliterate this outpost tonight!"

Fafhrd considered that for a bit, then said, in a tentative sort of voice, "You will both accompany me, I presume, to aid me with your wizardly sendings and castings in what I can see must be a most perilous operation, to serve me as a sort of sorcerous artillery and archery corps while I play assault battalion—"

"Oh My Gentle Son…" Ningauble interrupted in tones of deepest disappointment, shaking his head so that his eye-glows jogged in his cowl.

"You must do it alone!" Sheelba rasped.

"Without any help at all?" Fafhrd demanded. "No! Get someone else. Get this doltish brave man who always follows his scheming uncle's advice as slavishly as you tell me the Devourers' customers respond to their merchandising. Get *him!* But as for me—No, I say !"

"Then leave us, coward!" Sheelba decreed dourly, but Ningauble only sighed and said quite apologetically, "It was intended that you have a comrade in this quest, a fellow soldier against noisome evil—to wit, the Gray Mouser. But unfortunately he came early to his appointment with my colleague here and was enticed into the shop of the Devourers and is doubtless now deep in their snares, if not already extinct. So you can see that we do take thought for your welfare and have no wish to overburden you with solo quests. However, My Gentle Son, if it still be your firm resolve—"

Fafhrd let out a sigh more profound than Ningauble's. "Very well," he said in gruff tones admitting defeat, "I'll do it for you. Someone will have to pull that poor little gray fool out of the pretty-pretty fire—or the twinkly-twinkly water! —that tempted him. But how do I go about it?" He shook a big finger at Ningauble. "And no more Gentle-Sonning!"

Ningauble paused. Then he said only, "Use your own judgment."

Sheelba said, "Beware the Black Wall!"

Ningauble said to Fafhrd, "Hold, I have a gift for you," and held out to him a ragged ribbon a yard long, pinched between the cloth of the wizard's long sleeve so that it was impossible to see the manner of hand that pinched. Fafhrd took the tatter with a snort, crumpled it into a ball, and thrust it into his pouch.

"Have a greater care with it," Ningauble warned. "It is the Cloak of Invisibility, somewhat worn by many magic usings. Do not put it on until you near the Bazaar of the Devourers. It has two minor weaknesses: it will not make you altogether invisible to a master sorcerer if he senses your presence and takes certain steps. Also, see to it that you do not bleed during this exploit, for the cloak will not hide blood."

"I've a gift too!" Sheelba said, drawing from out of his black cowl-hole—with sleeve-masked hand, as Ningauble had done—something that shimmered faintly in the dark like...

Like a spiderweb.

Sheelba shook it, as if to dislodge a spider, or perhaps two.

"The Blindfold of True Seeing," he said as he reached it toward Fafhrd. "It shows all things as they really are! Do not lay it across your eyes until you enter the Bazaar. On no account, as you value your life or your sanity, wear it now!"

Fafhrd took it from him most gingerly, the flesh of his fingers crawling. He was inclined to obey the taciturn wizard's instructions. At this moment he truly did not much care to see the true visage of Sheelba of the Eyeless Face.

The Gray Mouser was reading the most interesting book of them all, a great compendium of secret knowledge written in a script of astrologic and geomantic signs, the meanings of which fairly leaped off the page into his mind.

To rest his eyes from that—or rather to keep from gobbling the book too fast—he peered through a nine-elbowed brass tube at a scene that could only be the blue heaven-pinnacle of the universe where angels flew shimmeringly like dragonflies and where a few choice heroes rested from their great mountain-climb and spied down critically on the antlike labors of the gods many levels below.

To rest his eye from *that*, he looked up between the scarlet (bloodmetal?) bars of the inmost cage at the most winsome, slim, fair, jet-eyed girl of them all. She knelt, sitting on her heels, with her upper body leaned back a little. She wore a red velvet tunic and had a mop of golden hair so thick and pliant that she could sweep it in a neat curtain over her upper face, down almost to her pouting lips. With the slim fingers of one hand she would slightly part these silky golden drapes to peer at the Mouser playfully, while with those of the other she rattled golden castanets in a most languorously slow rhythm, though with occasional swift staccato bursts.

The Mouser was considering whether it might not be as well to try a turn or two on the ruby-crusted golden crank next his elbow, when he spied for the first time the glimmering wall at the back of the shop. What could its material be? he asked himself. Tiny diamonds countless as the sand set in smoky glass? Black opal? Black pearl? Black moonshine?

Whatever it was, it was wholly fascinating, for the Mouser quickly set down his book, using the nine-crooked spy-tube to mark his place—a most engrossing pair of pages on dueling where were revealed the Universal

Parry and its five false variants and also the three true forms of the Secret Thrust—and with only a finger-wave to the ensorceling blonde in red velvet he walked quickly toward the back of the shop.

As he approached the Black Wall he thought for an instant that he glimpsed a silver wraith or perhaps a silver skeleton walking toward him out of it, but then he saw that it was only his own darkly handsome reflection, pleasantly flattered by the lustrous material. What had momentarily suggested silver ribs was the reflection of the silver lacings on his tunic.

He smirked at his image and reached out a finger to touch *its* lustrous finger when—Lo, wonder!—his hand went into the wall with never a sensation at all save a faint tingling coolth promising comfort like the sheets of a fresh-made bed.

He looked at his hand inside the wall and—Lo, another wonder!—it was all a beautiful silver faintly patterned with tiny scales. And though his own hand indubitably, as he could tell by clenching it, it was scarless now and a mite slimmer and longer fingered—altogether a more handsome hand than it had been a moment ago.

He wriggled his fingers and it was like watching small silver fish dart about—fingerlings!

What a droll conceit, he thought, to have a dark fishpond or rather swimming pool set on its side indoors, so that one could walk into the gracious erect fluid quietly and gracefully, instead of all the noisy, bouncingly athletic business of diving!

And how charming that the pool should be filled not with wet soppy cold water, but with a sort of moondark essence of sleep—an essence with beautifying cosmetic properties too!—a sort of mudbath without the mud. The Mouser decided he must have a swim in this wonder pool at once, but just then his gaze lit on a long high black couch toward the other end of the dark liquid wall, and beyond the couch a small high table set with viands and a crystal pitcher and goblet.

He walked along the wall to inspect these, his handsome reflection taking step for step with him.

He trailed his hand in the wall for a space and then withdrew it, the scales instantly vanishing and the familiar old scars returning.

The couch turned out to be a narrow high-sided black coffin lined with quilted black satin and piled at one end with little black satin pillows. It looked most invitingly comfortable and restful—not quite as inviting as the Black Wall, but very attractive just the same; there was even a rack of tiny black books nested in the black satin for the occupant's diversion and also a black candle, unlit.

The collation on the little ebony table beyond the coffin consisted entirely of black foods. By sight and then by nibbling and sipping the Mouser discovered their nature: thin slices of a very dark rye bread crusted with poppy seeds and dripped with black butter; slivers of charcoal-seared steak; similarly broiled tiny thin slices of calf's liver sprinkled with dark spices and liberally pricked with capers; the darkest grape jellies; truffles cut paper thin and mushrooms fried black; pickled chestnuts; and of course ripe olives and black fish eggs—caviar. The black drink, which foamed when he poured it, turned out to be stout laced with the bubbly wine of Ilthmar.

He decided to refresh the inner Mouser—the Mouser who lived a sort of blind soft greedy undulating surface-life between his lips and his belly—before taking a dip in the Black Wall.

Fafhrd re-entered the Plaza of Dark Delights walking warily and with the long tatter that was the Cloak of Invisibility trailing from between left forefinger and thumb and with the glimmering cobweb that was the Blindfold of True Seeing pinched even more delicately by its edge between the same digits of his right hand. He was not yet altogether certain that the trailing gossamer hexagon was completely free of spiders.

Across the Plaza he spotted the bright-mouthed shop—the shop he had been told was an outpost of the deadly Devourers—through a ragged gather of folk moving about restlessly and commenting and speculating to one another in harsh excited undertones.

The only feature of the shop Fafhrd could make out at all clearly at this distance was the red-capped red-footed baggy-trousered porter, not capering now but leaning on his long broom beside the trefoil-arched doorway.

With a looping swing of his left arm Fafhrd hung the Cloak of Invisibility around his neck. The ragged ribband hung to either side down his chest in its wolfskin jerkin only halfway to his wide belt which supported longsword and short-ax. It did not vanish his body to the slightest degree that he could see and he doubted it worked at all—like many another thaumaturge, Ningauble never hesitated to give one useless charms, not for any treacherous reason, necessarily, but simply to improve ones morale. Fafhrd strode boldly toward the shop.

The Northerner was a tall, broad-shouldered, formidable-looking man—doubly formidable by his barbaric dress and weaponing in supercivilized Lankhmar—and so he took it for granted that the ordinary run of city folk stepped out of his way; indeed it had never occurred to him that they should not.

He got a shock. All the clerks, seedy bravos, scullery folk, students, slaves, second-rate merchants and second-class courtesans who would automatically have moved aside for him (though the last with a saucy swing of the hips) now came straight at him, so that he had to dodge and twist and stop and even sometimes dart back to avoid being toe-tramped and bumped. Indeed one fat pushy proud-stomached fellow almost carried away his cobweb, which he could see now by the light of the shop was free of spiders—or if there were any spiders still on it, they must be very small.

He had so much to do dodging Fafhrd-blind Lankhmarians that he could not spare one more glance for the shop until he was almost at the door. And then before he took his first close look, he found that he was tilting his head so that his left ear touched the shoulder below it and that he was laying Sheelba's spiderweb across his eyes.

The touch of it was simply like the touch of any cobweb when one runs face into it walking between close-set bushes at dawn. Everything shimmered a bit as if seen through a fine crystal grating. Then the least shimmering vanished, and with it the delicate clinging sensation, and Fafhrd's vision returned to normal—as far as he could tell.

It turned out that the doorway to the Devourers' shop was piled with garbage—garbage of a particularly offensive sort: old bones, dead fish, butcher's offal, moldering gravecloths folded in uneven squares like badly bound uncut books, broken glass and potsherds, splintered boxes, large stinking dead leaves orange-spotted with blight, bloody rags, tattered discarded loincloths, large worms nosing about, centipedes a-scuttle, cockroaches a-stagger, maggots a-crawl—and less agreeable things.

Atop all perched a vulture which had lost most of its feathers and seemed to have expired of some avian eczema. At least Fafhrd took it for dead, but then it opened one white-filmed eye.

The only conceivably salable object outside the shop—but it was a most notable exception—was the tall black iron statue, somewhat larger than life-size, of a lean swordsman of dire yet melancholy visage. Standing on its square pedestal beside the door, the statue leaned forward just a little on its long two-handed sword and regarded the Plaza dolefully.

The statue almost teased awake a recollection in Fafhrd's mind—a recent recollection, he fancied—but then there was a blank in his thoughts and he instantly dropped the puzzle. On raids like this one, relentlessly swift action was paramount. He loosened his ax in its loop, noiselessly whipped out Graywand and, shrinking away from the piled and crawling garbage just a little, entered the Bazaar of the Bizarre.

The Mouser, pleasantly replete with tasty black food and heady black drink, drifted to the Black Wall and thrust in his right arm to the shoulder.

He waved it about, luxuriating in the softly flowing coolth and balm—and admiring its fine silver scales and more than human handsomeness. He did the same with his right leg, swinging it like a dancer exercising at the bar. Then he took a gently deep breath and drifted farther in.

Fafhrd on entering the Bazaar saw the same piles of gloriously bound books and racks of gleaming brass spy-tubes and crystal lenses as had the Mouser—a circumstance which seemed to overset Ningauble's theory that the Devourers sold only trash.

He also saw the eight beautiful cages of jewel-gleaming metals and the gleaming chains that hung them from the ceiling and went to the jeweled wall cranks.

Each cage held a gleaming, gloriously hued, black- or light-haired spider big as a rather small person and occasionally waving a long jointed claw-handed leg, or softly opening a little and then closing a pair of fanged down-swinging mandibles, while staring steadily at Fafhrd with eight watchful eyes set in two jewel-like rows of four.

Set a spider to catch a spider, Fafhrd thought, thinking of his cobweb, and then wondered what the thought meant.

He quickly switched to more practical questions then, but he had barely asked himself whether before proceeding further he should kill the very expensive-looking spiders, fit to be the coursing beasts of some jungle empress—another count against Ning's trash-theory!—when he heard a faint splashing from the back of the shop. It reminded him of the Mouser taking a bath—the Mouser loved baths, slow luxurious ones in hot soapy scented oil-dripped water, the small gray sybarite!—and so Fafhrd hurried off in that direction with many a swift upward overshoulder glance.

He was detouring the last cage, a scarlet-metalled one holding the handsomest spider yet, when he noted a book set down with a crooked spy-tube in it—exactly as the Mouser would keep his place in a book by closing it on a dagger.

Fafhrd paused to open the book. Its lustrous white pages were blank. He put his impalpably cobwebbed eye to the spy-tube. He glimpsed a scene that could only be the smoky red hell-nadir of the universe, where dark devils scuttled about like centipedes and where chained folk gazing yearn-ingly upward as the damned writhed in the grip of black serpents whose eyes shone and whose fangs dripped and whose nostrils breathed fire.

As he dropped tube and book, he heard the faint sonorous quick dull report of bubbles being expelled from a fluid at its surface. Staring instantly toward the dim back of the shop, he saw at last the pearl-shim-mering Black Wall and a silver skeleton eyed with great diamonds receding into it. However, this costly bone-man—once more Ning's trash-theory disproven!—still had one arm sticking part way out of the wall and this arm was not bone, whether silver, white, brownish or pink, but live-looking flesh covered with proper skin.

As the arm sank into the wall, Fafhrd sprang forward as fast as he ever had in his life and grabbed the hand just before it vanished. He knew then he had hold of his friend, for he would recognize anywhere the Mouser's grip, no matter how enfeebled. He tugged, but it was as if the Mouser were mired in black quicksand. He laid Graywand down and grasped the Mouser by the wrist too and braced his feet against the rough black flags and gave a tremendous heave.

The silver skeleton came out of the wall with a black splash, metamorphosing as it did into a vacant-eyed Gray Mouser who without a look at his friend and rescuer went staggering off in a curve and pitched head over heels into the black coffin.

But before Fafhrd could hoist his comrade from this new gloomy predicament, there was a swift clash of footsteps and there came racing into the shop, somewhat to Fafhrd's surprise, the tall black iron statue. It had forgotten or simply stepped off its pedestal, but it had remembered its two-handed sword, which it brandished about most fiercely while shooting searching black glances like iron darts at every shadow and corner and nook.

The black gaze passed Fafhrd without pausing, but halted at Graywand lying on the floor. At the sight of that longsword the statue started visibly, snarled its iron lips, its black eyes narrowed, it shot glances more ironly stabbing than before, and it began to move about the shop in sudden zigzag rushes, sweeping its darkly flashing sword in low scythe-strokes.

At that moment the Mouser peeped moon-eyed over the edge of the coffin, lifted a limp hand and waved it at the statue, and in a soft sly foolish voice cried, "Yoo-hoo!"

The statue paused in its searchings and scythings to glare at the Mouser in mixed contempt and puzzlement.

The Mouser rose to his feet in the black coffin, swaying drunkenly, and dug in his pouch.

"Ho, slave!" he cried to the statue with maudlin gayety, "your wares are passing passable. I'll take the girl in red velvet." He pulled a coin from his pouch, goggled at it closely, then pitched it at the statue. "That's one penny. And the nine-crook'd spy-tube. That's another penny." He pitched it. "And *Gron's Grand Compendium of Exotic* Lore—another penny for you! Yes, and here's one more for supper—very tasty, 'twas. Oh and I almost forgot—here's for tonight's lodging!" He pitched a fifth large copper coin at the demonic black statue and, smiling blissfully, flopped back out of sight. The black quilted satin could be heard to sigh as he sank in it.

Four-fifths of the way through the Mouser's penny-pitching Fafhrd decided it was useless to try to unriddle his comrade's nonsensical behavior
and that it would be far more to the point to make use of this diversion to
snatch up Graywand. He did so on the instant, but by that time the black
statue was fully alert again, if it had ever been otherwise. Its gaze switched
to Graywand the instant Fafhrd touched the longsword and it stamped its
foot, which rang against the stone, and cried a harsh metallic "Ha!"

Apparently the sword became invisible as Fafhrd grasped it, for the black
statue did not follow him with its iron eyes as he shifted position across
the room. Instead it swiftly laid down its own mighty blade and caught up
a long narrow silver trumpet and set it to its lips.

Fafhrd thought it wise to attack before the statue summoned reinforce-
ments. He rushed straight at the thing, swinging back Graywand for a great
stroke at the neck—and steeling himself for an arm-numbing impact.

The statue blew and instead of the alarm blare Fafhrd had expected,
there silently puffed out straight at him a great cloud of white powder that
momentarily blotted out everything, as if it were the thickest of fogs from
Hlal-river.

Fafhrd retreated, choking and coughing. The demon-blown fog cleared
quickly, the white powder falling to the stony floor with unnatural swiftness,
and he could see again to attack, but now the statue apparently could see
him too, for it squinted straight ay him and cried its metallic "Ha!' again and
whirled its sword around its iron head preparatory to the charge—rather
as if winding itself up.

Fafhrd saw that his own hands and arms were thickly filmed with the
white powder, which apparently clung to him everywhere except his eyes,
doubtless protected by Sheelba's cobweb.

The iron statue came thrusting and slashing in. Fafhrd took the great
sword on his, chopped back, and was parried in return. And now the combat assumed the noisy deadly aspects of a conventional longsword duel,
except that Graywand was notched whenever it caught the chief force of a
stroke, while the statue's somewhat longer weapon remained unmarked.
Also, whenever Fafhrd got through the other's guard with a thrust—it was
almost impossible to reach him with a slash—it turned out that the other
had slipped his lean body or head aside with unbelievably swift and infallible anticipations.

It seemed to Fafhrd—at least at the time—the most fell, frustrating, and
certainly the most wearisome combat in which he had ever engaged, so
he suffered some feelings of hurt and irritation when the Mouser reeled
up in his coffin again and leaned an elbow on the black-satin-quilted side
and rested chin on fist and grinned hugely at the battlers and from time to

time laughed wildly and shouted such enraging nonsense as "Use Secret Thrust Two-and-a-Half, Fafhrd—it's all in the book!" or "Jump in the oven!—there'd be a master stroke of strategy!" or—this to the statue— "Remember to sweep under his feet, you rogue!"

Backing away from one of Fafhrd's sudden attacks, the statue bumped the table holding the remains of the Mouser's repast—evidently its anticipatory abilities did not extend to its rear—and scraps of black food and white potsherds and jags of crystal scattered across the floor.

The Mouser leaned out of his coffin and waved a finger waggishly. "You'll have to sweep that up!" he cried and went off into a gale of laughter.

Backing away again, the statue bumped the black coffin. The Mouser only clapped the demonic figure comradely on the shoulder and called, "Set to it again, clown! Brush him down! Dust him off!"

But the worst was perhaps when, during a brief pause while the combatants gasped and eyed each other dizzily, the Mouser waved coyly to the nearest giant spider and called his inane "Yoo-hoo!" again, following it with, "I'll see you, dear, after the circus."

Fafhrd, parrying with weary desperation a fifteenth or a fiftieth cut at his head, thought bitterly, *This comes of trying to rescue small heartless madmen who would howl at their grandmothers hugged by bears. Sheelba's cobweb has shown me the Gray One in his true idiot nature.*

The Mouser had first been furious when the sword-skirling clashed him awake from his black satin dreams, but as soon as he saw what was going on he became enchanted at the wildly comic scene.

For, lacking Sheelba's cobweb, what the Mouser saw was only the zany red-capped porter prancing about in his ridiculous tip-curled red shoes and aiming with his broom great strokes at Fafhrd, who looked exactly as if he had climbed a moment ago out of a barrel of meal. The only part of the Northerner not whitely dusted was a shadowy dark masklike stretch across his eyes.

What made the whole thing fantastically droll was that miller-white Fafhrd was going through all the motions—and emotions!—of a genuine combat with excruciating precision, parrying the broom as if it were some great jolting scimitar or two-handed broadsword even. The broom would go sweeping up and Fafhrd would gawk at it, giving a marvelous interpretation of apprehensive goggling despite his strangely shadowed eyes. Then the broom would come sweeping down and Fafhrd would brace himself and seem to catch it on his sword only with the most prodigious effort—and then pretend to be jolted back by it!

The Mouser had never suspected Fafhrd had such a perfected theatric talent, even if it were acting of a rather mechanical sort, lacking the broad sweeps of true dramatic genius, and he whooped with laughter.

Then the broom brushed Fafhrd's shoulder and blood sprang out.

Fafhrd, wounded at last and thereby knowing himself unlikely to outendure the black statue—although the latter's iron chest was working now like a bellows—decided on swifter measures. He loosened his hand-ax again in its loop and at the next pause in the fight, both battlers having outguessed each other by retreating simultaneously, whipped it up and hurled it at his adversary's face.

Instead of seeking to dodge or ward off the missile, the black statue lowered its sword and merely wove its head in a tiny circle.

The ax closely circled the lean black head, like a silver wood-tailed comet whipping around a black sun, and came back straight at Fafhrd like a boomerang—and rather more swiftly than Fafhrd had sent it.

But time slowed for Fafhrd then and he half ducked and caught it lefthanded as it went whizzing past his cheek.

His thoughts too went for a moment fast as his actions. He thought of how his adversary, able to dodge every frontal attack, had not avoided the table or the coffin behind him. He thought of how the Mouser had not laughed now for a dozen clashes and he looked at him and saw him, though still dazed-seeming, strangely pale and sober-faced, appearing to stare with horror at the blood running down Fafhrd's arm.

So crying as heartily and merrily as he could, "Amuse yourself! Join in the fun, clown!—here's your slap-stick," Fafhrd tossed the ax toward the Mouser.

Without waiting to see the result of that toss—perhaps not daring to—he summoned up his last reserves of speed and rushed at the black statue in a circling advance that drove it back toward the coffin.

Without shifting his stupid horrified gaze, the Mouser stuck out a hand at the last possible moment and caught the ax by the handle as it spun lazily down.

As the black statue retreated near the coffin and poised for what promised to be a stupendous counterattack, the Mouser leaned out and, now grinning foolishly again, sharply rapped its black pate with the ax.

The iron head split like a coconut, but did not come apart. Fafhrd's handax, wedged in it deeply, seemed to turn all at once to iron like the statue and its black haft was wrenched out of the Mouser's hand as the statue stiffened up straight and tall.

The Mouser stared at the split head woefully, like a child who hadn't known knives cut.

The statue brought its great sword flat against its chest, like a staff on which it might lean but did not, and it fell rigidly forward and hit the floor with a ponderous clank.

At that stony-metallic thundering, white wildfire ran across the Black Wall, lightening the whole shop like a distant levin-bolt, and the iron-basalt thundering echoed from deep within it.

Fafhrd sheathed Graywand, dragged the Mouser out of the black coffin—the fight hadn't left him the strength to lift even his small friend—and shouted in his ear, "Come on! Run!"

The Mouser ran for the Black Wall.

Fafhrd snagged his wrist as he went by and plunged toward the arched door, dragging the Mouser after him.

The thunder faded out and there came a low whistle, cajolingly sweet.

Wildfire raced again across the Black Wall behind them—much more brightly this time, as if a lightning storm were racing toward them.

The white glare striking ahead imprinted one vision indelibly on Fafhrd's brain: the giant spider in the inmost cage pressed against the bloodred bars to gaze down at them. It had pale legs and a velvet red body and a mask of sleek thick golden hair from which eight jet eyes peered, while its fanged jaws hanging down in the manner of the wide blades of a pair of golden scissors rattled together in a wild staccato rhythm like castanets.

That moment the cajoling whistle was repeated. It too seemed to be coming from the red and golden spider.

But strangest of all to Fafhrd was to hear the Mouser, dragged unwillingly along behind him, cry out in answer to the whistling, "Yes, darling, I'm coming. Let me go, Fafhrd! Let me climb to her! Just one kiss! Sweetheart!"

"Stop it, Mouser," Fafhrd growled, his flesh crawling in mid-plunge. "It's a giant spider!"

"Wipe the cobwebs out of your eyes, Fafhrd," the Mouser retorted pleadingly and most unwittingly to the point. "It's a gorgeous girl! I'll never see her ticklesome like—and I've paid for her! *Sweetheart!*"

Then the booming thunder drowned his voice and any more whistling there might have been, and the wildfire came again, brighter than day, and another great thunderclap right on its heels, and the floor shuddered and the whole shop shook, and Fafhrd dragged the Mouser through the trefoil-arched doorway, and there was another great flash and clap.

The flash showed a semicircle of Lankhmarians peering ashen-faced overshoulder as they retreated across the Plaza of Dark Delights from the remarkable indoor thunderstorm that threatened to come out after them.

Fafhrd spun around. The archway had turned to blank wall.

The Bazaar of the Bizarre was gone from the World of Nehwon.

The Mouser, sitting on the dank flags where Fafhrd had dragged him, babbled wailfully, "The secrets of time and space! The lore of the gods! The mysteries of Hell! Black nirvana! Red and gold Heaven! Five pennies gone forever!"

Fafhrd set his teeth. A mighty resolve, rising from his many recent angers and bewilderments, crystallized in him.

Thus far he had used Sheelba's cobweb—and Ningauble's tatter too—only to serve others. Now he would use them for himself! He would peer at the Mouser more closely and at every person he knew. He would study even his own reflection! But most of all, he would stare Sheelba and Ning to their wizardly cores!

There came from overhead a low "Hssst!"

As he glanced up he felt something snatched from around his neck and, with the faintest tingling sensation, from off his eyes.

For a moment there was a shimmer traveling upward and through it he seemed to glimpse distortedly, as through thick glass, a black face with a cobwebby skin that entirely covered mouth and nostrils and eyes.

Then that dubious flash was gone and there were only two cowled heads peering down at him from over the wall top. There was chuckling laughter.

Then both cowled heads drew back out of sight and there was only the edge of the roof and the sky and the stars and the blank wall.

MIDNIGHT BY THE
MORPHY WATCH

BEING WORLD CHESS CHAMPION, (crowned or uncrowned) puts a more deadly and maddening strain on a man even than being President of the United States. We have a prime example enthroned right now. For more than ten years the present champion was clearly the greatest chess player in the world, but during that time he exhibited such willful and seemingly self-destructive behavior—refusing to enter crucial tournaments, quitting them for crankish reasons while holding a commanding lead, entertaining what many called a paranoid delusion that the whole world was plotting to keep him from reaching the top—that many informed experts wrote him off as a contender for the highest honors. Even his staunchest supporters experienced agonizing doubts—until he finally silenced his foes and supremely satisfied his friends by decisively winning the crucial and ultimate match on a fantastic polar island.

Even minor players bitten by the world's-championship bug—or the fantasy of it—experience a bit of that terrible strain, occasionally in very strange and even eerie fashion...

Stirf Ritter-Rebil was indulging in one of his numerous creative avocations—wandering at random through his beloved downtown San Francisco with its sometimes dizzily slanting sidewalks, its elusive narrow courts and alleys, and its kaleidoscope of ever-changing store- and restaurant-fronts amongst the ones that persist as landmarks. To divert his gaze, there were interesting almond and black faces among the paler ones. There was the dangerous surge of traffic threatening to invade the humpy sidewalks.

The sky was a careless silvery gray, like an expensive whore's mink coat covering bizarre garb or nakedness. There were even wisps of fog, that Bay Area benison. There were bankers and hippies, con men and corporation men, queers of all varieties, beggars and sports, murderers and saints (at least in Ritter's freewheeling imagination). And there were certainly alluring girls aplenty in an astounding variety of packages—and pretty girls are the essential spice in any really tasty ragout of people. In fact there may well have been Martians and time travelers.

Ritter's ramble had taken on an even more dreamlike, whimsical and unpredictable quality than usual—with an unflagging anticipation of mystery, surprise, and erotic or diamond-studded adventure around the very next corner.

He frequently thought of himself by his middle name, Ritter, because he was a sporadically ardent chess player now in the midst of a sporad. In German "Ritter" means "knight," yet Germans do not call a knight a Ritter, but a springer, or jumper (for its crookedly hopping move), a matter for inexhaustible philological, historical, and socioracial speculation. Ritter was also a deeply devoted student of the history of chess, both in its serious and anecdotal aspects.

He was a tall, white-haired man, rather thin, saved from the look of mere age by ravaged handsomeness, an altogether youthful though worldly and sympathetically cynical curiosity in his gaze (when he wasn't daydreaming), and a definitely though unobtrusively theatrical carriage.

He was more daydreamingly lost than usual on this particular ramble, though vividly aware of all sorts of floating, freakish, beautiful and grotesque novelties about him. Later he recollected that he must have been fairly near Portsmouth Square and not terribly far from the intersection of California and Montgomery. At all events, he was fascinatedly looking into the display window of a secondhand store he'd never recalled seeing before. It must be a new place, for he knew all the stores in the area, yet it had the dust and dinginess of an *old* place—its owner must have moved in without refurbishing the premises or even cleaning them up. And it had a delightful range of items for sale, from genuine antiques to mod facsimiles of same. He noted in his first scanning glance, and with growing delight, a Civil War saber, a standard promotional replica of the starship *Enterprise*, a brand-new deck of tarots, an authentic shrunken head like a black globule of detritus from a giant's nostril, some fancy roach-clips, a silver lusterware creamer, a Sony tape recorder, a last year's whiskey jug in the form of a cable car, a scatter of Gene McCarthy and Nixon buttons, a single brass Lucas "King of the Road" headlamp from a Silver Ghost Rolls Royce, an electric toothbrush, a 1920s radio, a last month's copy of the *Phoenix*, and three dime-a-dozen plastic chess sets.

And then, suddenly, all these were wiped from his mind. Unnoticed were the distant foghorns, the complaining prowl of slowed traffic, the shards of human speech behind him mosaicked with the singsong chatter of

Chinatown, the reflection in the plate glass of a girl in a grandmother dress selling flowers, and of opening umbrellas as drops of rain began to sprinkle from the mist. For every atom of Stirf Ritter-Rebil's awareness was burningly concentrated on a small figure seeking anonymity among the randomly set-out chessmen of one of the plastic sets. It was a squat, tarnished silver chess pawn in the form of a barbarian warrior. Ritter knew it was a chess pawn—and what's more, he knew to what fabulous historic set it belonged, because he had seen one of its mates in a rare police photograph given him by a Portuguese chess-playing acquaintance. He knew that he had quite without warning arrived at a once-in-a-lifetime experience.

Heart pounding but face a suave mask, he drifted into the store's interior. In situations like this it was all-essential not to let the seller know what you were interested in or even that you were interested at all.

The shadowy interior of the place lived up to its display window. There was the same piquant clutter of dusty memorables and among them several glass cases housing presumably choicer items, behind one of which stood a gaunt yet stocky elderly man whom Ritter sensed was the proprietor, but pretended not even to notice.

But his mind was so concentrated on the tarnished silver pawn he must possess that it was a stupefying surprise when his automatically flitting gaze stopped at a second and even greater once-in-a-lifetime item in the glass case behind which the proprietor stood. It was a dingy, old-fashioned gold pocket watch with the hours not in Roman numerals as they should have been in so venerable a timepiece, but in the form of dull gold and silver chess pieces as depicted in game-diagrams. Attached to the watch by a bit of thread was a slim, hexagonal gold key.

Ritter's mind almost froze with excitement. Here was the big brother of the skulking barbarian pawn. Here, its true value almost certainly unknown to its owner, was one of the supreme rarities of the world of chess-memorabilia. Here was no less than the gold watch Paul Morphy, meteorically short-reigned King of American chess, had been given by an adoring public in New York City on May 25, 1859, after the triumphal tour of London and Paris which had proven him to be perhaps the greatest chess genius of all time.

Ritter veered as if by lazy chance toward the case, his eyes resolutely fixed on a dull silver ankh at the opposite end from the chess watch. He paused like a sleepwalker across from the proprietor after what seemed like a suitable interval and—hoping the pounding of his heart wasn't audible—made a desultory inquiry about the ankh. The proprietor replied in as casual a fashion, though getting the item out for his inspection.

Ritter brooded over the silver love-cross for a bit, then shook his head and idly asked about another item and still another, working his insidious way toward the Morphy watch.

The proprietor responded to his queries in a low, bored voice, though in each case dutifully getting the item out to show Ritter. He was a very old and completely bald man with a craggy Baltic cast to his features. He vaguely reminded Ritter of someone.

Finally Ritter was asking about an old silver railroad watch next to the one he still refused to look at directly.

Then he shifted to another old watch with a complicated face with tiny windows showing the month and the phases of the moon, on the other side of the one that was keeping his heart a-pound.

His gambit worked. The proprietor at last-dragged out the Morphy watch, saying softly, "Here is an odd old piece that might interest you. The case is solid gold. It threatens to catch your interest, does it not?"

Ritter at last permitted himself a second devouring glance. It confirmed the first. Beyond shadow of a doubt this was the genuine relic that had haunted his thoughts for two-thirds of a lifetime.

What he said was "It's odd, all right. What are those funny little figures it has in place of hours?"

"Chessmen," the other explained. "See, that's a King at six o'clock, a Pawn at five, a Bishop at four, a Knight at three, a Rook at two, a Queen at one, another King at midnight, and then repeat, eleven to seven, around the dial."

"Why midnight rather than noon?" Ritter asked stupidly. He knew why.

The proprietor's wrinkled fingernail indicated a small window just above the center of the face. In it showed the letters P.M. "That's another rare feature," he explained. "I've handled very few watches that knew the difference between night and day."

"Oh, and I suppose those squares on which the chessmen are placed and which go around the dial in two and a half circles make a sort of check-erboard?"

"Chessboard," the other corrected. "Incidentally, there are exactly sixty-four squares, the right number."

Ritter nodded. "I suppose you're asking a fortune for it," he remarked, as if making conversation.

The other shrugged. "Only a thousand dollars."

Ritter's heart skipped a beat. He had more than ten times that in his bank account. A trifle, considering the stake.

But he bargained for the sake of appearances. At one point he argued, "But the watch doesn't run, I suppose."

"But it still has its hands," the old Balt with the hauntingly familiar face countered. "And it still has its works, as you can tell by the weight. They could be repaired, I imagine. A French movement. See, there's the hexagonal winding-key still with it."

A price of seven hundred dollars was finally agreed on. He paid out the fifty dollars he always carried with him and wrote a check for the remainder. After a call to his bank, it was accepted.

The watch was packed in a small box in a nest of fluffy cotton. Ritter put it in a pocket of his jacket and buttoned the flap.

He felt dazed. The Morphy watch, the watch Paul Morphy had kept his whole short life, despite his growing hatred of chess, the watch he had willed to his French admirer and favorite opponent Jules Arnous de Riviere, the watch that had then mysteriously disappeared, the watch of watches—was his!

He felt both weightless and dizzy as he moved toward the street, which blurred a little.

As he was leaving he noticed in the window something he'd forgotten—he wrote a check for fifty dollars for the silver barbarian pawn without bargaining.

He was in the street, feeling glorious and very tired. Faces and umbrellas were alike blurs. Rain pattered on his face unnoticed, but there came a stab of anxiety.

He held still and very carefully used his left hand to transfer the heavy little box—and the pawn in a twist of paper—to his trouser pocket, where he kept his left hand closed around them. Then he felt secure.

He flagged down a cab and gave his home address.

The passing scene began to come unblurred. He recognized Rimini's Italian Restaurant where his own chess game was now having a little renaissance after five years of foregoing tournament chess because he knew he was too old for it. A chess-smitten young cook there, indulged by the owner, had organized a tourney. The entrants were mostly young people. A tall, moody girl he thought of as the Czarina, who played a remarkable game, and a likeable, loudmouthed young Jewish lawyer he thought of as Rasputin, who played almost as good a game and talked a better one, both stood out. On impulse Ritter had entered the tournament because it was such a trifling one that it didn't really break his rule against playing serious chess. And, his old skills reviving nicely, he had done well enough to have a firm grip on third place, right behind Rasputin and the Czarina.

But now that he had the Morphy watch…

Why the devil should he think that having the Morphy watch should improve his chess game? he asked himself sharply. It was as silly as faith in the power of the relics of saints.

In his hand inside his left pocket the watch box vibrated eagerly, as if it contained a big live insect, a golden bee or beetle. But that, of course, was his imagination.

Stirf Ritter-Rebil (a proper name, he always felt, for a chess player, since they specialize in weird ones, from Euwe to Znosko-Borovsky, from Noteboom to Dus-Chotimirski) lived in a one-room and bath, five blocks west of Union Square and packed with files, books and also paintings wherever the wall space allowed, of his dead wife and parents, and of his son. Now that he was older, he liked living with clues to all of his life in view. There was a fine view of the Pacific and the Golden Gate and their fogs to the west, over a sea of roofs. On the orderly cluttered tables were two fine chess sets with positions set up.

Ritter cleared a space beside one of them and set in its center the box and packet. After a brief pause—as if for propitiatory prayer, he told himself sardonically—he gingerly took out the Morphy watch and centered it for inspection with the unwrapped silver pawn behind it.

Then, wiping and adjusting his glasses and from time to time employing a large magnifying glass, he examined both treasures exhaustively.

The outer edge of the dial was circled with a ring or wheel of twenty-four squares, twelve pale and twelve dark alternating. On the pale squares were the figures of chessmen indicating the hours, placed in the order the old Balt had described. The Black pieces went from midnight to five and were of silver set with tiny emeralds or bright jade, as his magnifying glass confirmed. The White pieces went from six to eleven and were of gold set with minute rubies or amethysts. He recalled that descriptions of the watch always mentioned the figures as being colored.

Inside that came a second circle of twenty-four pale and dark squares.

Finally, inside *that*, there was a two-thirds circle of sixteen squares below the center of the dial.

In the corresponding space above the center was the little window showing P.M.

The hands on the dial were stopped at 11:57—three minutes to midnight.

With a paperknife he carefully pried open the hinged back of the watch, on which were floridly engraved the initials PM—which he suddenly realized also stood for Paul Morphy.

On the inner golden back covering the works was engraved "France H&H"—the old Balt was right again—while scratched in very tiny—he used his magnifier once more—were a half-dozen sets of numbers, most of the sevens having the French slash. Pawnbrokers' marks. Had Arnous de Riviere pawned the treasure? Or later European owners? Oh well, chess players were an impecunious lot. There was also a hole by which the watch could be wound with its hexagonal key. He carefully wound it but of course nothing happened.

He closed the back and brooded on the dial. The sixty-four squares—twenty-four plus twenty-four plus sixteen—made a fantastic circular board. One of the many variants of chess he had played once or twice was cylindrical.

"Les échecs fantasques." he quoted. "It's a cynical madman's allegory with its doddering monarch, vampire queen, gangster knights, double-faced bishops, ramming rooks and inane pawns, whose supreme ambition is to change their sex and share the dodderer's bed."

With a sigh of regret he tore his gaze away from the watch and took up the pawn behind it. Here was a grim little fighter, he thought, bringing the tarnished silver figure close to his glasses. Naked longsword clasped against his chest, point down, iron skullcap low on forehead, face merciless as Death's. What did the golden legionaries look like?

Then Ritter's expression grew grim too, as he decided to do something he'd had in mind ever since glimpsing the barbarian pawn in the window. Making a long arm, he slid out a file drawer and after flipping a few tabs drew out a folder marked "Death of Alekhine." The light was getting bad. He switched on a big desk lamp against the night.

Soon he was studying a singularly empty photograph. It was of an un-occupied old armchair with a peg-in chess set open on one of the flat wooden arms. Behind the chess set stood a tiny figure. Bringing the mag-nifying glass once more into play, he confirmed what he had expected: that it was a precise mate to the barbarian pawn he had bought today.

He glanced through another item from the folder—an old letter on onionskin paper in a foreign script with cedillas under half the "C's" and tildes over half the "A's."

It was from his Portuguese friend, explaining that the photo was a repro-duction of one in the Lisbon police files.

The photo was of the chair in which Alexander Alekhine had been found dead of a heart attack on the top floor of a cheap Lisbon rooming house in 1946.

Alekhine had won the World's Chess Championship from Capablanca in 1927. He had held the world's record for the greatest number of games played simultaneously and blindfolded—thirty-two. In 1946 he was prepar-ing for an official match with the Russian champion Botvinnik, although he had played chess for the Axis in World War II. Though at times close to psychosis, he was considered the profoundest and most brilliant attacking player who had ever lived.

Had he also, Ritter asked himself, been one of the players to own the Morphy silver-and-gold chess set and the Morphy watch?

He reached for another file folder labeled "Death of Steinitz." This time he found a brownish daguerreotype showing an empty, narrow, old-fashioned hospital bed with a chessboard and set on a small table beside it. Among the chess pieces, Ritter's magnifier located another one of the unmistakable barbarian pawns.

Wilhelm Steinitz, called the Father of Modern Chess, who had held the world's championship for twenty-eight years, until his defeat by Emanuel Lasker in 1894. Steinitz, who had had two psychotic episodes and been hospitalized for them in the last years of his life, during the second of which he had believed he could move the chess pieces by electricity and challenged God to a match, offering God the odds of Pawn and Move. It was after the second episode that the daguerreotype had been taken which Ritter had acquired many years ago from the aged Emanuel Lasker.

Ritter leaned back wearily from the table, took off his glasses and knuckled his tired eyes. It was later than he'd imagined.

He thought about Paul Morphy retiring from chess at the age of twenty-one after beating every important player in the world and issuing a challenge, never accepted, to take on any master at the odds of Pawn and Move. After that contemptuous gesture in 1859 he had brooded for twenty-five years, mostly a recluse in his family home in New Orleans, emerging only fastidiously dressed and becaped for an afternoon promenade and regular attendance at the opera. He suffered paranoid episodes during which he believed his relatives were trying to steal his fortune and, of all things, his clothes. And he never spoke of chess or played it, except for an occasional game with his friend Maurian at the odds of Knight and Move.

Twenty-five years of brooding in solitude without the solace of playing chess, but with the Morphy chess set and the Morphy watch in the same room, testimonials to his world mastery.

Ritter wondered if those circumstances—with Morphy constantly thinking of chess, he felt sure—were not ideal for the transmission of the vibrations of thought and feeling into inanimate objects, in this case the golden Morphy set and watch.

Material objects intangibly vibrating with twenty-five years of the greatest chess thought and then by strange chance (chance alone?) falling into the hands of two other periodically psychotic chess champions, as the photographs of the pawns hinted.

An absurd fancy, Ritter told himself. And yet one to the pursuit of which he had devoted no small part of his life.

And now the richly vibrant objects were in *his* hands. What would be the effect of that on *his* game?

But to speculate in that direction was doubly absurd.

A wave of tiredness went through him. It was close to midnight.

He heated a small supper for himself, consumed it, drew the heavy window drapes tight, and undressed.

He turned back the cover of the big couch next to the table, switched off the light, and inserted himself into bed.

It was Ritter's trick to put himself to sleep by playing through a chess opening in his thoughts. Like any talented player, he could readily contest one blindfold game, though he could not quite visualize the entire board and often had to count moves square by square, especially with the bishops. He selected Breyer's Gambit, an old favorite of his.

He made a half-dozen moves.

Then suddenly the board was brightly illuminated in his mind, as if a light had been turned on there. He had to stare around to assure himself that the room was still dark as pitch. There was only the bright board inside his head.

His sense of awe was lost in luxuriant delight. He moved the mental pieces rapidly, yet saw deep into the possibilities of each position.

Far in the background he heard a church clock on Franklin boom out the dozen strokes of midnight. After a short while he announced mate in five by White. Black studied the position for perhaps a minute, then resigned.

Lying flat on his back he took several deep breaths. Never before had he played such a brilliant blindfold game—or game with sight even. That it was a game with himself didn't seem to matter—his personality had split neatly into two players.

He studied the final position for a last time, returned the pieces to their starting positions in his head, and rested a bit before beginning another game.

It was then he heard the ticking, a nervous sound five times as fast as the distant clock had knelled. He lifted his wristwatch to his ear. Yes, it was ticking rapidly too, but this was another ticking, louder.

He sat up silently in bed, leaned over the table, switched on the light.

The Morphy watch. That was where the louder ticks were coming from. The hands stood at twelve ten and the small window showed A.M.

For a long while he held that position—mute, motionless, aghast, wondering, fearing, doubting, dreaming dreams no mortal ever dared to dream before.

Let's see, Edgar Allan Poe had died when Morphy was twelve years old and beating his uncle, Ernest Morphy, then chess king of New Orleans.

It seemed impossible that a stopped watch with works well over one hundred years old should begin to run. Doubly impossible that it should begin to run at approximately the right time—his wristwatch and the Morphy watch were no more than a minute apart.

Yet the works might be in better shape than either he or the old Balt had guessed; watches did capriciously start and stop running. Coincidences were only coincidences. Yet he felt profoundly uneasy. He pinched himself and went through the other childish tests.

He said aloud, "I am Stirf Ritter-Rebil, an old man who lives in San Francisco and plays chess, and who yesterday discovered an unusual curio. But really, everything is perfectly normal..."

Nevertheless, he suddenly got the feeling of "A man-eating lion is a-prowl." It was the childish form terror still took for him on rare occasions. For a minute or so everything seemed *too* still, despite the ticking. The stirring of the heavy drapes at the window gave him a shiver, and the walls seemed thin, their protective power nil.

Gradually the sense of a killer lion moving outside them faded and his nerves calmed.

He switched off the light, the bright mental board returned, and the ticking became reassuring rather than otherwise. He began another game with himself, playing for Black the Classical Defense to the Ruy Lopez, another of his favorites.

This game proceeded as brilliantly and vividly as the first. There was the sense of a slim, man-shaped glow standing beside the bright board in the mental dark. After a while the shape grew amorphous and less bright, then split into three. However, it bothered him little, and when he at last announced mate in three for Black, he felt great satisfaction and profound fatigue.

Next day he was in exceptionally good spirits. Sunlight banished all night's terrors as he went about his ordinary business and writing chores. From time to time he reassured himself that he could still visualize a mental chessboard very clearly, and he thought now and again about the historical chess mystery he was in the midst of solving. The ticking of the Morphy watch carried an exciting, eager note. Toward the end of the afternoon he realized he was keenly anticipating visiting Rimini's to show off his new-found skill.

He got out an old gold watch chain and fob, snapped it to the Morphy watch, which he carefully wound again, pocketed them securely in his vest, and set out for Rimini's. It was a grand day—cool, brightly sunlit and a little windy. His steps were brisk. He wasn't thinking of all the strange happenings but of *chess*. It's been said that a man can lose his wife one day and forget her that night, playing *chess.*

Rimini's was a good, dark, garlic-smelling restaurant with an annex devoted to drinks, substantial free pasta appetizers and, for the nonce, chess. As he drifted into the long L-shaped room, Ritter became pleasantly aware of the row of boards, chessmen, and the intent, mostly young, faces bent above them.

Then Rasputin was grinning at him calculatedly and yapping at him cheerfully. They were due to play their tournament game. They checked out a set and were soon at it. Beside them the Czarina also contested a crucial game, her moody face askew almost as if her neck were broken, her bent wrists near her chin, her long fingers pointing rapidly at her pieces as she calculated combinations, like a sorceress putting a spell on them.

Ritter was aware of her, but only peripherally. For last night's bright mental board had returned, only now it was superimposed on the actual board before him. Complex combinations sprang to mind effortlessly. He beat Rasputin like a child. The Czarina caught the win from the corner of her eye and growled faintly in approval. She was winning her own game; Ritter beating Rasputin bumped her into first place. Rasputin was silent for once.

A youngish man with a black mustache was sharply inspecting Ritter's win. He was the California state champion, Martinez, who had recently played a simultaneous at Rimini's, winning fifteen games, losing none, drawing only with the Czarina. He now suggested a casual game to Ritter, who nodded somewhat abstractedly.

They contested two very hairy games—a Sicilian Defense by Martinez in which Ritter advanced all his pawns in front of his castled king in a wild-looking attack, and a Ruy Lopez by Martinez that Ritter answered with the Classical Defense, going to great lengths to preserve his powerful king's bishop. The mental board stayed superimposed, and it almost seemed to Ritter that there was a small faint halo over the piece he must next move or capture. To his mild astonishment he won both games.

A small group of chess-playing onlookers had gathered around their board. Martinez was looking at him speculatively, as if to ask, "Now just where did you spring from, old man, with your power game? I don't recall ever hearing of you."

Ritter's contentment would have been complete, except that among the kibitzers, toward the back, there was a slim young man whose face was always shadowed when Ritter glimpsed it. Ritter saw him in three different places, though never in movement and never for more than an instant. Somehow he seemed one onlooker too many. This disturbed Ritter obscurely, and his face had a thoughtful, abstracted expression when he finally quit Rimini's for the faintly drizzling evening streets. After a block he looked around, but so far as he could tell, he wasn't being followed. This time he walked the whole way to his apartment, passing several landmarks of Dashiell Hammett, Sam Spade, and *The Maltese Falcon.*

Gradually, under the benison of the foggy droplets, his mood changed to one of exaltation. He had just now played some beautiful chess, he was in the midst of an amazing historic chess mystery he'd always yearned to penetrate, and somehow the Morphy watch was working *for* him—he could actually hear its muffled ticking in the street, coming up from his waist to his ear.

Tonight his room was a most welcome retreat, *his* place, like an extension of his mind. He fed himself. Then he reviewed, with a Sherlock Holmes smile, what he found himself calling "The Curious Case of the Morphy Timepiece." He wished he had a Dr. Watson to hear him expound. First, the appearance of the watch after Morphy returned to New York on the *Persia* in 1859. Over paranoid years Morphy had imbued it with psychic energy and vast chessic wisdom. Or else—mark this, Doctor—he had set up the conditions whereby subsequent owners of the watch would *think* he had done such, for the supernatural is not our bailiwick, Watson. Next (after de Riviere) great Steinitz had come into possession of it and challenged God and died mad. Then, after a gap, paranoid Alekhine had owned it and devised diabolically brilliant, hyper-Morphian strategies of attack, and died all alone after a thousand treacheries in a miserable Lisbon flat with a peg-in chess set and the telltale barbarian pawn next to his corpse. Finally, after a hiatus of almost thirty years (Where had the watch and set been then? Who'd had their custody? Who was the old Balt?) the timepiece and a pawn had come into his own possession. A unique case, Doctor. There isn't even a parallel in Prague in 1863.

The nighted fog pressed against the windowpane and now and again a little rain pattered. San Francisco was a London City and had its own resident great detective. One of Dashiell Hammett's hobbies had been chess, even though there was no record of Spade having played the game.

From time to time Ritter studied the Morphy watch as it glowed and ticked on the table space he'd cleared. P.M. once more, he noted. The time: White Queen, ruby glittering, past Black King, microscopically emerald studded—I mean five minutes past midnight, Doctor. The witching hour, as the superstitiously minded would have it.

But to bed, to bed, Watson. We have much to do tomorrow—and, paradoxically, tonight.

Seriously, Ritter was glad when the golden glow winked out on the watch face, though the strident ticking kept on, and he wriggled himself into his couch-bed and arranged himself for thought. The mental board flashed on once more and he began to play. First he reviewed all the best games he'd ever played in his life—there weren't very many—discovering variations he'd never dreamed of before. Then he played through all his favorite games in the history of chess, from McDonnell-La Bourdonnais to Fischer-Spassky, not forgetting Steinitz-Zukertort and Alekhine-Bogolyubov. They were richer masterpieces than ever before—the mental board saw very deep. Finally he split his mind again and challenged himself to an eight-game blindfold match, Black against White. Against all expectation, Black won with three wins, two losses, and three draws.

But the night was not all imaginative and ratiocinative delight. Twice there came periods of eerie silence, which the ticking of the watch in the dark made only more complete, and two spells of the man-eating lion a-prowl that raised his hair at the roots. Once again there loomed the slim, faint, man-shaped glow beside the mental board and he wouldn't go away. Worse, he was joined by two other man-shaped glows, one short and stocky, with a limp, the other fairly tall, stocky too, and restless. These inner intruders bothered Ritter increasingly—who were they? And wasn't there beginning to be a faint fourth? He recalled the slim young elusive watcher with shadowed face of his games with Martinez and wondered if there was a connection.

Disturbing stuff—and most disturbing of all, the apprehension that his mind might be racked apart and fragmented abroad with all its machine-gun thinking, that it already extended by chessic veins from one chess-playing planet to another, to the ends of the universe.

He was profoundly glad when toward the end of his self-match, his brain began to dull and slow. His last memory was of an attempt to invent a game to be played on the circular board on the watch dial. He thought he was succeeding as his mind at last went spiraling off into unconsciousness.

Next day he awoke restless, scratchy, and eager—and with the feeling that the three or four dim figures had stood around his couch all night vibrating like strobe lights to the rhythm of the Morphy watch. Coffee heightened his alert nervousness. He rapidly dressed, snapped the Morphy watch to its chain and fob, pocketed the silver pawn, and went out to hunt down the store where he'd purchased the two items.

In a sense he never found it, though he tramped and minutely scanned Montgomery, Kearny, Grant, Stockton, Clay, Sacramento, California, Pine, Bush, and all the rest.

What he did find at long last was a store window with a grotesque pattern of dust on it that he was certain was identical with that on the window through which he had first glimpsed the barbarian pawn day before yesterday.

Only now the display space behind the window was empty and the whole store too, except for a tall, lanky Black with a fabulous Afro hair-do, sweeping up.

Ritter struck up a conversation with the man as he worked, and slowly winning his confidence, discovered that he was one of three partners opening a store there that would be stocked solely with African imports.

Finally, after the Black had fetched a great steaming pail of soapy water and a long-handled roller mop and begun to efface forever the map of dust by which Ritter had identified the place, the man at last grew confidential.

"Yeah," he said, "there *was* a queer old character had a secondhand store here until yesterday that had every crazy thing you could dig for sale, some junk, some real fancy. Then he cleared everything out into two big trucks in a great rush, with me breathing down his neck every minute because he'd been supposed to do it the day before.

"Oh, but he was a fabulous cat, though," the Black went on with a reminiscent grin as he sloshed away the last peninsulas and archipelagos of the dust map. "One time he said to me, 'Excuse me while I rest,' and—you're not going to believe this—he went into a corner and stood on his head. I'm telling you he did, man. I'd like to bust a gut. I thought he'd have a stroke—and he did get a bit lavender in the face—but after three minutes exact—I timed him—he flipped back onto his feet neat as you could ask and went on with his work twice as fast as before, supervising his carriers out of their skulls. Wow, that was an event."

Ritter departed without comment. He had got the final clue he'd been seeking to the identity of the old Balt and likewise the fourth and most shadowy form that had begun to haunt his mental chessboard.

Casually standing on his head, saying "It threatens to catch your interest"—why, it had to be Aaron Nimzovich, most hyper-eccentric player of them all and Father of Hypermodern Chess, who had been Alekhine's most dangerous but ever-evaded challenger. Why, the old Balt had even looked exactly like an aged Nimzovich—hence Ritter's constant sense of a facial familiarity. Of course, Nimzovich had supposedly died in the 1930s in his home city of Riga in the U.S.S.R., but what were life and breath to the forces with which Ritter was now embroiled?

It seemed to him that there were four dim figures stalking him relentlessly as lions right now in the Chinatown crowds, while despite the noise he could hear and feel the ticking of the Morphy watch on his waist.

He fled to the Danish Kitchen at the St. Francis Hotel and consumed cup on cup of good coffee and two orders of Eggs Benedict, and had his mental chessboard flashing on and off in his mind like a strobe light, and wondered if he shouldn't hurl the Morphy watch into the Bay to be rid of the influence racking his mind apart and destroying his sense of reality.

But then with the approach of evening, the urge toward *chess* gripped him more and more imperiously and he headed once again for Rimini's.

Rasputin and the Czarina were there and also Martinez again, and with the last a distinguished silver-haired man whom Martinez introduced as the South American international master, Pontebello, suggesting that he and Ritter have a quick game.

The board glowed again with the superimposed mental one, the halos were there once more, and Ritter won as if against a tyro.

At that, chess fever seized him entirely and he suggested he immediately play four simultaneous blindfold games with the two masters and the Czarina and Rasputin, Pontebello acting also as referee.

There were incredulous looks aplenty at that, but he *had* won those two games from Martinez and now the one from Pontebello, so arrangements were quickly made, Ritter insisting on an actual blindfold. All the other players crowded around to observe.

The simul began. There were now four mental boards glowing in Ritter's mind. It did not matter now—that there were four dim forms with them, one by each. Ritter played with a practiced brilliance, combinations bubbled, he called out his moves crisply and unerringly. And so he beat the Czarina and Rasputin quickly. Pontebello took a little longer, and he drew with Martinez by perpetual check.

There was silence as he took off the blindfold to scan a circle of astonished faces and four shadowed ones behind them. He felt the joy of absolute chess mastery. The only sound he heard was the ticking, thunderous to him, of the Morphy watch.

Pontebello was first to speak. To Ritter, "Do you realize, master, what you've just done?" To Martinez, "Have you the scores of all four games?" To Ritter again, "Excuse me, but you look pale, as if you've just seen a ghost." "Four," Ritter corrected quietly. "Those of Morphy, Steinitz, Alekhine, and Nimzovich."

"Under the circumstances, most appropriate," commented Pontebello, while Ritter sought out again the four shadowed faces in the background. They were still there, though they had shifted their positions and withdrawn a little into the varied darknesses of Rimini's.

Amid talk of scheduling another blindfold exhibition and writing a multiple-signed letter describing tonight's simul to the U.S. Chess Federation—not to mention Pontebello's searching queries as to Ritter's chess career—he tore himself away and made for home through the dark streets, certain that four shadowy figures stalked behind him. The call of the mental *chess* in his own room was not to be denied.

Ritter forgot no moment of that night, for he did not sleep at all. The glowing board in his mind was an unquenchable beacon, an all-demanding mandala. He replayed all the important games of history, finding new moves. He contested two matches with himself, then one each with Morphy, Steinitz, Alekhine and Nimzovich, winning the first two, drawing the third, and losing the last by a half point. Nimzovich was the only one to speak, saying, "I am both dead and alive, as I'm sure you know. Please don't smoke, or threaten to."

He stacked eight mental boards and played two games of three-dimensional chess, Black winning both. He traveled to the ends of the universe, finding chess everywhere he went, and contesting a long game, more complex than 3-D chess, on which the fate of the universe depended. He drew it.

And all through the long night the four were with him in the room and the man-eating lion stared in through the window with black-and-white checkered mask and silver mane. While the Morphy watch ticked like a death-march drum. All figures vanished when the dawn came creeping, though the mental board stayed bright and busy into full daylight and showed no signs of vanishing ever. Ritter felt overpoweringly tired, his mind racked to atoms, on the verge of death.

But he knew what he had to do. He got a small box and packed into it, in cotton wool, the silver barbarian pawn, the old photograph and daguerrotype, and a piece of paper on which he scribbled only:

Morphy, 1859–1884
de Riviere, 1884–?
Steinitz, ?–1900
Alekhine, ?–1946
Nimzovich, 1946–now
Ritter-Rebil, 3 days

Then he packed the watch in the box too, it stopped ticking, its hands were still at last, and in Ritter's mind the mental board winked out.

He took one last devouring gaze at the grotesque, glittering dial. Then he shut the box, wrapped and sealed and corded it, boldly wrote on it in black ink "Chess Champion of the World" and added the proper address.

He took it to the post office on Van Ness and sent it off by registered mail. Then he went home and slept like the dead.

Ritter never received a response. But he never got the box back either. Sometimes he wonders if the subsequent strange events in the Champion's life might have had anything to do with the gift.

And on even rarer occasions he wonders what would have happened if he had faced the challenge of death and let his mind be racked to bits, if that was what was to happen.

But on the whole he is content. Questions from Martinez and the others he has put off with purposefully vague remarks.

He still plays chess at Rimini's. Once he won another game from Martinez, when the latter was contesting a simul against twenty-three players.

BELSEN EXPRESS

GEORGE SIMISTER WATCHED THE BLUE FLAMES writhe beautifully in the grate, like dancing girls drenched with alcohol and set afire, and congratulated himself on having survived well through the middle of the twentieth century without getting involved in military service, world-saving, or any activities that interfered with the earning and enjoyment of money. Outside rain dripped, a storm snarled at the city from the outskirts, and sudden gusts of wind produced in the chimney a sound like the mourning of doves. Simister shimmied himself a fraction of an inch deeper in his easy chair and took a slow sip of diluted scotch—he was sensitive to most cheaper liquors. Simister's physiology was on the delicate side; during his childhood certain tastes and odors, playing on an elusive heart weakness, had been known to make him faint.

The outspread newspaper started to slip from his knee. He detained it, let his glance rove across the next page, noted a headline about an uprising in Prague like that in Hungary in 1956 and murmured, "Damn Slavs," noted another about border fighting around Israel and muttered, "Damn Jews," and let the paper go. He took another sip of his drink, yawned, and watched a virginal blue flame flutter frightenedly the length of the log before it turned to a white smoke ghost. There was a sharp *knock-knock*.

Simister jumped and then got up and hurried tight lipped to the front door. Lately some of the neighborhood children had been trying to annoy him probably because his was the most respectable and best-kept house on the block. Doorbell ringing, obscene sprayed scrawls, that sort of thing. And hardly children—young rowdies rather, who needed rough handling and a trip to the police station. He was really angry by the time he reached the door and swung it wide. There was nothing but a big wet empty darkness.

245

A chilly draft spattered a couple of cold drops on him. Maybe the noise had come from the fire. He shut the door and started back to the living room, but a small pile of books untidily nested in wrapping paper on the hall table caught his eye and he grimaced.

They constituted a blotchily addressed parcel which the postman had delivered by mistake a few mornings ago. Simister could probably have deciphered the address, for it was clearly on this street, and rectified the postman's error, but he did not choose to abet the activities of illiterates with leaky pens. And the delivery must have been a mistake for the top book was titled *The Scourge of the Swastika* and the other two had similar titles, and Simister had an acute distaste for books that insisted on digging up that satisfactorily buried historical incident known as Nazi Germany.

The reason for this distaste was a deeply hidden fear that George Simister shared with millions, but that he had never revealed even to his wife. It was a quite unrealistic and now completely anachronistic fear of the Gestapo.

It had begun years before the Second World War, with the first small reports from Germany of minority persecutions and organized hoodlumism—the sense of something reaching out across the dark Atlantic to threaten his life, his security, and his confidence that he would never have to suffer pain except in a hospital.

Of course it had never got at all close to Simister, but it had exercised an evil tyranny over his imagination. There was one nightmarish series of scenes that had slowly grown in his mind and then had kept bothering him for a long time. It began with a thunderous knocking, of boots and rifle butts rather than fists, and a shouted demand: "Open up! It's the Gestapo." Next he would find himself in a stream of frantic people being driven toward a portal where a division was made between those reprieved and those slated for immediate extinction. Last he would be inside a closed motor van jammed so tightly with people that it was impossible to move. After a long time the van would stop, but the motor would keep running, and from the floor, leisurely seeking the crevices between the packed bodies, the entrapped exhaust fumes would begin to mount.

Now in the shadowy hall the same horrid movie had a belated showing. Simister shook his head sharply, as if he could shake the scenes out, reminding himself that the Gestapo was dead and done with for more than ten years. He felt the angry impulse to throw in the fire the books responsible for the return of his waking nightmare. But he remembered that books are hard to burn. He stared at them uneasily, excited by thoughts of torture and confinement, concentration and death camps, but knowing the nasty aftermath they left in his mind. Again he felt a sudden impulse, this time to bundle the books together and throw them in the trash can. But that would mean getting wet; it could wait until tomorrow. He put the screen in front of the fire, which had died and was smoking like a crematory, and went to bed.

Some hours later he waked with the memory of a thunderous knocking.

He started up, exclaiming, "Those damned kids!" The drawn shades seemed abnormally dark—probably they'd thrown a stone through the street lamp.

He put one foot on the chilly floor. It was now profoundly still. The storm had gone off like a roving cat. Simister strained his ears. Beside him his wife breathed with irritating evenness. He wanted to wake her and explain about the young delinquents. It was criminal that they were permitted to roam the streets at this hour. Girls with them too, likely as not.

The knocking was not repeated. Simister listened for footsteps going away, or for the creaking of boards that would betray a lurking presence on the porch.

After a while he began to wonder if the knocking might not have been part of a dream, or perhaps a final rumble of actual thunder. He lay down and pulled the blankets up to his neck. Eventually his muscles relaxed and he got to sleep.

At breakfast he told his wife about it.

"George, it may have been burglars," she said.

"Don't be stupid, Joan. Burglars don't knock. If it was anything it was those damned kids."

"Whatever it was, I wish you'd put a bigger bolt on the front door."

"Nonsense. If I'd known you were going to act this way I wouldn't have said anything. I told you it was probably just the thunder."

But the next night at about the same hour it happened again.

This time there could be little question of dreaming. The knocking still reverberated in his ears. And there had been words mixed with it, some sort of yapping in a foreign language. Probably the children of some of those European refugees who had settled in the neighborhood.

Last night they'd fooled him by keeping perfectly still after banging on the door, but tonight he knew what to do. He tiptoed across the bedroom and went down the stairs rapidly, but quietly because of his bare feet. In the hall he snatched up something to hit them with, then in one motion unlocked and jerked open the door.

There was no one.

He stood looking at the darkness. He was puzzled as to how they could have got away so quickly and silently. He shut the door and switched on the light. Then he felt the thing in his hand. It was one of the books. With a feeling of disgust he dropped it on the others. He must remember to throw them out first thing tomorrow.

But he overslept and had to rush. The feeling of disgust or annoyance, or something akin, must have lingered, however, for he found himself sensitive to things he wouldn't ordinarily have noticed. People especially. The swollen-handed man seemed deliberately surly as he counted Simister's pennies and handed him the paper. The tight-lipped woman at the gate hesitated suspiciously, as if he were trying to pass off a last month's ticket.

And when he was hurrying up the stairs in response to an approaching rumble, he brushed against a little man in an oversize coat and received in return a glance that gave him a positive shock.

Simister vaguely remembered having seen the little man several times before. He had the thin nose, narrow-set eyes and receding chin that is by a stretch of the imagination described as "rat-faced." In the movies he'd have played a stool pigeon. The flapping overcoat was rather comic.

But there seemed to be something at once so venomous and sly, so time-bidingly vindictive, in the glance he gave Simister that the latter was taken aback and almost missed the train.

He just managed to squeeze through the automatically closing door of the smoker after the barest squint at the sign to assure himself that the train was an express. His heart was pounding in a way that another time would have worried him, but now he was immersed in a savage pleasure at having thwarted the man in the oversize coat. The latter hadn't hurried fast enough and Simister had made no effort to hold open the door for him.

As a smooth surge of electric power sent them sliding away from the station Simister pushed his way from the vestibule into the car and snagged a strap. From the next one already swayed his chief commuting acquaintance, a beefy, suspiciously red-nosed, irritating man named Holstrom, now reading a folded newspaper one-handed. He shoved a headline in Simister's face. The latter knew what to expect.

"Atomic Weapons for West Germany," he read tonelessly. Holstrom was always trying to get him into outworn arguments about totalitarianism, Nazi Germany, racial prejudice and the like. "Well, what about it?"

Holstrom shrugged. "It's a natural enough step, I suppose, but it started me thinking about the top Nazis and whether we really got all of them."

"Of course," Simister snapped.

"I'm not so sure," Holstrom said. "I imagine quite a few of them got away and are still hiding out somewhere."

But Simister refused the bait. The question bored him. Who talked about the Nazis any more? For that matter, the whole trip this morning was boring; the smoker was overcrowded; and when they finally piled out at the downtown terminus, the rude jostling increased his irritation.

The crowd was approaching an iron fence that arbitrarily split the stream of hurrying people into two sections which reunited a few steps farther on. Beside the fence a new guard was standing, or perhaps Simister hadn't noticed him before. A cocky-looking young fellow with close-cropped blond hair and cold blue eyes.

Suddenly it occurred to Simister that he habitually passed to the right of the fence, but that this morning he was being edged over toward the left. This trifling circumstance, coming on top of everything else, made him boil. He deliberately pushed across the stream, despite angry murmurs and the hard stare of the guard.

He had intended to walk the rest of the way, but his anger made him forgetful and before he realized it he had climbed aboard a bus. He soon regretted it. The bus was even more crowded than the smoker and the standees were morose and lumpy in their heavy overcoats. He was tempted to get off and waste his fare, but he was trapped in the extreme rear and moreover shrank from giving the impression of a man who didn't know his own mind.

Soon another annoyance was added to the ones already plaguing him—a trace of exhaust fumes was seeping up from the motor at the rear. He immediately began to feel ill. He looked around indignantly, but the others did not seem to notice the odor, or else accepted it fatalistically.

In a couple of blocks the fumes had become so bad that Simister decided he must get off at the next stop. But as he started to push past her, a fat woman beside him gave him such a strangely apathetic stare that Simister, whose mind was perhaps a little clouded by nausea, felt almost hypnotized by it, so that it was several seconds before he recalled and carried out his intention.

Ridiculous, but the woman's face stuck in his mind all day.

In the evening he stopped at a hardware store. After supper his wife noticed him working in the front hall.

"Oh, you're putting on a bolt," she said.

"Well, you asked me to, didn't you?"

"Yes, but I didn't think you'd do it."

"I decided I might as well." He gave the screw a final turn and stepped back to survey the job. "Anything to give you a feeling of security."

Then he remembered the stuff he had been meaning to throw out that morning. The hall table was bare. "What did you do with them?" he asked.

"What?"

"Those fool books."

"Oh, those. I wrapped them up again and gave them to the postman."

"Now why did you do that? There wasn't any return address and I might have wanted to look at them."

"But you said they weren't addressed to us and you hate all that war stuff."

"I know, but—" he said and then stopped, hopeless of making her understand why he particularly wanted to feel he had got rid of that package himself, and by throwing it in the trash can. For that matter, he didn't quite understand his feelings himself. He began to poke around the hall.

"I did return the package," his wife said sharply. "I'm not losing my memory."

"Oh, all right!" he said and started for bed.

That night no knocking awakened him, but rather a loud crashing and rending of wood along with a harsh metallic *ping* like a lock giving.

In a moment he was out of bed, his sleep-sodden nerves jangling with anger. Those hoodlums! Rowdy pranks were perhaps one thing, deliberate destruction of property certainly another. He was halfway down the stairs before it occurred to him that the sound he had heard had a distinctly menacing aspect. Juvenile delinquents who broke down doors would hardly panic at the appearance of an unarmed householder.

But just then he saw that the front door was intact.

Considerably puzzled and apprehensive, he searched the first floor and even ventured into the basement, racking his brains as to just what could have caused such a noise. The water heater? Weight of the coal bursting a side of the bin? Those objects were intact. But perhaps the porch trellis giving way?

That last notion kept him peering out of the front window several moments. When he turned around there was someone behind him.

"I didn't mean to startle you," his wife said. "What's the matter, George?"

"I don't know. I thought I heard a sound. Something being smashed."

He expected that would send her into one of her burglar panics, but instead she kept looking at him.

"Don't stand there all night," he said. "Come on to bed."

"George, is something worrying you? Something you haven't told me about?"

"Of course not. Come on."

Next morning Holstrom was on the platform when Simister got there and they exchanged guesses as to whether the dark rainclouds would burst before they got downtown. Simister noticed the man in the oversize coat loitering about, but he paid no attention to him.

Since it was a bank holiday there were empty seats in the smoker and he and Holstrom secured one. As usual the latter had his newspaper. Simister waited for him to start his ideological sniping—a little uneasily for once; usually he was secure in his prejudices, but this morning he felt strangely vulnerable.

It came. Holstrom shook his head. "That's a bad business in Czechoslovakia. Maybe we were a little too hard on the Nazis."

To his surprise Simister found himself replying with both nervous hypocrisy and uncharacteristic vehemence. "Don't be ridiculous! Those rats deserved a lot worse than they got!"

As Holstrom turned toward him saying, "Oh, so you've changed your mind about the Nazis," Simister thought he heard someone just behind him say at the same time in a low, distinct, pitiless voice: "I heard you."

He glanced around quickly. Leaning forward a little, but with his face turned sharply away as if he had just become interested in something passing the window, was the man in the oversize coat.

"What's wrong?" Holstrom asked.

"What do you mean?"

"You've turned pale. You look sick."

"I don't feel that way."

"Sure? You know, at our age we've got to begin to watch out. Didn't you once tell me something about your heart?"

Simister managed to laugh that off, but when they parted just outside the train he was conscious that Holstrom was still eyeing him rather closely.

As he slowly walked through the terminus his face began to assume an abstracted look. In fact he was lost in thought to such a degree that when he approached the iron fence, he started to pass it on the left. Luckily the crowd was thin and he was able to cut across to the right without difficulty. The blond young guard looked at him closely—perhaps he remembered yesterday morning.

Simister had told himself that he wouldn't again under any circumstances take the bus, but when he got outside it was raining torrents. After a moment's hesitation he climbed aboard. It seemed even more crowded than yesterday, if that were possible, with more of the same miserable people, and the damp air made the exhaust odor particularly offensive.

The abstracted look clung to his face all day long. His secretary noticed, but did not comment. His wife did, however, when she found him poking around in the hall after supper.

"Are you still looking for that package, George?" Her tone was flat.

"Of course not," he said quickly, shutting the table drawer he'd opened.

She waited. "Are you sure you didn't order those books?"

"What gave you that idea?" he demanded. "You know I didn't."

"I'm glad," she said. "I looked through them. There were pictures. They were nasty."

"You think I'm the sort of person who'd buy books for the sake of nasty pictures?"

"Of course not, dear, but I thought you might have seen them and they were what had depressed you."

"Have I been depressed?"

"Yes. Your heart hasn't been bothering you, has it?"

"No."

"Well, what is it then?"

"I don't know." Then with considerable effort he said, "I've been thinking about war and things."

"War! No wonder you're depressed. You shouldn't think about things you don't like, especially when they aren't happening. What started you?"

"Oh, Holstrom keeps talking to me on the train."

"Well, don't listen to him."

"I won't."

"Well, cheer up then."

"I will."

"And don't let anyone make you look at morbid pictures. There was one of some people who had been gassed in a motor van and then laid out—"

"Please, Joan! Is it any better to tell me about them than to have me look at them?"

"Of course not, dear. That was silly of me. But do cheer up."

"Yes."

The puzzled, uneasy look was still in her eyes as she watched him go down the front walk next morning. It was foolish, but she had the feeling that his gray suit was really black—and he had whimpered in his sleep. With a shiver at her fancy she stepped inside.

That morning George Simister created a minor disturbance in the smoker, it was remembered afterwards, though Holstrom did not witness the beginning of it. It seems that Simister had run to catch the express and had almost missed it, due to a collision with a small man in a large overcoat. Someone recalled that trifling prelude because of the amusing circumstance that the small man, although he had been thrown to his knees and the collision was chiefly Simister's fault, was still anxiously begging Simister's pardon after the latter had dashed on.

Simister just managed to squeeze through the closing door while taking a quick squint at the sign. It was then that his queer behavior started. He instantly turned around and unsuccessfully tried to force his way out again, even inserting his hands in the crevice between the door frame and the rubber edge of the sliding door and yanking violently.

Apparently as soon as he noticed the train was in motion, he turned away from the door, his face pale and set, and roughly pushed his way into the interior of the car.

There he made a beeline for the little box in the wall containing the identifying signs of the train and the miniature window which showed in reverse the one now in use, which read simply EXPRESS. He stared at it as if he couldn't believe his eyes and then started to turn the crank, exposing in turn all the other white signs on the roll of black cloth. He scanned each one intently, oblivious to the puzzled or outraged looks of those around him.

He had been through all the signs once and was starting through them again before the conductor noticed what was happening and came hurrying. Ignoring his expostulations, Simister asked him loudly if this was really the express. Upon receiving a curt affirmative, Simister went on to assert that he had in the moment of squeezing aboard glimpsed another sign in the window—and he mentioned a strange name. He seemed both very positive and very agitated about it, the conductor said. The latter asked Simister to spell the name. Simister haltingly complied: "B-E-L-S-E-N..." The conductor shook his head, then his eyes widened and he demanded, "Say, are you trying to kid me? That was one of those Nazi death camps."

Simister slunk toward the other end of the car.

It was there that Holstrom saw him, looking "as if he'd just got a terrible shock." Holstrom was alarmed—and as it happened felt a special private guilt—but could hardly get a word out of him, though he made several attempts to start a conversation, choosing uncharacteristically neutral topics. Once, he remembered, Simister looked up and said, "Do you suppose there are some things a man simply can't escape, no matter how quietly he lives or how carefully he plans?" But his face immediately showed he had realized there was at least one very obvious answer to this question, and Holstrom didn't know what to say. Another time he suddenly remarked, "I wish we were like the British and didn't have standing in buses," but he subsided as quickly. As they neared the downtown terminus Simister seemed to brace up a little, but Holstrom was still worried about him to such a degree that he went out of his way to follow him through the terminus. "I was afraid something would happen to him, I don't know what," Holstrom said. "I would have stayed right beside him except he seemed to resent my presence."

Holstrom's private guilt, which intensified his anxiety and doubtless accounted for his feeling that Simister resented him, was due to the fact that ten days ago, cumulatively irritated by Simister's smug prejudices and blinkered narrow-mindedness, he had anonymously mailed him three books recounting with uncompromising realism and documentation some of the least pleasant aspects of the Nazi tyranny. Now he couldn't but feel they might have helped to shake Simister up in a way he hadn't intended, and he was ashamedly glad that he had been in such a condition when he sent the package that it had been addressed in a drunken scrawl. He never discussed this matter afterwards, except occasionally to make strangely feelingful remarks about "what little things can unseat a spring in a man's clockworks!"

So, continuing Holstrom's story, he followed Simister at a distance as the latter dejectedly shuffled across the busy terminus. "Terminus?" Holstrom once interrupted his story to remark. "He's a god of endings, isn't he?—and of human rights. Does that mean anything?"

When Simister was nearing an iron fence a puzzling episode occurred. He was about to pass it to the right, when someone just ahead of him lurched or stumbled. Simister almost fell himself, veering toward the fence. A nearby guard reached out and in steadying him pulled him around the fence to the left.

Then, Holstrom maintains, Simister turned for a moment and Holstrom caught a glimpse of his face. There must have been something peculiarly frightening about that backward look, something perhaps that Holstrom cannot adequately describe, for he instantly forgot any idea of surveillance at a distance and made every effort to catch up.

But the crowd from another commuters' express enveloped Holstrom. When he got outside the terminus it was some moments before he spotted Simister in the midst of a group jamming their way aboard an already crowded bus across the street. This perplexed Holstrom, for he knew Simister didn't have to take the bus and he recalled his recent complaint.

Heavy traffic kept Holstrom from crossing. He says he shouted, but Simister did not seem to hear him. He got the impression that Simister was making feeble efforts to get out of the crowd that was forcing him onto the bus, but, "They were all jammed together like cattle."

The best testimony to Holstrom's anxiety about Simister is that as soon as the traffic thinned a trifle he darted across the street, skipping between the cars. But by then the bus had started. He was in time only for a whiff of particularly obnoxious exhaust fumes.

As soon as he got to his office he phoned Simister. He got Simister's secretary and what she had to say relieved his worries, which is ironic in view of what happened a little later.

What happened a little later is best described by the same girl. She said, "I never saw him come in looking so cheerful, the old grouch—excuse me. But anyway he came in all smiles, like he'd just got some bad news about somebody else, and right away he started to talk and kid with everyone, so that it was awfully funny when that man called up worried about him. I guess maybe, now I think back, he did seem a bit shaken underneath, like a person who's just had a narrow squeak and is very thankful to be alive.

"Well, he kept it up all morning. Then just as he was throwing his head back to laugh at one of his own jokes, he grabbed his chest, let out an awful scream, doubled up and fell on the floor. Afterwards I couldn't believe he was dead, because his lips stayed so red and there were bright spots of color on his cheeks, like rouge. Of course it was his heart, though you can't believe what a scare that stupid first doctor gave us when he came in and looked at him."

Of course, as she said, it must have been Simister's heart, one way or the other. And it is undeniable that the doctor in question was an ancient, possibly incompetent dispenser of penicillin, morphine and snap diagnoses swifter than Charcot's. They only called him because his office was in the same building. When Simister's own doctor arrived and pronounced it heart failure, which was what they'd thought all along, everyone was much relieved and inclined to be severely critical of the first doctor for having said something that sent them all scurrying to open the windows.

For when the first doctor had come in, he had taken one look at Simister and rasped, "Heart failure? Nonsense! Look at the color of his face. Cherry red. That man died of carbon monoxide poisoning."

CATCH THAT ZEPPELIN!

THIS YEAR ON A TRIP TO NEW YORK CITY to visit my son who is a social historian at a leading municipal university there, I had a very unsettling experience. At black moments, of which at my age I have quite a few, it still makes me distrust profoundly those absolute boundaries in Space and Time which are our sole protection against Chaos, and fear that my mind—no, my entire individual existence—may at any moment at all and without any warning whatsoever be blown by a sudden gust of Cosmic Wind to an entirely different spot in a Universe of Infinite Possibilities. Or, rather, into another Universe altogether. And that my mind and individuality will be changed to fit.

But at other moments, which are still in the majority, I believe that my unsettling experience was only one of those remarkably vivid waking dreams to which old people become increasingly susceptible, generally waking dreams about the past in which at some crucial point one made an entirely different and braver choice than one actually did, or in which the whole world made such a decision with a completely different future resulting. Golden glowing might-have-beens nag increasingly at the minds of some older people.

In line with this interpretation I must admit that my whole unsettling experience was structured very much like a dream. It began with startling flashes of a changed world. It continued into a longer period when I completely accepted the changed world and delighted in it and, despite fleeting quivers of uneasiness, wished I could bask in its glow forever. And it ended in horrors, or nightmares, which I hate to mention, let alone discuss, until I must.

Opposing this dream notion, there are times when I am completely convinced that what happened to me in Manhattan and in a certain famous building there was no dream at all, but absolutely real, and that I did indeed visit another Time Stream.

Finally, I must point out that what I am about to tell you I am necessarily describing in retrospect, highly aware of several transitions involved and, whether I want to or not, commenting on them and making deductions that never once occurred to me at the time.

No, at the time it happened to me—and now at this moment of writing I am convinced that it did happen and was absolutely real—one instant simply succeeded another in the most natural way possible. I questioned nothing.

As to why it all happened to me, and what particular mechanism was involved, well, I am convinced that every man or woman has rare brief moments of extreme sensitivity, or rather vulnerability, when his mind and entire being may be blown by the Change Winds to Somewhere Else. And then, by what I call the Law of the Conservation of Reality, blown back again.

I was walking down Broadway somewhere near 34th Street. It was a chilly day, sunny despite the smog—a bracing day—and I suddenly began to stride along more briskly than is my cautious habit, throwing my feet ahead of me with a faint suggestion of the goose step. I also threw back my shoulders and took deep breaths, ignoring the fumes which tickled my nostrils. Beside me, traffic growled and snarled, rising at times to a machine-gun rata-tat-tat. While pedestrians were scuttling about with that desperate ratlike urgency characteristic of all big American cities, but which reaches its ultimate in New York, I cheerfully ignored that too. I even smiled at the sight of a ragged bum and a furcoated, gray-haired society lady both independently dodging across the street through the hurtling traffic with a cool practiced skill one sees only in America's biggest metropolis.

Just then I noticed a dark, wide shadow athwart the street ahead of me. It could not be that of a cloud, for it did not move. I craned my neck sharply and looked straight up like the veriest yokel, a regular *Hans-Kopf-in-die-Luft* (Hans-Head-in-the-Air, a German figure of comedy).

My gaze had to climb up the giddy 102 stories of the tallest building in the world, the Empire State. My gaze was strangely accompanied by the vision of a gigantic, long-fanged ape making the same ascent with a beautiful girl in one paw—oh, yes, I was recollecting the charming American fantasy-film *King Kong*, or as they name it in Sweden, *Kong King*.

And then my gaze clambered higher still, up the 222-foot sturdy tower, to the top of which was moored the nose of the vast, breathtakingly beautiful, streamlined, silvery shape which was making the shadow.

Now here is a most important point. I was not at the time in the least startled by what I saw. I knew at once that it was simply the bow section of the German Zeppelin *Ostwald*, named for the great German pioneer of physical chemistry and electrochemistry, and queen of the mighty passenger and light-freight fleet of luxury airliners working out of Berlin, Baden-Baden, and Bremerhaven. That matchless Armada of Peace, each titanic airship named for a world-famous German scientist—the *Mach*, the *Nernst*, the *Humboldt*, the *Fritz Haber*, the French-named *Antoine Henri Becquerel*, the American-named *Edison*, the Polish-named *Sklodowska*, the American-Polish *T. Sklodowska Edison*, and even the Jewish-named *Einstein*! The great humanitarian navy in which I held a not unimportant position as international sales consultant and *Fachman*—I mean expert. My chest swelled with justified pride at this *edel*—nobel—achievement of *der Vaterland*.

I knew also without any mind-searching or surprise that the length of the *Ostwald* was more than one half the 1,472-foot height of the Empire State Building plus its mooring tower, thick enough to hold an elevator. And my heart swelled again with the thought that the Berlin Zeppelinturm (dirigible tower) was only a few meters less high. Germany, I told myself, need not strain for mere numerical records—her sweeping scientific and technical achievements speak for themselves to the entire planet.

All this literally took little more than a second, and I never broke my snappy stride. As my gaze descended, I cheerfully hummed under my breath *Deutschland, Deutschland über alles*.

The Broadway I saw was utterly transformed, though at the time this seemed every bit as natural as the serene presence of the *Ostwald* high overhead, vast ellipsoid held aloft by helium. Silvery electric trucks and buses and private cars innumerable purred along far more evenly and quietly, and almost as swiftly, as had the noisy, stenchful, jerky gasoline-powered vehicles only moments before, though to me now the latter were completely forgotten. About two blocks ahead, an occasional gleaming electric car smoothly swung into the wide silver arch of a quick-battery-change station, while others emerged from under the arch to rejoin the almost dreamlike stream of traffic.

The air I gratefully inhaled was fresh and clean, without trace of smog.

The somewhat fewer pedestrians around me still moved quite swiftly, but with a dignity and courtesy largely absent before, with the numerous blackamoors among them quite as well dressed and exuding the same quiet confidence as the Caucasians.

The only slightly jarring note was struck by a tall, pale, rather emaciated man in black dress and with unmistakably Hebraic features. His somber clothing was somewhat shabby, though well kept, and his thin shoulders were hunched. I got the impression he had been looking closely at me, and then instantly glanced away as my eyes sought his. For some reason I recalled what my son had told me about the City College of New York—CCNY—being referred to surreptitiously and jokingly as Christian College Now Yiddish. I couldn't help chuckling a bit at that witticism, though I am glad to say it was a genial little guffaw rather than a malicious snicker. Germany in her well-known tolerance and noble-mindedness has completely outgrown her old, disfiguring anti-Semitism—after all, we must admit in all fairness that perhaps a third of our great men are Jews or carry Jewish genes, Haber and Einstein among them—despite what dark and, yes, wicked memories may lurk in the subconscious minds of oldsters like myself and occasionally briefly surface into awareness like submarines bent on ship murder.

My happily self-satisfied mood immediately reasserted itself, and with a smart, almost military gesture I brushed to either side with a thumbnail the short, horizontal black mustache which decorates my upper lip, and I automatically swept back into place the thick comma of black hair (I confess I dye it) which tends to fall down across my forehead.

I stole another glance up at the *Ostwald*, which made me think of the matchless amenities of that wondrous deluxe airliner: the softly purring motors that powered its propellers—electric motors, naturally, energized by banks of lightweight TSE batteries and as safe as its helium; the Grand Corridor running the length of the passenger deck from the Bow Observatory to the stern's like-windowed Games Room, which becomes the Grand Ballroom at night; the other peerless rooms letting off that corridor—the *Gesellschaftraum der Kapitän* (Captain's Lounge) with its dark woodwork, manly cigar smoke and *Damentische* (Tables for Ladies), the Premier Dining Room with its linen napery and silver-plated aluminum dining service, the Ladies' Retiring Room always set out profusely with fresh flowers, the Schwartzwald bar, the gambling casino with its roulette, baccarat, chemmy, blackjack (*ving-et-un*), its tables for skat and bridge and dominoes and sixty-six, its chess tables presided over by the delightfully eccentric world's champion Nimzovitch, who would defeat you blindfold, but always brilliantly, simultaneously or one at a time, in charmingly baroque brief games for only two gold pieces per person per game (one gold piece to nutsy Nimzy, one to the DLG), and the supremely luxurious staterooms with costly veneers of mahogany over balsa; the hosts of attentive stewards, either as short and skinny as jockeys or else actual dwarfs, both types chosen to save weight; and the titanium elevator rising through the countless bags of helium to the two-decked Zenith Observatory, the sun deck windscreened but roofless to let in the ever-changing clouds, the mysterious fog, the rays of the stars and good old Sol, and all the heavens. Ah, where else on land or sea could you buy such high living?

I called to mind in detail the single cabin which was always mine when I sailed on the *Ostwald*—*meine Stammkabine.* I visualized the Grand Corridor thronged with wealthy passengers in evening dress, the handsome officers, the unobtrusive ever-attentive stewards, the gleam of white shirt fronts, the glow of bare shoulders, the muted dazzle of jewels, the music of conversations like string quartets, the lilting low laughter that traveled along.

Exactly on time I did a neat *"Links, marschieren!"* ("To the left, march!") and passed through the impressive portals of the Empire State and across its towering lobby to the mutedly silver-doored bank of elevators. On my way I noted the silver-glowing date: 6 May 1937 and the time of day: 1:07 P.M. Good!—since the *Ostwald* did not cast off until the tick of three P.M., I would be left plenty of time for a leisurely lunch and good talk with my son, if he had remembered to meet me—and there was actually no doubt of that, since he is the most considerate and orderly minded of sons, a real German mentality, though I say it myself.

I headed for the express bank, enjoying my passage through the clusters of high-class people who thronged the lobby without any unseemly crowding, and placed myself before the doors designated "Dirigible Departure Lounge" and in briefer German *"Zum Zeppelin."*

The elevator hostess was an attractive Japanese girl in a skirt of dull silver with the DLG, Double Eagle and Dirigible insignia of the German Airship Union emblazoned in small on the left breast of her mutedly silver jacket. I noted with unvoiced approval that she appeared to have an excellent command of both German and English and was uniformly courteous to the passengers in her smiling but unemotional Nipponese fashion, which is so like our German scientific precision of speech, though without the latter's warm underlying passion. How good that our two federations, at opposite sides of the globe, have strong commercial and behavioral ties!

My fellow passengers in the lift, chiefly Americans and Germans, were of the finest type, very well dressed—except that just as the doors were about to close, there pressed in my doleful Jew in black. He seemed ill at ease, perhaps because of his shabby clothing. I was surprised, but made a point of being particularly polite towards him, giving him a slight bow and brief but friendly smile, while flashing my eyes. Jews have as much right to the acme of luxury travel as any other people on the planet, if they have the money—and most of them do.

During our uninterrupted and infinitely smooth passage upward, I touched my outside left breast pocket to reassure myself that my ticket—first class on the *Ostwald!*—and my papers were there. But actually I got far more reassurance and even secret joy from the feel and thought of the documents in my tightly zipped inside left breast pocket: the signed preliminary agreements that would launch America herself into the manufacture of passenger zeppelins. Modern Germany is always generous in sharing her great technical achievements with responsible sister nations, supremely confident that the genius of her scientists and engineers will continue to keep her well ahead of all other lands; and after all, the genius of two Americans, father and son, had made vital though indirect contributions to the development of safe airship travel (and not forgetting the part played by the Polish-born wife of the one and mother of the other).

The obtaining of those documents had been the chief and official reason for my trip to New York City, though I had been able to combine it most pleasurably with a long overdue visit with my son, the social historian, and with his charming wife.

These happy reflections were cut short by the jarless arrival of our elevator at its lofty terminus on the 100th floor. The journey old love-smitten King Kong had made only after exhausting exertion we had accomplished effortlessly. The silvery doors spread wide. My fellow passengers hung back for a moment in awe and perhaps a little trepidation at the thought of the awesome journey ahead of them, and I—seasoned airship traveler that I am—was the first to step out, favoring with a smile and nod of approval my pert yet cool Japanese fellow employee of the lower echelons.

Hardly sparing a glance toward the great, fleckless window confronting the doors and showing a matchless view of Manhattan from an elevation of 1,250 feet minus two stories, I briskly turned, not right to the portals of the Departure Lounge and tower elevator, but left to those of the superb German restaurant *Krahenest* (Crow's Nest).

I passed between the flanking three-foot-high bronze statuettes of Thomas Edison and Marie Sklodowska Edison niched in one wall and those of Count von Zeppelin and Thomas Sklodowska Edison facing them from the other, and entered the select precincts of the finest German dining place outside the Fatherland. I paused while my eyes traveled searchingly around the room with its restful, dark wood paneling deeply carved with beautiful representations of the Black Forest and its grotesque supernatural denizens—kobolds, elves, gnomes, dryads (tastefully sexy) and the like. They interested me since I am what Americans call a Sunday painter, though almost my sole subject matter is zeppelins seen against blue sky and airy, soaring clouds.

The *Oberkellner* came hurrying toward me with menu tucked under his left elbow and saying, "*Mein Herr!* Charmed to see you once more! I have a perfect table-for-one with porthole looking out across the Hudson."

But just then a youthful figure rose springily from behind a table set against the far wall, and a dear and familiar voice rang out to me with "*Hier, Papa!*"

"*Nein, Herr Ober,*" I smilingly told the head waiter as I walked past him, "*heute hab ich ein Gesellschafter. Mein Sohn.*"

I confidently made my way between tables occupied by well-dressed folk, both white and black.

My son wrung my hand with fierce family affection, though we had last parted only that morning. He insisted that I take the wide, dark, leather-upholstered seat against the wall, which gave me a fine view of the entire restaurant, while he took the facing chair.

"Because during this meal I wish to look only on you, Papa," he assured me with manly tenderness. "And we have at least an hour and a half together, Papa—I have checked your luggage through, and it is likely already aboard the *Ostwald.*" Thoughtful, dependable boy!

"And now, Papa, what shall it be?" he continued after we had settled ourselves. "I see that today's special is *Sauerbraten mit Spätzle* and sweet-sour red cabbage. But there is also *Paprikahuhn* and—"

"Leave the chicken to flaunt her paprika in lonely red splendor today," I interrupted him. "*Sauerbraten* sounds fine."

Ordered by my Herr Ober, the aged wine waiter had already approached our table. I was about to give him directions when my son took upon himself that task with an authority and a hostfulness that warmed my heart. He scanned the wine menu rapidly but thoroughly.

"The Zinfandel 1933," he ordered with decision, though glancing my way to see if I concurred with his judgment. I smiled and nodded.

"And perhaps *ein Tröpfchen Schnapps* to begin with?" he suggested.

"A brandy?—yes!" I replied. "And not just a drop, either. Make it a double. It is not every day I lunch with that distinguished scholar, my son."

"Oh, Papa," he protested, dropping his eyes and almost blushing. Then firmly to the bent-backed, white-haired wine waiter, "*Schnapps* also. *Doppel.*" The old waiter nodded his approval and hurried off.

We gazed fondly at each other for a few blissful seconds. Then I said, "Now tell me more fully about your achievements as a social historian on an exchange professorship in the New World. I know we have spoken about this several times, but only rather briefly and generally when various of your friends were present, or at least your lovely wife. Now I would like a more leisurely man-to-man account of your great work. Incidentally, do your find the scholarly apparatus—books, *und so weiter* (et cetera)—of the Municipal Universities of New York City adequate to your needs after having enjoyed those of Baden-Baden University and the institutions of high learning in the German Federation?"

"In some respects they are lacking," he admitted. "However, for my purposes they have proved completely adequate." Then once more he dropped his eyes and almost blushed. "But, Papa, you praise my small efforts far too highly." He lowered his voice. "They do not compare with the victory for international industrial relations you yourself have won in a fortnight."

"All in a day's work for the DLG," I said self-deprecatingly, though once again lightly touching my left chest to establish contact with those important documents safely sowed in my inside left breast pocket. "But now, no more polite fencing!" I went on briskly. "Tell me all about those 'small efforts,' as you modestly refer to them."

His eyes met mine. "Well, Papa," he began in suddenly matter-of-fact fashion, "all my work these last two years has been increasingly dominated by a firm awareness of the fragility of the underpinnings of the good world-society we enjoy today. If certain historically minute key-events, or cusps, in only the past one hundred years had been decided differently—if another course had been chosen than the one that was—then the whole world might now be plunged in wars and worse horrors then we ever dream of. It is a chilling insight, but it bulks continually larger in my entire work, my every paper."

I felt the thrilling touch of inspiration. At that moment the wine waiter arrived with our double brandies in small goblets of cut glass. I wove the interruption into the fabric of my inspiration. "Let us drink then to what you name your chilling insight," I said. *"Prosit!"*

The bite and spreading warmth of the excellent *schnapps* quickened my inspiration further. "I believe I understand exactly what you're getting at…" I told my son. I set down my half-emptied goblet and pointed at something over my son's shoulder.

He turned his head around, and after one glance back at my pointing finger, which intentionally waggled a tiny bit from side to side, he realized that I was not indicating the entry of the *Krahenest*, but the four sizable bronze statuettes flanking it.

"For instance," I said, "if Thomas Edison and Marie Sklodowska had not married, and especially if they had not had their supergenius son, then Edison's knowledge of electricity and hers of radium and other radioactives might never have been joined. There might never have been developed the fabulous T. S. Edison battery, which is the prime mover of all today's surface and air traffic. Those pioneering electric trucks introduced by the *Saturday Evening Post* in Philadelphia might have remained an expensive freak. And the gas helium might never have been produced industrially to supplement Earth's meager subterranean supply."

My son's eyes brightened with the flame of pure scholarship. "Papa," he said eagerly, "you are a genius yourself! You have precisely hit on what is perhaps the most important of those cusp-events I referred to. I am at this moment finishing the necessary research for a long paper on it. Do you know, Papa, that I have firmly established by researching Parisian records that there was in 1894 a close personal relationship between Marie Sklodowska and her fellow radium researcher Pierre Curie, and that she might well have become Madame Curie—or perhaps, Madame Becquerel, for he too was in that work—if the dashing and brilliant Edison had not most opportunely arrived in Paris in December 1894 to sweep her off her feet and carry her off to the New World to even greater achievements?

"And just think, Papa," he went on, his eyes aflame, "what might have happened if their son's battery had not been invented—the most difficult technical achievement, hedged by all sorts of seemingly scientific impossibilities, in the entire millennium-long history of industry. Why, Henry Ford might have manufactured automobiles powered by steam or by exploding natural gas or conceivably even vaporized liquid gasoline, rather than the mass-produced electric cars which have been such a boon to mankind everywhere—not our smokeless cars, but cars spouting all sorts of noxious fumes to pollute the environment."

Cars powered by the danger-fraught combustion of vaporized liquid gasoline!—it almost made me shudder and certainly it was a fantastic thought, yet not altogether beyond the bounds of possibility, I had to admit.

Just then I noticed my gloomy, black-clad Jew sitting only two tables away from us, though how he had got himself into the exclusive *Krahenest* was a wonder. Strange that I had missed his entry—probably immediately after my own, while I had eyes only for my son. His presence somehow threw a dark though only momentary shadow over my bright mood. Let him get some good German food inside him and some fine German wine, I thought generously—it will fill that empty belly of his and even put a bit of a good German smile into those sunken Yiddish cheeks! I combed my little mustache with my thumbnail and swept the errant lock of hair off my forehead.

Meanwhile my son was saying, "Also, Father, if electric transport had not been developed, and if during the last decade relations between Germany and the United States had not been so good, then we might never have gotten from the wells in Texas the supply of natural helium our Zeppelins desperately needed during the brief but vital period before we had put the artificial creation of helium onto an industrial footing. My researches at Washington have revealed that there was a strong movement in the U.S.

military to ban the sale of helium to any other nation, Germany in particular. Only the powerful influence of Edison, Ford, and a few other key Americans, instantly brought to bear, prevented that stupid injunction. Yet if it had gone through, Germany might have been forced to use hydrogen instead of helium to float her passenger dirigibles. That was another crucial cusp."

"A hydrogen-supported Zeppelin!—ridiculous! Such an airship would be a floating bomb, ready to be touched off by the slightest spark," I protested.

"Not ridiculous, Father," my son calmly contradicted me, shaking his head. "Pardon me for trespassing in your field, but there is an inescapable imperative about certain industrial developments. If there is not a safe road of advance, then a dangerous one will invariably be taken. You must admit, Father, that the development of commercial airships was in its early stages a most perilous venture. During the 1920s there were the dreadful wrecks of the American dirigibles *Roma*, *Shenandoah*, which broke in two, *Akron*, and *Macon*, the British R-38, which also broke apart in the air, and R-101, the French *Dixmude*, which disappeared in the Mediterranean, Mussolini's *Italia*, which crashed trying to reach the North Pole, and the Russian *Maxim Gorky*, struck down by a plane, with a total loss of no fewer than 340 crew members for the nine accidents. If that had been followed by the explosions of two or three hydrogen Zeppelins, world industry might well have abandoned forever the attempt to create passenger airships and turned instead to the development of large propeller-driven, heavier-than-air craft."

Monster airplanes, in danger every moment of crash from engine failure, competing with good old unsinkable Zeppelins?—impossible, at least at first thought. I shook my head, but not with as much conviction as I might have wished. My son's suggestion was really a valid one.

Besides, he had all his facts at his fingertips and was complete master of his subject, as I also had to allow. Those nine fearful airship disasters he mentioned had indeed occurred, as I knew well, and might have tipped the scale in favor of long-distance passenger and troop-carrying airplanes, had it not been for helium, the T. S. Edison battery, and German genius.

Fortunately I was able to dump from my mind these uncomfortable speculations and immerse myself in admiration of my son's multisided scholarship. That boy was a wonder!—a real chip off the old block, and, yes, a bit more.

"And now, Dolfy," he went on, using my nickname (I did not mind), "may I turn to an entirely different topic? Or rather to a very different example of my hypothesis of historical cusps?"

I nodded mutely. My mouth was busily full with fine *Sauerbraten* and those lovely, tiny German dumplings, while my nostrils enjoyed the unique aroma of sweet-sour red cabbage. I had been so engrossed in my son's revelations that I had not consciously noted our luncheon being served. I swallowed, took a slug of the good, red Zinfandel, and said, "Please go on."

"It's about the consequences of the American Civil War, Father," he said surprisingly. "Did you know that in the decade after that bloody conflict, there was a very real danger that the whole cause of Negro freedom and rights—for which the war was fought, whatever they say—might well have been completely smashed? The fine work of Abraham Lincoln, Thaddeus Stevens, Charles Sumner, the Freedmen's Bureau, and the Union League Clubs put to naught? And even the Ku Klux Klan underground allowed free reign rather than being sternly repressed? Yes, Father, my thoroughgoing researchings have convinced me such things might easily have happened, resulting in some sort of re-enslavement of the Blacks, with the whole war to be refought at an indefinite future date, or at any rate Reconstruction brought to a dead halt for many decades—with what disastrous effects on the American character, turning its deep simple faith in freedom to hypocrisy, it is impossible to exaggerate. I have published a sizable paper on this subject in the *Journal of Civil War Studies*."

I nodded somberly. Quite a bit of this new subject matter of his was *terra incognita* to me; yet I knew enough of American history to realize he had made a cogent point. More than ever before, I was impressed by his multifaceted learning—he was indubitably a figure in the great tradition of German scholarship, a profound thinker, broad and deep. How fortunate to be his father. Not for the first time, but perhaps with the greatest sincerity yet, I thanked God and the Laws of Nature that I had early moved my family from Braunau, Austria, where I had been born in 1889, to Baden-Baden, where he had grown up in the ambience of the great new university on the edge of the Black Forest and only 150 kilometers from Count Zeppelin's dirigible factory in Württemberg, at Friedrichshafen on Lake Constance.

I raised my glass of *Kirschwasser* to him in a solemn, silent toast—we had somehow got to that stage in our meal—and downed a sip of the potent, fiery, white, cherry brandy.

He leaned toward me and said, "I might as well tell you, Dolf, that my big book, at once popular and scholarly, my *Meisterwerk*, to be titled *If Things Had Gone Wrong*, or perhaps *If Things Had Turned for the Worse*, will deal solely—though illuminated by dozens of diverse examples—with my theory of historical cusps, a highly speculative concept but firmly footed in fact." He glanced at his wristwatch, muttered, "Yes, there's still time for it. So now—" His face grew grave, his voice clear though small—"I will venture to tell you about one more cusp, the most disputable and yet most crucial of them all." He paused. "I warn you, dear Dolf, that this cusp may cause you pain."

"I doubt that," I told him indulgently. "Anyhow, go ahead."

"Very well. In November of 1918, when the British had broken the Hindenburg Line and the weary German army was defiantly dug in along the Rhine, and just before the Allies, under Marshal Foch, launched the final crushing drive which would cut a bloody swath across the heartland to Berlin—"

I understood his warning at once. Memories flamed in my mind like the sudden blinding flares of the battlefield with their deafening thunder. The company I had commanded had been among the most desperately defiant of those he mentioned, heroically nerved for a last-ditch resistance. And then Foch had delivered that last vast blow, and we had fallen back and back and back before the overwhelming numbers of our enemies with their field guns and tanks and armored cars innumerable and above all their huge aerial armadas of De Havilland and Handley-Page and other big bombers escorted by insect-buzzing fleets of Spads and other fighters shooting to bits our last Fokkers and Pfalzes and visiting on Germany a destruction greater far than our Zeps had worked on England. Back, back, back, endlessly reeling and regrouping, across the devastated German countryside, a dozen times decimated yet still defiant until the end came at last amid the ruins of Berlin, and the most bold among us had to admit we were beaten and we surrendered unconditionally.

These vivid, fiery recollections came to me almost instantaneously.

I heard my son continuing, "At that cusp moment in November 1918, Dolf, there existed a very strong possibility—I have established this beyond question—that an immediate armistice would be offered and signed, and the war ended inconclusively. President Wilson was wavering, the French were very tired, and so on.

"And if that had happened in actuality—harken closely to me now, Dolf—then the German temper entering the decade of the 1920s would have been entirely different. She would have felt she had not been really licked, and there would inevitably have been a secret recrudescence of pan-German militarism. German scientific humanism would not have won its total victory over the Germany of the—yes!—Huns.

"As for the Allies, self-tricked out of the complete victory which lay within their grasp, they would in the long run have treated Germany far less generously than they did after their lust for revenge had been sated by that last drive to Berlin. The League of Nations would not have become the strong instrument for world peace that it is today; it might well have been repudiated by America and certainly secretly detested by Germany. Old wounds would not have healed because, paradoxically, they would not have been deep enough.

"There, I've said my say. I hope it hasn't bothered you too badly, Dolf."

I let out a gusty sigh. Then my wincing frown was replaced by a brow serene. I said very deliberately, "Not one bit, my son, though you have certainly touched my own old wounds to the quick. Yet I feel in my bones that your interpretation is completely valid. Rumors of an armistice were indeed running like wildfire through our troops in that black autumn of 1918. And I know only too well that if there had been an armistice at that time, then officers like myself would have believed that the German soldier had never really been defeated, only betrayed by his leaders and by red incendiaries, and we would have begun to conspire endlessly for a resumption of the war under happier circumstances. My son, let us drink to your amazing cusps."

Our tiny glasses touched with a delicate ting, and the last drops went down of biting, faintly bitter *Kirschwasser*. I buttered a thin slice of pumpernickel and nibbled it—always good to finish off a meal with bread. I was suddenly filled with an immeasurable content. It was a golden moment, which I would have been happy to have go on forever, while I listened to my son's wise words and fed my satisfaction in him. Yes, indeed, it was a golden nugget of pause in the terrible rush of time—the enriching conversation, the peerless food and drink, the darkly pleasant surroundings—

At that moment I chanced to look at my discordant Jew two tables away. For some weird reason he was glaring at me with naked hate, though he instantly dropped his gaze—

But even that strange and disquieting event did not disrupt my mood of golden tranquility, which I sought to prolong by saying in summation, "My dear son, this has been the most exciting though eerie lunch I have ever enjoyed. Your remarkable cusps have opened to me a fabulous world in which I can nevertheless utterly believe. A horridly fascinating world of sizzling hydrogen Zeppelins, of countless—evil-smelling gasoline cars built by Ford instead of his electrics, of re-enslaved American blackamoors, of Madame Becquerels or Curies, a world without the T. E. Edison battery and even T. S. himself, a world in which German scientists are sinister pariahs instead of tolerant, humanitarian, great-souled leaders of world thought, a world in which a mateless old Edison tinkers forever at a powerful storage battery he cannot perfect, a world in which Woodrow Wilson doesn't insist on Germany being admitted at once to the League of Nations, a world of festering hatreds reeling toward a second and worse world war. Oh, altogether an incredible world, yet one in which you have momentarily made me believe, to the extent that I do actually have the fear that time will suddenly shift gears and we will be plunged into that bad dream world, and our real world will become a dream—"

I suddenly chanced to see the face of my watch.

At the same time my son looked at his own left wrist—

"Dolf," he said, springing up in agitation, "I do hope that with my stupid chatter I haven't made you miss—"

I had sprung up too—

"No, no, my son," I heard myself say in a fluttering voice, "but it's true I have little time in which to catch the *Ostwald. Auf Wiedersehen, mein Sohn, auf Wiedersehen!*"

And with that I was hastening, indeed almost running, or else sweeping through the air like a ghost—leaving him behind to settle our reckoning—across a room that seemed to waver with my feverish agitation, alternately darkening and brightening like an electric bulb with its fine tungsten filament about to fly to powder and wink out forever—

Inside my head a voice was saying in calm yet deathknell tones, "The lights of Europe are going out. I do not think they will be rekindled in my generation—"

Suddenly the only important thing in the world for me was to catch the *Ostwald*, get aboard her before she unmoored. That and only that would reassure me that I was in my rightful world. I would touch and feel the *Ostwald*, not just talk about her—

As I dashed between the four bronze figures, they seemed to hunch down and become deformed, while their faces became those of grotesque, aged witches—four evil kobolds leering up at me with a horrid knowledge bright in their eyes—

While behind me I glimpsed in pursuit a tall, black, white-faced figure, skeletally lean—

The strangely short corridor ahead of me had a blank end—the Departure Lounge wasn't there—

I instantly jerked open the narrow door to the stairs and darted nimbly up them as if I were a young man again and not forty-eight years old—

On the third sharp turn I risked a glance behind and down—

Hardly a flight behind me, taking great pursuing leaps, was my dreadful Jew—

I tore open the door to the 102nd floor. There at last, only a few feet away, was the silver door I sought of the final elevator and softly glowing above it the words, "*Zum Zeppelin.*" At last I would be shot aloft to the *Ostwald* and reality.

But the sign began to blink as the *Krahenest* had, while across the door was pasted askew a white cardboard sign which read "Out of Order."

I threw myself at the door and scrabbled at it, squeezing my eyes several times to make my vision come clear. When I finally fully opened them, the cardboard sign was gone.

But the silver door was gone too, and the words above it forever. I was scrabbling at seamless pale plaster.

There was a touch on my elbow. I spun around.

"Excuse me, sir, but you seem troubled," my Jew said solicitously. "Is there anything I can do?"

I shook my head, but whether in negation or rejection or to clear it, I don't know. "I'm looking for the *Ostwald*," I gasped, only now realizing I'd winded myself on the stairs. "For the zeppelin," I explained when he looked puzzled.

I may be wrong, but it seemed to me that a look of secret glee flashed deep in his eyes, though his general sympathetic expression remained unchanged.

"Oh, the zeppelin," he said in a voice that seemed to me to have become sugary in its solicitude. "You must mean the *Hindenburg*."

Hindenburg?—I asked myself. There was no zeppelin named *Hindenburg*. Or was there? Could it be that I was mistaken about such a simple and, one would think, immutable matter? My mind had been getting very foggy the last minute or two. Desperately I tried to assure myself that I was indeed myself and in my right world. My lips worked and I muttered to myself, *Bin Adolf Hitler, Zeppelin Fachmann...*

"But the *Hindenburg* doesn't land here, in any case," my Jew was telling me, "though I think some vague intention once was voiced about topping the Empire State with a mooring mast for dirigibles. Perhaps you saw some news story and assumed—"

His face fell, or he made it seem to fall. The sugary solicitude in his voice became unendurable as he told me, "But apparently you can't have heard today's tragic news. Oh, I do hope you weren't seeking the *Hindenburg* so as to meet some beloved family member or close friend. Brace yourself, sir. Only hours ago, coming in for her landing at Lakehurst, New Jersey, the *Hindenburg* caught fire and burned up entirely in a matter of seconds. Thirty or forty at least of her passengers and crew were burned alive. Oh, steady yourself, sir."

"But the *Hindenburg*—I mean the *Ostwald!*—couldn't burn like that," I protested. "She's a helium zeppelin."

He shook his head. "Oh, no. I'm no scientist, but I know the *Hindenburg* was filled with hydrogen—a wholly typical bit of reckless German risk-running. At least we've never sold helium to the Nazis, thank God."

I stared at him, wavering my face from side to side in feeble denial. While he stared back at me with obviously a new thought in mind.

"Excuse me once again," he said, "but I believe I heard you start to say something about Adolf Hitler. I suppose you know that you bear a certain resemblance to that execrable dictator. If I were you, sir, I'd shave my mustache."

I felt a wave of fury at this inexplicable remark with all its baffling references, yet withal a remark delivered in the unmistakable tones of an insult. And then all my surroundings momentarily reddened and flickered and I felt a tremendous wrench in the inmost core of my being, the sort of wrench one might experience in transiting timelessly from one universe into another parallel to it. Briefly I became a man still named Adolf Hitler, same as the Nazi dictator and almost the same age, a German-American born in Chicago, who had never visited Germany or spoken German, whose friends teased him about his chance resemblance to the other Hitler, and who used stubbornly to say. "No, I won't change my name! Let that *Führer* bastard across the Atlantic change his! Ever hear about the British Winston Churchill writing the American Winston Churchill, who wrote *The Crisis* and other novels, and suggesting he change his name to avoid confusion, since the Englishman had done some writing too? The American wrote back it was a good idea, but since he was three years older, he was senior and so the Britisher should change *his* name. That's exactly how I feel about that son of a bitch Hitler."

The Jew still stared at me sneeringly. I started to tell him off, but then I was lost in a second weird, wrenching transition. The first had been directly from one parallel universe to another. The second was also in time—I aged fourteen or fifteen years in a single infinite instant while transiting from 1937 (where I had been born in 1889 and was forty-eight) to 1973 (where I had been born in 1910 and was sixty-three). My name changed back to my truly own (but what is that?). And I no longer looked one bit like Adolf Hitler the Nazi dictator (or dirigible expert?), and I had a married son who was a sort of social historian in a New York City municipal university, and he had many brilliant theories, but none of historical cusps.

And the Jew—I mean the tall, thin man in black with possibly Semitic features—was gone. I looked around and around but there was no one there.

I touched my outside left breast pocket, then my hand darted tremblingly underneath. There was no zipper on the pocket inside and no precious documents, only a couple of grimy envelopes with notes I'd scribbled on them in pencil.

I don't know how I got out of the Empire State Building. Presumably by elevator. Though all my memory holds for that period is a persistent image of King Kong tumbling down from its top like a ridiculous yet poignantly pitiable giant teddy bear.

I do recollect walking in a sort of trance for what seemed hours through a Manhattan stinking with monoxide and carcinogens innumerable, half waking from time to time (usually while crossing streets that snarled, not purred) and then relapsing into trance. There were big dogs.

When I at last fully came to myself, I was walking down a twilit Hudson Street at the north end of Greenwich Village. My gaze was fixed on a distant and unremarkable pale-gray square of a building top. I guessed it must be that of the World Trade Center, 1,350 feet tall.

And then it was blotted out by the grinning face of my son, the professor.

"Justin!" I said.

"Fritz!" he said. "We'd begun to worry a bit. Where did you get off to, anyhow? Not that it's a damn bit of my business. If you had an assignation with a go-go girl, you needn't tell me."

"Thanks," I said, "I do feel tired, I must admit, and somewhat cold. But no, I was just looking at some of my old stamping grounds," I told him, "and taking longer than I realized. Manhattan's changed during my years on the West Coast, but not all that much."

"It's getting chilly," he said. "Let's stop in at that place ahead with the black front. It's the White Horse. Dylan Thomas used to drink there. He's supposed to have scribbled a poem on the wall of the can, only they painted it over. But it has the authentic sawdust."

"Good," I said, "only we'll make mine coffee, not ale. Or if I can't get coffee, then cola."

I am not really a *Prosit!*-type person.

HORRIBLE IMAGININGS

"Present fears are less than horrible imaginings." —MACBETH

OLD RAMSEY RYKER ONLY COMMENCED THINKING about going to see (through one-way glass) the young women fingering their genitals *after* he started having the low-ceilinged dreams without light—the muttering dull black nightmares—but *before* he began catching glimpses of the vanishing young-old mystery girl, who wore black that twinkled, lurking in the first-floor ground-level corridors, or disappearing into the elevator, and once or twice slipping along the upstairs halls of the apartment tree (or skeleton) that is, with one exception, the sole scene of the action in this story, which does not venture farther, disturb the privacy of the apartments themselves, or take one step out into the noisy metropolitan street. Here all is hushed.

I mean by the *apartment tree* all the public or at least tenant-shared space within the thirteen-floor building where Ryker lived alone. With a small effort you can visualize that volume of connected space as a rather repetitious tree (color it red or green if it helps, as they do in "You are *here*" diagrammatic maps; I see it as pale gray myself, for that is the color of the wallpaper in the outer halls, pale gray faintly patterned with dingy silver): its roots the basement garage where some tenants with cars rented space along with a few neighborhood shopkeepers and businessmen; its trunk the central elevator shaft with open stairway beside it (the owner of the building had periodic difficulties with the fire inspectors about the latter—they wanted it walled off with heavy self-closing doors at each floor; certainly a building permit would never have been granted today—or in the last three decades, for that matter—for such a lofty structure with an open stairwell); its branches the three halls, two long, one short, radiating out from the shaft-stairwell trunk and identical at each level except for minor features; from the top floor a sort of slanted, final thick branch of stairs led, through a stout door (locked on the outside but open on the inside—another fire regulation), to the roof and the strong, floored weatherproof shed holding the elevator's motor and old-fashioned mechanical relays. But we won't stir through that door either to survey the besmogged but nonetheless impressive cityscape and hunt for the odd star or (rarer still) an interesting window.

At ground level one of the long corridors led to the street door; on the floors above, to the front fire escape. The other long ones led to the alley fire escape. The short hall was blind (the fire inspector would shake his head at that feature too, and frown).

And then of course we should mention, if only for the sake of completists, the apartment tree's micro-world, its tiniest twigs and leaflets, in a sense: all the cracks and crevices (and mouse- and rat-holes, if any) going off into the walls, ceilings, and floors, with perhaps some leading to more spacious though still cramped volumes of space.

But it would be discourteous of us to wander—and so frivolously— through the strange labyrinthine apartment tree with its angular one- and two-bedroom forbidden fruit, when all the time Ramsey Ryker, a lofty, gaunt old man somewhat resembling a neatly dressed scarecrow, is waiting impatiently for us with his equally strange and tortuous problems and concerns. Of these, the black nightmares were the worst by far and also in a way the cause of, or at least the prelude to, all the others.

Actually they were the worst nightmares in a restrained sort of way that Ramsey ever remembered having in the seven decades of his life and the only ones, the only dreams of any sort for that matter, without any visual element at all (hence the "black"), but only sound, touch, intramuscular feelings, and smell. And the black was really inky, midnight, moonless and starless, sooty, utter—all those words. It didn't even have any of those faint churning points of light we see, some of them tinted, when we shut our eyes in absolute darkness and when supposedly we're seeing rods and cones of our retina fire off without any photons of outside light hitting them. No, the only light in his nightmares, if any, was of the phantom sort in which *memories* are painted—a swift, sometimes extensive-seeming flash which starts to fade the instant it appears and never seems to be in the retina at all, something far more ghostly even than the nebular churnings that occur under the eyelids in the inkiest dark.

He'd been having these nightmares every two or three nights, regular almost as clockwork, for at least a month now, so that they were beginning to seriously worry and oppress him. I've said "nightmares" up to now, but really there was only *one,* repeated with just enough changes in its details to convince him that he was experiencing new nightmares rather than just remembering the first. This made them more ominously terrifying; he'd know what was coming—up to a point—and suffer the more because of that.

Each "performance" of his frightening lightless dream, on those nights when his unconscious decided to put on a show, would begin the same way. He would gradually become aware, as though his mind were rising with difficulty from unimaginable depths of sleep, that he was lying stretched out naked on his back with his arms extended neatly down his sides, but that he was *not* in his bed—the surface beneath him was too ridged and hard for that. He was breathing shallowly and with difficulty—or rather he discovered that if he tried to investigate his breathing, speed or slow it, expand his chest more fully, he ran the danger of bringing on a strangling spasm or coughing fit. This prospect frightened him; he tried never to let it happen.

To check on this, explore the space around him, he would next in his dream try to lift up a hand and arm, stretch a leg sideways—and find out that he could *not,* that so far as any gross movement of limbs went he was paralyzed. This naturally would terrify him and push him toward panic. It was all he could do not to strain, thrash (that is, try to), gasp, or cry out.

Then as his panic slowly subsided, as he schooled himself to quietly endure this limitation on his actions, he would discover that his paralysis was not complete, that if he went about it slowly he could move a bit, wag his head about an inch from side to side, writhe a little the superficial muscles and skin under his shoulders and down his back and buttocks and legs, stir his heels and fingertips slightly. It was in this way that he discovered that the hard surface under him consisted of rough laths set close together, which were very dusty—no, *gritty.*

Next in his dream came an awareness of sound. At first it would seem the normal muttering hum of any big city, but then he'd begin to distinguish in it a faint rustling and an infinitesimal rapid clicking that was very much closer and seemed to get nearer each moment and he'd think of insects and spiders and he'd feel new terror gusting through him and there'd be another struggle to stave off hysteria. At this point in his dream he'd usually think of cockroaches, armies of them, as normal to big cities as the latter's muttering sounds, and his terror would fade though his revulsion would mount. Filthy creatures! but who could be frightened of them? True, his dear wife, now dead five years, had had a dread of stepping on one in the dark and hearing it crunch. (That reaction he found rather hard to understand. He was, well, if not exactly pleasured, then well satisfied to step on cockroaches, or mash them in the sink.)

His attention would then likely return to the muttering, growling, faintly buzzing, somehow *nasal* component of the general sound, and he'd begin to hear voices in it, though he could seldom identify the words or phrases—it was like the voices of a crowd coming out of a theater or baseball park or meeting hall and commenting and arguing droningly and wearily about what they'd just seen or heard. *Male* voices chiefly, cynical, sarcastic, deprecating, mean, sleepily savage, and ignorant, very ignorant, he'd feel sure. And never as loud or big as they ought to be; there was always a *littleness* about them. (Was his hearing impaired in his nightmares? Was he dreaming of growing deaf?) Were they the voices of depraved children? No, they were much too low—deep throat tones. Once he'd asked himself, "Midgets?" and had the thought, rich in dream wisdom, "A man lying down is not even as tall as a midget."

After sound, odor would follow, as his senses were assaulted cumulatively. First dry, stale, long-confined—somehow so natural seeming he would be unaware of the scents. But then he would smell smoke and know a special pang of fright—was he to be burned alive, unable to move? And the fire sirens when the engines came, tinied by distance and by muffling walls, no larger than those of toys?

But then he would identify it more precisely as tobacco smoke, the reeking smoke of cigars chiefly. He remembered how his dead wife had hated that, though smoking cigarettes herself.

After that, a whole host of supporting odors: toilet smells and the cheap sharp perfumes used to balance those out, stinking old flesh, the fishy reek of unwashed sex, locker rooms, beer, disinfectants, wine-laden vomit—all fitting very nicely, too, with the ignorant low growling.

After sound and odor, touch, living touch. Behind the lobe of his right ear, in his jaw's recessed angle, where a branch of the carotid pulses close to the surface, there'd come an exploring prod from the tip of something about as big as a baby's thumb, a pencil's eraserhead, snout of a mouse or of a garter snake, an embryo's fist, an unlit cigarette, a suppository, the phallus of a virile mannequin—a probing and a thrusting that did not stop and did not go away.

At that point his dream, if it hadn't already, would turn into full nightmare. He'd try to jerk his head sideways, throw himself over away from it, thrash his arms and legs, yell out unmindful of what it did to his breathing—and find that the paralysis still gripped him, its bonds growing tighter the more he struggled, his vocal cords as numb as if these were his life's last gaspings.

And then—more touches of the same puppet sort: his side, his thigh, between two fingers, up and down his body. The sounds and odors would get darker still as a general suffocating oppression closed in. He'd visualize grotesquely in imagination's lightless lightning flashes, which like those of memory are so utterly different from sight, a crowd of squatty, groping male Lilliputians, a press of dark-jowled, thickset, low-browed, unlovely living dolls standing or leaning in locker-room attitudes, each one nursing with one hand beneath his paunch a half-erect prick with a casual lasciviousness and with the other gripping a beer can or cigar or both, while all the while they gargled out unceasingly a thick oozy stream of shitty talk about crime and sports and sex, about power and profit. He envisioned their tiny prick nubs pressing in on him everywhere, as if he were being wrapped tighter and tighter in a rubber blanket that was all miniscule elastic knobs.

At this moment he would make a supreme effort to lift his head, reckless of heart attack, fighting for each fraction of an inch of upward movement, and find himself grinding his forehead and nose into a rough gritty wooden surface that had been there, not three inches above him, all the while, like the lid of a shallow coffin.

Then, and only then, in that moment of intensest horror, he'd wake at last, stretched out tidily in his own bed, gasping just a little, and with a totally unjoyous hard-on that seemed more like the symptom of some mortal disease than any prelude to pleasure.

The reader may at this point object that by entering Ramsey's bedroom we have strayed beyond the apartment-tree limits set for the actions of this story. Not so, for we have been examining only his memories of his nightmares, which never have the force of the real thing. In this fashion we peered into his dream, perhaps into his bedroom, but we never turned on the light. The same applies to his thoughts about and reactions to those erections which troubled his nightmare wakings and which seemed to him so much more like tumorous morbid growths—almost, cancers—than any swellings of joy.

Now Ramsey was sufficiently sophisticated to wonder whether his night-mares were an expression, albeit an unusual and most unpleasant one, of a gathering sexual arousal in himself, which his invariable waking hard-ons would seem to indicate, and whether the discharge of that growing sexual pressure would not result in the nightmares ceasing or at least becoming fewer in number and of a lesser intensity. On the one hand, his living alone was very thoroughgoing; he had formed no new intimacies since his wife's death five years earlier and his coincidental retirement and moving here. On the other, he had a deep personal prejudice against masturbation, not on moral or religious grounds, but from the conviction that such acts demanded a living accomplice or companion to make them effectively real, no matter how distant and tenuous the relation between the two par-ties, an adventuring-out into the real world and some achievement there, however slight.

Undoubtedly there were guilty shadows here—his life went back far enough for him to have absorbed in childhood mistaken notions of the unhealthiness of auto-eroticism that still influenced his feelings if not his intellect. And also something of the work-ethic of Protestantism, whereby everything had its price, had to be worked and sweated and suffered for.

With perhaps—who knows?—a touch of the romantic feeling that sex wasn't worth it without the spice of danger, which also required a venturing out beyond one's private self.

Now on the last occasion—about eight months ago—when Ramsey had noted signs of growing sexual tension in himself (signs far less grotesquely inappropriate, frightening, oppressive, and depressing than his current nightmares—which appeared to end with a strong hint of premature burial), he had set his imagination in a direction leading toward that tension's relief by venturing some four blocks into the outer world (the world beyond the apartment tree's street door) to a small theater called Ultrabooth, where for a modest price (in these inflated times) he could make contact with three living girls (albeit a voiceless one through heavy one-way glass), who would strip and display themselves intimately to him in a way calculated to promote arousal.

(A pause to note we've once more gone outside the apartment tree, but only by way of a remembered venturing—and memory is less real even than dream, as we have seen.)

The reason Ramsey had not at once again had recourse to these young ladies as soon as his nightmares began with their telltale terminal hard-ons, providing evidence of growing sexual pressure even if the peculiar nightmare contents did not, was that he had found their original performance, though sufficient for his purpose as it turned out, rather morally troubling and aesthetically unsatisfying in some respects and giving rise to various sad and wistful reflections in his mind as he repeated their performance in memory.

Ducking through a small, brightly lit marquee into the dim lobby of Ultrabooth, he'd laid a $10 bill on the counter before the bearded young man without looking at him, taken up the $2 returned with the considerate explanation that this was a reduction for senior citizens, and joined the half-dozen or so silent waiting men who mostly edged about restlessly yet slowly, not looking at each other.

After a moderate wait and some small augmentation of their number, there came a stirring from beyond the red velvet ropes as the previous audience was guided out a separate exit door. Ryker gravitated forward with the rest of the new audience. After a two-minute pause, a section of red rope was hooked aside, and they surged gently ahead into a shallow inner foyer from which two narrow dark doorways about fifteen feet apart led onward.

Ryker was the fourth man through the left-hand doorway. He found himself in a dim, curving corridor. On his left, wall. On his right, heavy curtains partly drawn aside from what looked like large closets, each with a gloomy window at the back. He entered the first that was unoccupied (the second), fumbled the curtains shut behind him, and clumsily seated himself facing the window on the cubicle's sole piece of furniture, a rather low barstool.

Actually his booth wasn't crampingly small. Ryker estimated its floor space as at least one-half that of the apartment tree's elevator, which had a six-person capacity.

As his eyes became accommodated to the darkness of his booth and the dimness of the sizable room beyond, he saw that the latter was roughly circular and walled by rectangular mirrors, each of which, he realized, must be the window of a booth such as his own—except one window space was just a narrow curtain going to the floor. A wailing bluesy jazz from an unseen speaker gently filled his ears, very muted.

The windows were framed with rows of frosted light bulbs barely turned on—must have them on a rheostat, he thought. The floor was palely and thickly carpeted, and there were a few big pale pillows set about. From the ceiling hung four velvet-covered ropes thinner than those in the lobby. Each ended in a padded leather cuff. He also noted uneasily two velvet-covered paddles, no larger than Ping-Pong ones, lying on one of the big pillows. The dimness made everything seem grimy, as though fine soot were falling continuously from the ceiling like snow.

He sensed a stirring in the other booths, and he saw that a girl had entered the room of mirrors while he'd been intent on the paddles. At first he couldn't tell whether she was naked or not, but then as she slowly walked out, hardly glancing at the mirrors, face straight ahead like a sleepwalker's, the music began to come up and the lights too, brighter and brighter. He saw she was a blonde, age anywhere from nineteen to twenty-nine—how could you know for sure? He hoped nineteen. And she was wearing a net brassiere bordered by what looked like strips of white rabbit's fur. A tiny apron of the same kind of fur hung down over her crotch, attached to some sort of G-string, and she wore short white rabbit's fur boots.

She yawned and stretched, looked around, and then swiftly removed these items of apparel, but instead of letting them fall or laying them down on one of the pillows, she carried them over to the curtained doorway which interrupted the wall of mirrors and handed them through to someone. They were taking no chances on the fur getting dirty—how many performances a day was it the girls gave? He also realized that the right- and left-hand passages to the booths didn't join behind, as he'd imagined at first—there had to be an entry passage for the performer. Good thing he hadn't tried to go all the way around and check on all the booths before picking one—and maybe lost his.

The vertical slit in the curtain widened, and the now naked blonde was joined by a naked brunette of the same undetermined youth. They embraced tenderly yet perfunctorily, as if in a dream, swaying with the music's wails, then leaned apart, brushing each other's small breasts, fingers lingering at the erecting nipples, then trailing down to touch each other's clefts. They separated then and began to work their way around the booths, facing each mirror in turn, swaying and writhing, bumping and grinding, arching back, bellying toward. The brunette was across from him, the blonde off to his left and coming closer. His mouth was dry, his breaths came faster. He was getting a hard-on, he told himself, or about to. He was jealous about the time the blonde spent at each other window and yet somehow dreaded her coming.

And then she was writhing in front of him, poker-faced, looking down toward him. Could she see him? Of course not!—he could see the windows across from him, and they just reflected his blank window. But suppose she bent down and pressed her face and flattening nose-tip against the glass, cupping her hands to either side to shut out light? Involuntarily he flinched backward, caught himself and almost as swiftly stretched his face forward to admire her breasts as she preened, trailing her fingers across them. Yes, yes, he thought desperately, dutifully, they were small, firm, not at all pendulous, big nippled with large aureoles, splendid, yes splendid, yes splendid…

And then he was forcing his gaze to follow her hands down her slender waist past her belly button and pale pubic hair and stretch open the lips of her cleft.

It was all so very confusing, those flaps and those ribbons of membrane, of glistening pinkish-red membrane. Really, a man's genitals were much neater, more like a good and clear diagram, a much more sensible layout. And when you were young you were always in too much of a hurry to study the female ones, too damn excited, keyed up, overwhelmed by the importance of keeping a hard-on. That, and the stubborn old feeling that you mustn't look, that was against the rules, this was dirty. With his wife he'd always done it in the dark, or almost. And now when you were old and your eyesight wasn't so good any more. One slender finger moved out from the bent stretching ones to point up, then down, to indicate clitoris and cunt. Whyn't she point out her urethra too? It was somewhere there, in between. The clitoris was hard to make out in the midst of all that red squirming...

And then without warning she had spun around, bent over, and was looking at him from between her spread legs, and her hand came back around her side to jab a finger twice at the shadowed sallow pucker of her anus, as if she were saying, "And here's my asshole, see? My God, how long does it take you dumb bastards to get things straight?"

Really, it was more like an anatomy lesson taught by a bored, clown-white cadaver than any sort of spicy erotic cocktail. Where was the faintest hint of the flirtatious teasing that in old times, Ryker recalled, gave such performances a point? Why, this girl had come in almost naked and divested herself of the scant remainder with all the romance of someone taking out dental plates before retiring. My God, was that how they got ready for the full act in private? Where was the slow unbuttoning, the sudden change of mind and buttoning up again? Where was the enthusiastic self-peek down her pulled-forward bodice followed by the smile and knowing wink that said, "Oh, boy, what I got down there! Don't you wish...?" Where was the teasing that overreached itself, the accidental exposure of a goody, pretended embarrassment, and the overhasty hiding of it, leading to further revelations, as one who covering her knees bares her rear end? Where the feigned innocence, prudish or naive? the sense of wicked play, precocious evil? Above all, where was the illusion that her body's treasures were just that? her choicest possessions and her chiefest pride, secret 'tween her and you, hoarded like miser's gold, though shared out joyously and generously at the end?

The girl, instead of graciously overhearing his racing thoughts (they must be audible!) and at least attempting to make some corrections for them in her behavior, last of all seized handholds at the corners of the window and set the soles of her feet against the sides and dangled there spread open and bent for a short while, rocking back and forth, like a poker-faced slender ape, so he could see it all at once after a fashion: asshole, cunt, and clitoris—and urethra—wherever that was.

That was the show's highpoint of excitement, or shock at any rate, for Ryker. Although a third girl appeared and the other two got her undressed and strung up by the padded straps on the velvet ropes, and did some things to her with their lips and tongues and the lightly brushing velvet paddles, that was the high point—or whatever.

Afterward he slipped out into the street feeling very conspicuous, but even more relieved. He swore he'd never visit the ignorant place again. But that night he had awakened ejaculating in a wet dream. Afterward he couldn't be quite sure whether his hand mightn't have helped and what sort of dream it had been otherwise, if any—certainly not one of his troll-haunted, buried-alive nightmares.

No, they were gone forever, or at any rate for the next five months.

And then when they did come back, against all his hopes, and when they continued on, and when he found himself balanced between the nightmares and Ultrabooth, and the days seemed dry as dust, there had come the welcome interruption of the Vanishing Lady.

The first time Ryker had seen her, so far as he could recall, they'd been at opposite ends of the long, low entry hall, a good forty feet apart. He had been fumbling for his key outside the street door, which was thick oak framing a large glass panel backed by metal tracery. She'd been standing in profile before the gray elevator door, the small window of which was lit, indicating the cage was at this floor. His gaze approved her instantly (for some men life is an unceasing beauty contest); he liked the way her dark knee-length coat was belted in trimly and the neat look of her head, either dark hair drawn in rather closely or a cloche hat. Automatically he wondered whether she was young and slender or old and skinny.

And then as he continued to look at her, key poised before the lock, she turned her head in his direction and his heart did a little fillip and shiver. *She looked at me,* was what he felt, although the corridor was dimly lit and from this far away a face was little more than a pale oval with eye-smudges—and now her hair or hat made it a shadowed oval. It told you no more about her age than her profile had. Just the same, it was now turned toward him.

All this happened quite swiftly.

But then he had to look down at the lock in order to fit his key into it (a fussy business that seemed to take longer with each passing year) and turn it (he sometimes forgot which way) and shove the door open with his other hand, and by that time she'd moved out of sight.

She couldn't have taken the elevator up or down, he told himself as he strode the corridor a little more briskly than was his wont, for the small glass window in its door still shone brightly. She must have just drifted out of sight to the right, where the stairs were and the brass-fronted mailboxes and the window and door to the manager's office and, past those, the long and short back corridors of the ground floor.

But when he reached that foyer, it was empty and the manager's window unoccupied, though not yet dark and shuttered for the night. She must have gone up the stairs or to a back apartment on this floor, though he'd heard no receding footsteps or shutting door confirm that theory.

Just as he opened the elevator door he got the funniest hunch that he'd find her waiting for him there—that she'd entered the cage while he'd been unlocking the front door, but then not pushed a button for a floor. But the cage was as empty as the foyer. So much for hunches! He pushed the 14 button at the top of the narrow brass panel, and by the time he got there, he'd put the incident out of his mind, though a certain wistfulness clung to his general mood.

And he probably would have forgotten it altogether except that late the next afternoon, when he was returning from a rather long walk, the same thing happened to him all over again, the whole incident repeating itself with only rather minor variations. For instance, this time her eyes seemed barely to stray in his direction; there wasn't the same sense of a full look. And something flashed faintly at her chest level, as if she were wearing jewelry of some sort, a gemmed pendant—or brooch more likely, since her coat was tightly shut. He was sure it was the same person, and there was the same sense of instant approval or attraction on his part, only stronger this time (which was natural enough, he told himself later). And he went down the hall faster this time and hurried on without pausing to check the stairs and the back corridor, though his chance of hearing footsteps or a closing door was spoiled by the siren of an ambulance rushing by outside. Returning thoughtfully to the foyer, he found the cage gone, but it came down almost immediately, debarking a tenant he recognized—third or fourth floor, he thought—who said rather puzzledly in answer to a question by Ryker that he thought he'd summoned the elevator directly from One and it had been empty when it had reached his floor.

Ryker thanked him and boarded the elevator.

The cage's silvered gray paper and polished fittings made it seem quite modern. Another nice touch was the little window in its door, which matched those in the floor doors when both were shut, so that you got a slow winking glimpse of each floor as you rose past—as Ryker now glimpsed the second floor go down. But actually it was an ancient vehicle smartened up, and so was the system that ran it. You had to hold down a button for an appreciable time to make the cage respond, because it worked by mechanical relays in the elevator room on the roof, not by the instant response to a touch of electronic modern systems. Also, it couldn't remember several instructions and obey them in order as the modern ones could; it obeyed one order only and then waited to be given the next one manually.

Ryker was very conscious of that difference between automatic and manual. For the past five years he had been shifting his own bodily activities from automatic to manual: running (hell, trotting was the most you could call it!—a clumping trot), going down stairs, climbing them, walking outside, even getting dressed and—almost—writing. Used to be he could switch on automatic for those and think about something else. But now he had to do more and more things a step at a time, and watching and thinking about each step too, like a baby learning (only you never did learn; it never got automatic again). And it took a lot more time, everything did. Sometimes you had to stand very still even to think.

Another floor slowly winked by. Ryker caught the number painted on the shaft side of its elevator door just below that door's little window—5. What a slow trip it was!

Ryker did a lot of his real thinking in this elevator part of the apartment tree. It wasn't full of loneliness and ambushing memories the way his apartment was, or crawling with the small dangers and hostilities that occupied most of his mind when he was in the street world outside. It was a world between those, a restful pause between two kinds of oppression, inhabited only by the mostly anonymous people with whom he shared his present half-life, his epilogue life, and quite unlike the realer folk from whom he had been rather purposefully disengaging himself ever since his wife's and his job's deaths.

They were an odd lot, truly, his present fellow-inhabitants of the apartment tree. At least half of them were as old as he, and many of them engaged in the same epilogue living as he was, so far as he could judge. Perhaps a quarter were middle-aged; Ryker liked them least of all—they carried tension with them, things he was trying to forget. While rather fewer than a quarter were young. These always hurried through the apartment tree on full automatic, as if it were a place of no interest whatever, a complete waste of time.

He himself did not find it so, but rather the only place where he could think and observe closely at the same time, a quiet realm of pause. He saw nothing strange in the notion of ghosts (if he'd believed in such) haunting the neighborhood where they'd died—most of them had spent their last few years studying that area in greatest detail, impressing their spirits into its very atoms, while that area steadily grew smaller, as if they were beetles circling a nail to which they were tethered by a thread that slowly wound up, growing shorter and shorter with every circumambulation they made.

Another floor numeral with its little window slid into and out of view—8 only. God, what snail-like, well-frog pace!

The only denizen of the apartment tree with whom Ryker had more than a recognition acquaintance (you could hardly call the one he had with the others nodding, let alone speaking) was Clancy, rough-cut manager-janitor of the building, guardian of the gates of the apartment tree and its historian, a retired fireman who managed to make himself available and helpful without becoming oppressive or officious. Mrs. Clancy was an altogether more respectable and concierge-like character who made Ryker feel uncomfortable. He preferred always to deal with her husband, and over the years a genuine though strictly limited friendship (it never got beyond "Clancy" and "Mr. Ryker") had sprung up between them.

The figure 12 appeared and disappeared in the window. He kept his eyes on the empty rectangle and gave an accustomed chuckle when the next figure was 14, with none intervening. Superstition, how mighty, how undying! (Though somehow the travel between the last two floors, Twelve and Fourteen, always seemed to take longest, by a fraction. There was food for thought there. Did elevators get tired?—perhaps because the air grew more rarified with increased altitude?)

The window above the 14 steadied. There was a clicking; the gray door slid open sideways, he pushed through the outer door, and as he did so, he uttered another chuckle that was both cheerful and sardonic. He'd just realized that after all his journeying in the apartment tree, he'd at last become interested in one of his nameless traveling companions. The elevator-tree world also held the Vanishing Lady.

It was surprising how lighthearted he felt.

As if in rebuke for this and for his springing hopes not clearly defined, he didn't see the Vanishing Lady for the next three days, although he devised one or two errands for himself that would bring him back to the apartment tree at dusk, and when he did spot her again on the fourth day, the circumstances were altered from those of their first two encounters.

Returning from another of his little twilight outings and unlocking the heavy street door, he noted that the hall and distant foyer were a little bit dimmer than usual, as if some small, normal light source were gone, with the effect of a black hole appearing suddenly in the fabric of reality.

As he started forward warily, he discerned the explanation. The doors to the elevator were wide open, but the ceiling light in the cage had been switched (or gone) off, so that where a gray door gleaming by reflection should have been, there was an ominous dark upright rectangle.

And then, as he continued to advance, he saw that the cage wasn't empty. Light angling down into it from the foyer's ceiling fixture revealed the slender figure of the Vanishing Lady leaning with her back against the cage's wall just behind the column of buttons. The light missed her head, but showed the rest of her figure well enough, her dejected posture, her motionless passivity.

As he imperceptibly quickened his stride straight toward her, the slanting light went on, picking up bits of detail here and there in the gloom, almost as if summoning them: the glossy gleam of black oxfords, the muted one of black stockings, and the in-between sheen of her sleek coat. The nearest black-gloved hand appeared to be clutching that together snugly, and from the closure there seemed to come faint diamond glimmers like the faint-est ghost of a sparkler shower, so faint he couldn't be sure whether it was really there, or just his own eyes making the churning points of light there are in darkness. The farthest jetty hand held forward a small brass object which he first took for an apartment door key got out well in advance (as some nervous people will) but then saw to be a little too narrow and too long for that.

He was aware of a mounting tension and breathlessness—and sense of strangeness too. And then without warning, just as he was about to enter the cage and simultaneously switch its light on, he heard himself mutter apologetically, "Sorry, I've got to check my mailbox first," and his footsteps veered sharply but smoothly to the right with never a hesitation.

For the next few seconds his mind was so occupied with shock at this sudden rush of timidity, this flinching away from what he'd thought he wanted to do, that he actually had his keys out, was advancing the tiny flat one toward the brass-fronted narrow box he'd checked this noon as always, before he reversed his steps with a small growl of impatience and self-rebuke and hurried back past the manager's shuttered window and around the stairs.

The elevator doors were closed and the small window glowed bright. But just as he snatched at the door to open it, the bright rectangle nar-rowed from the bottom and winked out, the elevator growled softly as the cage ascended, and the door resisted his yank. Damn! He pressed himself against it, listening intently. Soon—after no more than five or six seconds, he thought—he heard the cage stop and its door *clump* open. Instantly he was thumbing the button. After a bit he heard the door *clump* shut and the growling recommence. Was it growing louder or softer—coming down or going away? Louder! Soon it had arrived, and he was opening the door—rather to the surprise of its emerging occupant, a plump lady in a green coat.

Her eyebrows rose at his questions, rather as had happened on the previ-ous such occasion. She'd been on Three when she'd buzzed for the elevator, she said. No, there'd been no one in it when it arrived, no one had got off, it had been empty. Yes, the light *had* been off in the elevator when it had come up, but she hadn't missed anyone on account of that—and she'd turned it on again. And then she'd just gotten in and come down. Had he been buzzing for it? Well, she'd been pushing the button for One, too. What did it matter?

She made for the street door, glancing back at Ryker dubiously, as if she were thinking that, whatever he was up to, she didn't ever want that excited old man tracking *her* down.

Then for a while Ryker was so busy trying to explain that to himself (Had there been time for her to emerge and shut the doors silently and hurry down the long hall or tiptoe up the stairs before the cage went up to Three? Well, just possibly, but it would have had to be done with almost incredible rapidity. Could he have *imagined* her—projected her onto the gloom inside the cage, so to speak? Or had the lady in green been lying? Were she and the Vanishing Lady confederates? And so on…) that it was some time before he began to try to analyze the reasons for his self-betrayal.

Well, for one thing, he told himself, he'd been so gripped by his desire to see her close up that he'd neglected to ask himself what he'd do once he'd achieved that, how he'd make conversation if they were alone together in the cage—and that these questions popping up in his mind all at once had made him falter. And then there was his lifelong habit, he had to admit, of automatically shrinking from all close contact with women save his mother and wife, especially if the occasion for it came upon him suddenly. Or had he without knowing it become just a little frightened of this mysterious person who had stirred him erotically—the apartment tree was always dimly lit, there'd never been anyone else around when she'd appeared, there'd been something so woeful-melancholy about her attitude (though that was probably part of her attraction), and finally she *had* vanished three times unaccountably—so that it was no wonder he had veered aside from entering the elevator, its very lightlessness suggesting a trap. (And that made him recall another odd point. Not only had the light inside the elevator been switched off but the door, which always automatically swung shut unless someone held it open or set a fairly heavy object, such as a packed suitcase or a laden-large shopping bag, against it, had been standing open. And he couldn't recall having seen any such object or other evidence of propping or wedging. Mysterious. In fact, as mysterious as his suffocation dreams, which at least had lessened in number and intensity since the Vanishing Lady had turned up.)

Well, he told himself with another effort at being philosophical, now that he'd thought all these things through, at least he'd behave more courageously if a similar situation arose another time.

But when the Vanishing Lady next appeared to Ramsey, it was under conditions that did not call for that sort of courage. There were others present.

He'd come in from outside and found the empty cage ready and waiting, but he could hear another party just close enough behind him that he didn't feel justified in taking off without them—though there'd been enough times, God knows, when he'd been left behind under the same circumstances. He dutifully waited, holding the door open. There had been times, too, when this politeness of his had been unavailing—when the people had been bound for a ground-floor apartment, or when it had been a lone woman and she'd found an excuse for not making her journey alone with him.

The party finally came into view—two middle-aged women and a man— and the latter insisted on holding the door himself. Ryker relinquished it without argument and went to the back of the cage, the two women following. But the man didn't come inside; he held the door for yet a third party he'd evidently heard coming behind them.

The third party arrived, an elderly couple, but that man insisted on holding the door in his turn for the second man and his own ancient lady. They were six, a full load, Ryker counted. But then, just as the floor door was swinging shut, someone caught it from the outside, and the one who slipped in last was the Vanishing Lady.

Ramsey mightn't have seen her if he hadn't been tall, for the cage was now almost uncomfortably crowded, although none of them were conspicuous heavyweights. He glimpsed a triangle of pale face under dark gleaming eyes, which fixed for an instant on his, and he felt a jolt of excitement, or something. Then she had whipped around and was facing front, like the rest. His heart was thudding and his throat was choked up. He knew the sheen of her black hair and coat, the dull felt of her close-fitting hat, and watched them raptly. He decided from the flash of face that she was young or very smoothly powdered.

The cage stopped at the seventh floor. She darted out without a backward glance and the elderly couple followed her. He wanted to do something but he couldn't think what, and someone pressed another button.

As soon as the cage had resumed its ascent, he realized that he too could have gotten out on Seven and at least seen where she went in, discovered her apartment number. But he hadn't acted quickly enough and some of these people probably knew he lived on Fourteen and would have wondered.

The rest got out on Twelve and so he did the last floor alone—the floor that numerically was two floors, actually only one, yet always seemed to take a bit too long, the elevator growing tired, ha-ha-ha.

Next day he examined the names on the seventh-floor mailboxes, but that wasn't much help. Last names only, with at most an initial or two, was the rule. No indication of sex or marital status. And, as always, fully a third were marked only as OCCUPIED. It was safer that way, he remembered being told (something about anonymous phone calls or confidence games), even if it somehow always looked suspicious, vaguely criminal.

Late the next afternoon, when he was coming in from the street, he saw a man holding the elevator door open for two elderly women to enter. He hurried his stride, but the man didn't look his way before following them.

But just at that moment, the Vanishing Lady darted into view from the foyer, deftly caught the closing door, and with one pale glance over her shoulder at Ryker, let herself in on the heels of the man. Although he was too far away to see her eyes as more than twin gleams, he felt the same transfixing jolt as he had the previous day. His heart beat faster too.

And then as he hurried on, the light in the little window in the gray door winked out as the elevator rose up and away from him. A few seconds later he was standing in front of the electrically locked door with its dark little window and staring ruefully at the button and the tiny circular telltale just above it, which now glowed angry red to indicate the elevator was in use and unresponsive to any summons.

He reproached himself for not having thought to call out, "Please wait for me," but there'd hardly been time to think, and besides it would have been such a departure from his normal, habitually silent behavior. Still, another self-defeat, another self-frustration, in his pursuit of the Vanishing Lady! He wished this elevator had, like those in office buildings or hotels, a more extensive telltale beside or over its door that told which floor it was on or passing, so you could trace its course. It would be helpful to know whether it stopped at Seven again this time—it was hard to hear it stop when it got that far away. Of course you could run up the stairs, racing it, if you were young enough and in shape. He'd once observed two young men who were sixth-floor residents do just that, pitting the one's strong legs and two-or-three-steps-at-a-time against the other's slow elevator—and never learned who won. For that matter, the young tenants, who were mostly residents of the lower floors, where the turnover of apartments was brisker, quite often went charging blithely up the stairs even when the elevator was waiting and ready, as if to advertise (along with their youth) their contempt for its tedious *elderly* pace. If *he* were young again now, he asked himself, would he have raced up after a vanished girl?

The telltale went black. He jabbed the button, saw it turn red again as the cage obediently obeyed his summons.

Next afternoon found him staring rather impatiently at the red telltale on the fourteenth floor, this time while waiting to travel to the ground floor and so out. And this time it had been red for quite some while, something that happened not infrequently, since the cage's slow speed and low capacity made it barely adequate to service a building of this size. And while it stayed red it was hard to tell how many trips it was making and how long people were holding the door at one floor. He'd listened to numerous speculative conversations about "what the elevator was doing," as if it had a mind and volition of its own, which one humorist had indeed suggested. And there were supposed to be certain people (sometimes named and sometimes not) who did outrageous and forbidden things, such as jamming the floor door open while they went back to get things they'd forgotten, or picked up friends on other floors as they went down (or up), organizing an outing or party or having secret discussions and arguments before reaching the less private street. There were even said to be cases of people "pulling the elevator away" from other people who were their enemies, just to spite them.

The most colorful theory, perhaps, was that held by two elderly ladies, both old buffs of elevator travel, whom Ramsey had happened to overhear on two or three occasions. The cornerstone of their theory was that all the building's troubles were caused by its younger tenants and the teenage sons and daughters of tenants. "Mrs. Clancy told me," one of them had whispered loudly once, "that they know a way of stopping the thing between floors so they can smooch together and shoot dope and do all sorts of other nasty things—even, if you can believe, go the whole way with each other." Ryker had been amused; it gave the cage a certain erotic aura.

And every once in a while the elevator did get stuck between floors, sometimes with people in it and sometimes not, especially between the twelfth and fourteenth floors, Clancy had once told him, "like it was trying to stop at the thirteenth!"

But now the elevator's vagaries weren't all that amusing to Ramsey standing alone on the top floor, so after one more session of pettish button-pushing—the telltale had gone briefly black, but evidently someone else had beat him to the punch—he decided to "walk down for exercise," something he'd actually done intentionally upon occasion.

As he descended the apartment tree (he thought of himself as an old squirrel sedately scampering zigzag down the barky outside of the trunk the elevator shaft made), he found himself wondering how the elevator could be so busy when all the corridors were so silent and empty. (But maybe things were happening just before his footstep-heralded arrivals and after his departures—they heard him coming and hid themselves until he was by. Or maybe there was some sort of basement crisis.) The floors were all the same, or almost so: the two long corridors ending in doors of wire-reinforced glass which led to the front and alley fire escapes; these were also lit midway by frosted glass spheres like full moons hanging in space; in either wall beside these handsome globes were set two narrow full-length mirrors in which you could see yourself paced along by two companions.

The apartment tree boasted many mirrors, a luxury note like its silver-arabesqued gray wallpaper. There was a large one opposite each elevator door and there were three in the lobby.

As he ended each flight, Ramsey would look down the long alley corridor, make a U-turn, and walk back to the landing (glancing into the short corridor and the elevator landing, which were lit by a central third moon and one large window), all this while facing the long front corridor, then make another U-turn and start down the next flight.

(He did discover one difference between the floors. He counted steps going down, and while there were nineteen between the fourteenth and the twelfth floors, there were only seventeen between all the other pairs. So the cage had to travel a foot and a bit farther to make that Fourteen–Twelve journey; it didn't just *seem* to take longer, it *did*. So much for tired elevators!)

So it went for nine floors.

But when he made his U-turn onto the third floor he saw that the front corridor's full moon had been extinguished, throwing a gloom on the whole passageway, while silhouetted against the wired glass at the far end was a swayed, slender figure looking very much like that of the Vanishing Lady. He couldn't make out her pale triangle of face or gleaming eyes because there was no front light on her; she was only shaped darkness, yet he was sure it was she.

In walking the length of the landing, however, there was time to think that if he continued on beyond the stairs, it would be an undeniable declaration of his intention to meet her, he'd have to keep going, he had no other excuse; also, there'd be the unpleasant impression of him closing in ominously, relentlessly, on a lone trapped female.

As he advanced she waited at the tunnel's end, silent and unmoving, a shaped darkness.

He made his customary turn, keeping on down the stairs. He felt so wrenched by what was happening that he hardly knew what he was thinking or even feeling, except his heart was thudding and his lungs were gasping as if he'd just walked ten stories upstairs instead of down.

It wasn't until he had turned into the second floor and seen through the stairwell, cut off by ceiling, the workshoes and twill pants of Clancy, the manager, faced away from him in the lobby, that he got himself in hand. He instantly turned and retraced his steps with frantic haste. He'd flinched away again, just when he'd sworn he wouldn't! Why, there were a dozen questions he could politely ask her to justify his close approach. Could he be of assistance? Was she looking for one of the tenants? Some apartment number? Etcetera.

But even as he rehearsed these phrases, he had a sinking feeling of what he was going to find on Three.

He was right. There was no longer a figure among the shadows filling the dark front corridor.

And then, even as he was straining his eyes to make sure, with a flicker and a flash the full moon came on again and shone steadily.

Showing no one at all.

Ramsey didn't look any further but hurried back down the stairs. He wanted to be with people, anyone, just people in the street.

But Mr. Clancy was still in the lobby, communing with himself. Ramsey suddenly felt he simply had to share at least part of the story of the Vanishing Lady with someone.

So he told Clancy about the defective light bulb inside the front globe on Three, how it had started to act like a globe that's near the end of its lifetime, arcing and going off and on by itself, unreliable. Only then did he, as if idly, an afterthought, mention the woman he'd seen and then got to wondering about and gone back and not seen, adding that he thought he'd also seen her in the lobby once or twice before.

He hadn't anticipated the swift seriousness of the manager's reaction. Ramsey'd hardly more than mentioned the woman when the ex-fireman asked sharply, "Did she look like a bum? I mean, for a woman—"

Ramsey told him that no, she didn't, but he hadn't more than sketched his story when the other said, "Look, Mr. Ryker, I'd like to go up and check this out right away. You said she was all in black, didn't you? Yeah. Well, look, you stay here, would you do that? And just take notice if anybody comes down. I won't be long."

And he got in the elevator, which had been waiting there, and went up. To Four or Five, or maybe Six, Ramsey judged from the cage's noises and the medium-short time the telltale flared before winking out. He imagined that Clancy would leave it there and then hunt down the floors one by one, using the stairs.

Pretty soon Clancy did reappear by way of the stairs, looking thoughtful. "No" he said, "she's not there any more, at least—not in the bottom half of the building—and I don't see her doing a lot of climbing. Maybe she got somebody to take her in, or maybe it was just one of the tenants. Or…?" He looked a question at Ramsey, who shook his head and said, "No, nobody came down the stairs or elevator."

The manager nodded and then shook his own head slowly. "I don't know, maybe I'm getting too suspicious," he said. "I don't know how much you've noticed, Mr. Ryker, living way on top, but from time to time this building is troubled by bums—winos and street people from south of here—trying to get inside and shelter here, especially in winter, maybe go to sleep in a corner. Most of them are men, of course, but there's an occasional woman bum." He paused and chuckled reflectively. "Once we had an invasion of women bums, though they weren't that exactly."

Ramsey looked at him expectantly.

Clancy hesitated, glanced at Ramsey, and after another pause said, "That's why we turn the buzzer system off at eleven at night and keep it off until eight in the morning. If we left it on, why, any time in the night a drunken wino would start buzzing apartments until he got one who'd buzz the door open (or he might push a dozen at once, so somebody'd be sure to buzz the door), and once he was inside, he'd hunt himself up an out-of-the-way spot where he could sleep it off and be warm. And if he had cigarettes, he'd start smoking them to put him to sleep, dropping the matches anywhere, but mostly under things. There's where your biggest danger is—fire. Or he'd get an idea and start bothering tenants, ringing their bells and knocking on their doors, and then anything could happen. Even with the buzzer system off, some of them get in. They'll stand beside the street door and then follow a couple that's late getting home, or the same with the newsboy delivering the morning paper before it's light. Not following them directly, you see, but using a foot (sometimes a cane or crutch) to block the door just before it locks itself, and then coming in soon as the coast's clear."

Ramsey nodded several times appreciatively, but then pressed the other with "But you were going to tell me something about an invasion of female bums?"

"Oh, that," Clancy said doubtfully. A look at Ramsey seemed to reassure him. "That was before your time—you came here about five years ago, didn't you? Yeah. Well, this happened… let's see… about two years before that. The Mrs. and I generally don't talk about it much to tenants, because it gives… gave the building a bad name. Not really any more now, though. Seven years and all's forgotten, eh?"

He broke off to greet respectfully a couple who passed by on their way upstairs. He turned back to Ramsey. "Well, anyway," he continued more comfortably, "at this time I'm talking about, the Mrs. and I had been here ourselves only a year. Just about long enough to learn the ropes, at least some of them.

"Now there's one thing about a building like this I got to explain," he interjected. "You never, or almost never, get any disappearances—you know, tenants sneaking their things out when they're behind on the rent, or just walking out one day, leaving their things, and never coming back (maybe getting mugged to death, who knows?)—like happens all the time in those fleabag hotels and rooming houses south of us. Why, half of *their* renters are on dope or heavy medication to begin with, and come from prisons or from mental hospitals. Here you get a steadier sort of tenant, or at least the Mrs. and I try to make it be like that.

"Well, back then, just about the steadiest tenant we had, though not the oldest by any means, was a tall, thin, very handsome and distinguished-looking youngish chap, name of Arthur J. Stensor, third floor front. Very polite and soft-spoken, never raised his voice. Dark complected, but with blond hair which he wore in a natural—not so common then; once I heard him referred to by another tenant as 'that frizzy bleached Negro,' and I thought they were being disrespectful. A sharp dresser but never flashy—he had class. He always wore a hat. Rent paid the first of the month in cash with never a miss. Rent for the garage space too—he kept a black Lincoln Continental in the basement that was always polished like glass; never used the front door much but went and came in that car. And his apartment was furnished to match: oil paintings in gold frames, silver statues, hi-fi, *big*-screen TV and the stuff to record programs and films off it when that *cost*, all sorts of fancy clocks and vases, silks and velvets, more stuff like that than you'd ever believe.

"And when there was people with him, which wasn't too often, they were as classy as he and his car and his apartment, especially the women—high society and always young. I remember once being in the third-floor hall one night when one of those stunners swept by me and he let her in, and thinking, 'Well, if that filly was a call girl, she sure came from the best stable in town.' Only I remember thinking at the same time that I was being disrespectful, because A. J. Stensor was just a little too respectable for even the classiest call girl. Which was a big joke on me considering what happened next."

"Which was?" Ramsey prompted, after they'd waited for a couple more tenants to go by.

"Well, at first I didn't connect it at all with Stensor," Clancy responded, "though it's true I hadn't happened to see him for the last five or six days, which was sort of unusual, though not all that much so. Well, what happened was this invasion—no, goddammit! this *epidemic*—of good-looking hookers, mostly tall and skinny, or at least skinny, through the lower halls and lobby of this building. Some of them were dressed too respectable for hookers, but most of them wore the street uniform of the day—which was high heels, skintight blue jeans, long lace blouses worn outside the pants, and lots of bangles—and when you saw them talking together palsy-walsy, the respectable-looking and the not, you knew they all had to be."

"How did it first come to you?" Ramsey asked. "Tenants complain?"

"A couple," Clancy admitted. "Those old biddies who'll report a young and good-looking woman on the principle that if she's young and good-looking she can't be up to any good purpose. But the really funny thing was that most of the reports of them came in just by way of gossip—either to me direct, or by way of the Mrs., which is how it usually works—like it was something strange and remarkable—which it was, all right! Questions too, such as what the hell they were all up to, which was a good one to ask, by the way. You see, they weren't any of them *doing* anything to complain of. It was broad day and they certainly weren't trying to pick anyone up, they weren't plying their trade at all, you might say, they weren't even smiling at anybody, especially men. No, they were just walking up and down and talking together, looking critical and angry more than anything, and very serious—like they'd picked our apartment building for a hookers' convention, complete with debates, some sort of feminist or union thing, except they hadn't bothered to inform the management. Oh, when I'd cough and ask a couple of them what they were doing, they'd throw me some excuse without looking at me—that they had a lunch date with a lady here but she didn't seem to be in and they couldn't wait, or that they were shopping for apartments but these weren't suitable—and at the same time they'd start walking toward the street door, or toward the stairs if they were on the third or second floor, still gabbing together in private voices about whatever it was they were debating, and then they'd sweep out, still not noticing me even if I held the door for them.

"And then, you know, in twenty minutes they'd be back inside! or at least I'd spot one of them that was. Some of them *must* have had front door keys, I remember thinking—and as it turned out later, some of them did."

By this time Mr. Clancy had warmed to his story and was giving out little chuckles with every other sentence, and he almost forgot to lower his voice next time a tenant passed.

"There was one man they took notice of. I forgot about that. It could have given me a clue to what was happening, but I didn't get it. We had a tenant then on one of the top floors who was tall and slim and rather good-looking—young looking too, although he wasn't—and always wore a hat. Well, I was in the lobby and four or five of the hookers had just come in the front door, debating of course, when this guy stepped out of the elevator and they all spotted him and made a rush for him. But when they got about a dozen feet away from him and he took off his hat—maybe to be polite, he looked a little scared, I don't know what he thought—showing his wavy black hair which he kept dyed, the hookers all lost interest in him—as if he'd looked like someone they knew, but closer up turned out not to be (which *was* the case, though I still didn't catch on then)—and they swept past him and on up the stairs as if that was where they'd been rushing in the first place.

"I tell you, that was some weird day. Hookers dressed all ways—classy-respectable, the tight-jeans and lacy-blouse uniform, mini-skirts, one in what looked like a kid's sailor suit cut for a woman, a sad one all in black looking like something special for funerals… you know, maybe to give first aid to a newly bereaved husband or something." He gave Ryker a quick look, continuing, "And although almost all of them were skinny, I recall there was a fat one wearing a mumu and swinging gracefully like a belly dancer.

"The Mrs. was after me to call the police, but our owner sort of discourages that, and I couldn't get him on the phone.

"In the evening the hookers tapered off and I dropped into bed, all worn out from the action, the wife still after me to call the police, but I just conked out cold, and so the only one to see the last of the business was the newsboy when he came to deliver at four-thirty about. Later on he dropped back to see me, couldn't wait to tell me about it.

"Well, he was coming up to the building, it seems, pushing his shopping cart of morning papers, when he sees this crowd of good-looking women (he wasn't wise to the hookers' convention the day before) around the doorway, most of them young and all of them carrying expensive-looking objects—paintings, vases, silver statues of naked girls, copper kitchenware, gold clocks, that sort of stuff—like they were helping a wealthy friend move. Only there is a jam-up, two or three of them are trying to maneuver an oversize dolly through the door, and on that dolly is the biggest television set the kid ever saw and also the biggest record player.

"A woman at the curb outside, who seems a leader, sort of very cool, is calling directions to them how to move it, and close beside her is another woman, like her assistant or gopher maybe. The leader's calling out directions, like I say, in a hushed voice, and the other women are watching, but they're all very quiet, like you'd expect people to be at that hour of the morning, sober people at any rate, not wanting to wake the neighbors.

"Well, the kid's looking all around, every which way, trying to take in everything—there was a lot of interesting stuff to see, I gather, and more inside—when the gopher lady comes over and hunkers down beside him—he was a runt, that newsboy was, and ugly too—and wants to buy a morning paper. He hauls it out for her and she gives him a five-dollar bill and tells him to keep the change. He's sort of embarrassed by that and drops his eyes, but she tells him not to mind, he's a handsome boy and a good hard-working one, she wished she had one like him, and he deserves everything he gets, and she puts an arm around him and draws him close and all of a sudden his downcast eyes are looking inside her blouse front and he's getting the most amazing anatomy lesson you could imagine.

"He has some idea that they're getting the dolly clear by now and that the other women are moving, but she's going on whispering in his ear, her breath's like steam, what a good boy he is and how grateful his parents must be, and *his* only worry, she'll hug him so tight he won't be able to look down her blouse.

"After a bit she ends his anatomy lesson with a kiss that almost smothers him and then stands up. The women are all gone and the dolly's vanishing around the next corner. Before she hurries after it, she says, 'So long, kid. You got your bonus. Now deliver your papers.'

"Which, after he got over his daze, is what he did, he said.

"Well, of course, as soon as he mentioned the big television and player, I flashed on what I'd been missing all yesterday, though it was right in front of my eyes if I'd just looked. Why they'd been swarming on Three, why they rushed the guy from Seven and then lost interest in him when he took off his hat and they saw his hair was black dyed (instead of frizzy blond), and why the hookers' convention wasn't still going on today. All that loot could have only come from one place—Stensor's. In spite of him being so respectable, he'd been running a string of call girls all the time, so that when he ran out on them owing them all money (I flashed on that at the same time), they'd collected the best way they knew how.

"I ran to his apartment, and you know the door wasn't even locked—one of them must have had a key to it too. Of course the place was stripped and of course no sign of Stensor.

"Then I did call the police of course but not until I'd checked the basement. His black Continental was gone, but there was no way of telling for sure whether he'd taken it or the gals had got that too.

"It surprised me how fast the police came and how many of them there were, but it showed they must have had an eye on him already, which maybe explained why he left so sudden without taking his things. They asked a lot of questions and came back more than once, were in and out for a few days. I got to know one of the detectives, he lived locally, we had a drink together once or twice, and he told me they were really after Stensor for drug dealing, he was handling cocaine back in those days when it was first getting to be the classy thing, they weren't interested in his call girls except as he might have used them as pushers. They never did turn him up though, far as I know, and there wasn't even a line in the papers about the whole business."

"So that was the end of your one-day hooker invasion?" Ryker commented, chuckling rather dutifully.

"Not quite," Clancy said, and hesitated. Then with a "What-difference-can-it-make?" shrug, he went on, "Well, yes, there was a sort of funny follow-up but it didn't amount to much. You see, the story of Stensor and the hookers eventually got around to most of the tenants in the building, as such things will, though some of them got it garbled, as you can imagine happens, that he was a patron and maybe somehow victim of call girls instead of running them. Well, anyhow, after a bit, we (the Mrs. mostly) began to get these tenant reports of a girl—a young woman—seen waiting outside the door to Stensor's apartment, or wandering around in other parts of the building, but mostly waiting at Stensor's door. And this was after there were other tenants in that apartment. A sad-looking girl."

"Like, out of all those hookers," Ryker said, "she was the only one who really loved him and waited for him. A sort of leftover."

"Yeah, or the only one who hadn't got her split of the loot," Clancy said. "Or maybe he owed her more than the others. I never saw her myself, although I went chasing after her a couple of times when tenants reported her. I wouldn't have taken any stock in her except the descriptions did seem to hang together. A college-type girl, they'd say, and mostly wearing black. And sort of sad. I told the detective I knew, but he didn't seem to make anything out of it. They never did pick up any of the women, he said, far as he knew. Well, that's all there is to the follow-up—like I said, nothing much. And after two or three months tenants stopped seeing her."

He broke off, eyeing Ryker just a little doubtfully.

"But it stuck in your mind," that one observed, "for all these years, so that when I told you about seeing a woman in black near the same door, you rushed off to check up on her, just on the chance? Though you'd never seen her yourself, even once?"

Clancy's expression became a shade unhappy. "Well, no," he admitted, glancing up and down the hall, as though hoping someone would come along and save him from answering. "There was a little more than that," he continued uneasily, "though I wouldn't want anyone making too much of it, or telling the Mrs. I told them.

"But then, Mr. Ryker, you're not the one to be gossiping or getting the wind up, are you?" he continued more easily, giving his tenant a hopeful look.

"No, of course I'm not," Ryker responded, a little more casually than he felt. "What was it?"

"Well, about four years ago we had another disappearance here, a single man living alone and getting on in years but still active. He didn't own any of the furniture, his possessions were few, nothing at all fancy like Stensor's, no friends or relations we knew of, and he came to us from a building that knew no more; in fact we didn't realize he was gone until the time for paying the rent came round. And it wasn't until then that I recalled that the last time or two I spoke to him he'd mentioned something about a woman in an upstairs hall, wondering if she'd found the people or the apartment number she seemed to be looking for. Not making a complaint, you see, just mentioning, just idly wondering, so that it wasn't until he disappeared that I thought of connecting it up with Stensor's girl at all."

"He say if she was young?" Ryker asked.

"He wasn't sure. She was wearing a black outside coat and hat or scarf of something that hid her face, and she made a point of not noticing him when he looked at her and thought of asking if she needed help. He did say she was thin, though, I remember."

Ryker nodded.

Clancy continued, "And then a few years ago there was this couple on Nine that had a son living with them, a big fat lug who looked older than he was and was always being complained about whether he did anything or not. One of the old ladies in the apartment next to their bathroom used to kick to us about him running water for baths at two or three in the morning. And he had the nerve to complain to us about *them,* claiming they pulled the elevator away from him when he wanted to get it, or made it go in the opposite direction to what he wanted when he was in it. I laughed in his pimply face at that. Not that those two old biddies wouldn't have done it to him if they'd figured a way and they'd got the chance.

"His mother was a sad soul who used to fuss at him and worry about him a lot. She'd bring her troubles to the Mrs. and talk and talk—but I think really she'd have been relieved to have him off her mind.

"His father was a prize crab, an ex-army officer forever registering complaints—he had a little notebook for them. But half the time he was feuding with me and the Mrs., wouldn't give us the time of day—or of course ask it. I know *he'd* have been happy to see his loud-mouthed dumb son drop out of sight.

"Well, one day the kid comes down to me here with a smart-ass grin and says, 'Mr. Clancy, you're the one who's so great, aren't you, on chasing winos and hookers out of here, not letting them freeload in the halls for a minute? Then how come you let—'

" 'Go on,' I tell him, 'what do you know about hookers?'

"But that doesn't faze him, he just goes on (he was copying his father, I think, actually), 'Then how come you let this skinny little hooker in a black fur coat wander around the halls all the time, trying to pick guys up?'

" 'You're making this up,' I tell him flat, 'or you're imagining things, or else one of our lady tenants is going to be awful sore at you if she ever hears you've been calling her a hooker.'

" 'She's nobody from this building,' the kid insists, 'she's got more class. That fur coat cost money. It's hard to check out her face, though, because she never looks at you straight on and she's got this black hat she hides behind. I figure she's an old bag—maybe thirty, even—and wears the hat so you can't see her wrinkles, but that she's got a young bod, young and wiry. I bet she takes karate lessons so she can bust the balls of any guy that gets out of line, or maybe if he just doesn't satisfy her—'

" 'You're pipe-dreaming, kid,' I tell him.

" 'And you know what?' he goes on. 'I bet you she's got nothing on but black stockings and a garter belt under that black fur coat she keeps wrapped so tight around her, so when she's facing a guy she can give him a quick flash of her bod, to lead him on—'

" 'And you got a dirty mind,' I say. 'You're making this up.'

" 'I am not,' he says. 'She was just now up on Ten before I came down and leering at me sideways, giving me the come on.'

" 'What were you doing up on Ten?' I ask him loud.

" 'I always go up a floor before I buzz the elevator,' he answers me quick, 'so's those old dames won't know it's me and buzz it away from me.'

" 'All right, quiet down, kid,' I tell him. 'I'm going up to Ten right now, to check this out, and you're coming with me.'

"So we go on up to Ten and there's nobody there and right away the kid starts yammering, 'I bet you she picked up a trick in this building and they're behind one of these doors screwing, right now. Old Mr. Lucas—'

"I was really going to give him a piece of my mind then, tell him off, but on the way up I'd been remembering that girl of Stensor's who lingered behind, maybe for a long time, if there was anything to what the other guy told me. And somehow it gave me a sort of funny feeling, so all I said was something like 'Look here, kid, maybe you're making this up and maybe not. Either way, I still think you got a dirty mind. But if you did see this hooker and you ever see her again, don't you have anything to do with her—and don't go off with her if she should ask you. You just come straight to me and tell me, and if I'm not here, you find a cop and tell him. Hear me?'

"You know, that sort of shut him up. 'All right, all right!' he said and went off, taking the stairs going down."

"And did *he* disappear?" Ryker asked after a bit. He seemed vaguely to remember the youth in question, a pallid and lumbering lout who tended to brush against people and bump into doorways when he passed them.

"Well, you know, in a way that's a matter for argument," Clancy answered slowly. "It was the last time I saw him—that's a fact. And the Mrs. never saw him again either. But when she asked his mother about him, she just said he was off visiting friends for a while, but then a month or so later she admitted to the Mrs. that he had gone off without telling them a word—to join a commune, she thought, from some of the things he'd been saying, and that was all right with her, because his father just couldn't get along with him, they had such fights, only she wished he'd have the consideration to send her a card or something."

"And that was the last of it?" Ryker asked.

Clancy nodded slowly, almost absently. "That was damn all of it," he said softly. "About ten months later the parents moved. The kid hadn't turned up. There was nothing more."

"Until now," Ryker said, "when I came to you with my questions about a woman in black—and on Three at that, where this Stensor had lived. It wasn't a fur coat, of course, and I didn't think of her being a hooker—" (Was that true? he wondered) "—and it brought it all back to you, which now included what the young man had told you, and so you checked out the floors and then very kindly told me the whole story so as to give me the same warning you gave him?"

"But you're an altogether different sort of person, Mr. Ryker," Clancy protested. "I'd never think— But yes, allowing for that, that about describes it. You can't be too careful."

"No, you can't. It's a strange business," Ryker commented, shaking his head, and then added, making it sound much more casual, even comical, than he felt it, "You know, if this had happened fifty years ago, we'd be thinking maybe we had a ghost."

Clancy chuckled uneasily and said, "Yeah, I guess that's so."

Ryker said, "But the trouble with that idea would have been that there's nothing in the story about a woman disappearing, but three men—Stensor, and the man who lived alone, and the young man who lived with his parents."

"That's so," Mr. Clancy said.

Ryker stirred himself. "Well, thanks for telling me all about it," he said as they shook hands. "And if I should run into the lady again, I won't take any chances. I'll report it to you, Clancy. But not to the Mrs."

"I know you will, Mr. Ryker," Clancy affirmed.

Ryker himself wasn't nearly so sure of that. But he felt he had to get away to sort out his impressions. The dingy silvery walls were becoming oppressive.

Ryker made his walk a long one, brisk and thoughtful to begin with, dawdling and mind-wandering to finish, so that it was almost sunset by the time he reentered the apartment tree (and our story), but he had his impressions sorted. Clancy had—possibly—given the Vanishing Lady a history, funny to start with (that "hookers' convention"!) but then by stages silly, sad, sinister. Melancholy, moody, and still mysterious.

The chief retroactive effect of Clancy's story on his memories of his own encounters with the Vanishing Lady had been to intensify their sexual color, give them a sharper, coarser erotic note—an Ultrabooth note, you could say. In particular Ryker was troubled that ever since hearing Clancy narrate the loutish youth's steamy adolescent imagining that his "little hooker" had worn nothing but black stockings and a garter belt under her black fur coat, he was unable to be sure whether he himself had had similar simmering fantasy flashes during his encounters with her.

Could he be guilty, at his age, he asked himself, of such callow and lurid fantasies? The answer to that was, of course, "Of course." And then wasn't the whole romantic business of the Vanishing Lady just a retailoring of Ultrabooth to his own taste, something that made an Ultrabooth girl his alone? Somehow, he hoped not. But had he any real plan for making contact with her if she ever did stop vanishing? His unenterprising behavior when he'd had the chance to get into the elevator with her alone, and later the chance to get off the elevator at the same floor as she, and today the opportunity to meet her face to face on the third floor, indicated clearly that the answer to that question was "No." Which depressed him.

To what extent did Clancy believe in his story and in the reality of the girl who'd reportedly lingered on? He obviously had enjoyed telling it, and likely (from his glibness) had done so more than once, to suitable appreciative listeners. But did he believe she was one continuing real entity, or just a mixture of suggestion, chance, and mistaken resemblances, gossip, and outright lies? He'd never seen her himself—had this made Clancy doubt her reality, or contrariwise given him a stubborn hankering to catch sight of her himself for once at least? On the whole, Ryker thought Clancy was a believer—if only judging by his haste to search for her.

And as for the ghost idea, which you couldn't get around because it fitted her appearing and disappearing behavior so well, no matter how silly and unfashionable such a suggestion might be—Clancy's reaction to that had seemed uneasy skepticism rather than outright "Nonsense!" rejection.

Which was very much like Ryker's own reaction to it, he realized. He knew there'd been some feelings of fear mixed in with the excitement during all his later encounters with her, before he'd heard Clancy's story. How would he feel now, after hearing it, if he should see her again, he wondered uncomfortably. More fear? Or would he now spot clues to her unreality? Would she begin to melt into mist? Would she look different simply because of what he'd heard about her?

Most likely, reality being the frustrating thing it was, he thought with an unamused inward guffaw, he'd simply never glimpse her again and never know. The stage having been set, all manifestations would cease.

But then, as he let the front door slip from his hand and swing toward its click-solemnized self-locking, he saw the Vanishing Lady forty feet away exactly as he had the first two times, real, no ghostliness anywhere (the name for the material of her coat came to his mind—velour), her shadowed face swung his way, or almost so, and modestly reaverted itself, and she moved out of sight on her black oxfords.

He reached the foyer fast as he could manage, its emptiness neither startling nor relieving him, nor the emptiness of the long back hall. He looked at the Clancys' door and the shuttered office window and shook his head and smiled. (Report this adventure? Whyever?) He started toward the stairs, but shook his head again and smiled more ruefully—he was already breathing very hard. He entered the elevator, and as he firmly pressed the 14 button with his thumb and heard the cage respond, he saw the dark gleaming eyes of the Vanishing Lady looking in at him anxiously, imploringly—they were open very wide—through the narrowing small window in the doors.

The next thing he was aware of, the cage was passing Three and he had just croaked out a harsh "Good evening"—the chalky aftertaste of these words was in his throat. The rest of the trip seemed interminable.

When the cage reached Fourteen, his thumb was already pressing the One button—and that trip seemed interminable too.

No sign of anyone anywhere, on One. He looked up the stairs, but he was breathing harder than even before. Finally he got back into the elevator and hovered his thumb over the 14 button. He could touch but not press it down. He brought his face close to the empty little window and waited and waited—and waited.

His thumb did not press down then, but the cage responded. The little window slipped shut. "It's out of my hands," he told himself fatalistically; "I'm being pulled somewhere." And from somewhere the thought came to him: What if a person were confined to this apartment tree forever, never leaving it, just going up and down and back and forth, and down and up and forth and back?

The cage didn't stop until Twelve, where the door was opened by a white-haired couple. Responding to their apologies with a reassuring head-shake and a signed "It's all right," Ryker pressed past them and, gasping gently and rapidly, mounted the last flight of stairs very slowly, very slowly. The two extra steps brought on a fit of swirling dizziness, but it passed and he slowly continued on toward his room. He felt frustrated, confused and very tired. He clung to the thoughts that he had reversed the elevator's course as soon as he could, despite his fright, and returned downstairs to hunt for her, and that in his last glimpse of them, her eyes had looked frightened too.

That night he had the muttering black nightmare again, all of it for the first time in weeks, and stronger, he judged afterward, than he'd ever before experienced it. The darkness seemed more impenetrable, solid, an ocean of black concrete congealing about him. The paralysis more complete, black canvas mummy wrappings drawn with numbing tightness, a spiral black cocoon tourniquet-tight. The dry and smoky odors more intense, as though he were baking and strangling in volcanic ash, while the sewer-stenches vied in disgustingness with fruity-flowery reeks meant to hide them. The sullen ghost-light of his imagination showed the micro-males grosser and more cockroachlike in their hordes. And when finally under the goad of intensest horror he managed to stir himself and strain upward, feeling his heart and veins tearing with the effort, he encountered within a fraction of an inch his tomb's coarsely lined ceiling, which showered gritty ash into his gasping mouth and sightless eyes.

When he finally fought his way awake it was day, but his long sleep had in no way rested him. He felt tired still and good for nothing. Yesterday's story and walk had been too long, he told himself, yesterday's elevator encounter too emotionally exhausting. "Prisoners of the apartment tree," he murmured.

The Vanishing Lady was in very truth an eternal prisoner of the apart-ment tree, knowing no other life than there and no sleep anywhere except for lapsings that were as sudden as a drunkard's blackouts into an uncon-sciousness as black as Ryker's nightmares, but of which she retained no memory whatever save for a general horror and repulsion which colored all her waking thoughts.

She'd come awake walking down a hall, or on the stairs or in the moving elevator, or merely waiting somewhere in the tall and extensive apartment tree, but mostly near its roots and generally alone. Then she'd simply con-tinue whatever she was doing for a while, sensing around her (if the episode lasted long enough, she might begin to wander independently), thinking and feeling and imagining and wondering as she moved or stood, always feeling a horror, until something would happen to swoop her back into black unconsciousness again. The something might be a sudden sound or thought, a fire siren, say, sight of a mirror or another person, encounter with a doorknob, or with the impulse to take off her gloves, the chilling sense that someone had noticed her or was about to notice her, the fear that she might inadvertently walk through a silver-gray, faintly grimy wall, or slowly be absorbed into the carpet, sink through the floor. She couldn't recall those last things ever happening, and yet she dreaded them. Surely she went *somewhere*, she told herself, when she blacked out. She couldn't just collapse down on the floor, else there'd be some clue to that next time she came awake—and she was always on her feet when that happened. Besides, not often, but from time to time, she noticed she was wearing different clothes—*similar* clothes, in fact always black or some very dark shade close to it, but of a definitely different cut or material (leather, for instance, instead of cloth). And she couldn't possibly change her clothes or, worse, have them changed for her, in a semi-public place like the apartment tree—it would be unthinkable, too horribly embarrassing. Or rather—since we all know that the unthinkable and the horribly embarrassing (and the plain horrible too, for that matter) *can* happen—it would be too *grotesque.*

That was her chief trouble about everything, of course, she knew so little about her situation—in fact, knew so little about herself and the general scheme of things that held sway in this area, period. That she suffered from almost total amnesia, that much was clear to her. Usually she assumed that she lived (alone?) in one of the apartments hanging on the tree, or else was forever visiting someone who did, but then why couldn't she remember the number or somehow get inside that apartment, or come awake inside, or else get out the door into the street if she were headed that way? Why, oh why, couldn't she once ever wake in a hospital bed?—that would be pure heaven! except for the thought of what *kind* of a hospital and what things they had passing as doctors and nurses.

But just as she realized her amnesia, she knew she must have some way of taking care of herself during her unconscious times, or be the beneficiary of another's or others' system of taking care of her, for she somehow got her rest and other necessary physical reliefs, she must somehow get enough food and drink to keep her functioning, for she never felt terribly tired or seriously sick or weak and dizzy—except just before her topplings into unconsciousness, though sometimes those came without any warning at all, as sudden as the strike of pentothal.

She remembered knowing drunks (but not their names—her memory was utterly worthless on names) who lived hours and days of their lives in states of total blackout, safely crossing busy streets, eating meals, even driving cars, without a single blink of remembered awareness, as if they had a guardian angel guiding them, to the point of coming awake in distant cities, not having the ghost of an idea as to how they'd got there. (Well, she could hardly be a drunk; she didn't stagger and there was never a bottle in her purse, the times she came awake clutching a purse.)

But those were all deductions and surmises, unanchored and unlabeled memories that bobbed up in her mind and floated there awhile. What did she really know about herself?

Pitifully little. She didn't know her name or that of any friend or relative. Address and occupation, too, were blanks. Ditto education, race, religion, and marital status. Oh Christ! she didn't even know what city she was in or how *old* she was! and whether she was good-looking, ugly, or merely nondescript. Sometimes one of those last questions would hit her so hard that she would forget and start to look into one of the many mirrors in the apartment tree, or else begin to take off her gloves, so she could check it that way—hey! maybe find a tag with her name on it sewed inside her coat!

But any of these actions would, of course, plunge her back into the black unconsciousness from which *this time* there might be no awakening.

And what about the general scheme of things that held sway in this area? What did she know about that? Precious little, too. There was this world of the apartment tree which she knew very well although she didn't permit herself to look at every part of it equally. Mirrors were taboo, unless you were so placed you couldn't see your own reflection in them; so mostly were people's faces. People meant danger. Don't look at them, they might look at you.

Then there was the outside world, a mysterious and wonderful place, a heaven of delights where there was everything desirable you could think or imagine, where there was freedom and repose. She took this on faith and on the evidence of most of her memories. (Though, sad to say, those memories' bright colors seemed to fade with time. Having lost names, they tended to lose other details, she suspected. Besides, it was hard to keep them vivid and bright when your only conscious life was a series of same-seeming, frantic, frightened little rushes and hidings and waits in the apartment tree, glued together at the ends like stretches of film—and the glue was black.)

But between those two worlds, the outside and the inside, separating them, there was a black layer (who knows how thick?) of unspeakable horrors and infinite terrors. What its outer surface was, facing the outside world, she could only guess, but its inside surface was clearly the walls, ceilings, and floors of the apartment tree. That was why she worried so much that she might become forgetful and step through them without intending to—she didn't know if she were insubstantial enough to do that (though she sometimes felt so), but she might be, or become so, and in any case she didn't intend to try! And why she had a dread of cracks and crevices and small holes anywhere and *things which could go through such cracks and holes,* leading logically enough to a fear of rats and mice and cockroaches and water bugs and similar vermin.

Deep down inside herself she felt quite sure, most of the time, that she spent all her unconscious life in the black layer, and that it was her experiences there, or her dreams there, that infected all her times awake with fear. But it didn't do to think of that, it was too terrible, and so she tried to occupy her mind fully with her normal worries and dreads, and with observing permitted things in the apartment tree, and with all sorts of little notions and fantasies.

One of her favorite fantasies, conceived and enjoyed in patches of clear thinking and feeling in the mostly on-guard, frantic stretches of her ragtag waking life, was that she really lived in a lovely modern hospital, occupied a whole wing of it, in fact, the favorite daughter of a billionaire no doubt, where she was cared for by stunningly handsome, sympathetic doctors and bevies of warm-hearted merry nurses who simply cosseted her to swooning with tender loving care, fed her the most delicious foods and drinks, massaged her endlessly, stole kisses sometimes (it was a rather naughty place), and the only drawback was that she was asleep throughout all these delightful operations.

Ah, but (she fantasized) you could tell just by looking at the girl—her eyes closed, to be sure, but her lips smiling—that somewhere deep within she knew all that was happening, *somewhere she enjoyed.* She was a sly one!

And then, when all the hospital was asleep, she would rise silently from her bed, put on her clothes, and still in a profound sleep sneak out of the hospital without waking a soul, hurry to this place, dive in an instant through the horror layer, and come awake!

But then, unfortunately, because of her amnesia, she would forget the snow-white hospital and all her specific night-to-night memories of its delights and her wonderfully clever escapes from it.

But she could daydream of the hospital to her heart's content, almost! That alone was a matchless reward, worth everything, if only you looked at it the right way.

And then after a while, of course, she'd realize it was time to hurry back to the hospital before anyone there woke up and discovered she was gone. So she would, generally without letting on to herself what she was doing, seek or provoke an incident which would hurtle her back into unconsciousness again, transform her into her incredibly clever blacked-out other self who could travel anywhere in the universe unerringly, do almost anything—and with her eyes closed! (It wouldn't do to let the doctors and nurses ever suspect she'd been out of bed. Despite their inexhaustible loving-kindness they'd be sure to do something about it, maybe even come here and get her, and bar her from the apartment tree forever.)

So even the nicest daydreams had their dark sides.

As for the worst of her daydreams, the nastiest of her imaginings, it didn't do to think of them at all—they were pure black-layer, through and through. There was the fantasy of the eraser-worms for instance—squirmy, crawling, sleek, horny-armored things about an inch long and of the thickness and semi-rigidity of a pencil eraser or a black telephone cord; once they were loose they could go anywhere, and there were hordes of them.

She would imagine them… Well, wasn't it better to imagine them outright than to pretend she'd had a dream about them? for that would be admitting that she might have dreamed about them in the black layer, which would mean she might actually have *experienced* them in the black layer, wasn't that so? Well, anyway, she would start by imagining herself in utter darkness.

It was strange, wasn't it, how, not often, but sometimes, you couldn't keep yourself from imagining the worst things? For a moment they became irresistible, a sort of nasty reverse delight.

Anyhow, she would imagine she was lying in utter darkness—sometimes she'd close her eyes and cup her hands over them to increase the illusion, and once, alone in the elevator, greatly daring, she had switched off the light—and then she'd feel the first worm touch her toe, then crawl inquisitively, peremptorily between her big toe and the next, as if it owned her. Soon they'd be swarming all over her, investigating every crevice and orifice they reached, finally assaulting her head and face. She'd press her lips tightly together, but then they'd block her nostrils (it took about two of them, thrusting together, to do each of those) and she'd be forced to part her lips to gasp and then they'd writhe inside. She'd squeeze her eyes tight shut, but nevertheless... and she had no way to guard her ears and other entries.

It was only bearable because you knew you were doing it to yourself and could stop any time you wanted. And maybe it was a sort of test to prove that, in a pinch, you *could* stand it—she wasn't sure. And although you told yourself it was nothing but imagination, it did give you ideas about the black layer.

She'd rouse from such a session shaking her head and with a little indrawn shudder, as if to say, "Who would believe the things she's capable of?" and "You're brooding, you're getting into yourself too much, child. Talk to others. Get out of yourself!" (And perhaps it was just as well there was seldom opportunity—long enough lulls—to indulge in such experimenting in the nervous, unpredictable, and sometimes breathless-paced existence of the apartment tree.)

There were any number of reasons why she couldn't follow her own advice and speak to others in the apartment tree, strike up conversations, even look at them much, do more than steal infrequent glances at their faces, but the overriding one was the deep conviction that *she had no right to be in the apartment tree* and that she'd get into serious trouble if she drew attention to herself. She might even be barred from the tree forever, sentenced to the black layer. (And if that was the ridiculous nonsense idea it sounded like—where was the court and who would pronounce sentence?—why did it give her the cold shivers and a sick depression just to mention it to herself?)

No, she *didn't* have an apartment here, she'd tell herself, or any friend in the building. That was why she never had any keys or any money either, or any little notebooks in which she could find out things about herself, or letters from others or even bills! No, she was a homeless waif and she had nothing. (The only thing she always or almost always carried was a complete riddle to her: a brass tube slim as a soda straw about four inches long which at one end went through a smooth cork not much bigger around than an eraser-worm—don't think of those!)

At other times she'd tell herself she needn't have any fear of being spotted, caught, unmasked, shown to be an illegal intruder by the other passers-through of the apartment tree, because she was *invisible* to them, or almost all of them. The proof of this (which was so obvious, right before your eyes, that you missed it) was simply that none of them noticed her, or spoke to her, or did her the little courtesies which they did each other, such as holding the elevator door for her. She had to move aside for them, not they for her!

This speculation about being invisible led to another special horror for her. Suppose, in her efforts to discover how old she was, she ever did manage to take off her gloves and found, not the moist hands of a young woman, nor yet the dry vein-crawling ones of a skinny old hag, but simply emptiness? What if she managed to open her coat and found herself, chin tucked in, staring down at lining? What if she looked into a mirror and saw nothing, except the wall behind her, or else only another mirror with reflections of reflections going back to infinity?

What if she were a ghost? Although it was long ago, or seemed long ago, she could recall, she thought, the dizzying chill that thought had given her the first time she'd had it. It fitted. Ghosts were supposed to haunt one place and to appear and disappear by fits and starts, and even then to be visible only to the sensitive few. None of the ghost stories she knew told it from the ghosts' side—what they thought and felt, how much they understood, and whether they ever knew what they were (ghosts) and what they were doing (haunting).

(And there even had been the "sensitive few" who had seemed to see her—and she looked back at them flirtatiously—though she didn't like to remember those episodes because they frightened her and made her feel foolish—whyever had she flirted? taken that risk?—and in the end made her mind go blurry. There'd been that big fat boy—whatever had she seen in him?—and before him a gentle old man, and before *him*—no, she certainly didn't have to push her memory back that far, no one could make her!)

But now that thought—that she might be a ghost—had become only one more of her familiar fancies, coming back into her mind every once in a while as regular as clockwork and with a little but not much of the original shock the idea had once given her. "Part of my repertoire," she told herself drolly. (God knows how she'd manage to stand her existence if things didn't seem funny to her once in a while.)

But most times weren't so funny. She kept coming back and coming back to what seemed after all the chief question: How *long* had her conscious life, *this* conscious life, lasted? And the only final answer she could get to this, in moments of unpanic, was that she couldn't tell.

It might be months or years. Long enough so that although not looking at their faces, she'd gotten to know the tenants of the apartment tree by their clothes and movements, the little things they said to each other, their gaits and favorite expressions. Gotten to know them well enough so that she could recognize them when they'd changed their clothes, put on new shoes, slowed down their gait, begun to use a cane. Sometimes completely new ones would appear and then slowly become old familiars—new tenants moving in. And then these old familiars might in their turn disappear—moved away, or died. My God, had she been here for decades? She remembered a horror story in which a beautiful young woman woke from a coma to find herself dying of old age. Would it be like that for her when she at last faced the mirror?

And if she *were* a ghost, would not the greatest horror for such a being be to die as a ghost?—to feel you had one tiny corner of existence securely yours, from which you could from time to time glimpse the passing show, and then be mercilessly swept out of that?

Or it might, on the other hand, be only minutes, hours, days at most—of strangely clear-headed fever dreaming, or of eternity-seeming withdrawal from a drug. Memory's fallible. Mind's capable of endless tricks. How could you be sure?

Well, whatever the truth was about the "How long?" business, she needn't worry about it for a while. The last few days (and weeks, or hours and minutes, who cared?) she'd been having a brand-new adventure. Yes, you could call it a flirtation if you wanted, but whatever you called it and in spite of the fact that it had its bad and scary parts, it had made her feel happier, gayer, braver, even more devil-may-care than she had in ages. Why, already it had revealed to her what she'd seen in the big fat boy and in the old man before him. My goodness, she'd simply *seen* them, felt interest in them, felt concern for them, yes, loved them. For that was the way it was now.

But that was then and this was now.

From the first time she'd happened to see Ryker (she didn't know his name then, of course) gazing so admiringly and wonderstruck at her from the front door, she'd known he couldn't possibly mean her harm, be one of the dangerous ones who'd send her back to the hospital or the black layer, or whatever. What had surprised her was the extent of her own inward reaction. She had a friend!—someone who thought she amounted to something, who *cared*. It made her dizzy, delirious. She managed to walk only a few steps, breasting the emotional tide, before she collapsed happily into the arms of darkness.

The second time it happened almost exactly the same way, only this time she was anticipating and needed only the barest glimpse—a flicker of her eyes his way—to assure herself that there hadn't been any mistake the first time, that he did feel that way about her, that he loved her.

By the time of their third meeting, she'd worked herself up into a really daring mood—she'd prepared a surprise for him and was waiting for him in the elevator. She'd even mischievously switched off the light (when she had the strength to do things like that, she knew she was in fine fettle), and was managing somehow to hold the door open (that surprised even her) so that she'd gradually be revealed to him as he came down the hall—a sort of hide-and-seek game. As to what happened after that, she'd take her chances!

Then when he'd walked past her, making a feeble excuse about his mailbox—that was one of the bad parts. What was the matter with him? Was he, a tenant, actually scared of her, a trespasser, a waif? And if so, how was he scared of her?—as a woman or as a possible criminal who'd try to rob or rape him, or maybe as a ghost? Was he shy, or had his smiles and admiration meant nothing, been just politeness? She almost lost her hold on the door then, but she managed not to. "Hurry up, hurry up, you old scaredy-cat!" she muttered perkily under her breath. "I can't hold this door forever!"

And then someone on an upper floor buzzed the elevator, startling her, and she did lose her hold on the doors and they closed and the cage moved upward. She felt a sudden surge of hopelessness at being thwarted by mere chance, and she blacked out.

But next time she came awake her spirits were soon soaring again. In fact, that was the time when on sheerest impulse, she'd darted into a crowded elevator after him, which was something she never did—too much chance of being forced against someone and revealing your presence that way even if invisible.

Well, *that* didn't happen, but only because she kept herself pressed as flat against the door as possible and had some luck. At the first stop she hopped out thankfully, and changing her plans simply flew up the stairs, outdistancing the creaking cage, and when he didn't get out at Twelve, went on to Fourteen, and changing her plans again (she had the feeling it was almost time to black out), she simply followed him as he plodded to his room and noted its number before she lost consciousness. That was how she learned his name—by going to the mailboxes next time and checking his number, which said: R. RYKER. Oh, she might be a stupid little orphan of the apartment tree, but she had her tricks!

resonant than he'd intended, so that it had a rather sepulchral sound. And his third movement was not completed, for just as he entered, she raised her head and simultaneously reached her black-gloved right hand and that arm across her body and the lower half of her face, apparently anticipating his intention to switch on the light, so that his own hand drew back.

He turned facing her as he stepped past her and settled his back against that of the elevator. Her outstretched arm concealed her lips, so he couldn't tell if she smiled or not, but her gleaming eyes followed him as he moved across the cage, and at least they didn't frown. The effect was provocative, alluring.

But her outreached hand did not turn on the light. Instead its black forefinger seemed to lay itself against the flat brass between the 12 and 14 buttons. But she must have pressed one or the other of those in so doing, for the doors growled shut and the cage moved upward.

That plunged the cage in gloom, but not quite as deeply as he would have expected, for the strange pale glimmering around her neck and her black coat's closure seemed to strengthen a little, almost sparkle (real or imagined? her body's aura, could it be? or only his old eyes dazzling?) and a twinkle of other light came in by the little window as they passed the second floor. In his state of heightened awareness he dimly yet distinctly saw her right hand drop away from the button panel and her other hand join it, creep a little way into its sleeve and then in one swift backward motion strip the glove from her right hand, which then uncurled gracefully toward him palm upward through the dark between them like a slender white sash ending in five slim white ribbons of unequal length. Advancing a step and bowing his head toward it, he gently received its cool weightless length upon his own fingers, touched his lips to the smooth slim palm, and withdrawing laid across it the white orchid he'd been carrying. Another little window winked by.

She pressed the slender spray against her throat and with her yet-gloved hand touched his as if in thanks. *She* wondered why she had pressed *between* the buttons and why the cage had responded, why she had not blacked out while drawing off her glove. Dark memories threatened opening, not without fear. She tugged a little at Ryker's hand in drawing her own away.

Emboldened, he advanced another step, bringing him almost against her. Her cat-triangular small face tilted up toward his, half of it pale, the other half dark mouth, gray gleaming eyes, their shadowed orbits under slim black brows. His left hand brushed her side and slid behind her, pressed her slim back. His right sought out the fingers at her throat holding his orchid and caressed them, playing with them gently. He felt her suede-soft gloved fingers creeping at the back of his neck.

She slid the orchid with its insubstantial spray inside her coat and her ungloved moist hand stroked his dry cheek. His hand felt out two large round buttons at her neck, tilted them through their thread-bordered slits, and the collar of her coat fell open. The diamond sparkling that had long puzzled him intensified, gushed up and poured out fountainlike, as if he had uncovered her aura's nest—or was his old heart blowing up a diamond hurricane? or his old eyes jaggedly spinning out a diamond migraine pattern? He gazed down through this ghostly scintillation, these microscopic stars, at a landscape pearly gray and cool as the moon's, the smooth valley where the orchid lodged between her small jutting breasts with their dark silver nipples, a scene that was not lost, though it swung and narrowed a little, when her small hands drew his head down to hers and their lips met in a leisurely kiss that dizzied him unalarmingly.

It occurred to him whimsically that although the pearly landscape he continued to admire might seem to stretch on and on, it had an exceedingly low black sky, an extremely low ceiling, air people would say. Now why should that fantasy carry overtones which were more sinister than amusing? he wondered idly.

It was at that moment that he became aware that he was smelling cigar smoke. The discovery did not particularly startle or alarm him, but it did awaken his other senses a little from their present great dreamy preoccupation, though not entirely. Indeed, in one sense that preoccupation deepened, for at that moment the tip of her tongue drew a very narrow line into their kiss. But at the same time, as he noted that the elevator had come to rest, that its creaking groan had been replaced by a growling mutter which he liked still less, while a wavering ruddy glow, a shadowed reddish flickering, was mounting the walls of the cage from some unknown source below, and that the thin reek of cigar smoke was becoming more acrid.

Unwillingly, wearily (he was anything but tired, yet this cost an effort), he lifted his gaze without breaking their kiss, without thinking of breaking it, and continuing to fondle her back and neck, until he was looking across her shoulder.

He saw, by the red glow, that the door of the cage had opened without his having noticed it and that the elevator was at the fourteenth floor.

But not *quite* at the fourteenth floor, for the outer door was closed tight and the little window in it that had the numeral 14 painted under it stood about eighteen inches higher than it should.

So the floor of the cage must be the same distance below the floor of Fourteen.

Still unalarmed, grudging each effort, he advanced his head across her shoulder until he could look down over it. As he did so, she leaned her head back and turned it a little sideways, accommodating, so that their kiss was still unbroken, meanwhile hugging him more tightly and making muffled and inarticulate crooning sounds as if to say "It is all right."

The space between the two floors (which was also the space between the ceiling of Twelve and the floor of Fourteen) was wide open, a doorway five feet wide and scarcely one foot high in the raw wall of the shaft, and through that doorway there was pouring into the bottom of the cage from the very low-ceilinged thirteenth floor a pulsing crimson glow which nevertheless seemed more steady in hue, more regular in its variations of intensity than that of any fire.

This furnace-light revealed, clustered around their ankles but spreading out more scatteredly to fill the elevator's carpeted floor, a horde of dark squat forms, a milling host of what appeared to be (allowing for the extreme foreshortening) stocky Lilliputian human beings, some lifting their white faces to peer up, others bent entirely to the business at hand. For instance, two pairs of them struggled with dull metal hooks almost as large as they were and to which stout cords were attached, others carried long prybars, one jauntily balanced on his shoulder what looked like a white paper packet about as big (relative to him) as an unfolded Sunday newspaper, while more than half of them held between two fingers tiny black cylinders from one end of which interweaving tiny tendrils of smoke arose, forming a thin cloud, and which when they applied the other ends to their tiny mugs, glowed winkingly red in the red light, as if they were a swarm of hellish lightless fireflies.

It may seem most implausible to assert that Ramsey Ryker did not feel terror and panic at this extremely grotesque sight (for he realized also that he had somehow penetrated the realm of his nightmares) and highly un-likely to record that his kiss and the Vanishing Lady's continued unbroken (save for the hurried puffings and inhalations normal in such a contact), yet both were so. True, as he wormed his head back across her shoulder to its first vantage point, his heart pounded alarmingly, there was a roaring in his ears, and waves of blackness threatened to overwhelm his vision and forced their way up into his skull, while the simple shifting movement he intended proved unexpectedly difficult to execute (his head felt heavy, not so much looking over her shoulder as slumped on it)—but these were physical reactions with many causes. His chief mental reactions to the beings he'd seen clustered around their feet were that they would have been interesting at another time and that they presumably had their own place, business, and concerns in the great scheme of things, and that just now he had his own great business and concerns he must return to, as hopefully they to theirs. Also, the Vanishing Lady's caresses and murmurings of reassurance and encouragement had their helpful and soothing effects.

But when he was once more gazing down into what we may call without any sarcasm his steep and narrow valley of delights, he could no longer tell whether the ghostly silver sparks that fountained from it were inside or outside his eyes and skull, the exquisite outlines wavered and were lost in mists, his fingers fondling her neck and her low back grew numb and powerless, all power save that of vision drained from his every part, he grew lax, and with her hands solicitously supporting and guiding him, he sank by degrees, his heavy head brushing her black coat entirely open and resting successively against her naked breasts, belly, and thighs, until he was laid out upon his back corner-to-corner in the small cage, head to the front of it, feet to the back, level with the hitherto unsuspected thirteenth floor, while the Vanishing Lady in assisting him had stooped until she now sat upon her heels, her upper body erect, her chin high, having never once looked down.

With a slow effortless movement she regained her full stature, her hands trailing limply down, one of them still gripping the brass tube. The jaunty homunculus lifted his white paper packet to the other, and she clipped it securely between thumb and forefinger, still without the slightest down-ward glance, raised it until it was before her eyes, and eagerly but carefully unfolded it.

Ryker watched her attentively from the floor. His entire consciousness, almost, had focused in on her until he saw only her face and shoulders, her busy hands and matchless breasts. They looked very clear but very far away, like something seen through the wrong end of a telescope. He was only most dimly aware of the movements closer to him, of the way the two large dull hooks were being effortfully fitted under his shoulders and beneath his armpits. He watched with great interest but no comprehension, aware only of the beauty of the sight, as she fitted the cork-protected end of the brass tube into one nostril, delicately applied the other end to the flat unfolded square of white paper, and slowly but deeply inhaled. He did not hear the distant windlass creaking nor feel the hooks tighten against his armpits as he was dragged out of the elevator into the thirteenth floor and his consciousness irised in toward nothingness.

Nor did the Vanishing Lady honor either his disappearance or his captors' with even one last glance as she impatiently shifted the brass tube to her other nostril and applied it to an edge of the diminished pile of crystals outspread on the white packet paper, the sight of which had instantly re-called to her mind the use of that tube and much more besides, not all of which she was tickled to relearn: the sullen waitings for Artie Stensor, her own entrapment by the thirteenth floor, the finding of Artie there in his new and degenerate imprisoned form, the sessions that reduced her also to such a form, her deal with the reigning homunculi, the three services (or was it four?) she'd promised them, the luring and entrapment of the other two tenants. She put all that out of her mind as she inhaled slowly, very evenly, and deeply, the mouth of the brass tube like that of some tiny reaping machine eating its way up and down the edge of the coke or "snow" or whatever else you might call the sovereign diamond sparkling dream drug, until the paper was empty.

She felt the atoms of her body loosening their hold on each other and those of her awareness and memory tightening theirs as with a fantastic feeling of liberation she slowly floated up through the ceiling of the cage into the stale air of the dark and cavernous shaft and then rose more and more swiftly along the black central cables until she shot through the shaft's ceiling, winked through the small lightless room in which were the elevator's black motor and relays, and burnt out of the apartment tree into the huge dizzying night.

South shone the green coronet of the Hilton, west the winking red light that outlined the tripod TV tower atop Sum Crest, northeast the topaz-sparkling upward-pointing arrow of the Transamerica Pyramid. Farther east, north, and west, all lapped in low fog, were the two great bridges, Bay and Golden Gate, and the unlimited Pacific Ocean. She felt she could see, go anywhere.

She spared one last look and sorrow pang for the souls entombed—or, more precisely, *immured*—in San Francisco and then, awareness sharpening and consciousness expanding, sped on up and out, straight toward that misty, nebula-swathed multiple star in Orion called the Trapezium.

THE CURSE OF THE SMALLS AND THE STARS

L ATE ONE NIPPY AFTERNOON OF EARLY RIME ISLE SPRING, Fafhrd and the Gray Mouser slumped pleasantly in a small booth in Salthaven's Sea Wrack Tavern. Although they'd been on the Isle for only a year, and patronizing this tavern for an eight-month, the booth was recognized as *theirs* when either was in the place. Both men had been mildly fatigued, the former from supervising bottom-repairs to *Seahawk* at the new moon's low tide—and then squeezing in a late round of archery practice, the latter from bossing the carpentering of their new warehouse-and-barracks—and doing some inventorying besides. But their second tankards of bitter ale had about taken care of that and their thoughts were beginning to float free.

Around them the livening talk of other recuperating laborers. At the bar they could see three of their lieutenants grousing together—Fafhrd-tall Skor, and the somewhat reformed small thieves Pshawri and Mikkidu. Behind it the keeper lit two thick wicks as the light dimmed as the sun set outside.

Frowning, as he pared a thumbnail with razor-keen Cat's Claw, the Mouser said, "I am minded of how scarce seventeen moons gone we sat just so in Silver Eel Tavern in Lankhmar, deeming Rime Isle a legend. Yet here we are."

"Lankhmar," Fafhrd mused, drawing a wet circle with the firmly socketed iron hook that had become his left hand after the day's bow bending, "I've heard somewhere of such a city, I do believe. 'Tis strange how oftentimes our thoughts do chime together, as if we were sundered halves of some past being, but whether hero or demon, wastrel or philosopher, harder to say."

"Demon, I'd say," the Mouser answered instantly, "a demon warrior. We've guessed at him before. Remember? We decided he always growled in battle. Perhaps a were-bear."

After a small chuckle at that, Fafhrd went on, "But then (that night twelve moons gone and five in Lankhmar) we'd had twelve tankards each of bitter instead of two, I ween, yes, and lacing them too with brandy, you can bet—hardly to be accounted best judges twixt phantasm and the veritable. Yes, and didn't two heroines from this fabled isle next moment stride into the Eel, as real as boots?"

Almost as if the Northerner hadn't answered, the small gray-smocked, gray-stockinged man continued in the same thoughtful reminiscent tones as he'd first used, "And you, liquored to the gills—agreed on that!—were ranting dolefully about how you dearly wanted work, land, office, sons, other responsibilities, and e'en a wife!"

"Yes, and didn't I get one?" Fafhrd demanded. "You too, you equally then-drunken destiny-ungrateful lout!" His eyes grew thoughtful also. He added, "Though perhaps comrade or co-mate were the better word—or even those plus partner."

"Much better all three," the Mouser agreed shortly. "As for those other goods your drunken heart was set upon—no disagreement there!—we've got enough of those to stuff a hog!—except, of course, far as I know, for sons. Unless, that is, you count our men as our grown-up unweaned babes, which sometimes I'm inclined to."

Fafhrd, who'd been leaning his head out of the booth to look toward the darkening doorway during the latter part of the Mouser's plaints, now stood up, saying, "Speaking of them, shall we join the ladies? Cif and Afreyt's booth 'pears to be larger than ours."

"To be sure. What else?" the Mouser replied, rising springily. Then, in a lower voice, "Tell me, did the two of them just now come in? Or did we blunder blindly by them when we entered, sightless of all save thirst-quench?"

Fafhrd shrugged, displaying his palm. "Who knows? Who cares?"

"*They* might," the other answered.

Many Lankhmar leagues east and south, and so in darkest moonless night, the archmagus Ningauble conferred with the sorceress Sheelba at the edge of the Great Salt Marsh. The seven luminous eyes of the former wove many greenish patterns within his gaping hood as he leaned his quaking bulk perilously downward from the howdah on the broad back of the forward-kneeling elephant which had borne him from his desert cave across the Sinking Land through all adverse influences to this appointed spot. While the latter's eyeless face strained upwards likewise as she stood tall in the doorway of her small hut, which had traveled from the Marsh's noxious center to the same dismal verge on its three long rickety (but now rigid) chicken-legs. The two wizards strove mightily to outshout (outbellow or outscreech) the nameless cosmic din (inaudible to human ears) which had hitherto hindered and foiled all their earlier efforts to communicate over greater distances. And now, at last, they strove successfully!

Ningauble wheezed, "I have discovered by certain infallible signs that the present tumult in realms magical, botching my spells, is due to the vanishment from Lankhmar of my servitor and sometimes student, Fafhrd the barbarian. All magics dim without his credulous and kindly audience, while high quests fail lacking his romantical and custard-headed idealisms."

Sheelba shot back through the murk, "While I have ascertained that my illspells suffer equally because the Mouser's gone with him, my protégé and surly errand boy. They will not work without the juice of his brooding and overbearing malignity. He must be summoned from that ridiculous rim-place of Rime Isle, and Fafhrd with him!"

"But how to do that when our spells won't carry? What servitor to trust with such a mission to go and fetch 'em? I know of a young demoness might undertake it, but she's in thrall to Khahkht, wizard of power in that frosty area—and he's inimical to both of us. Or should the two of us search out in noisy spirit realm to be our messenger that putative warlike ascendant of theirs and whilom forebear known as the Growler? A dismal task! Where'er I look I see naught but uncertainties and obstacles—"

"I shall send word of their whereabouts to Mog the spider god, the Gray One's tutelary deity!—this din won't hinder prayers," Sheelba interrupted in a harsh, clipped voice. The presence of the vacillating and loquacious over-sighted wizard, who saw seven sides to every question, always roused her to her best efforts. "Send you like advisos to Fafhrd's gods, stone-age brute Kos and the fastidious cripple Issek. Soon as they know where their lapsed worshippers are, they'll put such curses and damnations on them as shall bring them back squealing to us to have those taken off."

"Now why didn't I think of that?" Ningauble protested, who was indeed sometimes called the Gossiper of the Gods. "To work! To work!"

In paradisiacal Godsland, which lies at the antipodes of Nehwon's death pole and Shadowland, in the southernmost reach of that world's southernmost continent, distanced and guarded from the tumultuous northern lands by the Great eastward-rushing Equatorial Current (where some say swim the stars), sub-equatorial deserts, and the Rampart Mountains, the gods Kos, Issek, and Mog sat somewhat apart from the mass of more couth and civilized Nehwonian deities, who objected to Kos' lice, fleas, and crabs, and a little to Issek's effeminacy—though Mog had contacts among these, as he sarcastically called 'em, "higher beings."

Sunk in divine somnolent broodings, not to say almost deathlike trances, for prayers, petitions, and even blasphemous name-takings had been scanty of late, the three mismatched godlings reacted at once and enthusiastically to the instantaneously transmitted wizard missives.

"Those two ungodly swording rogues!" Mog hissed softly, his long thin lips stretched slantwise in a half spider grin. "The very thing! Here's work for all of us, my heavenly peers. A chance to curse again and to bedevil."

"A glad inspiro that, indeed, indeed!" Issek chimed, waving his limp-wristed hands excitedly. "*I* should have thought of that!—our chiefest lapsed worshippers, hidden away in frosty and forgotten far Rime Isle, farther away than Shadowland itself, *almost* beyond our hearing and our might. Such infant cunning! Oh but we'll make them pay!"

"The ingrate dogs!" Kos grated through his thick and populous black beard. "Not only casting us off, their natural heavenly fathers and rightful da's, but forsaking *all* decent Nehwonian deities and running with atheist men and gone a-whoring after stranger gods beyond the pall! Yes, by my lights and spleen, we'll make 'em suffer! Where's my spiked mace?"

(On occasion Mog and Issek had been known to have to hold Kos down to keep him from rushing ill-advised out of Godsland to seek to visit personal dooms upon his more disobedient and farther strayed worshippers.)

"What say we set their women against them, as we did last time?" Issek urged twitteringly. "Women have power over men almost as great as gods do."

Mog shook his humanoid cephalothorax. "Our boys are too coarse-tasted. Did we estrange from them Afreyt and Cif, they'd doubtless fall back on amorous arrangements with the Salthaven harlots Rill and Hilsa—and so on and so on." Now that his attention had been called to Rime Isle, he had easy knowledge of all overt things there—a divine prerogative. "No, not the women this time, I ween."

"A pox on all such subtleties!" Kos roared. "I want tortures for 'em! Let's visit on 'em the strangling cough, the prick-rot, and the Bloody Melts!"

"Nor can we risk wiping them out entirely," Mog answered swiftly. "We haven't worshippers to spare for that, you fire-eater, as you well know. Thrift, thrift! Moreover, as you should also know, a threat is always more dreadful than its execution. I propose we subject them to some of the moods and preoccupations of old age and of old age's bosom comrade, inseparable though invisible-seeming—Death himself! Or is that too mild a fear and torment, thinkest thou?"

"I'll say not," Kos agreed, suddenly sober. "I know that it scares *me*. What if the gods should die? A hellish thought."

"That infant bugaboo!" Issek told him peevishly. Then turning to Mog with quickening interest, "So, if I read you right, old Arach, let's narrow your silky Mouser's interests in and in from the adventure-beckoning horizon to the things closest around him: the bed table, the dinner board, the privy, and the kitchen sink. Not the far-leaping highway, but the gutter. Not the ocean, but the puddle. Not the grand view outside, but the bleared windowpane. Not the thunder-blast, but the knuckle-crack—or ear-pop."

Mog narrowed his eight eyes happily. "And for your Fafhrd, I would suggest a different old-age curse, to drive a wedge between them, so they can't understand or help each other: that we put a geas upon him to count the stars. His interests in all else will fade and fail; he'll have mind only for those tiny lights in the sky."

"So that, with his head in the clouds," Issek pictured, catching on quick, "he'll stumble and bruise himself again and again, and miss all opportunities of earthly delights."

"Yes, and make him memorize their names and all their patterns!" Kos put in. "There's busy-work for an eternity. I never could abide the things myself. There's such a senseless mess of stars, like flies or fleas. An insult to the gods to say that we created them!"

"And then, when those two have sufficiently humbled themselves to us and done suitable penance," Issek purred, "we will consider taking off or ameliorating their curses."

"I say, leave 'em on always," Kos argued. "No leniency. Eternal damnation!—that's the stuff !"

"That question can be decided when it arises," Mog opined. "Come, gentlemen, to work! We've some damnations to devise in detail and deliver."

Back at the Sea Wrack Tavern, Fafhrd and the Gray Mouser had, despite the latter's apprehensions, been invited to join with and buy a round of bitter ale for their lady-friends Afreyt and Cif, leading and sometimes office-holding citizens of Rime Isle, spinster-matriarchs of otherwise scionless dwindling old families in that strange republic, and Fafhrd's and the Mouser's partners and co-adventurers of a good year's standing in questing, business, and (this last more recently) bed. The questing part had consisted of the almost bloodless routing from the Isle of an invading naval force of maniacal Sea-Mingols, with the help of twelve tall berserks and twelve small warrior-thieves the two heroes had brought with them, and the dubious assistance of the two universes-wandering hobo gods Odin and Loki, and (minor quest) a small expedition to recover certain civic treasures of the Isle, a set of gold artifacts called the Ikons of Reason. And they had been *hired* to do these things by Cif and Afreyt, so business had been mixed with questing in their relationship from the very start. Other business had been a merchant venture of the Mouser (Captain Mouser for this purpose) in

Fafhrd's galley *Seahawk* with a mixed crew of berserks and thieves, and goods supplied by the ladies, to the oft-frozen port of No-Ombrulsk on Nehwonmainland—that and various odd jobs done by their men and by the women and girls employed by and owing fealty to Cif and Afreyt.

As for the bed part, both couples, though not yet middle-aged, at least in looks, were veterans of amorous goings-on, wary and courteous in all such doings, entering upon any new relationships, including these, with a minimum of commitment and a maximum of reservations. Ever since the tragic deaths of their first loves, Fafhrd's and the Mouser's erotic solacing had mostly come from a very odd lot of hard-bitten if beauteous slave-girls, vagabond hoydens, and demonic princesses, folk easily come by if at all and even more easily lost, accidents rather than goals of their weird adventurings; both sensed that anything with the Rime Isle ladies would have to be a little more serious at least. While Afreyt's and Cif's love-adventures had been equally transient, either with unromantic and hardheaded Rime Islanders, who are atheistical realists even in youth, or with sea-wanderers of one sort or another, come like the rain—or thunder-squall, and as swiftly gone.

All this being considered, things did seem to be working out quite well for the two couples in the bed area.

And, truth to tell, this was a greater satisfaction and relief to the Mouser and Fafhrd than either would admit even to himself. For each was indeed beginning to find extended questing a mite tiring, especially ones like this last which, rather than being one of their usual lone-wolf forays, involved the recruitment and command of other men and the taking on of larger and divided responsibilities. It was natural for them, after such exertions, to feel that a little rest and quiet enjoyment was now owed them, a little surcease from the batterings of fate and chance and new desire. And, truth to tell, the ladies Cif and Afreyt were on the verge of admitting in their secretest hearts something of the same feelings.

So all four of them found it pleasant during this particular Rime Isle twilight to take a little bitter ale together and chat of this day's doings and tomorrow's plans and reminisce about their turning of the Mingols and ask each other gentle questions about the times before they'd all four met—and each flirt privily and cautiously with the notion that each now had two or three persons on whom they might always rely fully, rather than one like-sexed comrade only.

During the course of this gossiping Fafhrd mentioned again his and the Mouser's fantasy that they were halves—or perhaps lesser fractions, fragments only—of some noted or notorious past being, explaining why their thoughts so often chimed together.

"That's odd," Cif interjected, "for Afreyt and I have had like notion and for like reason: that she and I were spirit-halves of the great Rimish witch-queen Skeldir, who held off the Simorgyans again and again in ancient times when that island boasted an empire and was above the waves instead of under them. What was your hero's name—or mighty rogue's?—if that likes you better."

"I know not, lady, perhaps he lived in times too primitive for names, when man and beast were closer. He was identified by his battle-growling—a leonine cough deep in the throat when'er he entered an encounter."

"Another like point!" Cif noted. "Queen Skeldir announced her presence by a short dry laugh—her invariable utterance when facing dangers, especially those of a sort to astound and confound the bravest."

"Gusorio's my name for our beastish forebear," the Mouser threw in. "I know not what Fafhrd thinks. Great Gusorio. Gusorio the Growler."

"Now he begins to sound like an animal," Afreyt broke in. "Tell me, have you ever been granted vision or dream of this Gusorio, or heard perhaps in darkest night his battle growl?"

But the Mouser was studying the dinted table top. He bent his head as his gaze traveled across it.

"No, milady," Fafhrd answered for his abstracted comrade. "At least not I. It's something we heard of a witch or fortuneteller, figment, not fact. Have you ever heard Queen Skeldir's short dry laugh, or had sight of that fabled warrior sorceress?"

"Neither I nor Cif," Afreyt admitted, "though she is in the Isle's history parchments."

But even as she answered him, Fafhrd's questioning gaze strayed past her. She looked behind and saw the Sea Wrack's open doorway and the gathering night.

Cif stood up. "So it's agreed we dine at Afreyt's in a half hour's time?"

The two men nodded somewhat abstractedly. Fafhrd leaned his head to the right as he continued to stare past Afreyt, who with a smile obligingly shifted hers in the opposite direction.

The Mouser leaned back and bent his head a little more as his gaze trailed down from the table top to its leg.

Fafhrd observed, "Astarion sets soon after the sun these nights. There's little time to observe her."

"God forbid I should stand in the evening star's way," Afreyt murmured humorously as she too arose. "Come, cousin."

The Mouser left off watching the cockroach as it reached the floor. It had limped interestingly, lacking a mid leg. He and Fafhrd drank off their bitters, then slowly followed their ladies out and down the narrow street, the one's eyes thoughtfully delving in the gutter, as if there might be treasure there, the other's roving the sky as the stars winked on, naming those he knew and numbering, by altitude and direction, those he didn't.

Their work well launched, Sheelba retired to Marsh center and Ningauble toward his cavern, the understorm abating, a good omen. While the three gods smiled, invigorated by their cursing. The slum corner of Heaven they occupied now seemed less chilly to Issek and less sweatily enervating to Kos, while Mog's devious mind spider stepped down more pleasant channels.

Yes, the seed was well planted and left to germinate in silence might have developed as intended, but some gods, and some sorcerers too, cannot resist boasting and gossiping, and so by way of talkative priests and midwives and vagabonds, word of what was intended came to the ears of the mighty, including two who considered themselves well rid of Fafhrd and the Mouser and did not want them back in Lankhmar at all. And the mighty are great worriers and spend much time preventing anything that troubles their peace of mind.

And so it was that Pulgh Arthonax, penurious and perverse overlord of Lankhmar, who hated heroes of all description, but especially fair-complected big ones like Fafhrd, and Hamomel, thrifty and ruthless grand master of the Thieves' Guild there, who detested the Mouser generally as a freelance competitor and particularly as one who had lured twelve promising apprentices away from the guild to be his henchmen—these two took counsel together and commissioned the Assassins Order, an elite within the Slayers' Brotherhood, to dispatch the Twain in Rime Isle before they should point toe toward Lankhmar. And because Arth-Pulgh and Hamomel were both most miserly magnates and insatiably greedy withal, they beat down the Order's price as far as they could and made it a condition of the commission that three-fourths of any portable booty found on or near the doomed Twain be returned to them as their lawful share.

So the Order drew up death warrants, chose by lot two of its currently unoccupied fellows, and in solemn secret ceremony attended only by the Master and the Recorder divested these of their identities and rechristened them the Death of Fafhrd and the Death of the Gray Mouser, by which names only they should henceforth be known to each other and within the profession until the death warrants were served and their commissions fulfilled.

Next day repairs to *Seahawk* continued, the low tide repeating, Witches Moon being only one day old. During a late morning break Fafhrd moved apart from his men a little and scanned the high bright sky toward north and east, his gaze ranging. Skor ventured to follow him across the wet sand and copy his peerings. He saw nothing in the gray-blue heavens, but experience had taught him his captain had exceptionally keen eyesight.

"Sea eagles?" he asked softly.

Fafhrd looked at him thoughtfully, then smiled, shaking his head, and confided, "I was imagining which stars would be there, were it now night."

Skor's forehead wrinkled puzzledly. "Stars by day?"

Fafhrd nodded. "Yes. Where think you the stars are by day?"

"Gone," Skor answered, his forehead clearing. "They go away at dawn and return at evening. Their lights are extinguished—like winter campfires! for surely it must be cold where the stars are, higher than mountaintops. Until the sun comes out to warm up things, of course."

Fafhrd shook his head. "The stars march west across the sky each night in the same formations which we recognize year after year, dozen years after dozen, and I would guess gross after gross. They do not skitter for the horizon when day breaks or seek out lairs and earth holes, but go on marching with the sun's glare hiding their lights—under cover of day, one might express it."

"Stars shining by day?" Skor questioned, doing a fair job of hiding his surprise and bafflement. Then he caught Fafhrd's drift, or thought he did, and a certain wonder appeared in his eyes. He knew his captain was a good general who made a fetish of keeping track of the enemy's position especially in terrain affording concealment, as forest on land or fog at sea. So by his very nature his captain had applied the same rule to the stars and studied 'em as closely as he'd traced the movements of the Mingol scouts fleeing across Rime Isle.

Though it was strange thinking of the stars as enemies. His captain was a deep one! Perhaps he did have foes among the stars. Skor had heard rumor that he'd bedded a queen of the air.

That night as the Gray Mouser and Cif leisurely prepared for bed in her low-eaved house tinted a sooty red on the northwestern edge of Salthaven City, and whilst that lady busied herself at her mirrored dressing table, the Mouser himself sitting on bed's edge set his pouch upon a low bedside table and withdrew from it a curious lot of commonplace objects—curious in part because they were so commonplace—and arranged them in a line on the table's dark surface.

Cif, made curious by the slow regularity of his movements she saw reflected cloudily in the sheets of silver she faced, took up a small flat black box and came over and sat herself beside him.

The objects included a toothed small wooden wheel as big almost as a Sarheenmar dollar with two of the teeth missing, a finch's feather, three look-alike gray round pebbles, a scrap of blue wool cloth stiff with dirt, a bent wrought iron nail, a hazelnut, and a dinted small black round that might have been a Lankhmar *tik* or Eastern halfpenny.

Cif ran her eye along them, then looked at him questioningly.

He said, "Coming here from the barracks at first eve, a strange mood seized me. Low in the sunset glow the new moon's faintest and daintiest silver crescent had just materialized like the ghost of a young girl—and just in the direction of this house, at that, as though to signal your presence here—but somehow I had eyes only for the gutter and the pathside. Which is where I found those. And a remarkable lot they are for a small northern seaport. You'd think Ilthmar at least…." He shook his head.

"But why collect 'em?" she queried. *Like an old ragpicker,* she thought.

He shrugged. "I don't know. I think I thought I might find a use for them," he added doubtfully.

She said, "They do look like oddments that might be involved in casting a spell."

He shrugged again, but added, "They're not all what they seem. *That,* for instance—" He pointed at one of three gray spherelets, "—is not a pebble like the other two, but a lead slingshot, perhaps one of my own."

Struck by his thrusting finger, *that* rolled off the table and hit the terrazzo floor with a little dull yet dinky thud, as if to prove his observation.

As he recovered it, he paused with his eyes close to the floor to study first the crushed black marble of the terrazzo flecked with dark red and gold, and second Cif's near foot, which he then drew up onto his lap and studied still more minutely.

"A strangely symmetric pentapod coral outcrop from sea's bottom," he observed and planted a slow kiss upon the base of her big toe, insinuated the tip of his tongue between it and the next.

"There's an eel nosed around in my reef," she murmured.

Laying his cheek upon her ankle, he sighted up her leg. She was wearing a singlet of fine brown linen that tied between her legs. He said, "Your hair has exactly the same tints as are in the flooring."

She said, "You think I didn't select the marble for crushing with that in mind? Or add in the gold flakes? Here's a present of sorts for you." And she pushed the small flat black box down her leg toward him from her groin to her knee.

He sat up to inspect it though keeping her foot in his lap.

On the black fabric lining it, there lay like a delicate mist cloud the slender translucent bladder of a fish.

Cif said, "I am minded to experience your love fully tonight. Yet not as fully, mind you, as to wish that we fashion a daughter together."

The Mouser said, "I've seen the like of this made of thinnest leather well oiled."

She said, "Not as effectual, I believe."

He said, "To be sure, here, it would be something from a fish, this being Rime Isle. Tell me, did harbor master Groniger fashion this, as thrifty with the Isle's sperm as with its coins?" Then he nodded.

He reached over and drew her other foot up on his lap also.

After saluting it similarly he rested the side of his face on both her ankles, and sighted up the narrow trough between her legs. "I am minded," he said dreamily but with a little growl in his voice, "to embark on another slow and intensely watchful journey, mindful of every step, such as that by which I arrived at this house this eve."

She nodded, wondering idly if the growl were Gusorio's, but it seemed too faint for that.

In the bow of a laden grainship sailing north from Lankhmar across the Inner Sea to the land of the Eight Cities, the Death of Fafhrd, who was tall and lank, dire as a steel scarecrow, said to his fellow passenger, "This incarnation likes me and likes me not. 'Tis a balmy journey now but it'll be long and by all accounts cold as witchcunt at the end, albeit summer. Arth-Pulgh's a mean employer, and unlucky. Hand me a medlar from the sack."

The Death of the Gray Mouser, lithe as a weasel and forever smiling, replied, "No meaner nor no curster than Hamomel. Working for whom, however, is the pits. I've not yet shaken down to this persona, know not its likings. Reach your own apples."

A week later, the evening being unseasonably balmy and Witches Moon at first quarter near the top of the sky, a hemispherical silver goblet brimful of stars and scattering them dimmed by moonwine all over the sky as it descended toward the lips of the west, drawn down by the same goddess who had lifted it, Afreyt and Fafhrd after supping alone at her violet-tinted pale house on Salthaven's northern edge were minded to wander across the great meadow in the direction of Elvenhold, a northward slanting slim rock spire two bowshots high, chimneyed and narrowly terraced, that thrust from the rolling fields almost a league away to the west.

"See how her tilt," Fafhrd observed of that slender mountainlet, "directs her at the dark boss of the Targe—" (naming the northernmost constellation in the Lankhmar heavens) "—as if she were granite arrow aimed at skytop by the gods of the underworld."

"Tonight the earth is full of the heat of these gods' forges, pressing summer scents from spring flowers and grasses. Let's rest a while," Afreyt answered, and truly although it was not yet May Eve, the heavy air was more like Midsummer's. She touched his shoulder and sank to the herby sward.

After a stare around the horizon for any sky wanderer on verge of rise or set, Fafhrd seated himself by her right side. A low lurhorn sounded faintly from the town behind them or the sea beyond that.

"Night fishers summoning the finny ones," he hazarded.

"I dreamed last night," she said, "that a beast thing came out of the sea and followed me dripping salt drops as I wandered through a dark wood. I could see its silver scales between the dark boles in the gloom. But I was not afeared, and it in turn seemed to respond to this cue, for the longer it followed me the less it became like a beast and the more like a seaperson, and come not to work a hurt on me but to warn me."

"Of what?" and when she was silent, "Its sex?"

"Why, female—" she answered at once, but then becoming doubtful "—I think. Had it sex? I wonder why I did not wait for it to catch up, or perhaps turn sudden and walk toward it? I think I felt, did I so, and although I feared it not, it would turn to a beast again, a deep-voiced beast."

"I too dreamed strangely last night, and my dream strangely chimed with yours, or was it by day I dreamed? For I have begun to do that," Fafhrd announced, dropping himself back at full length on the springy sward, the better to observe the seven spiraled stars of the Targe. "I dreamt I was pent in the greatest of castles with a million dark rooms in it, and that I searched for Gusorio (for that old legend between the Mouser and me is sometimes more than a joke) because I'd been solemnly told, perchance in a dream within the dream, that he had a message for me."

She turned and leaned over him, her eyes staring deep into his as she listened. Her palely golden hair fell forward in two sweeping smooth cascades over her shoulders. He readjusted his position slightly so that five of the stars of Targe rose in a semicircle from her forehead (his eyes straying now and again toward her shadowed throat and the silver cord lacing together the sides of her violet bodice) and he continued, "In the twelve times twelve times twelfth room there stood at the far door a figure clad all in silver scale mail (there's our dreams chiming) but its back was toward me and the longer I looked at it, the taller and skinnier it seemed than Gusorio should be. Nevertheless I cried out to it aloud and in the very instant of my calling knew that I'd made an irreparable mistake and that my voice would work a hideous change in it and to my harm. See, our dreams clink again? But then, as it started to turn, I awoke. Dearest princess, did you know that the Targe crowns you?" And his right hand moved toward the silver bow drooping below her throat as she bent down to kiss him.

But as he enjoyed those pleasures and their continuations and proliferations while the moon sank, which pleasures were greatly enhanced by their starry background, the far ecstasies complementing the near, he marveled how these nights he seemed to be walking at once toward brightest life and darkest death, while through it all Elvenhold loomed in the low distance.

"No question on it, Captain Mouser's changed," Pshawri said with certainty, yet also amazedly and apprehensively, to his fellow lieutenant Mikkidu as they tippled together two evenings later in a small booth of the Sea Wrack. "Here's yet another example if't be needed. You know the care he has for our grub, to see that cookie doesn't poison us. Normally he'll taste a spoon of stew, say what it lacks or not, even order it dumped (that happened once, remember?) and go dancing off. Yet this very afternoon I spied him standing before the roiling soup kettle and staring into it for as long as it takes to stow *Flotsam*'s mainsail and then rig it again, watching it bubble and seethe with greatest interest, the beans and fish flakes bobbing and the turnips and carrots turning over, as though he were reading there auguries and prognostics on the fate of the world!"

Mikkidu nodded, "Or else he's trotting about bent over like Mother Grum, seeing things even an ant ignores. He had me stooping about after him over a route that could have been the plan of a maze, pointing out in turn a tangle of hair combings, a penny, a pebble, a parchment scrap scribbled with runic, mouse droppings, and a dead cockroach."

"Did he make you eat it?" asked Pshawri.

Mikkidu shook his head wonderingly. "No chewings… and no chewings out either. He only said at the end, when my legs had started to cramp, "I want you to keep these matters in mind in the future—"

"And meantime Captain Fafhrd—"

The two semi-rehabilitated thieves looked up. Skor from the next booth had thrust over his balding head, worry-wrinkled, which now loomed above them. "—is so busy keeping watch on the stars by night—and by day too, somehow—that it's a wonder he can navigate Salthaven without breaking his neck. Think you some evil wight has put a spell on both?"

Normally the Mouser's and Fafhrd's men were mutually rivalrous, suspicious, and disparaging of each other. It was a measure of their present concern for their captains that they pooled their knowledge and took frank counsel together.

Pshawri shrugged as hugely as one so small was able. "Who knows? 'Tis such footling matters, and yet…"

"Chill ills abound here," Mikkidu intoned. "Khakht the Wizard of Ice, Stardock's ghost fliers, sunken Simorgya…"

At the same moment Cif and Afreyt in the former's sauna chatted together with even greater but more playful freedom. Afreyt confided with mock grandeur, "I'll have you know that Fafhrd compared my niplets to stars."

Cif chortled midst the steam and answered coarsely with mock pride, "The Mouser likened my arse hole to one. *And* to the stem dimple of a pome. And his own intrusive member to a stiletto! Whate'er ails them doesn't show in bed."

"Or does it?" Afreyt questioned laughingly. "In my case, stars. In yours, fruits and cutlery too."

As the Deaths of Fafhrd and the Mouser jounced on donkeyback at the tail of a small merchant troop to which they'd attached themselves traveling through the forested land of the Eight Cities from Kvarch Nar to Illik Ving, Witches Moon being full, the former observed, "The trouble with these long incarnations as the death of another is that one begins to forget one's own proper persona and best interests, especially if one be a dedicated actor."

"Not so, necessarily," the other responded. "Rather, it gives one a clear head (What head clearer than Death's?) to observe oneself dispassionately and examine without bias the terms of the contract under which one operates."

"That's true enough," Fafhrd's Death said, stroking his lean jaw while his donkey stepped along evenly for a change. "Why think you this one talks so much of booty we may find?"

"Why else but that Arth-Pulgh and Hamomel expect there will be treasure on our intendeds or about them? There's a thought to warm the cold nights coming!"

"Yes, and raises a nice question in our order's law, whether we're being hired principally as assassins or robbers."

"No matter that," Death of the Mouser summed up. "We know at least we must not hit the Twain until they've shown us where their treasure is."

"Or treasurers are, more like," the other amended, "if they distrust each other, as all sane men do."

Coming in opposite directions around a corner behind Salthaven's council hall after a sharp rainshower, the Mouser and Fafhrd bumped into each other because the one was bending down to inspect a new puddle while the other studied the clouds retreating from arrows of sunshine. After grappling together briefly with sharp growls that turned to sudden laughter, Fafhrd was shaken enough from his current preoccupations by this small surprise to note the look of puzzled and wondrous brooding that instantly replaced the sharp friendly grin on the Mouser's face—a look that was undersurfaced by a pervasive sadness.

His heart was touched and he asked, "Where've you been keeping yourself, comrade? I never seem to see you to talk to these past days."

"'Tis true," the Mouser replied with a sharp grimace, "we do seem to be operating on different *levels,* you and I, in our movings around Salthaven this last moon-wax."

"Yes, but where are your *feelings* keeping?" Fafhrd prompted.

Heart-touched in turn and momentarily impelled to seek to share deepest and least definable difficulties, the Mouser drew Fafhrd to the lane side and launched out, "If you said I were homesick for Lankhmar, I'd call you liar! Our jolly comrades and grand almost-friends there, yes, even those good not-to-be-trusted female troopers in memory revered, and all their perfumed and painted blazonry of ruby (or mayhap emerald?) lips, delectable tits, exquisite genitalia, they draw me not a whit! Not even Sheelba with her deep diggings into my psyche, nor your spicedly garrulous Ning. Nor all the gorgeous palaces, piers, pyramids, and fanes, all that marble and cloud-capped biggery! But oh…" and the underlook of sadness and wonder became *keen* in his face as he drew Fafhrd closer, dropping his voice, "…the *small things*—those, I tell you honest, *do* make me homesick, aye yearningly so. The little street braziers, the lovely litter, as though each scrap were sequined and bore hieroglyphs. The hennaed and the diamond-dusted footprints. I knew those things, yet I never looked at them closely enough, savored the *details.* Oh, the thought of going back and counting the cobblestones in the Street of the Gods and fixing forever in my memory the shape of each and tracing the course of the rivulets of rainy trickle between them! I'd want to be rat size again to do it properly, yes even ant size, oh there is no end to this fascination, the universe written in a pebble!"

And he stared desperately deep into Fafhrd's eyes to ascertain if that one had caught at least some shred of his meaning, but the big man whose questions had stirred him to speak from his inmost being had apparently lost the track himself somewhere, for his long face had gone blank again, blank with a faint tone of melancholia and eyes wandering doubtfully upward.

"Homesick for Lankhmar?" the big man was saying. "Well, I do miss her stars, I must confess, her southern stars we cannot see from here. But oh…" And now *his* face and eyes fired for the brief span it took him to say the following words, "…the thought of the still more southern stars we've never seen! The untraveled southern continent below the Middle Sea. Godsland and Nehwon's life pole and over 'em the stars a world of men have died and never seen. Yes, I am homesick for those lands indeed!"

The Mouser saw the flare in him dim and die. The Northerner shook his head. "My mind wanders," he said. "There are a many of good enough stars here. Why carry worries afar? Their sorting is sufficient."

"Yes, there are good pickings now here along Hurricane street and Salt, and leave the gods to worry over themselves," the Mouser heard himself say as his gaze dropped to the nearest puddle. He felt *his* flare die—if it had ever been. "Things will shake down, get done, sort themselves out, and feelings too."

Fafhrd nodded and they went their separate ways.

And so time passed on Rime Isle. Witches Moon grew full and waned and gave way to Ghostsmoon, which lived its wraith-short life in turn, and Midsummer Moon was born, sometimes called Murderers Moon because its full runs low and is the latest to rise and earliest to set of all full moons, not high and long like the full moons of winter.

And with the passage of time things did shake down and some of them got done and sorted out after a fashion, meaning mostly that the out of the way became the commonplace with repetition, as it has a way of doing.

Seahawk got fully repaired, even refitted, but Fafhrd's and Afreyt's plan to sail her to Ool Plerns and fell timber there for wood-poor Rime Isle got pushed into the future. No one said, "Next summer," but the thought was there.

And the barracks and warehouse got built, including a fine drainage system and a cesspool of which the Mouser was inordinately proud, but repairs to *Flotsam*, though hardly languishing, went slow, and Cif's and his plan to cruise her east and trade with the Ice Gnomes north of No-Ombrulsk even more visionary.

Mog, Kos, and Issek's peculiar curses continued to shape much of the Twain's behavior (to the coarse-grained amusement of those small-time gods), but not so extremely as to interfere seriously with their ability to boss their men effectively or be sufficiently amusing, gallant, and intelligent with their female co-mates. Most of their men soon catalogued it under the heading "captains' eccentricities," to be griped at or boasted of equally but no further thought of. Skor, Pshawri, and Mikkidu did not accept it quite so easily and continued to worry and wonder now and then and entertain dark suspicions as befitted lieutenants, men who are supposedly learning to be as imaginatively responsible as captains. While on the other hand the Rime Islers, including the crusty and measuredly friendly Groniger, found it a good thing, indicative that these wild allies and would-be neighbors, questionable protégés of those headstrong freewomen Cif and Afreyt, were settling down nicely into law-abiding and hard-headed island ways. The Gray Mouser's concern with small material details particularly impressed them, according with their proverb: rock, wood, and flesh; all else a lie, or, more simply still: Mineral, Vegetable, Animal.

Afreyt and Cif knew there had been a change in the two men, all right, and so did our two heroes too, for that matter. But they were inclined to put it down to the weather or some deep upheaval of mood as had once turned Fafhrd religious and the Mouser calculatedly avaricious. Or else—who knows?—these might be the sort of things that happened to anyone who settled down. Oddly, neither considered the possibility of a curse, whether by god or sorcerer or witch. Curses were violent things that led men to cast themselves off mountaintops or dash their children's brains out against rocks, and women to castrate their bed partners and set fire to their own hair if there wasn't a handy volcano to dive into. The triviality and low intensity of the curses misled them.

When all four were together they talked once or twice of supernatural influences on human lives, speaking on the whole more lightly than each felt at heart.

"Why don't you ask augury of Great Gusorio?" Cif suggested. "Since you are shards of him, he should know all about both of you."

"He's more a joke than a true presence one might address a prayer to," the Mouser parried and then riposted, "Why don't you or Afreyt appeal for enlightenment to that witch—or warrior-queen of yours, Skeldir, she of the silver scale-mail and the short dry laugh?"

"We're not on such intimate terms as that with her, though claiming her as ancestor," Cif answered, looking down diffidently. "I'd hardly know how to go about it."

Yet that dialogue led Afreyt and Fafhrd to recount the dreams they'd previously shared only with each other. Whereupon all four indulged in inconclusive speculations and guesses. The Mouser and Fafhrd promptly forgot these, but Cif and Afreyt stored them away in memory.

And although the curses on the Twain were of low intensity, the divine vituperations worked steadily and consumingly. Ensamples: Fafhrd became much interested in a dim hairy star low in the west that seemed to be slowly growing in brightness and luxuriance of mane and to be moving east against the current, and he made a point observing it early each eve. While it was noticed that the busily peering Captain Mouser had a favorite route for checking things out that led from the Sea Wrack, where he'd have a morning nip, to the low point in the lane outside, to the windy corner behind the council hall where he'd collided with Fafhrd, to his men's barracks and by way of the dormitory's closet, which he'd open and check for mouseholes, to his own room and shelfed closet and to the kitchen and pantry, and so to the cesspool behind them of which he was so proud.

So life went on tranquilly, busily, unenterprisingly in and around Salthaven as spring gave way to Rime Isle's short sharp summer. Their existence was rather like that of industrious lotus eaters, the others taking their cues from the bemused and somewhat absent-minded Twain. The only exception to this most regular existence promised to be the day of Midsummer Eve, a traditional Isle holiday, when at the two women's suggestion they planned a feast for all hands (and special Isle friends and associates) in the Great Meadow at Elvenhold's foot, a sort of picnic with dancing and games and athletic competitions.

If anyone could be said to have spent an unpleasant or unsatisfactory time during this period, it was the wizards Sheelba and Ningauble. The cosmic din had quieted down sufficiently for them to be able to communicate pretty well between the one's swamp hut and the other's cave and get some confused inkling of what Fafhrd and the Mouser and their gods were up to, but none of that inkling sounded very logical to them or favorable to their plot. The stupid provincial gods had put some unintelligible sort of curse on their two pet errand boys, and it was working after a fashion, but Mouser and Fafhrd hadn't left Rime Isle, nothing was working out according to the two wizards' wishes, while a disquieting adverse influence they could not identify was moving northwest across the Cold Wag north of the Land of the Eight Cities and the Trollstep Mountains. All very baffling and unsatisfactory.

At Illik Ving the Death of the Twain joined a caravan bound for No-Ombrulsk, changing their mounts for shaggy Mingo ponies inured to frost, and spent all of Ghostsmoon on that long traverse. Although early summer, there was sufficient chill in the Trollsteps and the foothills of the Bones of the Old One and in the plateau of the Cold Waste that lies between the ranges, for them to refer frequently to the seed bags of brazen apes and the tits of witches, and hug the cookfire while it lasted, and warm their sleep with dreams of the treasures their intendeds had laid up.

"I see this Fafhrd as a gold-guarding dragon in a mountain cave," his Death averred. "I'm into his character fully now, I feel. And onto it too."

"While I dream the Mouser as a fat gray spider," the other echoed, "with silver, amber, and leviathan ivory cached in a score of nooks, crannies, and corners he scuttles between. Yes, I can play him now. And play with him too. Odd, isn't it, how like we get to our intendeds at the end?"

Arriving at last at the stone-towered seaport, they took lodgings at an inn where badges of the Slayers' Brotherhood were recognized, and they slept for two nights and a day, recuperating. Then Mouser's Death went for a stroll down by the docks and when he returned, announced, "I've taken passage for us in an Ool Kroot trader. Sails with the tide day after morrow."

"Murderers Moon begins well," his wraith-thin comrade observed from where he still lay abed.

"At first the captain pretended not to know of Rime Isle, called it a legend, but when I showed him the badge and other things, he gave up that shipmasters' conspiracy of keeping Salthaven and western ports beyond a trade secret. By the by, our ship's called the *Good News.*"

"An auspicious name," the other, smiling, responded. "Oh Mouser, and oh Fafhrd, dear, your twin brothers are hastening toward you."

After the long morning twilight that ended Midsummer Eve's short night, Midsummer Day dawned chill and misty in Salthaven. Nevertheless there was an early bustling around the kitchen of the barracks, where the Mouser and Fafhrd had taken their repose, and likewise at Afreyt's house, where Cif and their nieces May, Mara, and Gale had stayed overnight.

Soon the fiery sun, shooting his rays from the northeast as he began his longest loop south around the sky, had burnt the milky mist off all Rime Isle and showed her clear from the low roofs of Salthaven to the central hills with the leaning tower of Elvenhold in the near middle distance and the Great Meadow rising gently toward it.

And soon after that an irregular procession set out from the barracks. It wandered crookedly and leisurely through town to pick up the men's women, chiefly by trade, at least in their spare time, sailorwives, and other island guests. The men took turns dragging a cart piled with hampers of barley cakes, sweetbreads, cheese, roast mutton and kid, fruit conserves and other Island delicacies, while at its bottom packed in snow were casks of the Isle's dark bitter ale. A few men blew woodflutes and strummed small harps.

At the docks Groniger, festive in holiday black, joined them with the news. "The *Northern Star* out of Ool Plerns came in last even to No-Ombrulsk. I spoke with her master and he said the *Good News* out of Ool Kroot was at last report sailing for Rime Isle one or two mornings after him."

At this point Ourph the Mingol begged off from the party, protesting that the walk to Elvenhold would be too much for his old bones and a new crick in his left ankle, he'd rest them in the sun here, and they left him squatting his skinny frame on the warming stone and peering steadily out to sea past where *Seahawk*, *Flotsam*, *Northern Star*, and other ships rode at anchor among the Island fishing sloops.

Fafhrd said to Groniger, "I've been here a year and more and it still wonders me that Salthaven is such a busy port while the rest of Nehwon goes on thinking Rime Isle a legend. I know I did for a half lifetime."

"Legends travel on rainbow wings and sport gaudy colors," the harbormaster answered him, "while truth plods on in sober garb."

"Like yourself?"

"Aye," Groniger grunted happily.

"And 'tis not a legend to the captains, guild masters, and kings who profit by it," the Mouser put in. "Such do most to keep legends alive." The little man (though not little at all among his corps of thieves) was in a merry mood, moving from group to group and cracking wise and gay to all and sundry.

Skullick, Skor's sub-lieutenant, struck up a berserk battle chant and Fafhrd found himself singing an Ilthmar sea chanty to it. At their next pick-up point tankards of ale were passed out to them. Things grew jollier.

A little ways out into the Great Meadow, where the thoroughfare led between fields of early ripening Island barley, they were joined by the feminine procession from Afreyt's. These had packed their contribution of toothsome edibles and tastesome potables in two small red carts drawn by stocky white bearhounds big as small men but gentle as lambs. And they had been augmented by the sailorwives and fisherwomen Hilsa and Rill, whose gift to the feast was jars of sweet-pickled fish. Also by the witchwoman Mother Grum, as old as Ourph but hobbling along stalwartly, never known to have missed a feast in her life's long history.

They were greeted with cries and new singings, while the three girls ran to play with the children the larger procession had inevitably accumulated on its way through town.

Fafhrd went back for a bit to quizzing Groniger about the ships that called at Salthaven port, flourishing the hook that was his left hand, for emphasis. "I've heard it said, and seen some evidence for it too, myself, that some of them hail from ports that are nowhere on Nehwon seas I know of."

"Ah, you're becoming a convert to the legends," the black-clad man told him. Then, mischievously, "Why don't you try casting the ships' horoscopes with all you've learned of stars of late, naked and hairy ones?" He frowned. "Though there was a black cutter with a white line that watered here three days ago whose home port I wish I could be surer of. Her master put me off from going below, and her sails didn't look enough for her hull. He said she hailed from Sayend, but that's a seaport we've had reliable word that the Sea-Mingols burned to ash less than two years agone. He knew of that, he claimed. Said it was much exaggerated. But I couldn't place his accent."

"You see?" Fafhrd told him. "As for horoscopes, I have neither skill or belief in astrology. My sole concern is with the stars themselves and the patterns they make. The hairy star's most interesting! He grows each night. At first I thought him a rover, but he keeps his place. I'll point him out to you come dark."

"Or some other evening when there's less drinking," the other allowed grudgingly. "A wise man is suspicious of his interests other than the most necessary. They breed illusions."

The groupings kept changing as they walked, sang, and danced—and played—their way up through the rustling grass. Cif took advantage of this mixing to seek out Pshawri and Mikkidu. The Mouser's two lieutenants had at first been suspicious of her interest in and influence over their captain—a touch of jealousy, no doubt—but honest dealing and speaking, the evident genuineness of her concern, and some furtherance of Pshawri's suit to an Island woman had won them over, so that the three thought of themselves in a limited way as confederates.

"How's Captain Mouser these days?" she asked them lightly. "Still running his little morning check-up route?"

"He didn't today," Mikkidu told her.

"While yesterday he ran it in the afternoon," Pshawri amplified. "And the day before that he missed."

Mikkidu nodded.

"I don't fret about him o'er much," she smiled at them, "knowing he's under watchful and sympathetic eyes."

And so with mutual buttering up and with singing and dancing the augmented holiday band arrived at the spot just south of Elvenhold that they'd selected for their picnic. A portion of the food was laid out on white-sheeted trestles, the drink was broached, and the competitions and games that comprised an important part of the day's program were begun. These were chiefly trials of strength and skill, not of endurance, and one trial only, so that a reasonable or even somewhat unreasonable amount of eating and drinking didn't tend to interfere with performance too much.

Between the contests were somewhat less impromptu dancings than had been footed earlier: Island stamps and flings, old-fashioned Lankhmar sways, and kicking and bouncing dances copied from the Mingols.

Knife-throwing came early—"so none will be mad drunk as yet, a sensible precaution," Groniger approved.

The target was a yard section of mainland tree-trunk almost two yards thick, lugged up the previous day. The distance was fifteen long paces, which meant two revolutions of the knife the way most contestants threw. The Mouser waited until last and then threw underhand as a sort of handicap, or at least seeming handicap, against himself, and his knife embedded deeply in or near the center, clearly a better shot than any of the earlier successful ones, whose points of impact were marked with red chalk.

A flurry of applause started, but then it was announced that Cif had still to throw; she'd entered at the last possible minute. There was no surprise at a woman entering; that sort of equality was accepted on the Isle.

"You didn't tell me beforehand you were going to," the Mouser said to her.

She shook her head at him, concentrating on her aim. "No, leave his dagger in," she called to the judges. "It won't distract me."

She threw overhand and her knife impacted itself so close to his that there was a *klir* of metal against metal along with the woody *thud*. Groniger measured the distances carefully with his beechwood ruler and proclaimed Cif the winner.

"And the measures on this ruler are copied from those on the golden Rule of Prudence in the Island treasury," he added impressively, but later qualified this by saying, "actually my ruler's more accurate than that ikon; doesn't expand with heat and contract with cold as metals do. But some people don't like to keep hearing me say that."

"Do you think her besting the captain is good for discipline and all?" Mikkidu asked Pshawri in an undertone, his new trust in Cif wavering.

"Yes, I do!" that one whispered back. "Do the captain good to be shook up a little, what with all this old-man scurrying and worrying and prying and pointing out he's going in for." *There*, he thought, *I've spoken it out to someone at last and I'm glad I did!*

Cif smiled at the Mouser. "No, I didn't tell you ahead of time," she said sweetly, "but I've been practicing—privately. Would it have made a difference?"

"No," he said slowly, "though I might have had second thoughts about throwing underhand. Are you planning to enter the slinging contest too?"

"No, never a thought of it," she answered. "Whatever made you think I might?"

Later the Mouser won that one, both for distance and accuracy, making the latter cast so powerful that it not only holed the center of the bull's-eye into the padded target box but went through the heavier back of the latter as well. Cif begged for the battered slug as a souvenir, and he presented it to her with elaborate flourishes.

"'Twould have pierced the cuirass of Mingsward!" Mikkidu fervently averred.

The archery contests were beginning, and Fafhrd was fitting the iron tang in the middle of his bow into the hardwood heading of the leather stall that covered half his left forearm, when he noted Afreyt approaching. She'd doffed her jacket, for the sun was beating down hotly, and was wearing a short-sleeved violet blouse, blue trousers wide-belted with a gold buckle, and purple-dyed short holiday boots. A violet handkerchief confined a little her pale gold hair. A worn green quiver with one arrow in it hung from her shoulder, and she was carrying a big longbow.

Fafhrd's eyes narrowed a bit at those, recalling Cif and the knife throwing. But "You look like a pirate queen," he greeted her and then only inquired, "you're entering one of the contests?"

"I don't know," she said with a shrug. "I'll watch along through the first."

"That bow," he said casually, "looks to me to have a very heavy pull and tall as you are, to be a touch long for you."

"Right on both counts," she agreed, nodding. "It belonged to my father. You'd be truly startled, I think, to see how I managed to draw it as a stripling girl. My father would doubtless have spanked me soundly if he'd ever caught me at it, or rather lived long enough to do that."

Fafhrd lifted his eyebrows inquiringly, but the pirate queen vouchsafed no more. He won the distance shot handily but lost the target shot (through which Afreyt also watched) by a fingersbreadth to Skor's other sub-lieutenant Mannimark.

Then came the high shot, which was something special to Midsummer Day on Rime Isle and generally involved the loss of the contestant's arrow, for the target was a grassy, nearly vertical stretch on the upper half of the south face of Elvenhold. The north face of the slanting rock tower actually overhung the ground a little and was utterly barren, but the south face, though very steep, sloped enough to hold soil to support herbage, rather miraculously. The contest honored the sun, which reached this day his highest point in the heavens, while the contesting arrows, identified by colored rags of thinnest silk attached to their necks, emulated him in their efforts.

Then Afreyt stepped forward, kicked off her purple boots, and rolled up her blue trousers above her knees. She plucked her arrow, which bore a violet silk, from her quiver and threw that aside. "Now I'll reveal to you the secret of my girlish technique," she said to Fafhrd.

Quite rapidly she sat down facing the dizzy slope, set the bow to her bare feet, laying the arrow between her big toes and holding it and the string with both hands, rolled back on to her shoulders, straightened her legs smoothly, and loosed her shot.

It was seen to strike the slope near Fafhrd's yellow, skid a few yards higher, and then lie there, a violet taunt.

Afreyt, bending her legs again, removed the bow from her feet, and rolling sharply forward, stood up in the same motion.

"You practiced that," Fafhrd said, hardly accusingly, as he finished screwing the hook back in the stall on his left arm.

She nodded. "Yes, but only for half a lifetime."

"The lady Afreyt's arrow didn't stick in," Skullick pointed out. "Is that fair? A breath of wind might dislodge it."

"Yes, but there is no wind and it somehow got highest," Groniger pointed out to him. "Actually it's accounted lucky in the high shot if your arrow doesn't embed itself. Those that don't sometimes are blown down. Those that do stay up there are never recovered."

"Doesn't someone go up and collect the arrows?" Skullick asked.

"Scale Elvenhold? Have you wings?"

Skullick eyed the rock tower and shook his head sheepishly. Fafhrd overheard Groniger's remarks and gave the harbormaster an odd look but made no other comment at the time.

Afreyt invited both of them over to the red dogcarts and produced a jug of Ilthmar brandy, and they toasted her and Fafhrd's victories—the Mouser's too and Cif's, who happened along.

"This'll put feathers in your wings!" Fafhrd told Groniger, who eyed him thoughtfully.

The children were playing with the white bearhounds. Gale had won the girls' archery contest and May the short race.

Some of the younger children were becoming fretful, however, and shadows were lengthening. The games and contests were all over now, and partly as a consequence of that the drinking was heavying up as the last scraps of food were being eaten. Among the whole picnic group there seemed to be a feeling of weariness but also (for those no longer very young but not yet old) new jollity, as though one party were ending and another beginning. Cif's and Afreyt's eyes were especially bright. Everyone seemed ready to go home, though whether to their own places or the Sea Wrack was a matter of age and temperament. There was a chill breath in the air.

Gazing east and down a little toward Salthaven and the harbor beyond, the Mouser opined that he could already see low mist gathering around the bare masts there, and Groniger confirmed that. But what was the small lone dark figure trudging up-meadow toward them in the face of the last low sunlight?

"Ourph, I'll be bound," said Fafhrd. "What's led him to make the hike after all?"

But it was hard to be sure the big northerner was right; the figure was still far off. Yet the signal for leaving had been given, things were gathered, the carts repacked, and all set out most staying near the carts, from which drinks continued to be forthcoming. And perhaps these were responsible for a resumption of the morning's impromptu singing and dancing though now it was not Fafhrd and the Mouser but others who took the lead in this. The Twain, after a whole day of behaving like old times, were slipping back under the curses they knew not of, the one's eyes forever on the ground, with the effect of old age unsure of its footing, the other's on the sky, indicative of old age's absent-mindedness.

Fafhrd turned out to be right about the up-meadow trudges but it was few words they got from Ourph as to why he'd made the hike he'd earlier begged off from.

The old Mingol said only to them, and to Groniger, who happed to be by, "The *Good News* is in." Then, eyeing the Twain more particularly, "Tonight stay away from the Sea Wrack."

But he would answer nothing more to their puzzled queries save, "I know what I know and I've told it," and two cups of brandy did not loosen his Mingol tongue one whit.

The encounter put them behind the main party, but they did not try to catch up. The sun had set some time back, and now their feet and legs were lapped by the ground mist that already covered Salthaven and into which the picnic party was vanishing, its singing and strumming already sounding tiny and far off.

"You see," Groniger said to Fafhrd and eyeing the twilit but yet starless sky while the mist lapped higher around them "you won't be able to show me your bearded star tonight in any case."

Fafhrd nodded vaguely but made no other answer save to pass the brandy jug as they footed it along: four men walking deeper and deeper, as it were, into a white silence.

Cif and Afreyt, very much caught up in the gayety of evening party and bright-eyed drunk besides, were among the first to enter the Sea Wrack and encounter arresting silence of another sort, and almost instantly come under the strange, hushing spell of the scene there.

Fafhrd and the Mouser sat at their pet table in the low-walled booth playing backgammon, and the whole tavern frightenedly watched them while pretending not to. Fear was in the air.

That was the first impression. Then, almost at once, Cif and Afreyt saw that Fafhrd couldn't be Fafhrd, he was much too thin; nor the Mouser the Mouser, much too plump (though every bit as agile and supple-looking, paradoxically).

Nor were the faces and clothing and accouterments of the two strangers

anything really like the Twain's. It was more their expressions and mannerisms, postures and general manner, self-confident manner, those and the
fact of *being at that table.* The sublime impression the two of them made
that they were who they were and that they were in their rightful place.

And the fear that radiated from them with the small sounds of their gaming: the muted rattle of shaken bone dice in one or the other's palm-closed
leather cup, the muted clatter as the dice were spilled into one or other of
the two low-walled felt-lined compartments of the backgammon box, the
sharp little clicks of the bone counters as they were shifted by ones and
twos from point to point. The fear that riveted the attention of everyone
else in the place no matter how much they pretended to be understanding the conversations they made, or tasting the drinks they swallowed, or
busying themselves with little tavern chores. The fear that seized upon and
recruited each picnic newcomer. Oh yes, this night something deadly was
coiling here at the Sea Wrack, make no mistake about it.

So paralyzing was the fear that it cost Cif and Afreyt a great effort to
sidle slowly from the doorway to the bar, their eyes never leaving that one
little table that was for now the world's hub, until they were as close as they
could get to the Sea Wrack's owner, who with downcast and averted eye
was polishing the same mug over and over.

"Keeper, what gives?" Cif whispered to him softly but most distinctly.
"Nay, sull not up. Speak, I charge you!"

Eagerly that one, as though grateful Cif's whiplash command had given
him opportunity to discharge some of the weight of dread crushing him,
whispered them back his tale in short, almost breathless bursts, though
without raising an eye or ceasing to circle his rag.

"I was alone here when they came in, minutes after the *Good News* docked.
They spoke no word, but as though the fat one were the lean one's hunting
ferret, they *scented out* our two captains' table, sat themselves down at it as
though they owned it, then spoke at last to call for drink.

"I took it them, and as they got out their box and dice cups and set up
their game, they plied me with harmless-seeming and friendly questions
mostly about the Twain, as if they knew them well. Such as: How fared they
in Rime Isle? Enjoyed they good health? Seemed they happy? How often
came they in? Their tastes in drink and food and the fair sex? What other
interests had they? What did they like to talk of? As though the two of them
were courtiers of some great foreign empire come hither our captains to
please and to solicit about some affair of state.

"And yet, you know, so *dire* somehow were the tones in which those
innocent questions were asked that I doubt I could have refused them if
they'd asked me for the Twain's hearts blood or my own.

"This too: The more questions they asked about the Twain and the more I answered them as best I might, the more they came to look like… to resemble our… you know what I'm trying to say?"

"Yes, yes!" Afreyt hissed. "Go on."

"In short, I felt I was their slave. So too, I think, have felt all those who came into the Sea Wrack after them, saw for old Mingo! Ourph, who shortly stayed, somehow then parted.

"At last they sucked me dry, bent to their game, asked for more drink. I sent the girl with that. Since then it's been as you see now."

There was a stir at the doorway through which mist was curling. Four men stood there, for a moment bemused. Then Fafhrd and the Mouser strode toward their table, while old Ourph settled down on his hams, his gaze unwavering, and Groniger almost totteringly sidled toward the bar, like a man surprised at midday by a sleepwalking fit and thoroughly astounded at it.

Fafhrd and the Mouser leaned over and looked down at the table and open backgammon box over which the two strangers were bent, surveying their positions. After a bit Fafhrd said rather loudly, "A good rilk against two silver smerduke on the lean one! His stones are poised to fleet swiftly home."

"You're on!" the Mouser cried back. "You've underestimated the fat one's back game."

Turning his chill blue eyes and flat-nosed skull-like face straight up at Fafhrd with an almost impossible twist of his neck, the skinny one said, "Did the stars tell you to wager at such odds on my success?"

Fafhrd's whole manner changed. "You're interested in the stars?" he asked with an incredulous hopefulness.

"Mightily so," the other answered him, nodding emphatically.

"Then you must come with me," Fafhrd informed him, almost lifting him from his stool with one fell swoop of his good hand and arm that at once assisted and guided, while his hook indicated the mist-filled doorway. "Leave off this footling game. Abandon it. We've much to talk of, you and I." By now he had a brotherly arm—the hooked one, this time—around the thin one's shoulders and was leading him back along the path he'd entered by. "Oh, there are wonders and treasures undreamed amongst the stars, are there not?"

"Treasures?" the other asked coolly, pricking an ear but holding back a little.

"Aye, indeed! There's one in particular under the silvery asterism of the Black Panther that I lust to show you," Fafhrd replied with great enthusiasm, at which the other went more willingly.

All watched astonishedly, but the only one who managed to speak out was Groniger, who asked, "Where are you going, Fafhrd?" in rather outraged tones.

The big man paused for a moment, winked at Groniger, and smiling said, "Flying."

Then with a "Come, comrade astronomer," said another great arm-sweep, he wafted the skinny one with him into the bulging white mist, where both men shortly vanished.

Back at the table the plump stranger said in loud but winning tones, "Gentle sir! Would you care to take over my friend's game, continue it with me?" Then in tones less formal, "And have you noticed that these mug dints on your table together with the platter burn make up the figure of a giant sloth?"

"Oh, so you've already seen that, have you?" the Mouser answered the second question, returning his gaze from the door. Then, to the second, "Why, yes, I will, sir, and double the bet!—it being my die cast. Although your friend did not stay long enough even to arrange a chouette."

"*Your* friend was most insistent," the other replied. "Sir, I take your bet."

Whereupon the Mouser sat down and proceeded to shake a masterly sequence of double fours and double threes so that the skinny man's stones, now his own, fleeted more swiftly to victory than ever Fafhrd had predicted. The Mouser grinned fiendishly, and as they set up the stones for another game, he pointed out to his more thinly smiling adversary in the table top's dints and stains the figure of a leopard stalking the giant sloth.

All eyes were now back on the table again save those of Afreyt. And of Fafhrd's lieutenant Skor. Those four orbs were still fixed on the mist-bulging doorway through which Fafhrd had vanished with his strangely unlike doublegoer. Since babyhood Afreyt had heard of those doleful nightwalkers whose appearance, like the banshee's, generally betokened death or near mortal injury to the one whose shape they mocked.

Now while she agonized over what to do, invoking the witch queen Skeldir and lesser of her own and (in her extremity) others' private deities, there was a strange growling in her ears—perhaps her rushing blood. Fafhrd's last word to Groniger kindled in her memory the recollection of an exchange of words between those two earlier today, which in turn gave her a bright inkling of Fafhrd's present destination in the viewless fog. This in turn inspired her to break the grip upon her of fear's and indecision's paralysis. Her first two or three steps were short and effortful ones but by the time she went through the doorway she was taking swift giant strides.

Her example broke the dread-duty deadlock in Skor and the lean, red-haired, balding giant followed her in a rush.

But few in the Sea Wrack except Ourph and perhaps Groniger noted either departure, for all gazes were fixed again on the one small table where now Captain Mouser in person contested with his dread were-brother, battling the Islanders' and his men's fears for them as it were. And whether by smashing attack, tortuous back game, or swift running one like the first, the Mouser kept winning again and again and again.

And still the games went on, as though the series might well outlast the night. The stranger's smile kept thinning. That was all, or almost all.

The only fly in this ointment of unending success was a nagging doubt, perhaps deriving from a growing languor on the Mouser's part, a lessening of his taunting joy at each new win, that destinies in the larger world would jump with those worked out in the little world of the backgammon box.

"We have reached the point in this night's little journey I'm taking you on where we must abandon the horizontal and embrace the vertical," Fafhrd informed his comrade astronomer, clasping him familiarly about the shoulders with his left hand and arm, and wagging the forefinger of his right before the latter's cadaver face, while the white mist hugged them both.

The Death of Fafhrd fought down the impulse to squirm away with a hawking growl of disgust close to vomiting. He abominated being touched except by outstandingly beautiful females under circumstances entirely of his own commanding. And now for a full half-hour he had been following his drunken and crazy victim (sometimes much too closely for comfort, but that wasn't his own choosing, Aarth forbid) through a blind fog, and mostly trusting the same madman to keep them from breaking their necks in holes and pits and bogs, and putting up with being touched and arm-gripped and back-slapped (often by that doubly disgusting hook that felt so like a weapon), and listening to a farrago of wild talk about long-haired asterisms and bearded stars and barley fields and sheep's grazing ground and hills and masts and trees and the mysterious southern continent until Aarth himself couldn't have held it, so that it was only the madman's occasional remention of a treasure or treasures he was leading his Death to that kept the latter tagging along without plunging exasperated knife into his victim's vitals.

And at least the loathsome cleavings and enwrappings expressive of brotherly affection that he had made himself submit to had allowed him to ascertain in turn that his intended wore no undergarment of chain mail or plate or scale to interfere with the proper course of things when knife time came. So the Death of Fafhrd consoled himself as he broke away from the taller and heavier man under the legitimate and friendly excuse of more closely inspecting the rock wall they now faced at a distance of no more than four or five yards. Farther off the fog would have hid it.

"You say we're to climb this to view your treasure?" He couldn't quite keep his incredulity out of his voice.

"Aye," Fafhrd told him.

"How high?" his Death asked him.

Fafhrd shrugged. "Just high enough to get there. A short distance, truly." He waved an arm a little sideways, as though dispensing with a trifle.

"There's not much light to climb by," his Death said somewhat tentatively.

Fafhrd replied, "What think you makes the mist whitely luminous an hour after sunset? There's enough light to climb by, never fear, and it'll get brighter as we go aloft. You're a climber, aren't you?"

"Oh, yes," the other admitted diffidently, not saying that his experience had been gained chiefly in scaling impregnable towers and cyclopean poisoned walls behind which the wealthier and more powerful assassin's targets tended to hide themselves—difficult climbs, some of them, truly, but rather artificial ones, and all of them done in the line of business.

Touching the rough rock and seeing it inches in front of his somewhat blunted nose, the Death of Fafhrd felt a measurable repugnance to setting foot or serious hand on it. For a moment he was mightily minded to whip out dagger and end it instanter here with the swift upward jerk under the breastbone, or the shrewd thrust from behind at the base of the skull, or the well-known slash under the ear in the angle of the jaw. He'd never have his victim more lulled, that was certain.

Two things prevented him. One, he'd never had the feeling of having an audience so completely under his control as he'd had this afternoon and evening at the Sea Wrack. Or a victim so completely eating out of his hand, so walking to his own destruction, as they said in the trade. It gave him a feeling of being intoxicated while utterly sober, it put him into an "I can do anything, I am God" mood, and he wanted to prolong that wonderful thrill as far as possible.

Two, Fafhrd's talk perpetually returning to treasure, and the way the invitation now to climb some small cliff to view it so fitted with his Cold Waste dreams of Fafhrd as a dragon guarding gold in a mountain cavern—combined to persuade him that the Fates were taking a hand in tonight's happening, the youngest of them drawing aside veil and baring her ruby lips to him and soon the more private jewelry of her person.

"You don't have to worry about the rock, it's sound enough, just follow in my footsteps and my handholds," Fafhrd told him impatiently as he advanced to the cliff's face and mounted past him, the hook making harsh metallic clashes.

His Death doffed the short cloak and hood he wore, took a deep breath and, thinking in a small corner of his mind, "Well, at least he won't be able to fondle me more while we're climbing—I hope!" went up after him like a giant spider.

It was as well for Fafhrd that his Death (and the Mouser's too) had neglected to make close survey of the landscape and geography of Rime Isle during this afternoon's sail in. (They'd been down in their cabin mostly, getting into their parts.) Otherwise he might have known that he was now climbing Elvenhold.

Back in the Sea Wrack the Mouser threw a double six, the only cast that would allow him to bear off his last four stones and leave his opponent's sole remaining man stranded one point from home. He threw up the back of a hand to mask a mighty yawn and over it politely raised an inquiring eyebrow at his adversary.

The Death of the Mouser nodded amiably enough, though his smile had grown very thin-lipped indeed, and said, "Yes, it's as well we write finished to my strivings. Was it eight games, or seven? No matter. I'll seek my revenge some other time. Fate is your girl tonight, cunt and arse hole, that much is proven."

A collective sigh of relief from the onlookers ended the general silence. They felt the relaxation of tension as much as the two players and to most of them it seemed that the Mouser in vanquishing the stranger had also dispersed all the strange fears that had been loose in the tavern earlier and running along their nerves.

"A drink to toast your victory, salve my defeat?" the Mouser's Death asked smoothly. "Hot Gahveh perhaps? With brandy in't?"

"Nay, sir," the Mouser said with a bright smile, collecting together his several small stacks of gold and silver pieces and funneling them into his pouch, "I must take these bright fellows home and introduce 'em to their cell mates. Coins prosper best in prison, as my friend Groniger tells me. But sir, would you not accompany me on that journey, help me escort 'em? We can drink there." A brightness came into his eyes that had nothing whatever in common with a miser's glee. He continued, "Friend who discerned the tree sloth and saw the black panther, we both know that there are mysterious treasures and matters of interest compared to which these clinking counters are no more than that. I yearn to show you some. You'll be intrigued."

At the mention of "treasure," his Death pricked up his ears much as his fellow assassin had at Fafhrd's speaking the word. Mouser's would-be nemesis had had his Cold Waste dreams too, his appetites whetted by the privations of long drear journeying, and by the infuriating losses he'd had to put up with tonight as well. And he too had the conviction that the fates must be on his side tonight by now, though for the opposite reason. A man who'd been so incredibly lucky at backgammon was bound to be hit by a great bolt of unluck at whatever feat he next attempted.

"I'll come with you gladly," he said softly, rising with the Mouser and moving with him toward the door.

"You'll not collect your dice and stones?" the one queried. "'Tis a most handsome box."

"Let the tavern have it as a memorial of your masterly victory," his Death replied negligently, with a sort of muted grandiloquence. He tossed aside an imaginary blossom.

Ordinarily *that* would have been too much to the Mouser, arousing all his worst suspicions. Only rogues pretended to be *that* carelessly munificent. But the madness with which Mog had cursed him was fully upon him again, and he forgot the matter with a smile and a shrug.

"Trifles both," he agreed.

In fact the manner of the two of them was so lightly casual for the moment, not to say la-di-da, that they might well have gotten out of the Sea Wrack and lost in the fog without anyone noticing, except of course for old Ourph, whose head turned slowly to watch the Mouser out the door, shook itself sadly, and then resumed its meditations or cogitations or whatever.

Fortunately there were those in the tavern deeply and intelligently concerned for the Mouser, and not bound by Mingolly fatalisms. Cif had no impulse to rush up to the Mouser upon his win. She'd had too strong a sense of something more than backgammon being at stake tonight, too lingering a conviction of something positively unholy about his were-adversary, and doubtless others in the tavern had shared those feelings. Unlike most of those, however, any relief she felt did not take her attention away from the Mouser for an instant. As he and his unwholesome doublegoer exited the doorway she hurried to it.

Pshawri and Mikkidu were at her heels.

They saw the two ahead of them as dim blobs, shadows in the white mist, as it were, and followed only swiftly enough to keep them barely in sight. The shadows moved across and down the lane a bit, paused briefly, then went on until they were traveling along back of the building made of gray timbers from wrecked ships that was the council hall.

Their pursuers encountered no other fog venturers. The silence was profound, broken only by the occasional *drip-drip* of condensing mist and a few very brief murmurs of conversation from ahead, too soft and fleeting to make out. It was eerie.

At the next corner the shadows paused another while, then turned it.

"He's following his regular morning route," Mikkidu whispered softly.

Cif nodded, but Pshawri gripped Mik's arm in warning, setting a finger to his lips.

But true enough to the second lieutenant's guess, they followed their quarry to the new-built barracks and saw the Mouser bow his doublegoer in. Pshawri and Mikkidu waited a bit, then took off their boots and entered in stocking feet most cautiously.

Cif had another idea. She stole along the side of the building, heading for the kitchen door.

Inside, the Mouser, who had uttered hardly a dozen words since leaving the Sea Wrack, pointed out various items to his guest and watched for his reactions.

Which threw his Death into a state of great puzzlement. His intended victim had spoken some words about a treasure or treasures, then taken him outside and with a mysterious look pointed out to him a low point in a lane. What could that mean? True, sunken ground sometimes indicated something buried there—a murdered body, generally. But who'd bury a treasure in the lane of a dinky northern seaport, or a corpse, for that matter? It didn't make sense.

Next the gray-clad baffler had gone through the same rigmarole at a corner behind a building built of strangely weathered, heavy-looking wood. That had for a moment seemed to lead somewhere, for there'd been an opalescent something lodged in one of the big beams, its hue speaking of pearls and treasure. But when he'd stooped to study it, it had turned out to be only a worthless seashell, worked into the gray wood Aarth knew how!

And now the riddlesome fellow, holding a lamp he'd lit, was standing in a bunkroom beside a closet he'd just opened. There didn't seem to be much of anything in it.

"Treasure?" the Mouser's Death breathed doubtfully, leaning forward to look more closely.

The Mouser smiled and shook his head. "No. Miceholes," he breathed back.

The other recoiled incredulously. Had the brains of the masterly backgammon player turned to mush? Had something in the fog stolen away his wits? Just what was happening here? Maybe he'd best out knife and slay at once, before the situation became too confusing.

But the Mouser, still smiling gleefully, as if in anticipation of wonders to behold, was beckoning him on with his free hand into a short hall and then a smaller room with two bunks only, while the lamp he held beside his head made shadows crawl around them and slip along the walls.

Facing his Death, he threw open the door of a wider closet, stretched himself to his fullest height and thrust his lamp aloft, as if to say, "Lo!"

The closet contained at least a dozen shallow shelves smoothly surfaced with black cloth, and on them were very neatly arrayed somewhere between a thousand and a myriad tiny objects, as if they were so many rare coins and precious gems. As if, yes... but as to what these objects really were... recall the nine oddments the Mouser had laid out on Cif's bed table three months past... imagine them multiplied by ten hundred... the booty of three months of ground peering... the loot of ninety days of floor delving... you'd have a picture of the strange collection the Mouser was displaying to his Death.

And as his Death leaned closer, running his gaze incredulously back and forth along the shelves, the triumphant smile faded from the Mouser's face and was replaced by the same look of desperate wondering he'd had on it when he told Fafhrd of his yearning for the small things of Lankhmar.

"We've reached our picnic ground," Afreyt told Skor as they strode through the mist. "See how the sward is trampled. Now cast we about for Elvenhold."

"'Tis done, lady," he replied as she moved off to the left, he to the right, "but why are you so sure Captain Fafhrd went there?"

"Because he told Groniger he was going flying," she called to him. "Earlier Groniger had said that none could climb Elvenhold without wings."

"But the captain could," Skor, taking her meaning, called back, "for he's scaled Stardock," thinking, though not saying aloud, *But that was before he lost a hand.*

Moments later he sighted vertical solidity, and was calling out that he'd found what they were seeking. When Afreyt caught up with him by the rock wall, he added, "I've also found proof that Fafhrd and the stranger did indeed come this way, as you deduced they would."

And he held up to her the hooded cloak of Fafhrd's Death.

Fafhrd, followed closely by his Death, climbed out of the fog into a world of bone-white clarity. He faced away from the rock to survey it.

The top of the mist was a flat white floor stretching east and south to the horizon, unbroken by treetop, chimney or spire of Salthaven, or mast top in the harbor beyond. Overhead the night shone with stars somewhat dimmed by the light of the round moon, which seemed to rest on the mist in the southeast.

"The full of Murderers Moon," he remarked oratorically, "the shortest and the lowest running full of the year, and come pat on Midsummer's Day

Night. I told you there'd be light enough to climb by."

His Death below him savored the appropriateness of the lunar situation but didn't care much for the light. He'd felt securer climbing in the fog with the height all hid. He was still enjoying himself, but now he wanted to get the killing done as soon as Fafhrd revealed where the cave or other treasure spot was.

Fafhrd faced around to the tower again. Soon they were edging up past the grassy stretch. He noted his white flagged arrow and left it where it was, but when he came to Afreyt's he reached over precariously, snagged it with his hook, and tucked it in his belt.

"How much further?" his Death called up.

"Just to the end of the grass," Fafhrd called down. "Then we traverse to the opposite edge of Elvenhold, where there's a shallow cave will give our feet good support as we view the treasure. Ah, but I'm glad you came with me tonight! I only hope the moon doesn't dim it too much."

"How's that?" the other asked, a little puzzled, though considerably enheartened by the mention of a cave.

"Some jewels shine best by their own light alone," Fafhrd replied somewhat cryptically. Clashing into the next hold, his hook struck a shower of white sparks. "Must be flint in the rock hereabouts," he observed. "See, friend, minerals have many ways of making light. On Stardock the Mouser and I found diamonds of so clear a water they revealed their shape only in the dark. And there are beasts that shine, in particular glowwasps, diamondflies, firebeetles, and nightbees. I know, I've been stung by them. While in the jungles of Klesh I have encountered luminous flying spiders. Ah, we arrive at the traverse." And he began to move sideways, taking long steps.

His Death copied him, hastening after. Footholds and handholds both seemed surer here, while back at the grass he'd twice almost missed a hold. Beyond Fafhrd he could see what he took to be the dark cave mouth at the end of this face of the rock pylon they'd mounted. Things seemed to be happening more quickly while simultaneously time stretched out for him—sure sign of climax approaching. He wanted no more talk—in particular, lectures on natural history! He loosened his long knife in its scabbard. Soon! Soon!

Fafhrd was preparing to take the step that would put him squarely in front of the shallow depression that looked at first sight like a cave mouth. He was aware that his comrade astronomer was crowding him. At that moment, although the two of them were clearly alone on the face, he heard a short dry laugh, not in the voice of either of them, that nevertheless sounded as if it came from somewhere very close by. And somehow that laugh inspired or stung him into taking, instead of the step he'd planned, a much longer one that took him just past the seeming cave mouth and put his left foot on the end of the ledge, while his right hand reached for a hold beyond the shallow depression so that his whole body would swing out past the end of this face, and he would hopefully see the bearded star which was currently his dearest treasure and which until this moment tonight Elvenhold itself had hid from him.

At the same moment his Death struck, who had perfectly anticipated his victim's every movement except the last inspired one. His dagger, instead of burying itself in Fafhrd's back, struck rock in the shallow depression and its blade snapped. Staggered by that and vastly surprised, he fought for balance.

Fafhrd, glancing back, perceived the treacherous attack and rather casually booted his threatener in the thigh with a free foot. By the bone-white light of Murderers Moon, the Death of Fafhrd fell off Elvenhold and, glancingly striking the very steep grassy slope once or twice, was silhouetted momentarily, long limbs writhing, against the floor of white fog before the latter swallowed him up and the scream he'd started. There was a distant *thud* that nevertheless had a satisfying finality to it.

Fafhrd swung out again around the end of the cliff. Yes, his bearded star, though dimmed by the moonlight, was definitely discernable. He enjoyed it. The pleasure was, somewhat remotely, akin to that of watching a beautiful girl undress in almost dark.

"Fafhrd!" Then again, "Fafhrd!"

Skor's shout, by Kos, he told himself. And Afreyt's! He pulled himself back on the ledge and, securely footed there, called, "Ahoy! Ahoy below!"

Back at the barracks things were moving fast and very nervously, notably on the part of the Mouser's Death. He almost dirked the vaunting idiot on sheer impulse in overpowering disgust at being shown that incredible mouse's museum of trash as though it were a treasure of some sort. Almost, but then he heard a faint shuffling noise that seemed to originate in the building they were in, and it never did to slay when witnesses might be nigh, were there another course to take.

He watched the Mouser, who looked somewhat disappointed now (had the idiot expected to be praised for his junk display?), shut the closet door and beckon him back into the short hall and through a third door. He followed, listening intently for any repetition of the shuffling noise or other sound. The moving shadows the lamp cast were a little unnerving now; they suggested lurkers, hidden observers. Well, at least the idiot hadn't deposited in his trash closet the gold and silver coins he'd won this night, so presumably there was still hope of seeing their "cell mates" and some real treasure.

Now the Mouser was pointing out, but in a somewhat perfunctory way, the features of what appeared to be a rather well-appointed kitchen: fireplaces, ovens, and so forth. He rapped a couple of large iron kettles, but without any great enthusiasm, sounding their dull, sepulchral tones.

His manner quickened a little, however, and the ghost at least of a gleeful smile returned to his lips, as he opened the back door and went out into the mist, signing for his Death to follow him. That one did so, outwardly seeming relaxed, inwardly alert as a drawn knife, poised for any action.

Almost immediately the Mouser stooped, grasped a ring, and heaved up a small circular trapdoor, meanwhile holding his lamp aloft, its beams reflecting whitely from the fog but not helping vision much. The Mouser's Death bent forward to look in.

Thereafter things happened very rapidly indeed. There was a scuffling sound and a thud from the kitchen. (That was Mikkidu tripping himself by stepping on the toe of his own stocking.) The Mouser's Death, his nerves tortured beyond endurance, whipped out his dirk, and next fell dead across the cesspool mouth with Cif's dagger in his ear, thrown from where she stood against the wall hardly a dozen feet away.

And somewhere, along with these actions, there were a brief growl and a short dry laugh. But those were things Cif and the Mouser claimed afterwards to have heard. At the present moment there was only the Mouser still holding his lamp and peering down at the corpse and saying as Cif and Pshawri and Mikkidu rushed up to him, "Well, he'll never get his revenge for tonight's gaming, that's for certain. Or do ghosts ever play backgammon, I wonder? I've heard of them contesting parties in chess with living mortals, by Mog."

Next day at the council hall Groniger presided over a brief but well-attended inquest into the demise of the two passengers in the *Good News*. Badges and other insignia about their persons suggested they were members not only of the Lankhmar Slayers' Brotherhood, but also of the even more cosmopolitan Assassins Order. Under close questioning, the captain of the *Good News* admitted knowing of this circumstance and was fined for not reporting it to the Rime Isle harbormaster immediately on making port. A bit later Groniger found that they were murderous rogues, doubtless hired by foreign parties unknown, and that they had been rightly slain on their first attempts to practice their nefarious trade on Rime Isle.

But afterwards he told Cif, "It's as well that you slew him, and with his dagger in his hand. That way, none can say it was a feuding of newcomers to the Isle with foreigners their presence attracted here. And that you, Afreyt, wcrc close witness to the other's death."

"I'll say I was!" that lady averred. "He came down not a yard from us, eh Skor? almost braining us. And with his hand death-gripping his broken dagger. Fafhrd, in future you should be more careful of how you dispose of your corpses."

When questioned about the cryptic warning he'd brought the Mouser and Fafhrd, old Ourph vouched, "The moment I heard the name *Good News* I knew it was an ill-omened ship, bearing watching. And when the two strangers came off and went into the Sea Wrack, I perceived them as dressed up, slightly luminous skeletons only, with bony hands and eyeless sockets."

"Did you see their corpses at the inquest so?" Groniger asked him.

"No, then they were but dead meat, such as all living become."

In Godsland the three concerned deities, somewhat shocked by the final turn of events and horrified to see how close they'd come to losing their chief remaining worshippers, lifted their curses from them as rapidly as they were able. Other concerned parties were slower to get the news and to believe it. The Assassins Order posted the two Deaths as "delayed" rather that "missing," but prepared to make what compensation might be unavoidable to Arth-Pulgh and Hamomel. While Sheelba and Ningauble, considerably irked, set about devising new stratagems to procure the return of their favorite errand boys and living touchstones.

The instant the gods lifted their curses, the Mouser's and Fafhrd's strange obsessions vanished. It happened while they were together with Afreyt and Cif, the four of them lunching al freso at Cif's. The only outward sign was that the Twain's eyes widened incredulously as they stared and then smiled at nothing.

"What deliciously outrageous idea has occurred to you two?" Afreyt demanded, while Cif echoed, "You're right! And it has to be something like that. We know you two of yore!"

"Is it that obvious?" the Mouser inquired, while Fafhrd fumbled out, "No, it's nothing like that. It's… No, you've all got to hear this. You know that thing about stars I've been having? Well, it's gone!" He lifted his eyes. "By Issek, I can look at the blue sky now without having it covered with the black flyspecks of the stars that would be there now if it were dark!"

"By Mog!" the Mouser exploded. "I had no idea, Fafhrd that your little madness was so like mine in the tightness of its grip. For I no longer feel the compulsion to try to peer closely at every tiny object within fifty yards of me. It's like being a slave who's set free."

"No more ragpicking, eh?" Cif said. "No more bent-over inspection tours?"

"No, by Mog," the Mouser asserted, then qualified that with a "Though of course little things can be quite as interesting as big things; in fact, there's a whole tiny world of—"

"Uh-uh, you better watch out," Cif interrupted, holding up a finger.

"And the stars too are of considerable interest, my unnatural infatuation with 'em aside," Fafhrd said stubbornly.

Afreyt asked, "What do you think it was, though? Do you think some wizard cast a spell on you? Perchance that Ningauble you told me of, Fafhrd?"

Cif said, "Yes, or that Sheelba you talk of in your sleep, Mouser, and tell me isn't an old lover?"

The two men had to admit that those explanations were distant possibilities.

"Or other mysterious or even otherworldly beings may have had a hand in it," Afreyt proposed. "We know Queen Skeldir's involved, bless her, from the warning laughter you heard. And, for all you make light of him, Gusorio. Cif and I did hear those growlings."

Cif said, the look in her eyes half-wicked, half-serious, "And has it occurred to any of you that, since Skeldir's warnings went to you two men, that you may be transmigrations of her? and we—Skeldir help us!—of Great Gusorio? Or does that shock you?"

"By no means," Fafhrd answered. "Since transmigration would be such a wonder, able to send the spirit of woman or man into animal, or vice versa, a mere change of sex should not surprise us at all."

The backgammon box of the two Deaths was kept at the Sea Wrack as a curiosity of sorts, but it was noted that few used it to play with, or got good games when they did.